THE
RESCUE
THE FIRST VISITATION
OF THURIA

JAMES TODD LEWIS
AUTHOR OF *THE THURIAN SAGA*

The Rescue: The First Visitation of Thuria

Copyright © 2014 by James Todd Lewis

(Revised and updated, 2020)

Front Cover Photo Credits:
Shannon Moon (wolf eyes)

Cover Background and Composition:
eBookLaunch.com

Editing and Review Assistance: James W. Lewis, Jr., Deborah Williford,
Shannon Moon, & Daniel Sherrett (SSJ3Mewtwo)

Illustrations, chapter and section breaks: Kat Miller
(www.furaffinity.net/user/foxenawolf)

"Honor to all. Honor from all. Honor … above all."

Revision 3.0.2

Contact e-mail: author @ jamestoddlewis.com

ISBN 978-1-940929-29-3

For
Ainslie, Sarah, and Alex
and for
the generations yet to come.

With thanks eternal to my God,
my family,
and my friends.

Books
by James Todd Lewis

THE THURIAN SAGA:

The Rescue: The First Visitation of Thuria

The Aftermath: Secrets of Thuria

The Ascent: Conflict on Thuria

The Summit: Rise of the Anati

Purebred: Soul of the Mixed Blood

The Fallen: Search for the Path

Trials of the Teldear

Beyond: Incarnation (Book 1)

Beyond: Resurrection (Book 2)

Beyond: Ascension (Book 3)

The Legacy of Aris

Enemy Deity

Table of Contents

Author's Note

Thank you for reading this book, and I hope you really enjoy yourself. After all, I enjoyed writing it.

This story is about events occurring on a planet far away from our own. It's so far away, in fact, that no humans are actually in this book. There aren't any stranded in a nearby star system, lingering in a legend, forgotten in a fossil, or sealed within the ice of a glacier. Everything within these pages happens somewhere else – a place without our hours, our days, our months, or our years. Our continents, our seas, our skies, and our stars are unknown there. This world is a different world.

Finally, this book contains some material not intended for children. Parents and other responsible adults are asked to do their part in ensuring that any story with mature subjects and themes does not end up in front of eyes too young and for which it was not intended. There are some episodes of violence, occurrences of suggestive material, and moments of coarse language; however, these are not prevalent.

Again, my sincere thanks. See you in the future.

James Todd Lewis

Introduction

A shining orb of golden-white light floated above a platform in the control center of a great starship. Intricate and beautiful patterns of luminescence rippled across the sphere's surface, through its interior, and out into the room. Had this radiant creature appeared in front of a lesser being, that individual might have been tempted to call such an awe-inspiring apparition "divine."

It was true, the creature – an Allarraen – had been mistaken for a god on more than one occasion, and there were good reasons why. By almost any standard of longevity, he was ancient – seemingly immortal. In his time, planets had formed and brought forth life, stars had grown old, and whole galaxies had collided and combined. Even more, his technology and abilities were so utterly fantastic that it was tempting to classify his actions in the category of miracles. Yet the Allarraen was not a god, nor did he pretend to be – he was something else.

There were those who believed that life started simply, biologically, and then through time and enlightenment found its way to ascension – the realization of a new level of existence above and beyond what simple, corporeal beings understood. Once transfigured into this new reality, such higher entities were supposed to shed any concerns about lower creatures or the universe in which they dwelt. The Allarrae had long since ascended, several times over. Yet through all of their various existences across the great expanse of time, they discovered that intelligent life had a commonality, regardless of its varying levels of grandeur and glory. The Allarrae believed that every self-aware species deserved respect, protection, and nurturing. That's why he was seeking them out. That's why he had brought his ship, the Tashar, to this particular location in the cosmos.

The great ship had been resting – absorbing energy in the stormy inferno of a galaxy's heart while it waited for the reconnaissance probes to report their findings. Most of those reports had been uninteresting and confirmed what the Tashar's sensors had already suggested; this galaxy was largely devoid of life, perhaps even completely barren. Every few moments, probes would appear, relay their findings in a microburst of information, and then wink out of existence as they journeyed to their next destination.

Suddenly, a distant probe requested the ship's attention. Relaying its observations through a narrow tunnel in space-time, the probe indicated that it had found life in a remote planetary system, and not merely living organisms; it had found intelligent life. It had found exactly what the ship and its inhabitant desired.

Having traversed the enormous distance from the galaxy's core to one of its spiral arms in an instant, the Tashar was soon drawing near to the outermost planet of that system. The orbiting probe's observations were now complimented by the full sensory capabilities of the great ship, and a torrent of raw information fed into its control center as the Tashar slowed to approach the fourth planet.

Within, the Allarraen easily absorbed the millions of sensor readings and measurements instantaneously. The first conclusions he reached were in relation to the basic aspects of the planet. Approximately fifty-eight percent of its surface was covered with water. The continental land masses in its temperate zones were of much the same size. The poles of the planet were capped with large amounts of floating ice, and while mild in comparison to many planetary environments, the climate of this world was somewhat cool. Each continent, to varying extents, had its mountains, rivers, lakes, and deserts; still, much of the land was arable. In comparison to its neighbors in this half of the galaxy, this world was one of the few favorable spots for life to flourish, and flourish it did! There was an abundance of plant life upon the land and in the seas, and non-sentient species proliferated in any moderately hospitable environment, even beneath the polar ice caps and in the harshest deserts.

The planet was unique in one other regard – the intelligent life that populated its surface consisted of no less than six major species. All were similar – anthropoid mammals standing erect on two legs covered with thick hair or fur, but there were very distinct differences from one species to the next. Body shape and color differed; tail length and size varied, as did ear height and muzzle length. Despite their physical differences, however, those who inhabited this planet, known to them as "Thuria," shared a common language with only minor variations in dialect from region to region, continent to continent.

It was also clear that there were common forms of hierarchy and association. Thurian society was organized not only by governments, but by large familial groupings. There were, as was frequently found, closely related individuals who lived together for support, nurturing the young and caring for the old. However, these nuclear families existed within a framework of named family houses. Some of these houses counted their numbers in the hundreds of thousands. Much of an individual's life and identity seemed to revolve around these familial institutions.

The Allarraen could easily get a sense of how these houses functioned by sampling the electronic communications flowing around the planet. A request from one family house, de Kestrick, floated across a network of communications satellites to another, de Khaetria, seeking a business relationship with one of its members. Another travelled between two houses of the same species, de Dothnar and de Orturu, seeking an agreement for the pairing of a male and female. Details were sent from an educational establishment to a family house about who was being accepted for the next cycle's course of instruction and who was not.

As the data continued to flow into the control room of the Tashar, other subtle patterns started to emerge. Beneath the orderly forms of governments and family houses were the quiet cries of those who could claim no family as their own. Individuals who resulted from a pairing of non-like species seemed adrift upon this world. It was clear that building any sort of life was far more challenging when no family house would claim you because of your mixed parentage. The computer communications network – "TransNet" as they called it – was one of the few places where the being could hear their desperation and resigned anger. Alongside them in trials and difficulties were the cast-outs, those who were once a part of some family house, but no longer. They had been disavowed because of a crime or an offense against the family, and all of the support that had once been theirs was ripped away. To those who were once their loved ones, it was almost as if they had died.

As the Allarraen contemplated these revelations, the ship noticed something. The probe's initial geological reports on the planet indicated that its two orbiting moons didn't exert much stress on the surface of the planet, so normally, volcanoes and ground quakes were comparatively rare events. However, only a few moments from now, an upwelling of molten rock was going to brush against an ancient continental fault line creating a moderate land quake.

Instantly, the thoughts of the ship were shared with the being shining above the dais. "Let us carefully observe and learn." The ship then emerged, still unseen, from behind the outermost of the two moons and started to move to a better position to watch events unfold.

Chapter 1: The Visitation

Time: 24.90 – 6.1 intervals before high night

Yarvea Mountain Range, Thuratan Continent, Planet Thuria

Sahnassa de Orturu was tired, from her pink nose all the way to her purplish-black tail-tip, but there was no way she could find relief. The dark purple fur of her chest and sides, accented by wide, silver-white stripes, was constantly being pinched and pulled by the safety harness tight across her chest. That device strapped her firmly into the passenger seat of her boss's sporty and expensive new hover. While Sahnassa supposed the racy little craft might be fun to drive, riding as a passenger down twisting mountain roads, at high speeds, and in the dark gave her even more feelings she just hated: tense anxiety and motion sickness. As the hover swished and swooshed in erratic directions, Sahnassa's claw tips slipped out of her paw fingers and dug hard into the grip bars on either side of her seat.

Opening tightly shut eyelids for a brief moment allowed her a glance at the speed indicator through her weary indigo eyes. That confirmed her worst suspicions; her boss was driving out her anger from the conference they had just left, or rather that they had been told to leave. Her employer, Vanarra Anasto, was beautiful, resourceful, smart, and more than a little proud, and when that pride was stung – watch out! Unfortunately, tonight, that had happened painfully and in public.

Vanarra's lucrative little "celebrations and catering" service was certainly something to be proud of, especially given the poor, sad past of its founder. Vanarra had grown up as an orphan on the streets of Shanandrae, begging or stealing food, sleeping where she could, and sneaking into the archives and family schools to steal books, since no school would have her. She had endured many tough seasons and humiliations, but her drive and her genetics came through for her.

Being a mix between two breeds of Thurian – Faelnar and Vulpi – Vanarra had been graced with the most desirable qualities of each. Covering a frame that was predominantly sleek, as was the case with most Faelnar, her fur bore the exotic coloration of a Vulpi – mostly a rich, reddish-brown, except where it turned white under her chin, went down the front of her neck, and then framed her ample chest and tight stomach. Golden furs were evenly scattered throughout both colors, making her coat nearly shine and shimmer in the light. A Vulpi's golden eyes and long tail – far more luxurious than that of any normal Faelnar, although not as full as a Vulpi – were among her most striking features. Taken as a whole, Vanarra's body was intensely attractive to most Faelnar and Vulpi males, not to mention those of several other species.

This attractiveness matched with a good mind and street-wise sensibilities soon allowed Vanarra to create a business that, while it may have started small and quite precariously in some respects, now thrived, and profitably. Traditional gatherings and corporate catering were the main businesses, intermixed with a little camera recording of the events. Everything her company did was executed with an artful touch one wouldn't expect from an owner so young and with so hard a history.

Van's "colleagues" in the business world had reportedly made their own assessment, voting her an award for all of her achievements, or so it seemed. Sahni – Vanarra's own pet name for Sahnassa – was supposed to be there to record Van's moment of triumph, had there been one. Tonight, the recognition, praise, and acceptance Sahni's boss had so longed for simply vanished. Instead, at the last instant, the Association of Service and Commerce (the ASC) pointedly snubbed Vanarra's company for the fastest growing business award (which it deserved), the most charitable (which it truly was), and the greatest new company success story (which Van had obvious claim to, given the age of the other businesses under consideration).

"Bigots! Prudes!" Vanarra thundered through bared teeth. "Hypocrites!" she growled, and they took another high gravity turn which almost pushed Sahnassa over the edge of nausea.

"Yes. They were awful. If you keep driving like that, it's going to get worse. I'm gonna be—" Sahni had to stop talking then, and Van looked at Sahnassa. The Nephti's eyes were clenched shut, and her paws held onto the grip bars as hard as they could. The fire drained out of Van as she looked back at the road; embarrassment and anger, as painful as they were, could not stand up to the thought she was inadvertently harming Sahnassa. Van would never do anything to hurt Sahni; she cared for her too much to allow that to happen.

Initially, Van was simply fascinated and amused by this young purebred, just out of academy. Sahnassa de Orturu was a winsome, high-society technophile whose blush furs rose at almost anything mildly suggestive. Here was someone who, growing up, had everything that Van didn't, but now this lovely, smart, and timid creature worked for her. Over time, however, they had actually settled into a genuine friendship. After all, working for Vanarra wasn't the type of job Sahni could tell her family of in detail, especially the family matriarch. Van knew Sahnassa would be undoubtedly disavowed if such a thing ever happened – a fact that made her feel Sahni stayed for more than just pay, and Van loved her for it. She was only a few seasons older than Sahni, which made their friendship all the stronger.

"I'm sorry," Van said, slowing their pace to something within the posted speeds. Her reddish-brown ears drooped down in apology. "Are you okay?"

"Just … about," Sahni uttered weakly, shifting her long, thickly furred tail and taking a big swallow. A few deep breaths later, she nodded.

Van stated decisively, "I'm pulling over." It was the kind of statement Sahni had learned long ago wasn't arguable, and she was secretly hoping for the chance to breathe fresh air, stretch arms, tail, and legs. The little craft glided to a stop and bobbed slightly as Van placed it in hover mode. "Better?"

"Much. I was hoping I could – what's that noise?" It was a low rumble that was growing louder. Without any other warning, Van's side of the vehicle crumpled with a loud bang, the lights went out, and they were thrown through the edge railing into a violent roll down the mountainside. Glass and dirt and noise and leaves and pain and blood and flame and blackness, and then … there was nothing.

Sahni awoke to an agony so terrible and intense, she instantly threw up. Her legs felt like she had blades stuck through them; her chest was painfully crushed against the console by a huge weight on her back. Her tail had to be gone; the pain told her that. Coughing through bloody spit and foul air, she realized what had happened; they were hit by a landslide. To her horror, she realized something else – they had been buried by it. The air was dusty, stale, and laced with the smell of burning electrics and singed fur. Worse, it was pitch black. Terror and panic raged in her with what little strength she had left. "Van? Van!?" There was no response. She would have reached out for her, but she couldn't move; her arms were pinned. She struggled, weeping hysterically and cried, "Oh no, no, no, no, no! Help us! Help! Help! Oh, please help—" At that moment, she felt her heart falter, and she knew she was going to die. She felt a strange buzzing sensation all about her, and then nothing.

Breathing. She wa sa felt the rise and fall of her own chest before perceiving anything else. Clean air, fresh air at that, with a light floral scent entered her nose. "That's really nice," she thought. The bed in which she rested was wonderfully soft and warm. As sensation began to return to the rest of her body, the memories did, as well. No longer protected by the forgetfulness of sleep, she sat bolt upright, eyes wide open. She was in a bed, in a large airy room decorated in very light pastels. It resembled a health care facility, but it was a step up, like health care for the very rich.

It took her a moment to realize someone was sitting beside her, holding her paw. A strong arm wrapped about her shoulders and gently pulled her back down to the bed. "There, there. Let's lie down now. You've been through a lot. You still need to rest." She had to admit she felt a little dizzy as her head softly landed on the pillow.

"Vanarra, is she?" Sahni managed in a weak voice.

"Badly injured, but alive. It was very close with her, and it will take some time." She looked over into the brilliant blue eyes of a very nice looking Vulpi, one she presumed was a doctor. His fur was almost the same reddish-brown shade as Vanarra, with much the same patterning of white under his chin, disappearing underneath his clothes. His paws were also white, an unusual coloration that made him look like he was wearing gloves of a sort, but Sahni thought it a nice feature. An athletic build, detectable even under his clothes, combined with a wonderfully keen face made her heartbeat quicken. Beyond her control, the fur on her cheeks raised slightly; she inwardly cursed at how quickly embarrassed she was. "Your pulse is racing; just close your eyes and take a few slow breaths. Calm. That's what you want to be. Deep breaths in, and deep breaths out. Very good."

The calm she felt lasted only for a moment, and she sat straight upright again, this time pulling the covering from her body. She was stunned by what she saw and felt; she was unharmed. She felt her chest through the soft, white shirt; her hips and legs, they were all fine. Her tail! "My tail! Oh no!" she gasped.

"It's fine," he said smiling warmly. "It's back there in all of its beauty and glory; it's just tucked into a special place in the bed so you could lie on your back without pinching it."

"I'm totally … fine? How's that possible?"

"You are completely well, Sahnassa. Oh, if you're wondering how I know your name, it was here on your identification card." He took the bent and crumpled card out of his pocket. "I'm afraid your other possessions are in as poor a condition."

"How long have I been here? It had to have been several moons! Does my family know?" She was feeling really light-headed now, and seeming to notice that, he gently pulled her back down again and replaced the covers.

"Now, now, now. Let's take it slow. As I said, you've been through a lot. Suffice it to say that your family believes, and rightly so, that you are safe. Now, that's all the questions you get answered until you eat and sleep again." With that, he walked to the door of her room, a room Sahni now realized could have easily held eight beds. After disappearing for a moment, he returned with a tray of food. Pushing a nearby cart over to her bed, he then warned her, "I'm going to sit you up." Sahni got ready to adjust, but it was like the bed simply cradled her into a reclining position. There was no sense of a mechanism or buzzing sound.

"Wow, nice bed," she mused.

"It's new. I'm glad you like it. Now, let's see how you like this." He raised the ornate covers off of the plates, and Sahni's mouth was instantly watering. Steamed creele grass, roasted swimmer fish, sweetened aster tree tea, and it just went on and on. Several of her other favorites were there too.

"Amazing! I hope it looks as good as it tastes," she said, and then caught herself fumbling the sentence, and giggled, sending her blush furs up almost at right angles. "Oh, sorry. What I meant to say was—"

He smiled and then joked "Drowned out by the sound of your chewing; come on now. I would hate for it to get cold."

She was a little embarrassed by his continued observation even as she took a skewer and carefully speared a small piece of creele. After tasting it, she found she was actually crooning in delight. "Oh, that is *so* good," she said, her mouth still full. When she swallowed, she looked at him and confessed, "There's no way my company health plan is going to pay for this."

"It doesn't have to. It's paid for by other sources. Don't worry about it. Now, I'll leave you to eat." She looked at him instinctively in a way she didn't intend to, pleading for him to stay. "Don't worry. I'll be back, but I do have another patient to attend to. Once you've finished eating, I'll be back to take the tray. We'll give you a little rest stop, a night cap, and then let you sleep."

"Thank you, Doctor," she said as he walked out of the room. She realized, belatedly, she didn't even get his name. She would ask later, she thought. In the meantime, she focused on the wonderful meal in front of her.

As she ate the last few bites, she started to look around. The room was very nicely decorated with soft abstract art, blooming plants, and she even heard soft music playing in the background. There was no sign of a LineCom or a VidStar or even worse, no computer. There were no books either, at least in sight. She looked around the room for a camera or intercom, but she couldn't see anything. The room had no windows – just soft, cove lighting. All of this comfort would normally have set her at ease, but her thoughts kept coming back to Vanarra. She earnestly wanted to ask about the condition of her friend as soon as the doctor returned.

Pushing the tray and cart off to the side, she shifted her body, and almost by reflex, flicked her tail around. It felt like there was a perfectly shaped hole in the bed which led to another bed underneath where her tail rested. Sahni remembered the intense pain and reached under herself to feel for any sign of injury, and she could not find the slightest hint of damage. Her tail felt completely normal.

Unfortunately, the swish of the door caused her to rapidly remove her paws and try to find something to do with them. "Great, he's coming back in, and he'll find me in here feeling up my own backside!" After a moment, he walked back in. "Gosh, he's cute," she thought to herself.

"Glad to see you enjoyed it," he said, replacing the lids on the plates.

"I muddled through," she dissembled coyly before confessing, "It was wonderful. Thank you. How's Vanarra?"

"A slight improvement, and I'm quite hopeful. I can give you more details after you've rested." He returned after disposing of the tray outside and stepped over to her bed. "Let's take a moment to get you back up on your hind paws and over to the facilities. Then, I want you straight back in bed. I have some medicine for you that will help you sleep, and sleep is what you need right now." Again, she had to fight her blush furs as she took his strong arm and gently slid out of the bed. She looked down as she carefully placed her three-toed paws onto the soft, carpeted floor. Watching her standing a little shakily, he asked, "Are you feeling alright?"

"Just ... don't go anywhere yet."

"Take as long as you need." She peeked behind her, grateful to actually set eyes on her tail, which looked fine – actually groomed. For the first time, she took account of the clothing she was wearing – soft white shorts and a soft, short sleeve shirt were welcome changes from the embarrassing gown she had worn on other medical occasions.

She looked at her legs. "I guess I'm feeling better."

"Let's try a few steps, nothing ambitious." They did just that, which she managed with nowhere near her normal grace; her legs were shaking and nearly threatening to fall out from under her. Nevertheless, his smooth, warm voice reassured her. "Very good. Let's wait a moment and try again."

"How bad were my legs and my tail ... when they brought me in?"

"You were in rough shape, all over," he told her gently as they took some more steps into the large bathroom. A full length mirror was before her; quickly glancing at herself, she thought she at least looked okay, even if she still felt a little shaky.

"Can't imagine what I must have looked like. They didn't take pictures, did they?"

He was a little stern in his reply. "No, and I don't want you to think about that, either. I want you to look in the mirror at that beautiful and graceful creature standing there, and then think about how wonderful it is that she has a second chance. Now, I'll give you some privacy. Call if you need me, but I'll wait for you to open the door otherwise. Please, take all the time you need." With that, he gently closed the door.

Almost without thinking, she took off the shorts and shirt and stood naked in front of the mirror. She turned left and right, touched her chest and legs, and felt and caressed her tail, not believing until now that she was actually okay – not until she could really see for herself. In many ways, she felt better than she ever had, and her coat seemed to look as good as she could remember seeing it in seasons. Her purplish-black pelt accented by her broad, silvery stripes looked and felt completely as it should.

She heard a sound outside, and it called her back to the task. She relieved herself, dressed, and cracked the door open. "Doctor?"

"Coming, Sahnassa; just a moment." She was glad he was only a few steps away. He appeared and offered her his arm. "Everything alright?"

"Yes," she said shyly, her blush fur again at full attention. "I'm sorry I took so long."

"Not at all. Now, let's get you back to where you can get some rest. I have some medicine waiting for you." He walked her back to the bed and gently sat her down. "Now, take a look behind you, and find the place to tuck your tail."

"Oh, right," she said, embarrassed again. As Sahnassa, with some concentration, did as he instructed, she commented, "This is really cool; I've never seen a bed like this." He smiled, but didn't respond. Once she was comfortably settled, he offered her a small drink. "Medicine?"

"Yes, diluted in the drink. No one wants the last taste in their mouth before bedtime to be sour."

She took a sniff and smiled. "Una juice. My favorite, thanks!" She drank it up quickly and smiled, again, as she returned the cup. She lay down as he put the glass on a nearby table. Sahni felt herself instantly relaxing into a warm and comfortable drowsiness. "Oh my! That was strong … I think."

"A little bit. It's important that you sleep. If you are doing well afterwards, we can talk some more."

"I'd *really* like that." She didn't mean to do it, but her head was so wonderfully foggy and comfortable that the words came out with a lot of affection in them. Despite her drowsiness, her blush furs raised again. She wasn't sure, but just as she dozed off, she thought she felt him take her paw and give it a gentle squeeze.

Sahnassa found herself riding in Vanarra's hover, moving faster and faster down twisting mountain roads, and again she felt frightened, cramped, and nauseous. The images ahead moved at blindingly fast speeds, and she began to scream at Vanarra to stop. When she looked towards the other seat, to her horror she found it empty. She started trying to free herself from the harness to slide over and take control, but the release was fused shut. A long, straight stretch appeared before her, heading for the edge of a cliff. Sahnassa knew she had only ticks to save herself, but as she struggled, the harness just seemed to hold her tighter and tighter. Now, all she could do was scream as the pilotless hover raced even faster towards a terrifyingly dark and cavernous abyss.

As the hover broke through the frail crash barrier and sailed into the open air, Sahnassa held on to the grip bars and shut her eyes, screaming at the feeling of weightlessness as she fell into darkness. Gently, though, the motion seemed to ease, and finally, it stopped. Panting, she opened her eyes and saw the walls of the crevice were not rushing upwards, but rather gently rolling down. She realized that the hover was now rising and not falling.

Looking to her side, she saw not Vanarra, but the Vulpi doctor. "You're fine, Sahnassa. You're just fine. Don't worry. Look, your harness is working."

Reaching down, she felt the harness loose around her and with little effort, she released and refastened it – its parts moving as if factory-new and well-lubricated.

"How?" she asked. "Hovers … can't fly!"

The keen-looking Vulpi smiled at her. "This one can. Look ahead." She did and saw, to her delight, that they were slipping above the edge of the chasm and drifting forward onto solid ground. A beautiful and peaceful forest surrounded them, with dappled sunlight passing through the branches of ancient aster and harlock trees. The most serene little path appeared in front of her, and she found herself sighing in relief after a moment.

Without realizing that it happened, she found herself walking down that same path beside the Vulpi doctor, the hover mysteriously gone. It didn't bother her, even though she half thought it should have. "Do you like this place?" he asked.

"Oh yes," she breathed. "It's so peaceful. So relaxing."

"I thought you might," he said. "Look over there." Sahni did, and she instantly gasped at a beautiful bed perfectly placed underneath the boughs of several trees. Gently, he escorted her to its side, and she wondered, with some growing excitement, what might happen next. As she reached its edge and sat down, and with drowsiness calling her strongly, she understood that it would be sleep that was coming. Again, without really noticing how the transition happened, she was under the covers, comfortable and happy.

Almost unable to keep her eyes open, she lolled her head to the side, looking for him. "Don't worry," his voice said, seeming to come from all around her as if carried by a gentle breeze. "I am here, and I am watching over you. Nothing will disturb you as you rest. Be at peace, Sahnassa de Orturu. Be at peace."

Sleep, for Sahnassa, was inescapable at that point, and it lowered her blissfully down into its warm recesses of contentment.

When she next opened her eyes, Sahnassa realized that someone was stroking the fur of her head ever so gently. Finally starting to process the sensations and sights around her, she realized she was resting in the hospital bed. Looking up slightly, she saw the Vulpi had moved his paws away and rested them on the side of the bed. "You had a bad dream," he observed softly.

Smiling back up at him, she replied, "It didn't end that way, though. It was this ... perfect place – so peaceful."

"Sounds nice. How do you feel?"

Sahnassa struggled a little to move, and she felt somewhat lethargic. "Still ... out of it, a bit. It's like my mind wants things to happen, but my body is just a little slow right now."

"Perfectly understandable," he assured her. "That feeling will last for a little bit longer, about a sol for you. That leads me to what you're going to be doing."

"Hopefully not ... running a race," Sahni said, groaning a little as she sat up.

"Perhaps more of an obstacle course, that is, when you're not sleeping. You're going to be doing a lot of that, trust me. Now, do you see the chairs and couch?"

"Yes."

"I want you to think of a little trail that leads from your bed to the chair on the left to the couch, to the chair on the right, and then back to your bed again. There are also a couple of books on the table there as well, you see? I want you to pick them up and read over them. It's not so much that there's anything in them you have to know; we're just working on fine-tuning your motor skills and seeing how well you can concentrate. As for reaction time, you'll find a small, portable game. Have you played electronic games before?"

"Oh yes, on computer, but I don't get to do that much. Too busy," she answered in a ragged voice as she tried to swing her legs around to the side of the bed. "Wow, that's … not that easy, and I sound awful."

"It will get better, I promise. Oh, and to help you work on your voice, this room has a feature. Computer?" he called. A soft tone sounded in the room. "Atrialli's *Transcendent Soul*, if you please. Medium volume."

The soft, almost undetectable background music gracefully altered to the opening strains of the popular orchestral piece. "Oh, wow!" Sahnassa exclaimed, wide-eyed. "You're kidding me? Voice recognition? Actual voice recognition?" She shook her head. "In a hospital?"

"Want to try it?"

"Oh, do I! What do I do?"

"Say the keyword 'computer' followed by the artist and/or the title, and then specify a volume – low, medium, or high. It should be easily able to understand you, and if it doesn't have the selection you wish in its repository, it will respond with a soft buzzing sound."

Sahnassa giggled a little as she replied, "Okay, here it goes. Computer?" The soft tone sounded in the room again. "Rebel Monster's Dream-catcher, medium volume." The current song faded, and a heavy fast drumbeat and string instrumentals sounded in the room. "Oh, that is terrific! This could keep me busy for intervals and intervals! What else can it do?"

"Music only in this version, but you can make general requests as well. Computer? Random choice, instrumental, volume medium." There was a pause, and beautiful if somewhat sad music started playing around them. "Computer? Announce artist and title."

An artificial voice sounded softly in the room, "Anonymous, The Lullaby for Myths."

Sahnassa gasped, "Wow! That's way too cool, and it's so pretty..." For a moment, she just listened. Then, she remembered Vanarra, as if the sad chords of the music had been trying to remind her. "How is Vanarra doing?"

"Doing better, and that's all I'll say. Now, why don't I help you to the facilities, and then you can begin your first run at the obstacle course.

I'll bring your food to the table in front of the couch. Why don't you try to get up on your hind legs all by yourself?"

She slipped off the bed, and her legs almost gave out. "Oh gosh. I'm not sure I can manage this alone."

"Take a couple of small steps, holding onto the bed. That's it. Give yourself a chance to get reacquainted with the feeling. Now, a little better?"

"Yes," she managed.

"Very good. Now, start to walk towards your destination."

"I'm … I feel like I'm going to plant my muzzle in the floor any tick," Sahnassa said, feeling very uncertain of her steps.

"Don't worry. I am here, and I am watching over you," he replied reassuringly, and the statement stunned her a bit. It echoed off the memories of her dream, and with his gentle paw under her wrist, it made her feel warm and secure.

Sahnassa awoke smiling, almost laughing to herself. Her progress, once the doctor had left, consisted only of making it to the chair, and then to the sofa. Several intervals of playing the paw-held video game and nibbling on the food meant she hadn't actually made it a full circuit around the room, even once. She brought herself to a sitting position and looked around, shaking her head. Everything here – the bed, the game, the music entertainment system – was just so much more advanced than anything she had ever seen or heard about. The furniture, the décor, and the food were so wonderful, not to mention her very lovely doctor.

She closed her eyes and chanted her mother's little mantra to herself. "Only a Nephti, only a Nephti, only a Nephti." Sahnassa sighed; it wasn't working. "Why does he have to be a Vulpi, and why does he have to be that keen-looking or that nice?" Except for Vanarra and a few other friends at work, Sahnassa was lonely; even relations between she and her parents were fairly strained and had been for some time. Absolutely nothing was happening for her on the romantic front; no one was interested in hunting her. It was so depressing when both of her sisters seemed to be the prized prey of nearly every male. "Well, they can't disavow you for having a fantasy," she thought to herself, shrugging.

Sahnassa then sat back and tried to figure out exactly what sort of place this was. It wasn't difficult to recall how badly injured she had been. Her paws went instinctively to her legs and felt up and down them searching for any signs of injury. There were none. She sat up straight and leaned over, stroking her leg fur against the grain to see the skin underneath. There were no injuries at all, not even signs of scars. "Incredible. How did they do it?" Keeping an ear turned towards the door, she shifted to her side and felt the base of her tail, carefully, slowly working her way back and forth where she remembered the terrible pain. Again, she was whole and healthy.

She sat there for a moment, in that position, thinking. Van was obviously in very bad shape, but improving, if the doctor could be believed. It followed, logically, that she was being worked on by a whole team of specialists. "I wonder how many of them worked on me." She had only seen the one doctor, but there had to be more. "I wonder where the nurses and attendants are?" she asked herself. Obviously, the place was very well funded, so it couldn't be that paying for them was a problem. Sahnassa then realized she was probably being monitored, and her blush furs lifted high. "Great, the nurse just saw me feel up my tail ... again!" she groaned inwardly.

After righting herself to a more appropriate position, the question still nagged at her about this place. A list of attributes played through her thoughts. "Well-equipped, well-funded, doctors actually the ones taking care of patients, so they have to be well paid, the latest cutting-edge health care ... a corporate pack? Perhaps a foundation ... like a partnership, between corporate packs, family houses, and the government, maybe even an academy or two?" That, of all the explanations, seemed to make the most sense, especially when she remembered his comment earlier. When Sahni had observed that there was no way Vanarra's frugal health insurer would cover such lavish care, he had told her that it didn't have to, that it was "paid for by other sources."

She felt sure she had arrived at the correct answer, and that answer made her feel a little guilty. She wasn't exactly following the doctor's orders, and this foundation was being very generous with the care she was receiving. "I'm sorry," she said aloud. "I'm going to get busy on my therapy now." No one answered, and she hoped as she stood and started to make her way to the next chair, that it also meant that no one had seen her feel up her tail.

When the doctor arrived delivering the next meal for Sahnassa, she was resting on the bed, breathing hard. She had thrown herself into her therapy and completed twenty full circuits, plus forced herself to play the game for a limited amount of time and also read through half of one book. "You might just be overdoing it a little," he observed, walking over to her after placing the tray on the table.

"I … was worried I was being lazy, especially given how much is being done for me," she explained.

"Why don't you lie on your back for me?" he asked. She did as he requested and closed her eyes. As he examined her, she tried not to show how much she was enjoying his attentions — the warm feeling of his paws on her legs and arms, his gentle touch on her neck, and the way he stroked the fur on top of her head as he spoke to her.

"How are you feeling, other than tired? That I can guess on my own," he joked softly.

She giggled back. "Alright, actually. I'm still a little weak, but I can tell I'm getting better. I had some problems focusing on the book – I mean concentrating not focusing, but I ate some more food and rested a little, then I was okay."

"That's good. You found the game engaging?"

"Oh, yes. I enjoyed it. I've never seen anything like it before. I … probably played it just a bit too much, though."

"Well, that was likely just your preference, and that's okay." He ceased his examinations and helped her sit back up. "Well, we're both right; you're a little exhausted, but otherwise, you're right on track, but you still have a strong need for rest. I want you to after you eat, okay? Lie down and sleep."

"Yes, Doctor," she said, opening her eyes and looking up at him. She then observed that, thanks to her naps and the lack of windows or clocks, she had no idea what interval of the sol it was. "I'm … finding it a little difficult not having some kind of timepiece to look at."

"It's hard, isn't it? However, for your recovery, you don't need to be on any schedule, either real or imagined. Listen to your body; do what it tells you to. If you're hungry, eat; if you're sleepy, rest. You'll make the fastest progress that way. Okay?" His admonishment was gentle, but firm.

"Okay," Sahnassa answered nodding.

"Don't worry," he reassured her. "You're doing well enough that it's only two more sols before you can go."

She hesitated before asking him, but Sahnassa felt she had to; she had worked out several things in her head about where she was, but Sahni was still curious. "And about that. Where am I? What kind of a place is this?"

He seemed unperturbed by the question. "You're in a health care facility; it's part of a larger complex."

"Corporate pack, house, or government?" she asked, finding his explanation very little more than a statement of the obvious.

"Oh, government," he added apologetically. "It's a secret, however, because of the technology involved. I'd ask you to keep what you see to yourself when you leave, if you wouldn't mind?"

"Certainly. I'm very grateful for what you've done for us. I apologize for my curiosity; I don't mean to press you on it."

"It's alright. Ask your questions. Since it's my job to give the answers, I'll make sure I keep us both out of trouble."

She looked around the room, her eyes again full of awe. "It's just that this is such an incredible place! Government, okay, I get that, but you've got some commercial sponsorship, though; I mean you'd have to."

He smiled a bit as he answered. "You'd be surprised. We don't get any corporate pack sponsorship, whatsoever. Mind you, I'm not saying we couldn't generate that type of interest if we wanted it, but strictly speaking, it's not needed. This facility is resourced and closely watched at the highest levels, and very few are ever afforded these services. It's … a bit of a rare honor, actually."

"I guess so. However, that makes me wonder … why us?" Sahnassa asked.

"Well, you were both badly injured, and I don't want to dwell on that, but we felt you could be helped by what we had to offer, and it seems to be paying good benefits for both you and Vanarra," he explained, with a little pride. Sahnassa couldn't help but think he looked cute; it was clear he was showing off a little.

"Well, thank you. Am … am I likely to have any long term, well, side effects from the treatment?" she asked, a little hesitantly.

"None at all," he answered with conviction. "At least from a physical sense; I know what you went through was traumatic and frightening. You may want to seek some counseling or at least a good friend to talk to, from time to time. I think, however, once your subconscious realizes that you came out of this episode okay, the bad dreams and fears will settle down, given time."

"I take it that the treatment … itself, is what's classified?" she asked.

"I'm afraid so. This level of technology is just a little bit more than most Thurian doctors are ready for. Then, there's idea rights and regulation and marketing and well, you know."

She actually chuckled, although it did strike her as a little strange that he said "most *Thurian* doctors." "I understand. I've seen what some computer device makers go through; it's not much fun – so many forms to fill out."

"Exactly!" he exclaimed so decisively that she had to laugh again. "And you think taxes and family dues are bad? Trust me, it wouldn't even begin to compare!"

She chuckled for a moment more before asking, "Can I try another question?"

"Well, you do need to rest," he warned, growing a little serious.

"Only one more," she promised. "Did you … did you develop the technology, uh, treatment?"

He again smiled at her, looking a little pleased. "I had a big part in it, but I didn't do it all on my own. I've got some very smart minds working on it with me. Now, let's get you to the facilities, back to the table for your meal, and after that, I want you to rest."

She smiled as she took his offered paw. "Thank you."

The sound of the doctor entering the room was the only thing that woke her from her nap. "Oh, hello," she said groggily as the lights slowly brightened.

"Hi there," he answered, bringing another plate of food to the table on the far side of the room.

Sahnassa shook her head. She ate so well before her nap that she wondered if she needed anymore food for the rest of the moon, let alone the rest of the sol. "I'm going to get spoiled; you know? You keep bringing such wonderful food every time you visit."

"Well, forgive me, but it's my pleasure. Right now, you're my only patient who can enjoy such things."

The tacit mention of Van brought Sahnassa to a sitting position on the bed. "How is Vanarra?"

"It's been a tough few intervals, but we're finally through it," he admitted. "The entire staff has been completely absorbed with her case in some fashion. It's frankly some of the best work they've ever done."

"Will ... will she be alright?" Sahnassa asked timidly. "Can I see her?"

"Yes and no," he answered a little apologetically. "I believe she's out of danger and will fully recover; I'm feeling pretty good about saying that, given present circumstances. Unfortunately, letting you see her now would require exposing you to some classified technology. I'll have to impose on your patience a little while longer."

Sahnassa shook her head. "Whatever it takes to get her well, please. That's all I want."

He nodded approvingly as he walked back to her bedside. "Now, lie back for me." Again, she had to lay there and just endure his wondrous touches, all the while trying not to let her embarrassment or sensual interest show. "Now, open your mouth," he bade, and she did so. "Good color; very good color. Could you get up and take a walk for me? One full circuit around?"

Sahnassa nodded and carefully slipped off the bed. This time, she felt much more her normal self. The weakness and lack of coordination she experienced before were beginning to fade, and she made it all the way around almost at a normal walk. "Hey, that's not bad, is it?"

"I think it's great," he said approvingly. "Balance feels alright?"

Sahni leaned a little left and right, and then forward and back. "I'd say so," she answered. "I can still feel it a little, in my knees and hips." She then concentrated as she swished her tail back and forth. "Maybe even in the base of my tail?" Sahni mused with honest curiosity before she realized what this would mean. "Uh, it's not bad, though," she stammered, backing up a little.

"Probably should still have a look. Back up on the bed, chest facing the floor." Unable to control her embarrassment any longer, she complied slowly. "Now, up on knees and elbows. Now, slowly lay the bottom of your muzzle on the bed."

As she complied, Sahnassa was almost shaking with humiliation and, she hated to admit, excitement. Gently, he felt down her back to where her tail began and thoroughly checked the base before taking several passes carefully palpitating its full length. It was all she could do to keep from sighing at his gentle touches, and she knew that this experience would definitely inspire some good fantasies later. "It's the same kind of fatigue you're experiencing in your legs. It's going to fade in time, but it will be tomorrow before it does. It's not a problem. You can get down now."

Sahnassa was so over-stimulated that she could barely breathe let alone move, but as the doctor turned away to lift the covers off her meal, she managed to right herself. Thoroughly embarrassed at her condition, she whispered, "I'll be back in a moment," and darted through the facilities door as quickly as she could manage.

After several deep breaths and many iterations of her Nephti mantra, Sahni finally emerged, calm enough to speak again and her tail now lowered back to a respectable level. "I'm sorry," she said to the Vulpi who had just finished changing the covers on her bed. "I just needed a moment."

"Oh, no, I apologize," he replied. "It's not your fault at all. I didn't mean to embarrass you. It's just that some of the fibrous muscle in your tail is a good indicator as to whether or not we did our jobs properly. It seems normal enough; you've nothing to worry about. I'll leave you alone to eat, and then you rest, okay?"

"Alright," Sahni agreed. "Thank you ... for taking such good care of me."

He nodded and then left her. As she made her way to the couch to begin eating, Sahnassa couldn't help but notice that her mother's Nephti-only mantra didn't seem to help very much.

The next time she awoke, Sahnassa was alone, but the room seemed to sense her waking and raised the lights for her. "Either that, or someone is actually watching me." After she had collected herself enough to think properly, she slipped off the bed and made her way – with ease this time, she noticed – to the facilities. Upon exiting, she decided to make a little closer examination of her room.

She started by walking around its circumference. Looking at the smooth walls, Sahni noticed something she was surprised she hadn't before – there were no outlets of any kind. That was at odds with every other medical facility she'd ever been to; walls covered with ports for air, power, computer communications, and many others were always commonplace. She reached for and felt the wall, sliding her sensitive paw pads along its slightly rough surface. It was perfectly regular. There were no seams and, leaning against the wall looking along its length, she saw no imperfections in its finish. Sahnassa tapped quietly along the wall, but her taps never changed tone. "No supports or, is it all supports?" she wondered.

Leaving the wall for a moment, she went to the couch and chairs. They looked normal enough, but when she pulled one of the cushions out, she noticed something else. "No seams here, either. Wow, this had to be expensive! Mom and Dad would just love this," she thought.

Remembering her parents for the first time made her sigh and feel quite sad. Losing interest in her investigations, she placed the cushion back where it belonged and sat on the couch. "It's not like they'd miss me much anyway, even if I *had* died," she thought despondently. Sahnassa remembered the arguments, the shouting matches, and then the sol she had left them. She remembered the stony silence that had lasted for seasons and how her father didn't support her in the academy. Their lack of attendance when she finally graduated and the cold, short note of congratulations when she had graced them with her first family dues payment – those still hurt.

Sahnassa dwelled on that pain awhile, but then realized that she almost made a horrible mistake. She had nearly died without making peace with them or at least apologizing for her part in the arguments, even if they would never apologize for theirs. Sahni bowed her head and cried. Perhaps after learning what happened to her; perhaps after sols and moons of waiting, maybe her dad would forgive her and hug her one more time. Perhaps her mother would stop worrying about what the dame or the matron or her friends thought and simply love her as a daughter once again.

As the tears continued, Sahnassa felt a presence at her side. "You okay, Sahnassa?" the doctor asked softly.

"When can I talk to my family?" she asked, trying to steady her voice.

"I'm hoping you'll be able to the sol after next," he answered. "May I ask what's bothering you? Are you in pain?"

She looked up at him, and his expression was so sympathetic towards her that she simply had to reassure the Vulpi. "It's ... it's not medical. I guess I'm just sort of realizing how close I actually came, and how I would have hated to have left things as they are, especially with my family."

He sat down beside her and placed his paw gently on her back. "I know. You'll get the chance now to change things, if you want to."

"I'm so grateful for that," she replied, brightening a little. "I ... I want to know how much I'm allowed to tell them about this wonderful place. I mean, I haven't ever seen anything like this room, the game, the bed, even the cushions. I haven't even read about this stuff. It's so cutting edge; it's like you've been salvaging alien spacecraft or something," she joked.

He looked at her and smiled. "No alien artifacts were salvaged to create what you see, that I can promise. We'll have a talk later about what can and can't be shared, but I wouldn't worry too much about it. You're alive and well, and that's all that matters."

"Thank you," she replied, "and whatever you and your team have done to make sure I get a second chance with my family again, thank you for that, too. Now, can you tell me about Vanarra?"

"Improving," he answered, pleased, "and she's showing good progress, as are you. I think tomorrow you'll be ready for some answers and a more serious discussion of what happened to you and Vanarra on that mountain, don't you?" She nodded, and he smiled at her agreement. "Now, just like last night, I have your meal outside, and I'll bring that in for you, and then I'll give you something else to help you rest through the night."

"Will I get to leave my room tomorrow?" she asked.

"Feeling a little caged, are we?" he teased. "We'll see what we can do."

"Can … can I ask you a favor?"

"Sure," he replied.

"Would you please give me a hug?" It was forward of her, she knew, but she just felt like she needed it, regardless if she wanted it or not.

Smiling, he lifted her to her hind paws, took her in his arms and gently hugged her. "It's going to be alright. I promise."

Accepting the comfort more than the sensuality of the action, she replied, "Thank you." With that, he guided her back to the bed before exiting the room to retrieve her meal. "He is the nicest doctor I've ever met, Vulpi or no," she said as she waited for him to return. "Somewhere, there had better be a really great Vulpi kit that can see how good he actually is."

She awoke in the same comfort she did before, this time alone. She felt really nice, almost "frisky." "Down Sahni," she told herself, snuggling against the pillow. Her thoughts returned to the doctor; she just *had* to ask his name. Idly she wondered if a nurse or attendant would ever come by.

She drifted off for what seemed to her only a moment and then awoke once again.

She was a little less comfortable this time, largely because her body was telling her that the desire to sleep and necessary relief were not completely in balance. Sahni stretched long and luxuriously before getting up and making her way, albeit shakily, to the bathroom.

Once done with the essentials, she looked at herself in the mirror once again. Reaching out, Sahnassa touched it intending only to make contact with her own image, but the whole mirror moved. "It's a door!" she thought to herself, and carefully, she pushed the door open, revealing a large, darkened room beyond. Lights came to life on the other side, beckoning her forward. As she stepped through, she had to shake her head in self-disgust. "There's a whole half of the bathroom I just missed!" Now, she couldn't help noticing the large shower, perhaps the largest she had ever seen. Water jets were spaced along all sides. "Oh, I've got to try this!"

She shucked out of her clothes and jumped into the shower, closing a glass door behind her. Soon, she was actually sighing at how good the pulsating jets of water felt against her body. She experimented with different jets and different settings, and it wasn't long before Sahni was slowly sinking to her knees from the sensuous pleasure afforded by the warm streams of water pelting her back and shoulders like an expert masseuse. With some effort, she was able to right herself, find the soap, and start to clean.

After more than half an interval of showering, Sahnassa finally rinsed herself. Opening the steam-covered door and looking around, she found a stack of thick towels, grabbed a few, and began slowly drying out her fur. Just as she reached that damp but not dripping stage, she noticed a full-body dryer – a rather nice one – attached to the wall. With a very pleased smile, she stepped from the shower and keyed the controls. After enjoying that luxury for almost a quarter interval and giving her fur a good thorough brushing, she put her clothes back on and returned to the bed. A new tray of food was waiting on the cart for her, but the doctor was nowhere in evidence. She settled down and had almost finished eating when he finally joined her. "Good morning; I hope you slept well."

"Yes," she said, her mouth not completely empty, and Sahni made a quick effort to swallow, embarrassed again.

"Good. So how do you feel this morning?" he asked cheerfully, but with an air of concern.

"Perfectly well, actually. How's Vanarra?"

He smiled and answered, "Slowly improving, but improving. I think we'll get her back all the way. Now, I know you have questions, and to save you the effort, why don't I hit some of the details? Alright?" Sahni nodded. "As far as what happened to you, it looks like the entire ridgeline you were parked beside just let go. The land had been cleared of deep-rooted vegetation by disease, insects, and recent brush fires. Heavy rains over the last moon combined with a moderate ground quake knocked loose huge amounts of dirt and other debris, sweeping you off the road, and pretty much demolishing it entirely. I hope the Meeting Den on top of the mountain has a plan to bypass the road damage and the bridges that collapsed. They're going to be pretty isolated up there for awhile. It looks like they took some serious building damage, as well."

"There's a little justice there. They weren't very kind to Vanarra," she thought. Outwardly, she just nodded.

"The quake brought down the bridge outside the entrance, so it's a fair guess they know they're trapped."

Sahni processed that for a moment and then quickly shook her head. "Hold it. I'm either not hearing you right or not understanding. How badly was I injured?" She saw his reluctance to tell her, and said, "Please. I need to know."

He shook his head in resignation, but answered. "Severely broken legs, crushed ribs, a nearly severed tail, crushed vertebrae, severe internal injuries, and a dangerous concussion. That's excluding numerous deep cuts, ligament tears, toxic fume and smoke inhalation, and minor crush injuries."

Feeling a little bit sick, Sahni pulled her legs close to her and asked, "Oh, how is that possible? I remember it, don't get me wrong, but I don't understand how those at the Meeting Den couldn't know … by now. It's been many sols, hasn't it? Maybe even a moon or two?"

He smiled, soft and sly. "Ah, you've hit the key point, and now is when your little experience here is going to get interesting. Let's try breaking it to you this way. It's only been half an interval since the landslide. When I brought you and Vanarra aboard, it was half an interval since the landslide, and it continues to be *exactly* half an interval since the landslide – in external, relative time." He ended the sentence exactly the same way an instructor from her academy might have done when posing a logic problem.

She sat quietly for a moment just staring at him. Sahnassa could almost hear his thoughts, "You're a smart kit; think it through." She shook her head; the only options coming to her mind were too fantastic, but her earlier musings about the bed, the room, the game, her treatment, and everything else actually pointed to a whole host of questions. "It's just – it's like – aboard a – how – either I'm – this isn't – I'm not – you're not – relative time?!"

He chuckled at her rapid-fire stream of consciousness. "Slow down; actually ask the questions you're thinking of, and only one at a time."

She took a breath and tried to calm herself. Finally, after a deep exhale, she asked, "You're not a doctor, are you?"

"My qualifications and knowledge far exceed any doctor you've ever met, or likely ever will." His expression was kind but certain.

Still not completely parsing what he meant, she tried again. "You said, you brought us aboard. This isn't a hospital?"

"It's the Tashar. It's my ship, and I consider it my home."

"Not like an on the water ship?" she asked, a little hesitantly.

"Not exclusively, no," he answered, smiling.

"And this really isn't a secret government health facility, is it?" she asked, realizing that everything he told her might have been a lie.

"No, this really is a health care facility *aboard the Tashar*, and it is a government secret, but just not a secret of *your* government." She could tell his answer emphasized the fact that he had been telling her the truth all along, even if she didn't understand the details.

"Am I hallucinating?"

His smile grew bigger at her question. "Generally speaking, such fine dining isn't offered in hallucinations," he answered, a slight smirk across his muzzle.

"Are you like … mentally…" she asked, making a looping motion with her paw finger to indicate "crazy."

Now, he was suppressing a laugh as he answered her. "You'll have to judge that for yourself, once you've seen some more evidence. Let's just say that most of the truly delusional can't cook as well as I do."

"And the whole half an interval since the landslide thing…"

He sat on the far corner of her bed. "The Tashar is 'holding position' in time. In short, if time was a flowing stream, we're swimming upstream at the exact speed that time is flowing downstream. Therefore, our relative position doesn't change. It's a temporal hover, if you will.

That's how your family believes you to be safe. Not enough time has gone by for them to worry."

"Oh." She hesitated and hugged herself a little tighter when asking her next question. "Where are you from?"

"Ah, yes. Here's the big answer. I'm not from your neighborhood, celestially speaking. The planet I come from is called Allarrae. It's a few universes and dimensions removed from your own."

His assertion struck her, as did all of his statements, as truly hard to believe. "You're like … an alien?" Sahni questioned dubiously. "But you look like a Thurian? You even smell like a Thurian. I mean … not bad" – her blush furs again – "just, and don't get me wrong, you look good, and you smell … fine but just … Thurian."

"True, this is what I look like, and smell like … right now," was his patient reply.

"Could you like change into something else, while I watch?" She knew she had him on this point. If he was a fake, he would say no.

"Certainly. Could you watch without losing consciousness?" he questioned warily.

"Fainting? Oh, sure. Don't worry about that. I've seen this kind of stuff on VidStar lots of times! I'm a real space fiction buff," she said with a little pride.

"It's different in the flesh, you know? Sit back in the bed, just in case. I've fixed your head once, already. Now, let's see, what to choose? How about me when I was your age?"

"Alright, go ahead," she agreed. He nodded, and his form began to glow and expand, larger and larger until it filled all of the open space in the room. A huge, seething, shimmering, winged, lizard-like being bent its long, serpentine head towards her and nodded. Its skin was iridescent purplish pink, and it seemed to almost glow with an inner power. She felt its hot breath on her body and in her face. Her eyes blurred a little, and her vision started to close in on her.

The great, wedged head gently nudged her so she would lie back in the bed. "Wow – okay, you're right, you're right! Just give me a tick or two," she pleaded, closing her eyes. "Oh, wow! I know, I know, deep breaths," she said in response to a rumbling that seemed like a combination of an admonishment and a reminder that he had warned her. "Give a kit a pass or two; I mean you could have just turned into a tree or something instead of a … whew! Oh, wow! Please, please, just don't change back, not yet! I've been waiting my whole life to see something like this … like you, I mean. I'm sorry." The rumble from the creature could hardly be interpreted as anything other than a deep chuckle.

After a few moments, the room stopped spinning, and the light-headed feeling faded away. "Okay. I'm going to try this again." Slowly, she opened her eyes and looked up. Propping herself on her elbows brought the great creature again into full view. "Wow!" she breathed, looking up and down its shimmering length. Again, she had to fight both her lightheadedness and her flight instincts. Her heart was racing, and she had to consciously struggle not to lose control. "You won't hurt me, will you?" The large beast shook its head in agreement. "Can ... can I touch you?"

The glowing violet eyes blinked, and the long head of the beast settled lightly across her legs. A river-fruit sized eye blinked at her from no more than arm's length away. Her soft paw pads reached out, almost on their own, to stroke ridges of purple-blue scales behind the eye. Sahni shook her head, open-mouthed. "They're *so* soft," she cooed. "You're just beautiful! I always wondered what it would be like. We have legends, stories of creatures like you, but nothing so marvelous!" The great head gently lifted away from her touch, looked at her, blinked, and then melted back into the keen-looking Vulpi.

"You did better than I thought you would," he said, seemingly proud of her.

"This bed, the room, it all makes sense! I can't believe it! It's real! It's all real! The alien abduction stories, shape changers that walk among us, the unidentified flyers in the sky, the secret government organizations!" Her excitement was almost frenzied as she contemplated the possibilities.

"Well, not exactly, and not how most of your fiction authors make it out to be. I'm real; the Tashar is real, but in truth, your galaxy is pretty devoid of life outside of your own planet. When I scanned your world, I couldn't find any other evidence of a visitation like mine or even other space faring civilizations within this half of your galaxy. It's probably going to be a very long time before your kind runs into someone new."

"Oh," Sahni said, obviously deflated.

"Don't be disappointed. That's a good thing, actually," he consoled. "Even in your history, when technically advanced civilizations wandered into the territories of those less advanced, the less advanced paid the price. That story is not unique to your world. Given some of what's out there, it wouldn't be a bad idea to get a little bit more advanced before that happens. Look at it this way: the price was high, but you and your friend Vanarra are perhaps the most fortunate beings on this planet ever to have lived. For the last ten thousand seasons and perhaps the next ten thousand, you are the only ones ever to see or be seen by an alien."

Sahni sat in quiet reflection for a moment. "Vanarra. I nearly forgot. You told me what happened to me..." She left her request unspoken, as it was obvious.

His expression grew serious and concerned. "I can tell you care very deeply for her. You asked about her first, even before your own tail. Are you sure you want to know?"

"Please, and I want to see her, too," she said, nearly begging.

The Vulpi had a grim expression on his face, but nodded. "Very well. She took the full impact of the rocks and other debris that hit your vehicle, and the first hits were very hard. She had massive head trauma and severe brain damage to her left side. The left side of her body was almost completely crushed, and her left arm was severed. If she were relying on the medicine of the best trauma team on your planet, and they were present immediately after the injury, she would be looking at many sols of surgery and a very sad and much shortened life. The individuality, the uniqueness of her, would be gone; there was simply too much damage for the spirit to survive. In truth, given where you were, she would have died almost immediately after you lost consciousness."

The images that came to Sahni's mind were horrific, imagining Vanarra in that condition for the rest of her life, and then imagining her being pulled from the wreckage dead made her cry. "It's hard to hear, I know. I know." He comforted her with a strong arm around her shoulder.

"How can even you heal that?" Sahnassa cried, and then looked up at him, aching for reassurance. "Can you heal that?"

"Yes," he said softly. "I can bring her back to full health, but I'm using more than just medical techniques here. I'm playing some games with time. So far, so good. Her ... reconstruction ... is far enough along that you can visit her. Would you like to go now?" Sahnassa nodded yes, and he guided her off the bed and out the door.

They passed into a nicely decorated hallway that was as inviting as her room – soft colors, carpeted floors, elegantly understated ornamental carvings on the wall. After walking for a few moments, Sahni noticed that some of the hallways they were passing were quite long.

"How big is the Tashar?" Sahni asked as she glanced behind her.

"Quite large. It's configurable, as well. I can change its arrangement, as needed, even to suit a special guest," he replied, looking down at her, kindly.

"So everything here was created … for me, I mean for us?" She looked again at the details of the carpet, the colors, and had to admit that this was very much in her taste.

"Yes, in this section of the ship."

She looked around again in renewed wonder, now that she knew he had created everything for her. "It's all so wonderful! I love my room. Thank you."

They were stopping at an ornately carved wooden door as he replied. "I'm glad you like it. We're here. Now, please understand that she is alive, regardless of what you see. Stay well back from the containment unit and don't try to touch it. It's protected by a force barrier, and they *hurt*. Keeping her perfectly still is very important. Are you ready?" She nodded, and the door in front of them slid open. The large, round room had what looked like a single large cylindrical aquarium in the center of it. Floating inside was the nude form of Vanarra. As Sahni walked forward holding his paw, it looked as if she was simply sleeping. Vanarra's long tail floated behind her, and the rest of her body looked unharmed – stunning, in fact, as Sahni had never seen her this way. Around her neck was a collar with a round, jewel-like disk attached to it, pulsating slowly on and off.

"She looks alright, at least on the outside," Sahnassa observed, hopefully.

"Healing the body is never the problem; it's healing the mind that's difficult. In this case, it means putting it back together."

"I don't understand."

An image appeared right in front of them, hovering in midair. It was a graph, with multiple wavy lines of information in different colors that pulsed from left to right. He explained, "This is a very small piece of what you would call a brain-wave pattern. You've probably seen things like this before?" She nodded in response. "Well, what you've seen up to now is a massive over-simplification. It looks more like this." The image changed to a three-dimensional brain outline rotating in front of them, with shifting colors and dazzling patterns firing in multiple directions within.

"Dropping the outline," he said. The brain image went away, leaving only the light patterns. "That, in many ways, is you. The incredible harmony of those patterns across all of your neurons and synapses make up who and what you are. The patterns control how memories are built, what areas of the brain are sought out for their information, and what areas are not. Mechanics vary from species to species, but for you, this is how it works. As you've seen, we can get the biology put back together fairly easily if we have a starting point of reference. A back-scan in time allowed me to get her pre-injury state in full detail. It's reestablishing those brain patterns that can take time. If you don't do it in the right way, then she really wouldn't be who she was." The image faded away.

"It's amazing. What's that around her neck?" Sahni asked, pointing to Van's only piece of clothing.

"That is a control collar," he answered, "and that is what's building new variations into her damaged patterns, in addition to keeping her alive. Right now, the collar has full control of all of her mental and bodily functions." Sahni felt herself become a little distracted by his statement. The "control collar" was triggering a favorite secret fantasy in her thoughts, even while he continued speaking. "What it's doing is a slow process, basically constrained by the brain chemistry of the subject. According to my estimates, we've got about two more sols before the collar is able to modify her thought patterns to match the moment just before the landslide. Take some comfort that, based on my scan of the events just before impact, *you* were responsible for establishing a stable and reproducible pattern."

That statement instantly pulled her out of her inward distraction. "Me?"

"She was very agitated, angry, it seemed. Then she was concerned for you, and it really calmed her down. Had she not pulled over, you would have still been hit by the landslide, and her patterns would have almost been irretrievable or unusable. You see, you can't separate the biology of this type of brain too far from the patterns within; there are problems when you do that. So, your friendship saved her – the simple fact she was concerned for you." Sahni couldn't help but start crying, and she hugged him, and he held her. "You've been a great friend to her, more than you ever thought you could. You helped save her life." It took her a few passes to collect herself, but eventually she let go and looked up into his eyes. "You can come back whenever you want."

"Thank you," she said softly, looking back at Vanarra again.

Patting her shoulder gently, he slowly led her away.

Chapter 2: Shared Discovery

As the door closed behind him, she asked, "Is there somewhere we can go and just talk?"

"Yes. There is a garden not far from here."

As they walked, Sahnassa tentatively spoke. "I realized just a moment ago that I probably shouldn't keep calling you Doctor. What's your name?"

"Hmm," he mused. "I always struggle with this part a little. You see, sometimes, it doesn't translate very well. Let me think. Theoreign de Draconis? Anarkus de Argilis? Polis de Arkus? It needs to be something that matches the forms of your culture. Okay, how's this: Theo de Allarrae? Will that do?"

Sahnassa laughed, "If you like it; I think it's very nice!"

"Thank you. I think Sahnassa is a very pretty name; what's its origin?"

"It's the name of a beautiful blooming plant that's my mother's favorite. Some of my friends started calling me Sahni, after Vanarra came up with it. My mother hates it when they do."

"Why is that?"

"Well, we're a very … formal family," she answered, a little embarrassed. "The purest of purebreds every one, as they say. Nearly all are in positions of respect or importance – teachers, arbiters, litigators, archive keepers, financiers, and so on. If one of our family wanted to become a groomer, for example, I think our matriarch would disavow them in a blink."

"Does what you do meet with her approval?"

Sahnassa hedged slightly. "Yes and no. Believe it or not, I'm the lone technologist of the family, and she doesn't quite know what to make of me. When she asks what I do, I tell her about all of the complex systems I manage, and how it's my job to make sure they keep running. She knows how much I make, and that seems to keep her satisfied. I just carefully avoid talking about who I actually work for."

"Vanarra?"

"Yes. Let's just say that might be a very difficult conversation. Vanarra's business comes very close to, well, being considered – well, let's just say it's not always the kind of business polite society likes to talk about. It's just a celebrations business, really, at the heart of it. We cater food, set up tables, make flower arrangements, and do VidStar recordings – that sort of thing. However, the kinds of celebrations we sometimes cater are a little fringe…"

"Oh, how so?" he asked.

Sahnassa was trying hard to walk through her description on paw tips. "Well, mostly because they involve … relationships, in a way. There's the obvious stuff, of course, like before a male and a female join themselves to one another, both will frequently want a final night of wildness before the tame sets in. No one ever tells their matriarchs that those parties happen or even worse, what happens *during* them. It's the kind of thing that you joke about and share with your friends, but don't ever speak of it around the family. Then, there are the Primalists."

"Oh, who are they?" he asked.

It took a moment to think of a good definition. "There are a very close-knit group of Thurians that, if you saw them on the street or in their jobs, you'd never know they were Primalists. Oh, wow!" Sahni was forced to stop talking as they had now entered the courtyard of the most beautiful indoor garden she had ever beheld. Not only were the grounds picturesque in every way, the enormous expanse above them was crowned by intricate vaulted ceilings that almost split the viewer in two, trying to look up and down at the same time. Cascading waterfalls beside winding paths lined with lush fruit trees and elegant blooming plants absorbed her complete attention.

"Shall we enter?" he asked, smiling at her reaction.

Sahnassa was wonder-struck. "Oh, Theo, it's just … I don't know! I've never seen anything so beautiful!" Realizing that he created it for her, she gripped his paw and wrapped her tail around his midsection. He walked them forward to a gazebo overlooking a small clearing wrapped in flowers just below. As she looked down, she first imagined being down there, and then thought about being down there with Theo, alone.

"The Primalists, you were saying?" Theo's voice and outstretched paw holding a glass of juice brought her back.

"Oh, yes. Thank you," Sahni said, sitting down. "I'm not totally familiar with everything they believe, but from what I understand, the core group thinks we have left too much of our *primal* selves behind over the seasons. Technological comforts, office jobs, and bank accounts take away from who they think we were truly meant to be. So, they have festivals or dances, they're called, where they … let their primal side out."

"Have you ever been? What do they do?"

Her blush furs rose up full. "Well, Vanarra talked me into going once. No cameras are allowed, so I was there just to help run things. It all starts innocently enough, with the herding. That's a formal banquet and dance about the eighth interval after mid-sol. It's really everyone checking each other out. The males and females try to check out their rivals and prospective … mates. If you didn't know any better, you might think it was a simple, innocent celebration. The young males of the wealthy classes are there, the star sports performers, along with the untitled daughters of prominent business leaders. Then, at the fifth interval before high night, there comes the shedding. They all follow two hooded guides. Males follow one, and females follow another to two separate camps. Generally, there's a great bonfire in each camp, and then … they all … disrobe. They're supposed to be shedding their modern age pretenses, which, ironically enough, they enjoyed quite nicely during the three prior intervals of eating and drinking and putting on airs."

Theo chuckled. "I see your point. Is there more?"

Sahnassa swallowed and tried to force both her tail and blush furs down before continuing. "Yes. After the shedding, come the contests. For the males, it is wrestling. They have several divisions, so at the end, you have six champions. For the females, there are contests of endurance, grace, appearance, and even some wrestling, but it's not as intense as the males. They pick six champions, too. After that, comes the hunt. This is where it gets a little – are you sure you still want to hear about all this?"

"If you are okay; it's very interesting." His serious nod and tone assured her his interest was purely scientific, sociological perhaps. There were no suggestions or overtones in what he was saying, but that still didn't make telling it any easier. After all, he might not be reacting, but Sahni was having a hard time keeping her tail down. She couldn't help thinking about how good he looked – Vulpi, mystic creature, or alien. She was really starting to just "like" him as well.

"I'll do my best. I apologize; I'm just a little embarrassed about this, but I'll go on." He smiled and nodded, and she said, "All of the champions are then *collared* and are taken to their *pens* to rest up for the hunt. Now, supposedly the champions are given some kind of performance enhancing drugs, all legal, but designed to highly stimulate their … natural drive. Vanarra said it was the same stuff they give to aging government officials, so how bad could it be, right? At the fourth interval after high night, each of the females is released, several ticks apart, into the hunting ground. They spread out and wait for the males to be released one interval later. Then, the males hunt out the females – and if a Vulpi wants to hunt a Nephti, so be it. That's the part that really twitches the matriarchs' tails. Now, all of the females are spiked, that is, given something to prevent gestation; it's a well-enforced rule. After all, a child would be, like, proof. When the females are caught, well, you can guess what happens, then."

"I see. Is that the end?" he asked, still seemingly curious.

Over the most difficult part of the description, Sahnassa was more relaxed as she answered. "Well, if they weren't chosen for the hunt, some just go back to their rooms and go to bed. Others pair up with a female or male they met earlier at the banquet, and some just sit naked around the fire all night talking about Primalism. The next morning, there's a final ceremony where those who have coupled are honored and toasted. The entire thing ends with a pledge that all that has happened will remain a secret. There isn't much talking about it, especially in front of the young, and *especially* not in the presence of parents, matrons, dames, or matriarchs. However, news is always circulating about rich Thurians who are now joined to someone they met at a dance. No one ever tells if it was a Primalist dance, but amongst the good looking and strong and wealthy, you always wonder."

"Interesting," Theo mused, considering what she had said. "So although attended by the famed and notable, primals are kept a strict societal secret – a contract of secrecy to which most of the attendees and staff also adhere?"

"That's one of the reasons Vanarra has done so well," Sahni offered. "She caters the banquet, provides the refreshments for the wrestling and so forth, and then for the final ceremony. Still, she keeps totally quiet about who was there or what they did and swears everyone who works with her to the same absolute secrecy. If you say *anything*, you're fired and, worse, everyone she does business with will know you can't keep your muzzle shut. For most of her employees, that would mean having to move to another city to find work and starting all over again without any references. Needless to say, secrecy isn't a problem."

"Have you participated in the shedding or the contests?"

Sahnassa was completely embarrassed. "Oh, no, I just couldn't! Besides, I was working. But Vanarra – well, perhaps I shouldn't say anything."

"It won't get back to her; I promise. So Vanarra did?"

Sahnassa cocked her head a bit and smiled, thinking of her friend. "I'm proud of her, in a way. She says this doesn't happen often, but the organizers were so pleased with her that they asked her to enter. No mistaking, she looks great; she works out. She's always turned them down, politely of course, but I know that she would just *love* to take on some of those purebreds. If she was chosen for the hunt, I'm not even sure who would be doing the hunting!" They both laughed at the joke.

"You really seem to admire her," Theo observed, curious.

"It didn't start out that way. She used to always tease me and call me 'purebred' after I first hired on. See, I was working two jobs and going to graduate academy at the same time, so I didn't exactly have the best marks. None of the pack-leading companies were interested. After being turned down dozens of times, Vanarra found me, by accident. She offered; I applied, and she hired me. I didn't even really know what they did, but when the first paycheck came, I figured I could live with it. As for Vanarra, it took a lot longer before I started to find out things about her, like she grew up being called Anati, or muddle-breed, by all of the other children, and that was even before her mother died. After that, there was nowhere for her to go and no family that would claim her. She scraped by, lived a really horrible life, but she still did everything she could to get educated and just stay alive. Regardless if Thurians don't think much of the business she runs, she's accomplished so much. She gives back, too. She's generous to all of her employees." Sahnassa's admiration and pride in her boss and friend was enthusiastic.

"That's very commendable," Theo said, appreciatively.

"And that's not all! The concept of a home for those kits and cubs with no family or matriarch isn't a popular one among Thurians, but there are a few good souls out there, and a lot of her profit goes to support an orphanage. She visits there and volunteers. When I watch her, I realize

I've led a very tame and mothered life. She's found the courage for things I may never have to face."

"But what made her so angry? She was intensely upset, enraged even."

Sahni groaned. "Oh, it's so bad – I don't even feel like we should talk about it here. It's too beautiful!"

"The beauty of a garden such as this can both ease pain and remind us of the joys in life. If the subject bothers you, perhaps we could talk about something else?"

"No, you asked, so I'll tell you." Sahni took a deep breath and sighed. "The Association of Service and Commerce holds a banquet at some fancy location every season. They're like their own corporate pack. This time, of course, it's an exclusive setting in the Yarvea Mountains. The only way you can attend is if you are one of the pack-leaders or you are recommended by a member of the pack. Every season, there are recognitions for the most charitable organization, the fastest growing, and the most promising new leader. If you look at Van's balance sheet, she's top of the mountain. She really knows how to please! Some wealthy pack member who was new to the area had us do a joining banquet for one of his cubs. Apparently, he had not been put wise to the other part of our business, namely the pre-joinings and the primals. So he recommended her, and Van was stunned. She finally thought she was being accepted. She spent sol after sol getting her submissions together, getting references – mostly from the socially acceptable clients, but a few from the wilder side, too. She just asked those to keep their comments focused on what her company did, catering wise. Keeping her clients happy and doing the volumes of work to get the submission together almost drove her feral, and everyone else around her, too."

"Sounds difficult. What happened when she tendered her submission?"

"For ten sols, nothing. However, a prestigious looking message arrived by private runner and indicated that the governing pack leaders would be 'honored to have her attend' and that 'a very positive result had been reached' and 'we look forward to honoring your accomplishments.' So, she spends ... just so much on the trip and on bringing me along to record it. It clearly meant everything to her."

"But it went wrong?" he asked.

She shrugged and answered, "We show up, and everything is going great. We register for the pack meeting, and they tell us we have a really great lair with a nice view, paid for by the ASC. We go to the watering hole, and then Van sees one of the rich young purebreds, a Faelnar, I think, who had a rather embarrassing loss at the last primal dance. She smiles and nods, and he gives her the coldest stare imaginable. After that, everything changed. The next time we walk by the registration desk, they call us over. They tell us that there was a mistake, and we're being relocated to different quarters."

"Oh dear," Theo groaned, sensing what was coming.

Sahnassa nodded grimly. "They put us in a building as far away from the conference as was possible. The lair wasn't even cleaned when we checked in, and even after, it never was! Also, we started seeing one or two Pantera security guards, big fellows, always stalking us, keeping an eye on us. So we try to drive on, only to find that the 'banquet room is at capacity', and we're told to wait outside. They never let us in, although Thurians are flowing in and out constantly. Van is just starting to get beside herself with anger. Finally, we show up for the presentation, and the Pantera sits us in the very last seats. The seats weren't even equipped with tail holes! Then, she sees the purebred on the platform. It's no surprise now that he's the honored cub of an ASC pack leader. They announce that the winner of this season's recognition had to be disqualified, and that the runner up would be the winner. Van stood up, and at that moment, the security guards bodily pulled us out, gave us our possessions, and told us to leave. We had to drag everything in the rain and find where our vehicle was, and they had parked it at the outer edge of the property. In every way they could think of, they made her feel like … complete trash."

Sahnassa was now upset as she continued to tell the tale. "By the time we finally get in and drive away, Van was angrier than I've ever seen her. She was almost nonsensical. For the first time, I was a little scared of her, up until the moment I told her I was sick. Then, she just looked at me and…"

Theo supplied the rest. "Her heart nearly broke for being so mad and not thinking of you. Her claws sheathed, her heart rate dropped, her back fur laid down, and she felt sick to her stomach. These were all observations of the sensors when I had the Tashar back-scan the event. I wasn't exaggerating when I said your friendship saved her."

Theo now leaned forward, and his tone, which had been affable and kind throughout, became serious. "Now, those very same individuals who worked so hard to insult her and treat you both so badly are in cold, dark buildings, isolated and with no communication. Some are injured, and some will soon have need of medicine. Their picturesque view is actually thanks to sheer cliffs on three sides, almost ensuring that they cannot escape down the mountain. The one road out was covered and destroyed by landslides not only where you were, but right outside the entrance to the Meeting Den, it's destroyed also. The other residents of the mountains and the valley below are in chaos, with little power and half of the communications grid off-line. TransNet is down throughout the region, to speak nothing of its condition within this territory. To make the situation even worse, an ice storm is coming in a little more than thirty-six intervals followed by a hard, lasting freeze. The authorities will be far too busy to know what's happened up at the conference. Unless someone tells them, it may be ten sols before anyone can attempt a rescue. The window for those Thurians to get out is very narrow. When I place you and Van back out on the mountain, you will be in one of the few places that still has some type of communications signal. What you choose to do is up to you, but I very much hope compassion and mercy are in your hearts."

Sahnassa looked away from him into the garden. "I hope Van will see it that way."

Theo's response was just above a whisper. "If not, then ask her this. How many more orphans would she create? There are joined pairs within those walls who left their cubs and kits at home, in the care of others. There are two matriarchs, dozens of children, and several honored dames who are going to starve or freeze to death on that mountain. If she really wants revenge on the purebreds, she can have it by simply pretending they aren't there."

"So, we'll remember this, when it's over?" she asked, looking at him expectantly.

His mood again turned sympathetic, and he eased back in his seat. "You will, Sahnassa, but Vanarra cannot. Part of restoring her normal patterns means that she must not experience or remember any of what happens here. You could try to tell her, of course, later – you could try to tell anyone else as well, but you know how you would be treated if you did." Sahnassa knew; VidStar programs ridiculing those who claimed such things were adequate testimony. "I will be long gone, and no one else will be coming. Regardless of how true your experience is, you'll leave here with no tangible proof any of this ever happened. If you want to, write it all up in a journal you keep to yourself. If anyone finds it, tell them it's space fiction. I've given both of your lives back to you; please, promise me you will not ruin yours by trying to tell others this happened. You could offer me no better thanks for anything I do than just living a normal life once this is over."

Sahni thought hard and looked back out into the garden. After a long moment, she asked, "Why not just make me forget what happened?"

"There are simply too many Thurians relying on you. Also, is that what you *really* want?"

Gazing across the beautiful expanse of the garden, Sahnassa knew she always wanted it in her memory. Then, looking at him, her expression became soft and dreamy as she realized she wanted to remember Theo as well, if for no other reason than to fuel her fantasies. "Sahnassa? You've got a very odd expression on your face," he observed almost bashfully.

She giggled and answered, "Sorry. I really do want to remember, and I do want to help those up at the Meeting Den." Just then, she had a little glimmer of an idea. "And if I'm going to remember, I want it to be more than of me just yammering about myself! I want to see more of your amazing ship – as much as I can!" She stood up and sat right beside him on the seat and grabbed his paw. "Can I at least get a quick tour? Please!" she pleaded like a little kit.

"Alright," he agreed, smiling down at her. "It would be my pleasure. Let's stroll the garden, first. There's an entrance on the other side, and you might enjoy the walk. As they walked away, paw in paw, Sahni felt her tail happily swish-swish, almost of its own accord.

They had been walking down a long, peaceful pathway under the loveliest boughs for some time when she finally asked a question that had started to weigh on her thoughts. "Theo, I am so thankful you found us and saved us, but I feel like I have to ask, why us?"

"What do you mean?"

"Well, there's a whole planet full of Thurians with troubles and tragedies. What made us so special?" she asked, shrugging a little.

"Three things, primarily, brought me to you. First, the Tashar was collecting information about your planet just beyond the orbit of your outer moon when we detected the massive upwelling from within your planet's core. You don't have these kinds of geologic events frequently on your world, so it was worth noting."

"Hold on a moment, you said 'we'? Who is 'we'?" Sahni asked, unable to keep a slight sense of betrayal out of the tone of her question.

Theo smiled knowingly as he answered. "I have three companions with me on the Tashar at all times. They are literally a part of it. You might be tempted to simply call them computers, but they are much more than that. They are all three sentient and have been my friends for many seasons. I'll introduce you later. One of them, Zeos, is actually the one restoring Vanarra. The other two are Haloizar and Tigherashar. Haloizar is generally responsible for tactics and research, and Tigherashar is responsible for ship's systems. They actually do a fair amount of messing about in each other's business, but they don't seem to mind. They just enjoy being together and working with one another."

"Amazing," she said. It was a relief, too, she thought. Then, she asked him in a completely normal tone of voice, "Okay, so what other two things attracted me to you?" Sahnassa almost dropped to the ground in tears at her fumbling of the sentence; she might as well just scream aloud she was developing a huge crush on him, she thought. Embarrassed completely and utterly, she inwardly shouted, "Why can't I ever be smooth and charming!? Why am I always such an idiot around keen males?!" She just couldn't flirt like Van did, let alone interest anyone worth being with, she thought grimly. "Oh, I'm so humiliated," she whispered turning away, her paws covering her fully raised blush, and her tail lying nearly flat upon the path.

Theo stopped her and gently held her shoulders. "Please, Sahni, don't worry about it. I have a friend on Veganas Nine who can't keep sentences straight no matter how hard he tries, but you'll never find a truer friend. Be honestly who you are, and the rest will attend to itself. Right?" She nodded, a little pitifully, but he took her paw again, and they walked on.

He then continued, "Once we gauged the magnitude of the quake, we pulled in closer to observe. It was only a few ticks later that the effects started to be felt above ground. To ensure we didn't miss anything, Tigherashar started slowing us in time. We watched, and although there was some significant loss of infrastructure near the quake, there was no immediate loss of life. That was true, until we detected your small vehicle rolling down the mountain. Once it stopped, we scanned within. The final thing that brought us to you and caused us to bring you aboard was *your* plea for help. You had to know no one could hear you, but still, you asked for help. We heard you. I heard you." He wrapped his arm around her shoulder, and she wrapped hers around his waist.

"It was so awful!" she said, horrified by the memory. "I just knew I was dead! I didn't want to die alone. Van didn't answer when I called, oh, and now I know why! Again, thank you, thank you!" After he accepted her thanks with a brief hug, they walked together quietly for a few more passes until they were midway through the garden. "May I ask another question, provided I can get it out of my mouth without making a complete fool of myself?"

"You may ask, please," he offered, kindly.

"Why were you scanning our planet?" she asked a little hesitantly.

"Even with all the knowledge we have, we are still driven to explore. You Thurians are a very rare species, in certain respects. Now, there are a lot of bipedal, opposing-thumb sentients out there, but almost none have progressed as far as you have mentally without significantly losing their more primal attributes. For most species, as soon as the brain gets big, the tail drops off."

Sahni had to laugh at that one. "Oh, no!"

"Oh, yes!" he countered, chuckling in return. "The fur falls out, the nose shortens to a stub, the eyes go, the hearing goes, and a few other things as well, if you follow. A few millennia later, it doesn't even look like the same species. You Thurians are an exciting anomaly! You've reached a stable plateau of physical development, but your mental development continues to increase. Hearing about a tradition such as a Primalist dance helps me understand the forces that are keeping your senses sharp, your primal attributes prominent and persistent. Now, thanks to the quake, my analysis of your culture is not yet complete; you could help me a little, if you don't mind an embarrassing question."

"Given what I've just said, I don't have any pride left to get embarrassed with," Sahnassa remarked, shaking her head and still utterly fruitless in the effort of trying to keep her blush furs down.

"Tell me, what physical aspects do you find attractive in your own kind?"

Looking up at him, startled, she wanted to say, "You", but she fought the urge and actually tried to think about it. "Well, if you're a Nephti, like me, then a good stripe pattern, good coloration, pronounced ears, a long tail with some fluff to it, and a strong (but not unpleasant) scent. Not being overweight or over-thin helps, too. Females need to have good hips and a … well, a good …" she said, motioning over her chest. "I guess that really caps off the package. If you're a Vulpi, which you are at the moment, then it's the strength and musculature in the upper body and … well … in the back side and legs, and a good puff of a tail. What we call a 'keen' or 'hunter' face doesn't hurt either. You know," she commented, looking up at him shyly, "for someone outside of the neighborhood and outside our species, you sure picked a good body. How does that work, exactly? Do you just copy someone or make one up?"

She half-expected a joke, but he answered her seriously. "You might say that each form I choose is like a piece of art I create, an expression of who I am within the norms and limitations of a species –

kind of like my name. So, when you see me in a form like this, you are still seeing me. There isn't anyone on your planet who looks exactly as I do, and (just in case you're curious) if your doctors looked me over, they wouldn't be able to tell me apart, biologically, from any other Thurian. Yet, I still am Allarraen. That part is hidden away, where no one can see."

He laughed a little and bent down towards her as if conveying a secret. "I have to hide so often it's nice to get a little direct praise now and then for my choice of a form. Now let me ask you another question; another interesting piece of trivia about your world is the cultural limitation against interspecies relations. You've used words like purebred and Anati. What drives that imperative? The species seem perfectly capable of interacting both on a social and on a professional level. They collaborate, discuss, disagree, and cohort – just like you and Van."

Sahnassa contradicted him, gently. "But never let a Pantera and a Vulpi get together or anything else that doesn't match up. Now, let me say that the children of such couplings are often incredibly beautiful. In a world full of conformity, they are exotic. Van is one of those mixed breeds, and I think she is beautiful. However, there are others who would look at her as a horror, and they would call her an Anati. Van tells me she has heard it all her life. It's a reference to a lower creature on Thuria that looks like it was all jumbled up."

"That's sad, and not very open minded," he observed.

"True. I've had really great friends that were from other species, ones I could have developed real feelings for, but I knew the moment I did and let it show, my tail-tip would be in front of my dame." She walked quietly for a moment, thinking about the times she had seen it happen to others, and times when she had been questioned and warned, by her mother. "I have to admit, there have been a few non-Nephti that I have really…" She paused, knowing she couldn't very well say that, and it took her a moment to find something safer. "…that I have thought about, well, dreamed of. Perhaps it's just because we're told we can't do it, that we want to do it all the more."

"That's not the first time I've heard that said," Theo remarked. "All sentience battles with curiosity, choice, and consequences. Our thirst, our fascination about the unknown can be our undoing. Understanding that, I still think curiosity is better than the alternative. There are cultures where simple exploration is beyond the pale. It's considered indecent by the Magok to even leave their village to explore. Of course, the only reason they have any commerce with others or avoid massive inbreeding is because they get 'lost' a lot. I thought that was amusing. When they asked me what I did, I simply told them I get lost on a regular basis." Sahni laughed. "What's funnier is that it worked!" They both laughed together.

He paused for a moment, and then a few steps later said, "The most important thing I guess is to fully understand the consequences of your actions and appreciate the risks you are taking. When presented with something or someone new, it can take us just a little time before we're able to do that properly. One should at least wait some time before making a difficult decision, if it's at all possible. Ah, here we are, the door to the core complex. I hope you enjoyed the walk through the garden."

"Oh yes," she said, "I did." Her mind was in chaos; was he really saying he liked her, and oh, how she liked him! As the door opened, they emerged into a completely different looking type of hallway, one that actually somewhat fit her expectation of a spaceship. "What will happen when you leave? Will you ever be back?"

"I can never say for sure, and it's not like I can take everyone I meet with me either. I can stay here for about thirty more of your sols, and then I have to return. That's in my time, not in the time that's frozen outside. It's already been seven for me."

Sahni's heart sank, and another fiction-driven fantasy of the star traveler who falls in passionate love and stays with his Thurian soul-mate fell away. "It must be hard, always leaving and never staying," she observed sadly.

"It can be," he agreed, "but I take some solace in the knowledge that I've left those I've come to care for better off than when I found them. I may have the opportunity to right a lifetime of injustices, repair an injury, heal an incurable disease, or grant some other special request or dream. I've become used to the fact that there are things I can do for others no one else can. With that, I also have to accept that I can't stay with them or keep them with me, no matter how much I might want to. If I did, I would fundamentally change who they are and the life they lead. In the end, all I want for those I help is for them to live a great life among friends and those they love. That's the best repayment I can receive for what I offer."

"Doesn't that make it sad for you?" she asked, beginning to wonder what kind of lonely life he led.

"Hardly," he said dismissively. "It's a great life travelling and helping others, and doing so has its own rewards. For example, on my last trip, I was able to return a lost son to his mother and father. It was just incredible to see; they were almost glowing with happiness! Now, it *was* six seasons after the fact, due to one of those 'laws of time'. If you're interested, I can tell you where your fiction authors have it right and, well, not so right."

"I would *really* like that. Thank you!" After all, the thought of spending more time in his company, let alone talking about her favorite subject, was too good an offer to pass by.

"You have a very keen mind, you know," he said with a hint of admiration in his voice. "Either that or you have an absolute talent for listening to things you don't understand while pretending that you do."

She laughed at his teasing. "No, I meant what I said! I am a space fiction buff, and although it's clear VidStar has it wrong in places, I at least know a few basics." A door slid open ahead of them, and they stepped through it into an oval shaped room. Uniformly colored in a single shade of off-white, the space had a short, round platform directly ahead with wide steps leading up to another raised platform supporting a large, U-shaped desk, its surface slanted almost like that of a drawing table. Facing them, a single chair waited in front of the desk.

"Ah, here we are. Do you have many friends who are as intelligent as you?"

Her blush furs went up again, "Well, some, but not many that I see often. Actually, in my office, I get a lot of teasing for being too brainy. So where are we?"

"You are in the control center of the Tashar," he said with just a hint of pride.

"Oh," she stated, looking around the largely vacant and rather bland-looking room. "It's a little … quieter … than I thought it would be."

"Really? How so?" he asked with a cocked eyebrow and a quizzical expression.

"Well, there aren't any humming sounds, blinking lights, or displays showing ship's status," she observed, trying not to sound disappointed.

He smiled at her as he explained. "Well, when the ship is taking care of itself and no one else is here, there really isn't much need for all that humming, blinking, and so forth. It makes for good VidStar, I suppose, but as for living with it sol in and sol out, it can be really annoying. Now, please come up here with me." She followed him onto the nearest platform and then up steps that could have easily accommodated three Thurians side-by-side. Upon reaching the second platform and standing behind Theo, seated now in the chair, Sahnassa noted that the height of the desk was well considered, at easy reach for someone either standing or sitting. Still, looking across its featureless surface, she just couldn't understand how this could possibly be the controls of a spaceship.

"Now, watch," Theo uttered in a hushed voice. The lights – which weren't coming from anywhere in particular – dimmed, and the walls just seemed to fade away, revealing the scene outside of the ship in full sunlight. The floor and ceiling then faded, as well. Because it appeared as if they were standing on a small platform hovering a hundred or more tracks in the air, Sahnassa tightly gripped Theo's shoulder with one paw and with the other the edge of the desk. Her mild acrophobia was making Sahni's pulse quicken rapidly. "Don't be afraid," he reassured her, looking over his shoulder and placing his paw on hers. "You were six tracks above the floor a moment ago, and you're still only that far off the floor right now."

Then, she gasped in surprise, as all around her, with just a slight swishing sound, the featureless desk became covered with multi-color controls and displays. Sahnassa's eyes were now wide with wonder as she looked all around. "This is so – like wow! This is so much more than I was expecting!" Sahni squealed in delight trying to take in every single switch and read-out. Looking over the edge of the desk to the ground far below, she blurted, "And who needs a view screen!? It's just like being at a scenic overlook!" Almost leaping to the other side, she looked down and saw a giant brown scar down one side of the mountain far below. Instantly sobered, she asked, "Is that the landslide?"

"Yes."

"Oh my gosh! I thought you said only half an interval had passed. It looks like mid-sol!"

Theo pressed a button while saying, "reducing to actual light levels." As smoothly as time-lapse, the night returned, and she could barely make out the ripped trees and torn landscape below. "Now, look over there." He pointed, and she saw just one small area in the valley below that wasn't dark, a single lit spire visible within. "That is the only functioning communications tower in range. It can barely reach where we are, but it cannot reach the Meeting Den. Speaking of which, look over there. Do you see anything interesting?"

She looked where he pointed and saw a faint orange glow on the bottom of the clouds that were hanging over the mountains some distance away. "That? What is that? Fast Trail lights?"

"No, those aren't vehicle lights. I'm going to move us in so you can see." The dark bulk of the mountain smoothly came closer and moved underneath them rapidly. Finally, she recognized the stark silhouette of the Meeting Den's main building, outlined by an eerie orange glow.

"Fire?" she asked, confused. The view pitched up before peering down on the center building of the complex, the main dining facility, which was fully engulfed in flames. "Did everyone get out?"

"It looks like it, although it appears that one of the food preparers was badly burned," Theo stated seriously. "Looks like a flammable gas explosion was set off by the quake."

"But there are drenchers in all the rooms, in every building!" Sahnassa exclaimed, protesting the obvious failure of such.

"All of the water at this altitude is pump-driven, and as there is no power, there are no fire suppression systems in operation. The cool, moist air will keep the fire from spreading to the other structures, so that's good news. They are already trying to empty the paddling ponds with buckets, but they can't hope to put out that large a blaze with what they have. The building and its underground storehouse will be a complete loss," he said, turning to face her.

"But that's where their food is!" she gasped, appalled at the scene in front of her.

"Certainly most of it. Unless they get help, they are looking at a real horror in under twenty-one intervals. Let's leave them for now—"

"No, wait! Look, right there! Can you bring them closer?" Sahni pointed at two figures, clutching each other in fear and lit starkly in the firelight. Theo nodded, and the two small forms became a close-up that their platform seemed to rotate around. Sahnassa was aghast as she looked at the two Nephti staring at the fire in horror. "By Thuria! That's the Grand Matriarch Rahnahi de Dothnar! She's practically a living legend, a cultural treasure! And ... and ... I think that's her tre-daughter she's holding; she can't be more than eight seasons! I didn't know they were at the conference! This is horrible!" Sahnassa was transfixed by the image of the two, both the elder poet matriarch and the frightened young kit with dark fur and light stripes that now appeared to glow orange, reflecting the intense glow from the blaze. Both sets of purplish-blue eyes were fixed forward in numb disbelief of what they were seeing.

"Scanning the Meeting Den records," Theo said quietly. A display changed in front of them with a whirl of information and images. "She's not here for the conference. She was set to depart in the middle of it, tomorrow. Her room key is coded for one of the large suites under a different name. Any idea why she would be here?" he asked.

Sahnassa thought for a moment and finally suggested, "According to rumor, the matriarchs often travel in disguise or under assumed names. It allows them to see things they wouldn't normally see. Some say they spy on others, but I've always thought it was because they can't get out and enjoy anything like a regular Thurian. Oh, Theo, we have to save them! I don't care who was at the conference or what they did. Look at the eyes of that little one! She's terrified!"

"Now, we'll pull back to an overview of the area," Theo said, and the image on the console changed to a graphical, map type view. "Overlay normal communications tower coverage. Highlight position of the Meeting Den and Vanarra's vehicle."

"Not much to begin with," Sahni observed, looking at the two pulsing circles whose outer fringe was all that covered the Meeting Den. "Perhaps they were relying on hard wiring, LineCom?"

"Overlay utility wiring prior to the event." A series of yellow lines trailed beside the access road on the map.

"Oh great! It went right along the same road we were using. Can you show me what it looks like now?" The image changed, showing the lines severed just outside the Meeting Den and in several places further along. There was only one circle of tower coverage remaining with Van's lost vehicle soundly within its outer boundary. "Oh my gosh."

Theo frowned. "I bet it gets worse. Overlay repair possibilities in the next sixteen intervals, based on all known data." Nothing changed, save one or two circles in the valley below. "If communications to the den aren't back up in twenty intervals, there's no force on your planet that could evacuate them before the storm. A food drop is a remote possibility, but not for so many. That's not to say how many will freeze to death or die from other causes if they try to weather the storm up there. When you and Van are back on the surface and time starts moving again, they'll need help and quickly."

Sahnassa backed up, looking at the images on the console screen and all around them. She looked down at Theo, shook her head, and breathed her realization in a whisper. "You could save them! You could save them all…"

Theo sighed and turned around in his chair to meet her gaze. Intently, he explained, "It's true, but that would mean letting hundreds of Thurians know about the presence of life outside their own world. How do you think that would change your culture? What kind of panic do you think that would cause? Unmask the Tashar right above them, and they would probably run over the cliffs in panic. Instantly transport them to the valley below, and a whole new religion would spring up trying to explain the miracle. We need a more conventional solution, and it needs to be you and Van who provide it."

"But we can't even reach them! Even if we weren't buried, we can only talk to the valley!"

He smiled, slyly, and in a much lighter tone said, "Ah, now here's where we start doing a little scene redressing! Let's get back to the landslide." The image all around them changed to the same false sunlight version as when they had started. "Here's Van's vehicle before, in an absolutely hopeless position, and here's Van's vehicle after."

The buried location of the hover changed and was now further up the mountainside, cradled in a group of aster trees. Theo explained, "Now, it's right side up, in open air, but far too damaged to move under its own power. However, all of the contents, including you two, will be in good order. I apologize in advance for the dirt and foliage in the cabin. You're actually right in the middle of a trail, so getting back up to the road shouldn't be a problem. Be careful on the trail, however. Van's vehicle might have *lost* a piece or two during its descent, and there will still be some loose stuff from the landslide to worry about. Just trips and falls to watch out for, nothing serious."

"Theo, this is so cool," Sahni said, drawing closer to him and touching his shoulder.

"I'm glad you like it. It gets better! Here's the inventory of your bags." The images all around them changed to an explosion of clothes, gadgets, and papers. "Let's remove some of the less useful items and look at yours first." Sahni's blush fur shot straight up as one particular, intimate item floated by. She tried to pretend she didn't see it, but he just looked at her and smiled. "I promise I won't tell. Now, first, you've got quite a little back-store of food. That's good. Dried meat, fruit bars, crackers, and a few bottled juices. Did anyone see you pack your bags? Did Van see inside of them?"

"Ahem. No, actually. There were a few *private* items I didn't want her to see," Sahnassa answered, still hopelessly embarrassed.

"Very good, because the amount of food you brought just tripled. It will easily be enough for a full sol for the both of you. We'll sacrifice one towel and one pillow for the space, if that's alright?" She nodded. "You already have enough to act as a pretty good emergency aid kit, but we'll plus that up a little, too. It's still completely within the realm of what you might have purchased. You've got a woven neck wrap here which can be unstrung for plenty of good tying material. Combine that with your rain gear plus some of what Van has, and you've got a great shelter! Your tool kit is very well equipped, and that mini torch will act as the perfect fire starter – you'll find it's fully fueled now. You'll also need the tools for another little project. Here is your communicator, your PawLink device. You and Van have similar models, but only yours can do this trick. Here is a TransNet site called 'Communi-cracker' that describes a way to trick your direct talk feature to bypass the towers. Now, look on the console behind you."

She did, and there sat her PawLink on a surface that was now suddenly flat. "Hey, it's my stuff!"

"Actually, they're all just recreations so you can practice. Take the cover off here using this one. That's right. Now, do you see this component? Using these pincers, carefully pull it out, and turn it around backwards. It won't actually fit unless you carve a notch right here to match the one on the other side, but if you put your knife in there, you'll see it just breaks away."

"It's a cut-out! Someone meant it to do that," Sahni observed excitedly.

"Exactly! Replace it in the socket, and close everything up. Good, now start up the PawLink. Press the keys like this for five ticks. Then, it will display an empty field for you to enter a number. It has to be the PawLink ID number of someone at the Meeting Den who uses the same network. I believe between Van and yourself, you have ten or so numbers. Look at business cards, stationary, whatever. Now, here are five more copies of your PawLink. I would suggest doing this a few more times until you can do it without thinking. Oh, and one more thing. We'll reduce the temperature to approximate the external conditions four intervals later." Sahni instantly picked up the little chill in the air, which grew to a genuine cold. "You can see where building a fire is going to be a really good idea. Now, reduce lighting by the same standard." All of the control panel lights dimmed and went out. "Provide one UltraBright, as found in Vanarra's possessions. Realistic, isn't it?"

Sahni shivered a little as she even felt a breeze. "I'll remember it for sure this way. Can you hold the light?"

"My pleasure. Why don't you sit, as well?" She smiled as he got up. Sahnassa settled into the comfortable seat (complete with tail hole she noted) and picked up her tools. "We'll reinforce this again before you leave, since it's so critical."

Sahni felt it was harder to work with cold, stiff paws, and she dropped the component on the first attempt. "Let me ask ... ask you another question."

"Please."

"So Van's PawLink will be able to talk to the valley, and mine will be able to talk to the Meeting Den. What do I say? I already know everything about what's happening there, and I shouldn't know, right? What do we do first?"

"First, start a fire and set up your shelter," Theo suggested. "If you get your fire going, it should be much easier to do this as you are practicing the hard way. Obviously, you'll try to contact the valley first. It will be tough since all of the locals will be trying to do the same thing. Keep at it. When you get in, tell them where you are and your situation. They'll probably say they'll send help as soon as they can, but that won't be very soon. Ask them if they've heard from the Meeting Den. You'll know already they haven't. Now, even while you're trying to get through to the valley, you can start trying to reach the Meeting Den. Tell Van that you remembered this technique and wanted to see if you could reach anyone up there who might send help."

"Oh, she won't like that," Sahnassa said, shaking her head.

"Maybe, but she wouldn't stop you either, I'd bet. When you get through, you're going to get the whole story from someone up there. Tell them that you'll try to get help. Call back down to the valley and give them the full horror story, including the weather."

"How would I have known about the weather?" she asked, not looking away from her task.

"You checked before you left the Meeting Den, right?" Theo asked slyly.

"Oh, right. I looked it up on TransNet." Sahni took a moment to look at him and wink, to which he smiled.

"Now, the locals might not have the ability to do this kind of a rescue. I am nearly sure they will not. Van keeps a little address and ID number book with her; have you seen it?"

Sahni remembered a fleeting glance or two over the seasons. "Yes. She keeps all of her most private contacts there; although she's not private about the fact she has a private contact book."

Theo nodded. "Good. Ask her if she knows anyone in the military who might help. My guess is she'll find the appropriate inspiration to get an airlift going. Make sure they pick you up first, since you know the lay of the land. Get what food you can into a bag and take it with you. When you see the flyers nearby, signal them with the fire or … I think Van has something in her vehicle that might do better. Contact the Meeting Den, and tell them to gather evacuation groups near the athletic field. It's big enough for a flyer rescue. Tell them to bring only medicine, water, and warm clothes. Nothing else."

"That's two. Onto number three," she said, shaking off a chill.

"You're getting better, too. You must do a lot of this kind of thing," complimented Theo.

"Not when it's this cold! Normally, though, I like wiring up my own computers from the boards up – makes me feel like they're really mine. What do we do next?" she asked, popping the cover off the third PawLink.

"It will take many round trips to get everyone off the mountain. You should both help with the evacuation, providing food and helping Thurians onto the flyers. You, however, must stay until the last flyer leaves. If things go well, you'll get out just intervals before the storm hits. If it doesn't go well, let's just say you'll be looked after."

"How will you keep from being discovered if it comes to that?" she wondered aloud.

Theo chuckled. "I'm pretty good at staying hidden and thinking on my … hind paws? I'll see what the situation calls for. That's it, you're ready for number four."

"Promise me, you'll help warm me up when this is over." Sahni couldn't believe she had just said that, but she was starting to get so cold she was desperate.

"Promise." He placed his paw on her shoulder, already dampening the cold.

"How … how long before you return us to the surface?"

He paused and then said, "We can check when we're done with these, but when I last inquired, Zeos said she's not comfortable letting Van out of her care for another thirty intervals, at least. I'd trust her on this."

"It's more time with you, uh … uh here, and that makes me happy. Provided it's warmer. I'm really starting to s-shake."

"You're doing fine. Now for number five. I don't mind having you here, myself. You're very bright company, and as I said earlier, you're truly both beautiful and graceful. Your species is, by nature, but I think you're even more so. I'm very glad we've met."

Although the room was icy, the compliment warmed her immensely. "For a space alien, you're not like anything I would have ever imagined. You're so nice, approachable. You've got all this power, but I feel like you live down the trail from me. I never thought it possible for someone to care so much who knows us so little. I can't thank you enough."

"You're worth it, and you're welcome."

She worked in silence for a few moments more and then exclaimed, "Done!" Instantly, the warmth and lighting returned. Bounding out of the chair, she looked up at him and said, "You did promise!" With that, she leaned stiffly up against him, and he held her tightly, gently rubbing the cold air out of her fur. "Oh, that's so nice." She buried her head in his neck. "How long have you been a Thurian?"

"About twenty intervals, total."

Sahni couldn't help herself; she was relaxing into him, and her tail was wrapping around his lovely hindquarters. She moaned almost involuntarily before she said quietly, "You're a quick study."

"I thought only Pantera and Faelnar were supposed to purr," he whispered back in jest.

She couldn't help but softly laugh at herself, as he started to rub and massage her back. "I know, but I don't know of a Nephti that's ever … had a massage as nice as this." She relaxed into him completely, enjoying the warmth, safety, and forbidden nature of being so entwined with a Vulpi. "Oh, this is so nice. Thank you for everything you've done for us. It's sad really," she said, her eyes closing with pleasure, "Vanarra would really have liked to meet you … I think."

"I'm not sure this is the place for it, and I don't think she would easily accept being here, like you do. You're unique in how well you accept such strange things, and you have a basic understanding of the concepts. It would seem Van's focus in life has been different. I think she would have a very tough time with all this, and she might be very afraid."

"You think? She just might get over her fear, after taking a look at you," Sahni suggested, almost slurring her words.

"She have an eye for males?"

"Both eyes, actually … oh," she moaned involuntarily as he stroked the center ridge of her back along both sides. Her legs twitched of their own accord, and she felt some surprise and alarm. "Oh Theo, that's, that's a trigger spot, like a reflex—"

"Does it bother you?"

"No, I'll just fall down if you keep that up, and maybe something else." He gently moved away. "Van's not a finicky predator, when it comes to males. As long as the species agree, she'll bed them. She stays spiked, she tells me. There are plenty of males, in particular where she throws her parties, who might be looking for a little forbidden dalliance. With her reputation for keeping her jaw shut, she has no problem finding someone to share a bed."

"Do you resent her for that?" Theo seemed to detect a complaint in her voice.

"No, I just want her to find someone who will stay with her, love her. She's ... my best friend, and I'm afraid she – attitudes being what they are ..."

"You're afraid that she'll never find anyone who will want to stay with her, and be joined to her?"

"Yeah," she said, sadly. His soft, strong paws moved up her neck to her ear ridges. Her tail tightened about him even more as he started gently stroking her ears. "That's so nice," Sahni breathed dreamily.

"Do *you* have a special someone?

"My last steady interest didn't work out. He had a problem with how intellectual I was."

He released her and looked down at her with unmistakable affection. "Don't settle for less than the best, Sahnassa. You're quite deserving, and should you and Van carry off this rescue, you might find your field of choice grows. You never know. Van may benefit, too. Nothing would please me more." She looked up at him and nuzzled and licked the side of his muzzle, a gentle thank you. "You're welcome. Now, speaking of our friend, let's have a look, yes?" Over the round raised section at the bottom of the stairs, the tank appeared with Vanarra still floating within. "How much longer, Zeos?"

A soft tone chimed, and a disembodied female voice sounded around them, "Thirty-one point one three intervals, using the standard Thurian measure."

"How is Van?" Sahni asked the voice.

"All autonomic and structural damage has been repaired, and the collar continues to make progress re-establishing her base patterns. Outlook is excellent for a complete recovery, with no loss of memory, motor skills, or variance of behavior or identity."

"Thank you, Zeos."

"You are welcome. Please let me know if you need any other assistance." Another tone clearly indicated the end of the conversation.

Sahni was staring at Van's nude form, nude save for the collar. "Does the image bother you?"

"No, I've always been curious about what she looks like. She is exotic, beautiful – I can see why she has no problems finding males. Can I ask you a question?" With his arm about her shoulder as they were standing, he nodded. "Does it hurt?"

"Does what hurt?"

"The control collar? Does it hurt?" Sahni asked timidly.

"Physically, no. It's very comfortable, so it can be worn for long periods like this. As far as what it's doing for her, any sensations she experiences are being instantly erased from her memory. For her, it's probably a mix of pleasant, unpleasant, and everything in-between. It vanishes like a dream a tick later."

Sahnassa couldn't stop staring at it. "What kind of things can it do, other than correcting brain patterns?"

"It can read a great deal from its subject, literally all memories and experiences. It can alter or delete memories, and it can regulate any part of the mind."

"It could actually–" She knew she was trembling again. Her blush furs were high, and she turned her head away in shame. "I ... I shouldn't be asking."

"Why not?"

"It's all a part of those silly stories and fantasies about alien abductions."

He was silent for a moment, but then reassured her. "Silly stories are one thing, but since I think you are important, I think your questions are important, too. I will not be offended by anything you ask; so ask."

It took all of her courage and trust to speak the words, but she managed it. "It could actually control someone, like me, make them do what they were told?"

She thought he seemed to pick up on her line of thought. "Oh, yes. Once around your neck, you could be made utterly helpless. It could leave you vacant of any higher thought, other than what is needed to breathe and stand upright. It could also leave your thoughts intact, but simply prevent you from acting on them, like speaking or moving. It could actually place sensations, images, sounds, and smells into your mind that weren't real, but your mind wouldn't be able to refuse them."

Sahnassa was trembling, unable to speak above a whisper. "Oh my…"

"It's just a tool, and how it's used is a choice. It's capable of miraculous healing or horrible malfeasance. You needn't be afraid. Unless your life was in danger as Vanarra's is, I would never use it on you, without your permission."

"I *want* you to use it on me," she nearly screamed in her thoughts, an adolescence full of fantasies of such things raged within her, brought so close to the surface by his excellent ministrations and the forbidden closeness to him. Sahni felt half entranced already, which was as delightful as she could have wished it to be. The image of Van disappeared, regaining her attention.

"Besides, I have a much lovelier piece of neckwear to give you." He reached behind his back and pulled out a gorgeous jeweled necklace. It had a large pendant at the center, precious metals, and ornate craftsmanship. To Sahnassa, it was simply jaw-dropping.

"Oh, my gosh! For me? Are, are they real?" Sahnassa gasped.

"Well, it depends on what you mean by real. Simple jewels can't do what this does. Take a look at the projector where Van's image was. What do you see?"

"I see us." She had to admit, she didn't look too bad, and not as embarrassingly enamored as she thought she might.

"Now watch this." He placed the necklace around her neck, and suddenly her image changed to that of a female Vulpi, with rich orange fur and sparkling green eyes. She gasped, and he removed the necklace, returning her to normal. "It's a changeling cloak. It can make you look, smell, sound, and touch like you were something else. We're going to need it, too. I think it would be wise to have a look around the Meeting Den about the time you were forced to leave. It would help you give instructions about where to meet for the aerial pick-up, and it will help you and Van as you guide the flyers down." He put it back around her neck and closed three locking clips. "The latches on this you can remove, but it's meant to take a beating without coming off or being detected. Unlike your fiction authors, I like for my little gadgets to work flawlessly without creating a major complication."

Sahni was amazed. She still had on the same clothes, but she looked like a very attractive female Vulpi, and she turned around to look at herself, her coloring, her tail, and her new face. "This is so strange. Whoa! Even my voice has changed! I sound like I'm foreign."

"The accent is within range, and I think it's considered elegant, so you will not have any problems charming others into thinking that you and I are some very well-moneyed purebreds on vacation. We'll have to be fast though; we'll only have about half an interval, and we'll probably need to dodge the meeting hall when you and Van are thrown out. Let's get you back to your room so you can get ready, if that's alright. I have some lovely attire picked out for you; I hope you like it."

"Oh, good sir, I'm *sure* I will." He laughed at the way she playfully accentuated her new accent. "Wow! This is fun, and I really sound the part!"

Chapter 2: Sewing the Past

Her heart swooning and her new Vulpi tail swishing high, Sahni was soon back in her room changing into the loveliest evening gown she had ever seen. While it was fun and exciting getting ready, that time also gave her an opportunity to think about everything that had happened since she was rescued. Sahnassa just couldn't keep her mind off that wonderful, mystical Vulpi who had saved her life. She wondered if Theo even knew what he was doing to her or how she felt about him – how *much* she wanted him. All of her upbringing and reason told her not to let her heart dream of such unreachable and forbidden possibilities, but still, he was just so special, so keen, so empathetic, not to mention sensitive, charming, and strong. Closing her eyes, she could just imagine the two of them entwined together, lost in passion.

Then, she remembered he couldn't stay. She also remembered what they were about to do, and the hundreds of innocents marooned on top of that mountain. She realized that all *he* wanted was to do some good, and for that, he wanted her help. "My help," she sighed aloud, in the elegant but false voice. Suddenly, she felt very disappointed by the course of her own thoughts. Sighing in frustration, she sat on a small stool looking at the lovely image of the false Vulpi in the mirror. She undid the three clips that held the necklace on, and once again she saw her true Nephti self.

It was a very hard moment, a moment Sahnassa knew she would never forget. She could imagine the Grand Matriarch Rahnahi de Dothnar, one of the most important Thurians of her time, standing behind her mirrored image, pleading for help. "And here I am all frisky just thinking about getting him into bed." She mulled over what it would be like once time moved forward again, and the tremendous number of things that could go wrong, even with Theo's help. Every Thurian up on that mountain, the kind and the unkind, the just and the unjust, the young and the old depended mostly on her, Sahnassa. Van would be there, a player for sure, but she would never have seen the script; Van wouldn't know what she knew. Sahni now realized she had to abandon her own selfish desires and her pointless dreaming, and focus upon putting the very real needs of others ahead of herself. If she didn't, then actual lives, including that of her friend, could well be lost, and her eyes drifted downwards to the floor in sad consideration of those consequences.

Looking back up into the mirror, into her own eyes, Sahni decided to choose the higher path. She stood, put the necklace back on, and watched the magical transformation happen, once again. Now, she was choosing to be better than she ever had, and Sahnassa thought she noticed that with or without the necklace, whether hued in Vulpi green or Nephti indigo, her own eyes looked back at her a little more focused, a little more honorable, and a little more determined.

As she turned away and walked towards the door, her inner self pleaded for some fulfillment for her own wants, if only a hope. She could hear the argument in her head, "You can't let him leave without at least asking! Can you really go through the rest of your life wondering what would have happened if you had only asked?" "Alright," she whispered, still angry at herself for such thoughts. She would ask, but only when everyone else was safe. That was the balance of needs and wants she felt she could manage.

Sahnassa opened the door and was about to apologize to Theo for being late when she realized he wasn't waiting on her. She heard footsteps coming down the corridor, and in a moment, he turned the corner and observed, "You look truly lovely, and forgive me please, but I can see you in the dress behind the false image. You're absolutely stunning, Sahni, a true beauty."

"Oh, thank you," she said in her rich accent, smiling playfully. "Although it makes me wonder what else you can see." She was doing it again, and she knew she had to stop. "Say, I … I need to ask something of you, a promise, if you don't mind?"

"Ask, please," he offered in gracious sincerity.

"I want you to know I am going to do all I can to save the Thurians marooned on top of that mountain. When everything is done, and everyone is safe, I want you to promise me that you'll entertain a request from me, in private, here. I want to be able to ask you when you still have some time left, if you could?" She paused, felt herself get desperate, and started to cry. "I … I've just read so many stories about those aliens who leave with no warning, and I…"

"Ah yes, the rude kind of alien!" he exclaimed in mock disgust.

She burst out laughing in her Vulpi voice, but was then stunned into silence. "Oh, no, that's my laugh? It's horrible! It makes me sound like I have the intelligence of a tree-screecher!"

"A perfect disguise for someone as smart as you." He placed his warm, strong paws on her shoulders again and said, "And as for your request, yes, I will not abandon you so thoughtlessly. Although I must go at some point, and you know that, there will be a fair share of time put aside for Sahni, and only Sahni."

She smiled and said, nearly at a whisper, "Thank you."

"Are you ready?"

Straightening up, she asserted, "I am."

"Alright, here we go."

Time: 23.75 – 6.25 intervals before high night

The next instant, they were standing inside of a closed evacuation stairway in the Meeting Den's main building. It took a moment for Sahnassa to realize what had happened. "Wow! I thought we would have to go to a transporting room or something."

"Another one of your authors' plot devices and drama builders that could really get tiresome after awhile." He paused for a moment, hearing some noise outside the nearby door. "There's no one in this stairway right now except for us, but as that could change at any moment, I suppose we had better start our little act."

"Which is?"

Theo smiled broadly, saying, "Why, two wealthy and ostentatious Vulpi who are obviously together, but whose relationship is not, shall we say, well defined."

"Positively scandalous," Sahni said in her new foreign accent.

"Let's start by going up. We're in the main building, and there's a wrap-around balcony up there that allows you to see pretty much everything within the grounds." As they opened the door at the top of the stairs, it emptied into a well-appointed hallway. "Actually, that door shouldn't have opened for us," he whispered quietly, "but it will open for me, and it and any other door will open for you while you're evacuating, since the Tashar will be watching."

"Very clever of you," Sahni said quietly as they started to walk down the hall. "I'm actually starting to get used to this."

"Excellent, because here is your first performance. The balcony is open, but it's open for a reception of business leaders. We'll bluff our way in." His tone of voice changed abruptly; obviously he now intended to be overheard. "So what I told Marlie was that if she wanted to diversify her portfolio of investments, that would be one thing, but diversifying her business would be unthinkable, unconscionable, given the market climate that's on the horizon." As they rounded the corner to face the wide doors of the banquet room, a young Pantera hostess, perhaps a shade off of purebred, and an elder Nephti male were acting as nominal guards.

"What did she say after that? She's not the sort who easily takes advice, no?" Sahni asked, jumping into her part.

"I would be interested as well, young sir," the elder Nephti said, his graying black fur, silver stripes, and silvery grey eyes making him look like the quintessential corporate leader. "Forgive my overhearing, but I would have a problem with that advice as well, as would most of the Harnard Business Academy."

Theo shifted his attention to the well-dressed Nephti with an air of politeness that Sahni found absolutely charming. "Please, I mean no disrespect to those of differing opinions, and I know it runs counter to conventional wisdom, but look at the objective evidence before you. The past thirty seasons have seen an enormous shift in the business climate, and those old rules of the past need some updating if medium to large size concerns want to survive in the new economic rangelands."

"What do you propose, exactly?" The elder Nephti wrinkled his mottled nose a bit, starting to betray some real interest. "For the past *forty* seasons, it's been the established maxim of the community, diversify or perish."

"A wholly valid standard in the business climate that's ending as we speak, but there is a detectable, and dare I say provable shift in the winds forthcoming. As counterintuitive as it seems, I would now hone my business by specialization and synergy. Before you think I'm a complete lunatic, consider two case studies—" Then, as if remembering his partner absent-mindedly, he said to Sahni, "Oh, I apologize, my dear, I'm so sorry. I have such the habit of jumping into this kind of discussion—"

"It's practically unavoidable with us business types," the male Nephti cut in, trying to aid his new friend, who had obviously struck on a matter of his intense interest. "There isn't a one of us that doesn't love a good argument about such things."

"It's perfectly alright," Sahni replied very sweetly, and her elegant voice put a pleased smile on the face of the older male.

Theo patted her shoulder, gratefully. "Dear, if you wouldn't mind going inside and finding us something to drink? I'll meet you on the balcony in a few passes."

"Certainly, darling one," she answered, and the female Pantera stepped out of the way, opening the door for her. "Thank you; you're such a dear," she said to her "companion." When she looked up and made pleasant eye contact with the Pantera, the female dropped her notebook, and her papers scattered everywhere. "Oh, please dear, let me help you."

The embarrassed server was horrified by what she had just done in front of an apparently wealthy and refined guest, and yet still more horrified that this elegant Vulpi was kneeling down to help her. Her silver eyes were wide with panic, and her longer than normal gray tail was nearly curling itself between her muscular legs. "Oh, no ma'am! I'll get it," the Pantera said, embarrassed.

"Please, I insist." She began helping the obviously intimidated, if not fearful, employee.

The elder Nephti looked incredulous at her behavior until Theo whispered, "Has got this *thing* about helping the less fortunate. She won't turn it off; I suppose it's because she thinks she's being fashionable and progressive."

Seeing the graceful Vulpi's beautiful features, especially those made more prominent by her kneeling and reaching down, his expression softened. "Still, with such a charming companion as you have, even I would be willing to make certain exceptions – you should be more patient with her. She seems sweet enough. I don't see as it does any real harm."

Theo sighed and shrugged, "I suppose you're right. Name's Theonat de Ackosar, by the way. Theo for short."

The elder Nephti was incredulous but impressed. "de Ackosar? I am Leoniry de Nestanum. You're with the family of the great southern matriarch?"

"We all love business, you do understand?" Theo asked, chuckling appropriately at his reaction.

"I should say so! You've got one of the most successful concerns on any of the southern continents. Now, as you were saying?" At his obvious beckoning, Theo continued to discuss business transformation strategies with the older male.

With all of the papers fully collected, the Pantera apologized, the blush furs of her thick muzzle at full salute. "Thank you so much ma'am. You really didn't have to!"

"I know, but I did, so there you have it. Thank you for all you are doing for us tonight," Sahnassa said, lightly touching the big shoulder of the hostess who only now smiled back at her timidly.

"Thank you, ma'am."

With that, Sahni nodded and slipped inside, completely impressed at how well that went. After entering the elegant room a few paw steps, she noticed the admiring looks that came her way, and she tried to walk as gracefully as she could manage. She found the watering hole, picked up two complimentary drinks that were discreetly ordered without any fermenta, and walked calmly towards the balcony, despite her nervousness. Smiling, she realized that the two drinks she now carried had signaled several males to stop looking her way and resume their conversations for fear of poaching someone else's date or, even worse, mate.

Back at the doorway, Leoniry was in a mode of high gratitude. "Theo, I can't thank you enough! Now, I'm not to mention you gave me the reference?"

"He's very diligent and buries all of his time on his clients' behalf. He doesn't mind the business I send his way, but he's deeply embarrassed that I keep doing it. While possessing one of the keenest analytical minds in economics, he's still rather young and wrapped up in that 'make it my own way' thing. He wanted to build his clientele himself, and while I appreciate that, we're his family, and well, you know. Introductions are important, but he'll prove his worth by what he actually does for his clients. Just say you saw his ad on TransNet, and you thought he would be worth considering. I don't think either of you will be displeased."

"I truly can't thank you enough! I've been looking for something like this for simply ages!" The Nephti was truly gratified and bowed slightly in respect.

Returning the somewhat unusual gesture, Theo said, "My pleasure. Now, I had better get in there before my lovely companion gets too upset with me. My respects to you."

"Certainly, certainly, and to you as well. Have a good evening, sir!" Theo nodded, and with that, he too was in.

After a moment, he joined Sahnassa on the balcony. "Sorry to keep you waiting my dear. Ah, thank you!"

"You are most welcome, my sweet! My *darling*!" She chuckled at her accent again. Then, looking up into the starry sky and the clouds blowing swiftly across, she sighed thinking about what was to come. "It's a shame. It's such a beautiful night."

Theo looked out into the circle of buildings surrounding the brightly lit dining facility. "I know. Some call it the calm before the storm. It's such an overused saying and so common that the same thought is found on many different worlds. Yet still, the same thought and metaphor comes into being because, as here, there are times when it fits with unfortunate perfection. This … ordered normalcy of recreation and business meetings and social expectations and veiled insults is just a few tender ticks from complete collapse." As they turned to look into the room behind, teeming with so many well-dressed Thurians, Theo added, "In less than one interval, they'll be fleeing for their very lives, wondering what they're going to eat, and how they are going to keep warm."

He turned to look at her and smiled. "I noticed, you know, the attention you attracted when you came in. I think that in the future, you'll get attention like that for the authentic Sahnassa." Her blush furs rose at his compliment. "Now, we had best focus on work."

"One question? What you told that older one by the door? Was any of it true?" Sahnassa asked.

"Everything but my identity was true. You do realize that it's never the most important member of a club who gets put on guard duty? He's got a good business; he's just not stylish, that's all. He needs and deserves some help. The fellow I paired him up with should serve him well."

"That's so kind."

"I hope so," Theo replied, looking back through the room to the entrance where Leoniry stood, his tail a little higher than it was before. Turning around, Theo pointed to the grounds and said, "Now, let's talk about the set-up here. As you know, it's one bridge in and one bridge out, and that one bridge won't survive the quake. We're in the main building, which sits on the western side. There are nine other buildings. Now, starting with that one on the southern side, they've numbered them. Building one, two, and then skipping over us, three, four, and so on all the way to building eight, which is again towards the south. The dining hall in the middle is the only other building, not counting the small concession stand at the athletic field. Now, take a look south towards that athletic field. You see the wide walking lane? It starts here, goes right down past the parking lot behind buildings one and two, and then heads to the edge of the field."

"I do. I see it," Sahnassa said, although she had to strain over the railing a bit.

"After the quake, the power will be out, but the flyers are going to need a clearly marked landing site. It will be worsening weather with poor visibility. They can't light bonfires to mark the site, since the thrusters the flyers use would blow flaming debris everywhere. When you speak with them, instruct them to drive vehicles to the edge of the field and create a ring of lights around it. Also, you should suggest that small children, young mothers, and the aged be put into the larger vehicles while they wait for rescue. Their hovers can't actually go anywhere, but the heaters will keep them in good shape far longer than cold buildings will. They should have someone going around checking on them every so often, as well."

"That's brilliant! Theo, could the groundskeepers remove the barricade poles to allow the vehicles up onto the field?"

"Yes. Exactly right! Now, that's the evacuation, but let's look to what's going on inside right now." Theo opened his paw and felt the light touch of rain striking it. "Time we left this lovely gathering."

Finishing their glasses, they left with over-the-shoulder apologies to the elder Nephti.

A short trip in the lift brought them down to the main lobby floor where the larger meeting rooms were. As the door opened, Theo led her out by the paw. "I have a special treat for you. Take a look in that direction in three, two, one." He turned the other way, still holding her paw.

The growing commotion in the attractive and well-decorated lobby had a strangely familiar sound to it. "You don't mean—" Before Sahni could get the rest out, two large Pantera were hauling Sahnassa and Vanarra out of the sizable meeting room and into the lobby. A stiff little tan Perratti was informing them both that they were to leave immediately, and they were being evicted from the premises. As the big gray Pantera began to push them out the rest of the way, Sahnassa caught her double's eye. Sadly, she waved to her embattled self, who could only offer an embarrassed shrug in return. Soon, though, they were gone. "I remember that Vulpi! That's so weird; I just waved to myself! Isn't that supposed to violate a rule—" She looked into his amused expression and shook her head. "Wrong again?"

"It's a little more complex than that. Come on, let's go check out the aftermath."

Just as they walked up to the meeting room entrance, the doors burst open as several very angry Thurians exited. Sahni peered through the doorway and saw most of the assembly on its hind legs issuing sounds of displeasure – to say the least; it was nearly a riot. Thinking she recognized some of those who were quitting the room, she asked, "Gentle sirs, what has happened?"

"What happened?! What happened?!" one Faelnar shouted, and she thought for sure she recognized him from somewhere. The keen-looking male had dark brown fur, nearly black, with just the slightest hint of a lighter brown under his chin. His golden eyes were snapping with anger, and his brown nose was twitching as he swore. "That mangy, rape-mated, stub-tailed, reeking, ill groomed—"

One of his friends, a light brown Perratti, placed a paw on his shoulder. "Now, Buck, no use shooting off at such a pretty one, uh, couple, you know what I mean." The upset Faelnar pulled away and stormed down the hall, swearing loudly. "I'm very sorry about that. You aren't even here for the conference, are you?"

"No, we're not. Sounds like it's not going well," Theo observed.

"Let's just say we've had a case of serious injustice, bigotry, nepotism, and vote-rigging all wrapped up together. I think our little association might now be looking for a new president," the Perratti said, nervously watching his friend stamping this way and that, ranting down the hallway.

Theo shook his head in sympathy. "That sounds very disappointing. It's hard when those we place our trust in disappoint us so blatantly."

"Good sir, that's not even the half of it, but I've got to catch Buck before he does something … inopportune. Please forgive me."

"No, no, please," Theo said, motioning that he should follow this "Buck."

"Best of chance to you, and to him, also," Sahnassa offered. Even as distracted as he was, the Perratti couldn't help but pause and smile at the elegantly delivered wish from such a beautiful Vulpi.

"Thank you, lovely one," he replied with an embarrassed smile and then turned away. "Buck! Hey Buck! Don't bother those – they're probably not even here for the conference!" He ran after the Faelnar who obviously had not heard him.

Sahnassa looked in disbelief at the continued flow of Thurians out of the meeting room. "All of that, for Van?"

"Surprising, isn't it? Unfortunate timing, too, since what my over-sensitive ears are hearing in that meeting room is not going to put this group in the best frame of mind to survive a disaster. Let's go." They started walking down the long hallway towards the center of the complex in the direction of the dining facility.

"Better to be an Anati than a lying shuck like you!" The loud call sounded over the unhappy din from the upcoming doorway, another entrance to the same chaos-filled room.

"Oh my gosh! I can't believe they'd all be so … angry."

He opened the door leading outside and asked, "It was an election, wasn't it? The members of the pack were supposed to vote, weren't they?" He grabbed a rain shield from a bin at the door and popped it open to cover them from the now drenching downpour.

"Yes, I think."

"I would say Vanarra won in a landslide, no humor intended," Theo said, almost having to yell over the rain.

"Ouch! Oh, and when that pureblood Vanarra saw at the dance tried to take it away—"

"Complete and utter rebellion. Look ahead, now. Overall, it's a good design," he commented, pointing ahead to the large dining pavilion in the center of the complex. "There's good separation of this building from the living spaces. The fire could burn itself out, and the buildings around would still have a good chance of making it. This rain will help that, too, as will the Tashar. Now, look up. The roof of every building is made of hard stone, so there's not too much to worry about from hot ash—" He dropped silent as a small entourage surrounding a hooded figure approached. Theo and Sahni were motioned to the side of the pathway as the group moved past them.

"The Grand Matriarch?" Sahni asked quietly in Theo's ear.

Theo held up his paw in warning until the group was well away. Then, he answered, "One of them; there are two here, remember? If I didn't know better, I would say she's been called to restore order to that little gathering that was about to come apart. That probably just saved her life. Come on."

They walked into the grand dining hall where a sparse crowd ate and talked. He motioned her towards a flight of stairs going down barred by a cloth rope, but the rope had been dropped on the floor and not replaced. Looking up at the vaulted ceiling, the magnificent banners, the chandeliers, and the graceful arches supporting the weight of the roof, Sahni sighed, "It's so beautiful. It's just so very sad."

"Not as sad as what we are about to find." They descended the stairs, replacing the rope as they went. "No reason for it to attract attention." In moments, they found themselves in a storeroom crowded full of spare tables, chairs, decorations, and serving ware.

"I don't see anything sad in here," Sahni noted, confused.

"One more level down. There's someone down here who needs our help, because if we don't get her out of here, she'll die. Come quick; we have to hurry. The quake is less than a quarter interval away."

"I thought you said everyone except the one who got burned made it out of here," Sahni asked, following behind him. "Wasn't that true?"

"It *was* true; now it's not," he explained. "This is just one reason why I chose to bring us here only half an interval before the quake. The very little we've done has already affected events. Let's hurry; time's running out for us."

She followed his quickening pace as best she could until they came to a locked door. At a wink from Theo, the door made the "thunk, thunk" sound of being unlocked. Again, a stairway took them to a mustier, more cave-smelling room with dim lights. As they walked down, a very large metal shape appeared in the light next to them. "That is a flammable gas tank," Theo whispered, "and it supplies the fuel for not only the dining hall, but for much of the complex as well. When this building succumbs to the flames, and the fire reaches here, well…"

"Boom?" Sahni ventured, quietly.

"A very big one. It will probably shatter all of the glass facing this direction."

"This is insane!" Sahni whispered harshly. "Who would build a restaurant, one that you know could catch fire, right on top of a huge fuel tank?"

Theo shrugged. "This is a very old facility, built in one of those waves of prosperity prior to any kind of safety laws. My guess is that local inspectors have either looked the other way or haven't forced the Meeting Den ownership to do anything because there's no new construction or some such excuse. Now, to the far corner, and call out for her; we don't want to startle her."

As they walked down between long racks filled with bottles of expensive fermentum, Sahni heard a voice crying. She called out in her rich Vulpi accent, "Hello there? Is anyone here?"

"Go away," a kit's voice said. The sound of her words led them right to her. "I want to be alone."

"Really, dear one, why?" Sahni asked, kneeling down. Tears stained and matted the cheek fur of the young Nephti.

"I lost my grandsire's honor ribbon, the one he gave me to remember him by when I was away. I can't find it, and grandama was called away. I was playing here, and—"

"You lost it; it went missing?" She nodded at Sahni's question.

"What's your name, little one?" Theo asked, now stooping down to her level.

"Carinthia de Doth – it's just Cari."

"Very well, just Cari, I'm Theo, and this is my friend, Celeste. What if I told you I was a conjuror, and that if you took my paw and thought very hard about what you lost, I could find it for you?"

"I'd say you're lying." Cari still took his paw, however.

Sahni had to laugh at the child's honesty. Theo was undeterred. "Oh really now?" He placed his other paw behind her ear and held something glimmering in his closed fist. Looking at her and winking, he opened his paw, and within, was the medallion and ribbon.

"His ribbon! His ribbon!" She took it from him. "Thank you!"

"You're welcome. Now, as much as I know you would like to stay here, it's very important that you go to the entrance of the Meeting Den right now. Your grandama was going in that direction, and she'll want to know the ribbon is safe, and that you're safe, too."

"Please, take my paw," Sahni said, "and we'll walk out together." Happy now, Cari did as she was asked. Sahnassa chatted back and forth with the adorable kit, but when the dark purple of her face came into full light, Sahni was startled. It was the same child she had seen from aboard the Tashar. "Cari, you have no idea how happy I am to meet you!"

"Lots of Thurians say that, but I don't know how many mean it."

Theo stepped in as he led them up the stairs back into the main hall, "I can assure you Cari, we are so very pleased to find you. Now, we'll stay here. You run along quick and tell her about the ribbon. I'm sure she'll be pleased to know."

"Thank you again! If I see you later, will you do another conjure for me?"

Theo bowed graciously. "Absolutely." With a smile, the little kit was off and heading toward the main building at a good speed through the diminishing rain. "We've got less than fifty ticks. Let's see if we can give these folks one last push out the door." His eyes went to a nearby alarm pull, and Sahni reached over, opened its covering, and pressed the alarm button. Instantly, sirens peeled through the room as startled Thurians tried to make out what was happening. Loudly, Theo yelled, "I think it's the fire siren! We should get out of the building! Hurry!" Some took their families and moved quickly towards the exits. In a voice only Sahni could hear, he said, "Ten ticks. Walk toward the center of the room with me. When the first blast occurs, it will shield our departure."

The ground beneath their hind paws started to shake, and now the exodus from the building moved with a panicked purpose. Everyone fled but the two solitary figures. A metal cylinder of flammable gas fell out of its holder, dropped to the floor, and sprung a violent leak until the sparking lights above ignited a bright fire all around them. Smoke and fire then covered all, and Cari, standing at the door to the main building, looked back in shock.

Chapter 4: Direction and Purpose

Time: 24.90 – 6.1 intervals before high night

As Theo held her paw, the fire all about them vanished when Sahni blinked, and then, they were back, standing on the raised dais of the Tashar's quiet and dimly lit control room. "Are you alright?"

"I'm ... alright, I think," she answered, albeit a little shakily. Sensing this, Theo gently guided her to the chair.

"I think you need to sit. After all, you've been rolled down a hill, buried, and now blown up. Brave you may be, but we'll have to find something a little more restful to do next; lunch perhaps? First, however, we need to know how well we faired. So, Haloizar?"

A soft tone sounded, a little lower than the one she had heard prior, and a male voice replied, "General temporal stability affirmed. Slight modification to overall time-line was non-impactful, and required changes have been made."

"Modification to time-line?" Sahni queried. "What does that mean?"

"It means you and I have now perceived something that wasn't before," Theo answered. "What's the variance, Haloizar?"

"Thurian cataloged as event strain 82601, severe injury, has now been reconstituted as injured, moderate."

"Show us a damage overlay, before and after, with tags in Thurian primary, if you please."

"Me Sha," Haloizar answered, and a diagram appeared on the wall ahead of them. Sahni could read these words, unlike those on the control panel earlier. It showed two images of a young Thurian male, a Vulpi mix of some type. One image had an overlay flashing red over most of his body, and the other was flashing red in only two small areas, with yellow in several others.

"Is that how badly burned he was before, and now, because we did what we did, he's less burned? How is that – because I saw Cari outside before, and you said he was badly burned and—"

"This time, I chose to control the falling of the canister, as well as where and how it would leak. By doing that, I gave us excellent cover to disappear, but I also redirected the bulk of the energy away from one of the nearby food preparers. If I hadn't, I don't think he would have made it off the mountain alive, given what's coming. As it is, he has a good chance at survival."

"So, time is okay? No rules broken?" Sahnassa asked, a mix of humor tinged with actual concern in her voice.

"The rules have a little bit of play in them; it's just important to know when the play runs out. Now, my good Sahnassa—" As he said that, she realized that she was again speaking in her own voice, not in that of Celeste. Surprised, she reached up and found the necklace was missing. With Sahnassa looking up at him with an obvious question, he explained, "I removed it during transport." Instantly, unbidden, she imagined being transported and finding herself aboard his ship, missing more than just a necklace. "You really didn't want to be a Vulpi, anymore, did you?"

She giggled again and then answered, "No, I was really over the laugh, anyway. I'm just glad you let me keep the dress. How's Vanarra?"

The Zeos tone sounded again. "Progress continues at the projected rate, no variance. Projections for a full recovery are unchanged, and not in question. She is doing quite well, Sahnassa."

"Oh, thank you, Zeos."

"You are welcome," the voice said sweetly.

"Now," Theo directed, pointing to the rounded platform at the other end of the room, "take a look back here." As he pressed some controls that had just appeared on the desk, the rotating sphere of her world now floated above the platform. "Here we are, but if we go back a few intervals in time, then this lovely spot on the globe is nearly at the mid-sol interval. Do you know of any good lunch spots along this stretch?"

The slice of her world now flashing on the image before them was one she actually knew quite well. Within was a favorite relaxation spot for the wealthiest Thurians, near the ocean. "There is Tapricia, and it has some of the best and most expensive lunches you could hope for. I've always dreamed of going there and having a really great meal!"

"It sounds nice, why don't we try it out?"

She frowned at him. "Notice I said 'expensive'? How will we pay for it? I can't afford—"

"You know, that's the funny thing about fire: it always seems to burn up some of the currency." After thinking for a moment, she looked at him with an accusatory look, to which he simply laughed. "Haloizar projected which currency would have been completely destroyed in the fire, so he *rescued* it as well. Instead of being burnt up uselessly, it will easily help feed a thoughtful and caring young Thurian, who looks like she could use a break just about as much as I do." He offered his paw, and smiling, she willingly accepted it.

As he led her down from the dais and out of the control room, he praised her for how well she conducted herself on their little excursion. "You did very well, you know. You continue to impress me, Sahni, and I think you'll do very well with what's to come." His praise warmed her inside, and almost without thinking about it, her tail searched for his and wrapped around it very gently.

"Oh, thanks," she said. "I'm just so glad you let me come. You're being so very kind to me, and to Van; I just hope you know how grateful I am. I know that you'll have to leave, at some point, but I want you to know how much I enjoy being with you right now." Her head rested on his shoulder as they walked, and he squeezed her paw gently, entwining his own tail gently around hers.

He smiled down at her as they approached her room. "I enjoy being with you, as well. Now, you should find some more travel-kind clothes waiting for you. Think you'll be ready in, say, half an interval?" She nodded, smiling as she untwined from him, holding his paw until the last moment as she broke away and entered her room.

As the door closed behind her, she stopped and hugged herself. Sahnassa knew she was falling so fast. Then, bitter memories intruded, and she felt like crying. The logical part of her saw her awe and fascination were quickly turning to affection, and her heart had been broken a few times before. All those times screamed in her head, warning her to do something to protect herself. As she stepped towards the bed, she knew how hard it would be now to say goodbye to him, but as Sahni touched the new clothes he had placed there, picked them up, and started to get dressed, some thoughts drew slowly into clarity. Every time in the past when her heart had been broken, she had thought "this might be the one" or even worse "this was the one." Now, this time, she knew from the start that this wouldn't be long term. There was comfort, of a sort, and a freedom that came from knowing that.

She loved being close to him; there was no denying it. "Tail tucking with a Vulpi, how scandalous," she mimicked aloud the voice of her mother in her head. With a little bit of astonishment, she then realized a society full of Thurians wasn't watching her every move while she was here; it was just the two of them. If she wanted to love him, adore him, cuddle, snuggle, or more, no one would ever know. At some point, all of this would end, and she would be back in her normal world, alive, with a heart full of memories and a life full of opportunities ahead, thanks to him.

Looking down at herself, feeling her legs and her tail reminded her of how close she was to being lost. He'd never said it directly, but she knew that she would have died beside Vanarra had he not saved her.

She stepped to the mirror and looked at herself, coming to another realization. The clothes he put her in made her look so beautiful. They fit perfectly, and tastefully showed off all of her better attributes, and seemed to make those things Sahni hated about herself almost invisible. He truly knew how to make her feel so wonderful. "Am I really that beautiful to you, graceful?" She had never before heard such spoken about her, but he said those things and made her feel that way. "There are packs of other Thurian females who are so much more beautiful than I."

She simply shook her head. It didn't matter; he was here, and she was here. There was a job to do, and it was important, and she had committed herself to it with her whole heart. Afterwards, however, Sahni knew that she would hold nothing back.

Chapter 5: Waking Up

Time: 25.10 – 5.9 intervals before high night

Dirty, dim, grassy, cold, humming, and foul-smelling. Vanarra's mind struggled to place itself in the world as she came out of unconsciousness; she tried to interpret the sensations that her paw pads, nose, ears, tail, and tongue were telling her. Starting to move, Van discovered she was sitting down in what felt like her vehicle's seat, but the angle was all wrong. Her seat restraint was holding her in, but she was leaning hard into it. She opened her eyes slowly and saw the familiar display of the dashboard in front of her, lit as if for night driving. A couple of warning lights were on, but it wasn't until she looked down that it started to dawn on her what happened. She saw that the Inflata-Straint had deployed and then had time to deflate completely. "Great," she thought. "Rape-mated twice in one night." Looking up, she saw the crumpled front of her precious baby was impaled and mangled with the soft outer layers of a huge aster tree. The light on the top of the vehicle shone forward, allowing her to see it. Only then did she realize that there was no plastishield in front of her.

She just stared ahead for a moment until she heard a faint groan beside her. "Sahni!" Whatever fogginess was in her head disappeared as she looked to the side and saw Sahnassa's limp body hanging from the restraint. "Oh little kit, please! Sahni, are you alright?" She reached out and stroked the Nephti's cheek. She thought to herself, "I'll never forgive myself if I dragged this poor kit all the way up here only to get her hurt, or worse!" Van slipped out of her harness and slid into a sitting position on the dashboard. "Come on, kit, you little purebred, give me a sign!"

Van kept stroking her friend's muzzle, even as a cool gust of wind blew Van's tail about.

Sahnassa stirred a little and whispered, "Van?"

"Yes, Sahni, it's me!" Van replied, voice shaking as she lifted Sahni's head up in her paws.

With some effort, the eyes opened, and a heartwarming smile played across Sahni's almost dreamy features. "Oh, Van, you're alright?"

Van choked back tears. "Of course I'm alright, kit; it's you I'm worried sick about! Are you hurt anywhere?"

Anxiously, Van watched as Sahnassa closed her eyes and seemed to take inventory. "I'll ... I'll be alright. I just need a moment. Can you get me out of this thing?"

"Sure, just a tick." Van pressed the harness release and gently guided the limp Sahnassa into a sitting position beside her. She was gratified to get a better look at the Nephti; at least she looked alright. "That okay?" she asked after having Sahni lean against her for support.

"Yes, much better. What happened?"

Van desperately tried to piece the events together. "I pulled over, and I was talking to you, and then ... tree. That's all I remember. You?"

"I remember us getting knocked off the road by something – we must have gone down the hill."

Van poked her head out and tried to see, but the roof-light was shining right in her face. Repositioning herself and putting her paws over the light to block it, she couldn't make out anything in the distance. However, when she started to pull her paws away, the reflected light showed that her almost new "Racerra 3000" was nearly buried in dirt and plants. "Maybe the road gave way. Hang on a pass." She ducked back in, pressed a control to turn off the outside lights and then fished between Sahni's legs for the storage compartment. "Sorry, don't mean to get overly friendly or anything." To her glad surprise, Sahni actually chuckled. Finally, Van found the UltraBright she had brought in case of an emergency. Slipping back outside again, she flicked it on. "Steaming piles of crap! The whole mountainside is gone!"

Sahni now felt mobile enough to slip out and stand beside Vanarra. Following the light as Vanarra moved it around, they both saw they were on the edge of a massive landslide. Just to the right of them, a huge flow of fresh mud had completely cleared the brush, broken smaller trees, and left larger ones bent, leaning, or with huge piles of dirt on one side.

Looking to the left, the ground was untouched after a track or two, and there was even a sign for a path.

Vanarra shook her head and exclaimed, "Whew! Are we lucky to be alive or what? I'm glad you got sick. If I hadn't pulled over, we might have been right in the middle of that!" Vanarra felt Sahni's arm around her, and she responded pulling her into a tight embrace. "Don't worry sweetie; we'll get out of this." While the hug was good for a number of reasons, Van realized quickly that warmth was one of them. "Mange, it's cold out here!" She broke the hug and asked, "You brought a coat, didn't you?"

"It's in with my luggage." Van shone the light towards the back of her hover, which was not visible underneath all the dirt and debris. "But how are we going to get to it?" Sahnassa asked.

"Don't worry. There's another way." Van ducked back inside, and Sahni watched as she folded seats back, climbed over them, and started working on the back panel. "Would you believe that they have an automatic snack dispenser you can rig up from the trunk? The liar that sold me this said you could remove this if you—" There was a loud snapping sound.

"Are you okay?"

"Yeah, I think I broke it. As the whole vehicle is pretty well rape-mated at this point, I'll just break the other..." Pop! "... ones and we should be in the trunk here ..." Pop! "... in just a tick." A few more pops later, she asked, "Can you take this panel and set it off to the left? Just make sure we don't lose it. That survival Thurian on VidStar says make sure you keep everything."

Sahni slid off the mound of dirt and happily placed her hind paws on firm ground again. She pressed the light button on her wrist-piece and smiled. It hadn't been a dream. Although Theo had mentioned she wouldn't have any tangible proof of his existence, there were certain signs he said he would use to reassure her. Her timepiece now bore three circles: one blue, one green, and one red. They looked as if they had always been there, inset enamel disks, each lined in a thin circle of gold. Yet, Sahni knew the truth. "Thanks, Theo," she said quietly and hugged herself in memory. Some shuffling and sliding brought her back to the task at paw, and she scrambled back up the mound just in time to catch a small bag sliding towards the trees.

"Sorry! That one got away from me," Van called down, seeming a little strained.

"I've got it. Let me set it on the ground, and I'll help you with the others."

"Hurry, I'm holding all this stuff up here," Van grunted. "I'm about to have my own luggage-slide on top of the landslide!"

Sahni laughed, but nonetheless moved quickly. "Alright, I'm ready for the next one." After a few passes, they had fully unloaded the Racerra, and, after getting their coats and what other warm clothes they could find, placed most of the luggage in a pile on the trail. "Now what do we do?" Sahni asked.

"Let's go up the trail and see if we can find the road. We'll just leave this stuff for right now. Doesn't seem like there's much chance of it being stolen." As they started walking together, Van took Sahni's paw. "I'm very happy you're all in one piece, you know?"

"You, too. I'm sorry about the Racerra."

"That's what insurance is for. Things can be fixed or replaced." A strong squeeze from Van implied again that she was glad Sahni was alright.

"What do you think we'll find at the top?"

"I don't know. Perhaps some of those jerks from the conference got stuck in the mud, too." Sahni didn't laugh at the joke, but simply followed behind Van as they worked their way up the trail. "Hey, look at that. It's a campsite! Now, we're getting somewhere." She shone her light on a small flat clearing with an old fire pit beside a set of stone benches and a table. "Come on; let's get up to the top."

Sahni lingered and looked up at the stars above them, knowing that they would spend more than a few intervals here. This part, Theo said, just had to play out. She started moving again and caught up with Van as she reached the small parking space, intended for the camp. Walking carefully onto the road, Van shone her light at the massive wall of dirt and loose stone that had covered and partially destroyed it. "Well, no one's going that way. It's probably three intervals or so to walk back to the Meeting Den; you up for it?"

"I can try." They started making their way around the turn in the mountain road. After a few passes went by, Sahni heard Van curse under her breath. "What's wrong?"

Vanarra was almost growling. "I'm a first-class idiot; that's what's wrong! I can just imagine how I'll look walking back up to those Pantera twins who threw us out, begging to be let in from the cold. I keep wondering if there are any other ways I can be humiliated tonight—" She was looking back at Sahni as she spoke.

"Van! Stop!" Sahni rushed up and grabbed Van by the shoulder. "Look!" Van looked forward, and not more than a few short steps away, the road just stopped, with a clean edge. "Shine your light across." Van did so, and a great distance away, the remnants of bridge supports bent towards the ground. Shining her light down showed the crumpled mass of the bridge, tangled and splintered in the canyon deep below.

"Now, I'm feeling sick," Van said, but then looked at Sahnassa in amazement. "Oh, by Thuria, thank you! You saved me!" She hugged her tightly, and said hopelessly, "Oh, Sahni, what are we going to do?"

"I don't think we have a choice. It looks like we're making camp." Sahni took her by the paw and led her away from the edge. "We'll get back and make a fire; it'll be alright." Van followed Sahni, completely willing to let her take the lead for once. As they walked back, Van took out her PawLink and tried to dial it several times. "Are you getting anything?"

Van's voice was still shaking. "It's got a signal. It's not great, but I can't get a free circuit."

"Try the StarSats."

Van pressed a few more controls. "Whoa, I've never seen that message before!"

"What?" Sahnassa came over and looked at the display. It read "Communications request denied. Regional Government Emergency Protocols in place." "I guess we have to keep trying the ground stations." Sahni walked ahead a little distance and then said, "Van?"

"Yes?"

"Shouldn't there be more down in the valley that's lit up?"

Van followed where Sahni was looking, through a stand of cold-cycle bared trees, and saw only one distant tower and a small huddling of lights around it. "You're right. There's a major road through there, and I remember seeing a couple of towns from the Meeting Den parking lot. This thing that brought the mountain down must have been pretty big. Big enough to rip a bridge apart – a land quake? Those don't happen around here, I didn't think."

Sahnassa shrugged. "Something did all of this, and that makes loads of sense. Looks like we'd better take care of ourselves. Help may be a long time in coming."

))((

Time: 26.60 – 3.4 intervals before high night

It took them nearly a full interval, but they carried all the luggage up the hillside away from the still imperiled vehicle, and Van, with the help of a small soldering torch from Sahni's toolkit, began working on the fire. By the time Sahni returned from the Racerra with the last of what wasn't fastened down, she had to remark, "Wow! Great job with the fire! The wood was wet. How did you manage it?"

Somewhat coquettishly, Van demurred, "You'd be surprised how well an acceptance speech burns! And then there's the rules, and the invitations, the example ballots, and the programs—" Sahni laughed at her. "They've just become more useful now than they ever might have been!"

A little more seriously, Sahni sat beside her on the bench in front of the fire. "I'm sorry. I know the award meant a lot to you. Until someone obviously changed the rules, do you think you might have won?"

Vanarra sighed. "I don't know. I thought so. I had so many customers tell me they voted for me, that they were proud of me. I was finally going to show the purebred aristocracy what Anati could mean and turn a curse into an adulation. Buck Harlock said that to me. I believed him." She was quiet and stared into the flames – eyes welling.

"It is true. I think he meant it, too. Don't look at me that way! I know your customers; they like you! You won that award, at least with them! More than a few of them were up there, don't you think?"

Van cocked her head to one side and nodded. "I suppose. I guess it doesn't matter now." Sahni hugged Van around the shoulder, and Van leaned into her. "Oh, Sahni, you're such a good kit – a good friend. I didn't realize until tonight how much it would have just killed me if something bad happened to you. You've stayed with me; you're the only avowed purebred who ever has."

"You're worth it." They hugged, tightly. As Sahni pulled away, she asked, "So, are you hungry?" Sahnassa got up and went for her luggage.

Somewhat stunned, Vanarra replied, "Well, as a matter of fact, yes. I certainly didn't get any food up there! I presume since you ask the question, you've actually got a little something?"

"More than a little, you'll be happy to know." Sahni opened the lid of a luggage container; it was almost two thirds full of food.

"Wow kit! What a haul!"

Sahni laughed, inwardly thanking Theo. "Go ahead, dig in! It's my healthy stuff though—"

"Sweetie, the tree bark over there was starting to look good! I've tried some of your stuff; it's not bad." Van was already opening a liquid container and peeling back a wrapper. "Oh, and when you're as hungry as I am—" Van stopped talking to bite into a meat bar. "It tastes better than the finest rulla eggs you could ever buy!"

Sahni grabbed some, as well, and lifted her drink to Van. "Here's to survivors!"

"Survivors!" they both shouted, and they both drank.

"I doubt they're eating as fine even at the Meeting Den," Van opined before taking another big bite.

As Van kept eating, Sahni stood up and looked to the sky. Far in the distance, up the ridge, she saw a soft, orange glow reflected against the clouds. "That's actually got me thinking. You know the maps to get up here?" Van signaled acknowledgement as best she could with a full mouth. "They only showed one road in and out – this road."

"What are you looking at?" Van asked between gulps of food. Sahni had stepped away from the fire and towards a short, stone wall meant to keep the unwary from going over the edge. Van got up and followed her. Tracing the line of Sahni's gaze, she also saw the strange glow reflected against the clouds. "What's that? Road lights?" Suddenly, the light grew much brighter, and a moment or two later, a sound like distant thunder rolled across the ridge line. "That's … that's not good, is it? What do you think just happened?"

Sahnassa's tone was grim. "Something bad. Something exploded. Fuel, gas … vehicles?" The glow slowly faded, but it did not disappear. "Want another piece of good news? I just remembered reading the weather forecast when we checked in. Late tomorrow evening, there's a really good chance of an ice storm – sleet and freezing rain followed by snow, a lot of snow. If everyone up there is trapped, and the den is burning down, they're—"

Van shook her head as she answered as grimly, "Really, really rape-mated. I bet their PawLinks are as blocked as ours are, at least from StarSats. I wonder if they can get out over—"

"The ground stations?" Sahnassa interrupted. "It depends if there's a tower near them that's got power. We've actually got a signal; we've just got to get through."

"What do you want to do?" Van asked, overwhelmed by the situation.

"Let's get back to the fire." They started walking back to their camp, and Sahni continued, "Why don't you keep trying to call the emergency number – as many times as it takes? After awhile, we're going to get through, even if it's in the middle of the night. I'm remembering something I read on TransNet once." As Van sat down and pulled out her PawLink and started pressing buttons, Sahni went digging through her bag for her tools. "My unit has a hack that will allow it to bypass the ground stations. Its range is short, but it may just reach the Meeting Den. We may ... actually ... be able to talk to them." Sahnassa was already sitting on a stone bench with an UltraBright, prying off the back of her PawLink with practiced skill.

"I knew I hired you for good reasons, Sahni. I just didn't know they were this good!"

The Nephti smirked as she shot back, "Ha, ha! I expect you'll remember that when we discuss raises, huh?" Van laughed, but not unkindly. As Sahnassa carefully placed the cover on the table, she asked, "How's your charge?"

Vanarra pressed a couple of controls. "Not so good, about halfway down. I could charge it in the Racerra, I suppose."

Sahni shook her head. "I've seen under the hood. I think I could get the power supply out through the back of the dash storage compartment, bring it up here, and rig your charger to it. I'll need your help, though. We're going to need these PawLinks to last a really long time. Besides, I'd rather have us both together here by the fire. It's going to get cold down there." She motioned down the trail to where Van's vehicle was nearly buried.

"Sahni! Is there anything you can't do?"

"Well," Sahnassa observed as she carefully pulled a small component out of her PawLink and placed it back in again, "this little trick depends on something I actually don't have."

"What? Do you need me to get something?"

"This only works," Sahni started to answer, but she paused again to carefully reattach the cover of her PawLink. "This only works if I have the number of another PawLink on the same network, but I don't have numbers for anyone up there." After a moment, she clicked the cover back on. "Got it! Press these buttons and ... yes! We're ready to talk! We just need someone to talk to."

Van raised her eyebrow fur as she thought and finally said, a little mysteriously, "You know, I may actually be able to find something for you."

Time: 25.00 – 5.0 intervals before high night

Honored Dame Dania de Dothnar was moving faster than she ever had before, with a stiff little Perratti, the Meeting Den's manager on duty, in tow. The removal of her shoulder scarf, revealing her house's rank emblem, was all it took to convince the irritating little male that he should immediately comply. They were now running through each of the buildings surrounding the inferno of the dining hall, pulling the evacuation alarms as they went. Other dames, matrons, and a group of strong males ran behind her, one dropping off every so often to help direct evacuees to the athletic field. "This is Mercea. We're making progress on the near side," a voice crackled in her earpiece. The only communication devices working were the short range TransCom sets carried by the Grand Matriarch's staff. "We've … we've got a good line of Thurians headed downstairs and out of the buildings away from the fire. We're directing them to the field! How on your side?"

Dania clicked the control in her dark purple paw to respond, "We're still making the traverse. Four buildings now, three to go! We'll let you know when we've got them all. Have the bucket details been pulled back?"

"Yes. Yes, we've got all of them."

"Have them gather on the near side of the field under protection. When the tank goes, it will be all we can do to save the rest of the buildings. We've got to save something to use as shelter! End." As they reached another junction, they pulled the alarm and three matrons bolted for the stairway, leaving one dame. As they dodged their way past those emerging from their rooms, she yelled, "Get coats and blankets, water if you have it, and get out of this building now!"

"Yes! Yes! Hurry!" was all the near breathless manager could add. It was clear he wasn't used to this level of physical exertion.

As they exited, Dania could hear the voice of the dame she just left behind pick up the call. Looking to her right, she could see the burning building, even feel its heat. They were fortunate that this facility had large gardens and pools surrounding that structure; it was the only hope for any of the other buildings to survive what was coming. The central dining building was now fully engulfed in flame, with gouts punching through the roof. "How long do you think we have?"

"There are ... (cough) ... two basements," the manager gasped. "When the roof collapses, the floor of the hall and the first basement floor may buy us a little time, maybe half an interval. One of the servers pushed the emergency shut off before they evacuated, so the fire actually has to reach the tank before—"

"Alright, alright. Any special suites in this building or the next? Anything we need you for?" Dania asked sharply, glaring at him with her dark purple eyes.

"No. These are economy class in the last three buildings."

"Alright, go back, organize your staff, and make sure everyone is cleared out of the main building! Go!" Struggling to jog, let alone run, the little Perratti was off. Looking toward the rest of the dames, she clicked her communicator and said, "This is Dame Dania de Dothnar. According to the hotel manager, the construction of the dining hall puts two floors between the fire and the flamgas tank. The fire has to reach the tank to breach it, so you may have half an interval. Control your evacuees, make sure they have enough to stay warm, but move them quickly. Keep order at all costs; panic will do us no good. When you clear your floors, follow the evacuees to the field. End." To the dames and matrons standing in front of her, she ordered, "All of you, take the last two buildings and call me when they are clear! I'm headed into the parking lot to start directing evacuees towards the field. Good chances to you!"

As the rest of the group ran off, she called one of them back – a dark brown Faelnar. "Hey, you're with me! I need you in the lot."

"Yes, Dame," the male replied as he turned and jogged back with ease.

The two scrambled over and through small bushes to reach the outer lots. "No! This way, this way!" Dania was shouting as soon as she saw small groups collecting and milling about. "Evacuate to the athletic field. Go all the way down to the last parking lot and look for the dames or matrons to direct you." The Faelnar ran after a group that was out of ear-shot, and he soon had them moving in the right direction, as well.

"If I go to the end," he asked, jogging back, "and direct them to you, would that work?"

"Yes, it would. What's your name?"

"Buck Harlock, Honored One."

"Disavowed?" she wondered. Still, he volunteered. "Mine's Dania. For tonight, let's drop all the titles." He nodded and sped off as he saw groups starting to pour out of the second to the last building.

Bam! Everyone instinctively ducked as the loud sound rocked the night. Instantly, her TransCom crackled, "That was not the main blast! That was not the main blast! This is Grand Matriarch Amyra de Gonari!" There was a brief pause. She was shouting to the groups to keep moving when the voice popped into her ears again. "Our observers are seeing smaller flammables go, but we have not had the main blast yet. Keep the evacuation moving! I say again, keep the evacuation to the athletic field moving with all purpose! End!"

Dania was impressed. While her Grand Matriarch was a noted poet and speaker, Amyra de Gonari had spent nearly a lifetime in disaster and famine relief. She had seen many tough situations, and obviously had a knack for taking charge during a crisis. Rahnahi de Dothnar, her own matriarch, had instantly turned over her entire staff to Amyra after the quake and fire. At the moment, she had a hard time knowing who to admire more, Amyra for her leadership or her own matriarch for her humility. Dania remembered Rahnahi's words when they had first crackled through her earpiece. "There must be but one paw that leads us to safety, and only one. Follow and obey her."

The TransCom crackled again after some loud crunching noises echoed through the night. Dania was startled when she looked at her timepiece; in what seemed like an instant, a quarter interval had passed by. "The roof has collapsed! Repeat, the roof has collapsed! Observers say – they say that the first basement has now been compromised and is now burning! We are running out of time! Get those buildings clear right now! End!"

Dania clicked talk on her TransCom. "Building eight, what's your status?"

"We're totally clear and following the last ones out."

"Building seven, what's your status?" she asked.

"We've got some hold-outs. Everyone else is out, but these six I'm standing here arguing with refuse to leave!"

Dania was outraged. "Put me on speaker! This is Honored Dame Dania de Dothnar! Tell them if they fail to comply, they WILL be imprisoned and disavowed as will their immediate family, no exceptions!" It was a stretch of her authority, but one she hoped she wouldn't have to use. Perhaps the matriarchs weren't listening at that particular moment.

There was a brief pause. "They heard you; they're moving."
"Glad to hear it. Tell them to run! End!"

After a moment, they could all hear a conversation on the TransCom between the two matriarchs.

"I told you she could scare an army into spontaneous defecation." Rahnahi de Dothnar's voice sounded faintly, as if she was speaking on the other side of a room. Dania's jaw dropped in utter shock.

"Rahnahi, the communicator was keyed when you said that!" Amyra said with a lilt of slyness in her voice.

"Oh, that … that wasn't too poetic, was it? Uh, sorry about that Dania."

Amyra laughed and then said, "Dania, don't worry about that one. We've needed to do this anyway. All matrons and dames, place your TransComs on speaker now with the volume up full!" Dania did as she was told. "Attention, all Thurians. This is the voice of the Grand Matriarch, Amyra de Gonari. Beside me is Grand Matriarch Rahnahi de Dothnar. We have decided that if you fail to instantly comply with the orders of any dame or matron, your immediate family will be disavowed and criminally punished for the endangerment of others. You are in extreme danger, and you are ordered to move calmly and quickly to the athletic field, NO EXCEPTIONS! That is all. Speakers off, please." There was a pause, and the matriarch spoke again, "Alright everyone, great job so far. Let's keep our full focus on completing this evacuation. End."

With that, the pace of all around her noticeably increased. Buck Harlock walked up, smiling. "Everyone's clear." Just then, the last group from building seven also emerged, making a straight line in the correct direction. Everyone assembled around Dania.

Collecting herself and ignoring the smirks from a few of the matrons, she asked, "That's it then? Alright, let's get ourselves evacuated, too. Spread out as we go; I want to make sure no one is hiding around these vehicles. Move quickly now!"

Soon, Dania stood amongst the huddled masses on the athletic field. For almost another full interval, nothing happened, except that it started getting much colder. The fiery glow from within the circle of buildings seemed to be fading. Then, with no preamble, the loudest sound she had ever heard blasted them like thunder, causing screams of terror from those ducking for cover all around her. An enormous orange fireball leapt out of the pit that had once been the dining facility, spraying debris far into the night sky. The ball of flame was quickly consumed by the low clouds above them in a singularly terrifying and stunning sight – a sickly, orange glow radiated through the clouds like a mini sunset.

As Dania tried to calm those around her, she saw the impromptu fire squads running with buckets and shovels back towards the flaming pit. She knew this was the critical moment. Would these few volunteers be able to find and extinguish all of the burning debris that threatened the rest of the buildings? Would there be any remaining shelter for these hundreds? Dania knew she, like everyone else, could only wait, watch, and pray.

Time: 27.00 – 3.0 intervals before high night

"How's it going Sahni?"

"About the same as you, I'm afraid. I'm going through the list, but no one's picking up. It's like they all have their PawLinks switched off."

Van thought for a moment. "Hmm. Probably most of them do to save the power cells. Hopefully someone forgot. Mange, it's getting cold! I'm glad we've got the fire." Even still, Vanarra was starting to shiver, and her tail was now really feeling the cold.

"We should probably build a shelter before too long. If I can't get anyone soon, I'll—"

"Wait a pass! Sahni, the call is going through!" Sahni rushed to Van's side as she put the call on speaker. The connection tone sounded for a long time before someone responded.

"Windston Emergency Management Center," a tired male voice answered. "We are already aware of the ground quake, the power failures, and the communications outages. Now, what is the nature of *your* emergency?"

Van looked at Sahni a little disbelievingly as she answered flatly. "Our vehicle was knocked off the road by a landslide, and now we're trapped up on a mountain with the road destroyed in both directions."

There was a pause on the other end. "Uh, what mountain? Can you be clearer about your position?"

"We're on the only road leading up through the Yarvea mountains to the Meeting Den conference center."

"How many of you are there?" The voice on the other end was starting to take them more seriously.

Sahni answered this time. "There are two of us here, but we think there are hundreds at the Meeting Den. Have you heard from them at all? We thought we heard something, like an explosion, earlier."

"No, we haven't. PawLink and LineCom coverage is out in that area. What you saw could have easily been lightening; we've had some of that tonight. Do you have any injuries?"

Van said, "No, other than being a little chilly. We have enough food, and we think we can put a shelter up."

"That's good. Can I have your names, please?" The operator covered his headset mouthpiece and called to someone else.

For a moment, Vanarra looked at her friend, unsure of what to do. Van worried this might end it for Sahni, especially if word ever got back to her family. Sahni smiled and nodded. When he finished talking, Sahni replied. "Sahnassa de Orturu and Vanarra Anasto."

A deeper voice came on the line. "This is Regional Emergency Manager Tedarri. With whom am I speaking?"

"I'm Vanarra."

"Vanarra—"

"Call me Van, sweetie. It'll save time." Sahnassa rolled her eyes at her boss's almost instinctual ability to flirt.

Obviously a little taken aback, Tedarri responded, "Okay, Van. What can you tell me about the condition of the mountain road?"

"It's in bad shape. Within a few passes' walk there's a giant bridge in pieces, and in the other direction there's a landslide that's completely covered and destroyed the road. We're caught between those two, and we can only imagine it's the same all over. We haven't seen or heard any vehicles coming down the road from the Meeting Den."

Tedarri was clearly unhappy at the news. "Mange! Van, I'm afraid you're going to have to hold out until sometime tomorrow."

Sahni spoke now. "I think we can do that, sir. We're also trying to contact the Meeting Den to figure out what their situation is."

"Don't waste your time. There isn't working coverage that will reach up there—"

Sahnassa interrupted him. "Sir, with all respect, there's a trick I can do with my PawLink that might work. I've already made the change, and we're just going from number to number until we find someone who'll answer."

"Hmm. Charlt, place Van's number on the priority list on the PawLink switch. Give her the back line so she can talk to us. Van, if you or your friend can find out the situation at the Meeting Den, we would greatly appreciate it. We know they lay in lots of food and flamgas for heat, so with a little luck they'll get through this in fair shape."

"Sir," the initial voice came in. "The command center wants to talk with you. Something just got relayed about the weather. It's not looking good."

Another sigh spoke volumes to both of them. Tedarri then said quietly, "We'll be in touch, Van. You two stay safe."

"We will." In only a few ticks, Van had the new number and had hung up. "Not bad, considering!"

"Top marks, boss," Sahni said as she hugged Van. "Hey, you want to try for a double? If you'll take over dialing the Meeting Den numbers, I'll go down and get the power cell for the charger. When I get back, I could start working on the shelter."

"Oh, no you don't! I'm coming with you, kit!" Van insisted, standing up. "You could get down there, lose your grip, get hurt, and then where would we be? Besides, I can dial just as well from down there as I can up here."

Sahni gently squeezed Van's shoulder before answering. "Alright then. Now, here's where I stopped on your list, and here's the two buttons you push before you put in the number. They should receive it like a regular call."

"Sounds like a winner to me, kit. Let me put a little more wood on the fire, and then we'll go."

Time: 27.00 – 3.0 intervals before high night

After intervals of shivering in the cold following the explosion, Dania walked alongside Buck as they escorted the last few stragglers back into the buildings. Once the fire squads reached the gardens surrounding what remained of the dining hall, they had been able to quickly put out any flaming debris that would have endangered the rest of the Meeting Den. Truly, they had been fortunate in that respect. However, as the squads surveyed the damage, three horrifying facts became apparent.

The first was that for the hundreds of rooms and halls facing inward, there were only ten pieces of glass still in place. Shards and fragments had been blown throughout these rooms, creating a dangerous hazard for anyone who tried to enter. A quick survey estimated that half of all rooms were now exposed to the elements. The other side had fared much better, thanks to two layers of closed doors.

The immense stores of food they had lost was what was really disheartening. Some was burnt, some was vaporized, and some was simply spoiled or covered in glass shards. Food that could have lasted eight sols, if need be, was gone. The water in the paddling pools were all they would have to drink from, saved from loss by covers placed on top of them at the last moment by an as yet unnamed benefactor. Without power, the deep well plunging through the mountain was useless. The stark truth of their situation was that they now had to survive on whatever was left in the rest of the facility. Dames and matrons were securing that now, before hoarding and looting set in. Everything from vending machines to the refrigerators in rooms had been searched, and what was found was confiscated and placed under armed guard.

That action, drastic though it was, was now necessary because of the third and final discovery: they were trapped. As the vigil on the athletic field began, two volunteers had almost been killed driving off a ledge where the bridge once stood. A quick check with the Meeting Den management confirmed their worst fears and added a new meaning to the words "dramatic view."

Her chief volunteer and new friend, Buck Harlock, had been an amazing help to her, even giving up his own coat when she was shivering so hard she couldn't even function. He was keen, even for a Faelnar. As they entered the building, the relative warmth, caused mostly by the bodies moving through the halls, allowed her teeth to stop clenching long enough to ask questions that had bothered her for intervals. She held his arm and pulled him quietly into the first empty parlor she could find. "I wanted to thank you for your kindness," she offered, returning his coat.

"It's alright. Happy to do it," he replied, a slight smile on his muzzle.

"Can I ask you a question?"

Buck's smile was now in earnest as he answered. "I'll save you the trouble. I twisted tails with a Vulpi when I was younger, and my matriarch found out. The great thing is that my business doesn't rely on good relations with any one family. I almost benefit by it."

"What do you do?" Dania was concerned she had entangled herself with someone she shouldn't have.

"Don't worry; I can't harm your reputation. I own a technical consultancy that services large corporate packs, and I'm good enough that my last name doesn't seem to matter. I actually have twenty or so who work for me, purebred and mixed alike. Some are avowed; most are not. Most are simply bright Thurians who made one very bad decision, and their families refuse to forgive them." Dania was embarrassed, and her raised blush fur made him smile. "It's alright. I'm used to it."

"Who – what was the name of your original family?" she asked carefully.

"I was de Caterra."

"Uh oh, sorry about that." The reputation of that grand matriarch bordered on infamy if not insanity. One could hold to rules and traditions too strictly. "That, actually … that wasn't my question."

Now, it was Buck's blush fur that rose. "Oops. Sorry."

She reassured him. "No, I won't lie to you; I did wonder. What I wanted to ask was why you kept looking down the mountain road. When we were in the field, everyone else was watching the fire, but you mostly kept your eyes on the entrance road. I thought you were looking for rescue, but once we found the bridge was out, you kept looking. Why?"

Dania saw the rage in Buck Harlock's face flare, and his lips pulled back across his teeth. "I was looking for a good friend of mine and her employee. Earlier tonight my friend, who is an 'Anati,' was supposed to be honored for the hard work she's put into her business – bringing herself up from beggar-hood and creating one of the fastest growing businesses in seasons. They were thrown out of this Meeting Den like common garbage just passes before all of this started."

"Thrown out? Why?"

"Because one of the Faelnar purebreds in charge decided he didn't want her to win what our assembly had voted for – in large majority. He disqualified her, and without so much as a second thought, he had her thrown into the cold night." She saw his rage disappear beneath sadness as he continued. "She's probably dead now or injured out there on the mountain. We at least have some food and shelter. We at least have others to help us. They're alone. They don't have anyone."

Dania remembered what seemed like a lifetime ago, though it was only a few intervals. "So that's why there was a near riot before the quake. The assembly found out what happened, didn't they?" He nodded. "As well they should have. Buck, your friends have each other. Perhaps it will be enough. I, for one, hope it will."

He closed his eyes and bowed his head. "I just keep getting these images in my head. Part of me hoped to see her walking back up that road, waving to us from the far side of the bridge. Part of me sees her buried under dirt and rock, or lost at the bottom of a ravine."

Dania's TransCom sounded in her ear. In the quiet of the room, Buck could hear it as well. "This is Dame Prattura de Gonari. We have the present situation stabilized. A general planning meeting has been called by Matriarch Amyra de Gonari in half an interval in meeting hall three. All honored dames will attend, with matrons helping the security volunteers keep order. Senior family and business leadership are summoned to discuss our current situation and the next steps we must take. Please insure all are notified. End."

"I'll have to go organize that," Dania said quietly. Looking up into his eyes, she added, "I hope your friends are alright. Come to this meeting Buck; I want you there. One other thing…" She placed a delicate kiss on one side of his muzzle. "Thank you." She smiled gently, and then left him standing there, feeling utterly bewildered.

Chapter 6: Contacts and Truth

Time: 27.50 – 2.5 intervals before high night

With exasperation, Van said, "I've tried nearly everyone. None of them are answering."

"Who haven't you tried?" Sahni asked from within their rapidly evolving shelter.

"Only one. I just can't bring myself to dial the number."

Sahni stuck her head out. "You're kidding, right? Who is it?"

"Arnat de Gonari," she growled through clenched teeth.

"Who is he?"

"Remember when you and I were having drinks? Remember the little cub Faelnar who stared at me the entire time?" Sahni nodded. "That's the one."

"Is he the one whose sire is in charge of the association?"

"The same." Van didn't face Sahni and just kept staring towards the fire, her flat tone belying her anger. Sahni didn't say anything, which made it all the worse for Van. "I can't do it. I can't call him." Sahni stopped what she was doing and sat beside her. Van stood up and walked to the other side of the fire. "I'm sorry! He put us here! He and his rape-mating, purebred, fully-avowed—" She turned to face Sahni, eyes flashing. "Why should I call? He's probably up there sipping fermentum on ice, his little tail all cozy by the fire while we're out here—"

Sahni looked at her again and then turned her head towards the Meeting Den and sniffed. There was no light there now, and the mountain was shrouded in clouds. A light wind blew gently from that direction, carrying the faint smell of burnt garbage. "What … what if he's not? I know. I thought of that, too." Van walked back around and sat beside Sahni. "I get it, really. I know that there are probably lots of others … children … old ones…" Sahni placed her paw on Van's arm and squeezed. "Mange, mange, mange! Okay! You're right! You're right!"

Sahnassa's voice was gentle. "No, you're right. It's worth risking your pride to make sure hundreds of Thurians are okay. I really think a lot of you for doing that."

"You don't know how much I don't want to do this," Van said, rubbing her head in her paws.

"You want to hurt him, like he hurt you?"

"Thurians like me never get those chances," Van sighed, resigned.

"Oh, yes they do!" Sahnassa corrected. "If he answers, be nice to him no matter what he says. Be genuinely concerned. There would be nothing worse for him!"

Van tilted her head back and forth, as if sifting the idea. "To be shown concern, pity … from an Anati? Maybe. Oh, what am I worried about? I've tried bunches of numbers already. There's no way he'll answer."

Time: 27.60 – 2.4 intervals before high night

Despite the intervals of cold they had all endured, the room they were in now was too warm, too humid, and too filled with the smells of others. Buck Harlock listened as Dame Dania de Dothnar stood on a raised platform and laid out their situation. Not much of it was new news to him, having shadowed her all evening, except for one, key fact: the ice storm. "Tomorrow evening," he thought and then looked as his timepiece marked the fast approaching transition into the next sol. "Soon it will be mid-sol, then late tomorrow night; a storm will cover this place in ice, and a driving snow storm will sack us in. This is going to turn into one of those legendary disasters – the kind they make VidStar of. It's the kind that doesn't end well for anyone." He buried his head in his paws as Dania tried to lay out the plan over the objections of others, including the vaunted head of the association, his annoying little cub Arnat dozing by his side.

"As I said, the food will remain under guard!" Dania's frustrated voice intruded into his tired distraction by its added volume. "Anyone caught hording or keeping food back will be disavowed. Food and water are to be rationed. There are no exceptions for anyone."

"What about sending someone down the mountain for help?"

"That's not possible, the bridge is—"

"PRIMAL RAGE, PRIMAL RAGE, YEAH GIVE INTO YOUR PRIMAL RAGE!" The tinny sound of a device playing a rather lurid song brought everyone in the hall to silence. "MATE ME LIKE I'M AN OPEN PAGE; GET ME HOT WITH YOUR PRIMAL RAGE!"

Finally, someone was elbowing Arnat de Gonari. The young, high-society Faelnar with yellow-brown fur blinked and tried to wake up.

"What the mange is that?" Dania wanted to know, angrily.

It took Buck just a moment to piece it together. "He's got a signal! He's got a signal! Check your PawLinks!" he yelled.

In the confused flurry of shuffling and beeps as everyone tried to see if they could connect, Arnat was desperately trying to find the pocket where his PawLink was still blaring, "I'M A BEAST, AND I'M HERE FOR THE FEAST! GIVE ME A TASTE OF YOUR PRIMAL RAGE!"

Finally, Arnat pressed the talk button, and the irritating song ended. "I've got nothing," several others said. "Nothing here! Nope, no signal."

Arnat raised the PawLink to his ear and answered shyly, knowing that he was now the center of the room's attention. "Hello, is someone there?"

An overly sweet female voice cooed back at him. "Arnat, sweet cakes! How are you? We just wanted to make sure you were all cozy up there, with the quake and all."

"Who is this?" he asked angrily, trying to keep his voice down.

"It's me, darling, Vanarra Anasto!"

Arnat's hazel eyes burned with indignation. "What the mange are you calling me for, you stinking Anati? Get the pit off my—"

"YOUNG SIR!" The voice from behind him was female, elderly, and stentorian enough not to be ignored. Looking behind him, he saw his own grand matriarch, Amyra de Gonari, standing, hood down, emblem rank displayed around her neck and shoulder, with her paw outstretched. "BRING THAT TO ME!" The whole room was in awe over the appearance of what some called the hero matriarch. The golden-brown fur of her face, tinged with hints of gray, framed piercing green eyes that stared down at him demanding instant and absolute obedience.

Somewhat reluctantly, he made his way as others opened a path for him, and he very gently placed the device into her paw. Amyra put it to her ear, only to hear a female voice say, "I don't know what happened. I don't hear anything now."

"I am Grand Matriarch Amyra de Gonari," she stated clearly and with the full force of her authority as she stepped towards the podium. "With whom am I speaking?"

There was a brief silence, and then a meek and trembling answer came. "Vanarra Anasto, Honored One."

"Interesting," she thought. Over PawLink or LineCom, Thurians often didn't believe she was actually a real matriarch at first. "Vanarra, where are you?" She let her tone soften somewhat, but kept a harsh edge to it just in case this was someone else at the Meeting Den playing the fool.

The voice answering sounded no less frightened than it had before. "We … (cough) … we were about five courses from the Meeting Den when we were knocked off the road by the quake. We've set up a camp and a shelter here. We've also been able to communicate with the emergency center in the valley below, Honored One."

Amyra's voice control slipped completely in her surprise and relief. "Oh sweet child, you are the answer we've been hoping for! Listen carefully! There's been a fire and an explosion up here. The Meeting Den is badly damaged; we can use less than half of the rooms now. Almost all of our food has been destroyed in the fire. We have no heat and very little water. The roads are out, and we have no other way down the mountain. If the last report holds, very bad weather is coming here in less than a sol. We have around fifteen hundred Thurians up here – families, children, and old ones – who need to be evacuated. Other than your call, we've not been able to get any word out as to our condition. Do you understand?"

Vanarra's voice now lost some of its fearfulness in exchange for empathy and urgency. "Yes, Honored One. We heard all of it. We're so very sorry. We'll relay your situation to the valley immediately. Yes. Put the call in now, please." The last was obviously directed away from the communicator to someone else.

"Yes, right away!" Sahni dialed the other PawLink, knowing that she would also impart a few additional details above and beyond what she had just heard. She also couldn't help but notice Van's distress with the conversation. She'd never before seen her boss act this way.

Amyra asked, "Who else is with you?" Again, Van looked at Sahni with an anxious expression. Van's PawLink was on speaker, and

Sahnassa nodded yes to Van's obvious question before she started talking to the valley emergency station.

Vanarra desperately hoped she wasn't about to ruin her friend's future. "Sahnassa de Orturu, Honored One. She was able to modify her communicator to reach you. We've taken the power cell out of my vehicle, so we should be able to talk to you again ... at least for the next several sols."

Amyra's relief increased all the more when she realized that they would be able to get out more than just this one message. "Clever, and very useful too! Vanarra, I just don't know what to tell you. I don't think I've ever been more pleased to hear someone's voice! Tell me, are either of you injured? Can you return here?"

"No to both, Honored One. Downed bridges and landslides have us trapped on this part of the road."

The mental picture Amyra formed in her mind was sobering. Two young Thurian females, all alone in the cold night and in dangerous conditions – they had to be scared out of their wits. "I'm so very sorry to hear that. Do you have any supplies?"

Vanarra's response was a little more cheerful than Amyra would have expected. "Yes, Honored One. We have a good fire, some food and drink, as well as a good shelter that Sahni ... uh ... Sahnassa made to keep us dry. I believe we have a good camp."

"Now, that's brave and sturdy stuff she's made out of," Amyra thought to herself. She was already starting to like this Vanarra, avowed or not. The name also tickled something in her mind, something she knew she ought to remember.

"Injured?" Sahni asked quietly, a concerned expression flashing across her features for Vanarra. Van was hunched down and nearly bowing, as if cowering before a matriarch who was standing right in front of her.

"Honored One, do you have any injured?"

"One moment Vanarra. Dame, the injury list?" Dania brought her a slip of paper, and she read it. "We may have lost two in the fire. We've got one with second and third degree burns, but only to about five percent of his body. Several cuts and bruises, but nothing else that's serious. A few are showing signs of exposure."

Vanarra called over to Sahni. "Did you get that? She got it. She's telling them right now, Honored One. If it would please you to wait a moment, *Sahnassa* will tell you what they say." Van looked at the young

Nephti with an expression that could be interpreted as nothing short of desperately pleading.

"I'll happily wait, Vanarra, dear."

"Okay. Thank you. I know you will," Sahni said. "I will tell them. Goodbye." Sahni stepped over to the PawLink Vanarra was holding. "Honored One, I'm Sahnassa de Orturu. I just spoke with Regional Emergency Manager Tedarri, and I relayed the details about your condition. He's going to do everything in his power to rescue you. I am to call him in one interval with an update on your status. He'll call us with anything he has for us to relay."

"Excellent. Did he say anything else?"

"He said to start planning for a rescue." Now was the time when Sahnassa pulled out some of that information from Theo. "For example, this rescue will have to be by flyer, so you need to make sure you have a large area cleared for them to land. The athletic field is the best choice. You have to make sure it's well-lit in case of bad weather or when it's dark. Get some of the vehicles up onto the edge of the field. Have them turn on their lights, some up and some into the field when we tell you the flyers are coming your way. Also, you should start deciding now who gets lifted out first and how to keep families together, Honored One."

Amyra's eyebrow fur raised; this Sahnassa sounded so calm and certain. "All excellent council, and we'll get to it straight away. Is there anything else you two can think of?"

Vanarra answered, nearly shaking with fear as if the matriarch could just reach through the PawLink and stab her in the heart. "Just this, Honored One. You have a whole pack of vehicles up there. It's going to be a long night, especially for the little ones. Perhaps you could put mothers and their young into those vehicles and run the heat for them. The roads are gone; no one is getting off the mountain that way. You might as well use up all the power packs you have keeping your most vulnerable warm until help arrives."

Sahnassa was filled with pride in her boss and thought to herself, "Theo's words exactly."

Amyra mentally chided herself for not thinking of it on her own. "We'll start that immediately. Vanarra, Sahnassa, I can't thank you enough." The matriarch's voice softened to her warmest and most grateful.

Van's tone was still effacing. "You are most welcome, Honored One. We'll be your relay station for any other information that needs to go up or down the mountain."

"You're far more than that. You're our only hope." As Amyra looked in front of her, Dania had brought forward a male Faelnar. Dania whispered in the matriarch's ear. "Just a moment, I believe there's someone here who wants to speak with you." She offered the communicator to Buck.

"Buck Harlock here. Van? Is that you?" he asked incredulously.

Immediate relief flooded Van's features. "Buck Harlock, you hotty!" It was something she said every time she saw him, but now, mortified, she cupped her paws over her mouth. "Oh, please tell me I just didn't say that on speaker!"

Buck laughed and said, "You're good. Oh, Van, I can't tell you how glad I am to hear your voice! I was really worried. What happened to you two?"

Van sighed, and her voice, still a little shaky, answered, "We were halfway down, and we got knocked for a loop by a landslide; my baby, the Racerra, is totally trashed!"

"Sorry to hear that. Do you need someone to come and get you?"

Always the gallant one, she thought. "Sweet offer, Bucky, but you couldn't. Don't worry. Sahni's really got us set up here. We're actually quite comfortable, and we probably have more food than you do. Hey, could you be the one we call from now on? I don't really want to talk to you-know-who unless I have to." She was hoping he understood that she meant the matriarch.

"I've got you. Just let me find out if he has a charger for this thing." Van realized he didn't understand, but she couldn't really blame him. It had been so long ago when she had told him. "I don't think he'll mind. In case he doesn't, what other communicators can you connect to?"

Sahni answered, stepping in for Van whom she could tell was barely holding it together. "Only ones on the WindStar network. When we call back in an interval or so, you could read us the numbers, and we could use those later in case we can't reach you on this one. Does that work?"

"Sounds great. So we'll talk to you what, once every interval?"

Van replied, "Let's start with that, Buck. We'll call you in one interval."

"Great. You two keep your heads down and stay warm, alright?"

"Sure thing; you too."

"One other thing, Van. You know what I told you earlier?"

"Yes."

"You remember that. I'm going to pass you back to the Matriarch." Looking up to the smiling elder Faelnar, he said, "Thank you, Honored One, very much. That meant a lot."

She nodded as she took the communicator back.   "Vanarra, Sahnassa, we'll hear from you in one interval. Stay safe."

"You too, Honored One. You too." Her voice breaking at the end, Van closed the channel, and then she closed her eyes. Sahni put her arm around her friend, who leaned into her and started crying. Sahni knew that Van was afraid of the matriarchs, and she guessed the interactions she had

with them in her early childhood were horrible experiences. Yet, this was not the time to ask. It was just a time to give comfort.

The Grand Matriarch touched the off key and just stared at the display for a moment. She had that strange feeling again, like a memory half forgotten: important, but sad. Amyra put that thought away for the present, and she lowered the device to address the hushed audience. In a strong and determined voice, she gave them the good news. "The authorities now know our plight, and they are working to rescue us." An instant cheer went up, with even Arnat smiling.

After an appropriate delay, she raised her paw. "True, this is good news, but we still have a tough ordeal ahead. There are over a thousand of us here. It will take some time for help to reach us, and until then, we must help ourselves and prepare. The dames will organize you into teams. One team will secure everything we need to ensure that we are able to maintain communication. At all costs, this lifeline must stay open. Buck Harlock, will you do this for us, take charge of our communications with Vanarra and Sahnassa?"

"It would be my pleasure, Honored One," he answered, respectfully, but smiling.

"Thank you. Second, our rescue, when it comes, will be from the air. The athletic field is to be prepared as a landing zone. Make sure it is completely clear of debris or any hazards, and place vehicles all along its edges to act as lights should the evacuation stretch into the intervals of darkness or into foul weather." She nodded at a nearby dame who stepped forward.

"Third, we have young here and the sick – those who cannot deal easily with cold or discomfort, our most vulnerable. Vehicles parked around these buildings that are not being used for the landing zone activity will act as heat shelters. As there will be no way to drive down the mountain for several moons, we will expend the vehicles' energies to ensure everyone survives. The dames and matrons will enforce, with your help, that this shelter is not abused by those simply seeking comfort. We will meet again in three intervals to discuss progress."

The other grand matriarch, Rahnahi, stood up beside her, previously unseen underneath her cowl and shielded by her attendants. Gasps of awe rippled through the crowd. She placed her paw upon the shoulder of Amyra and said boldly, "Now is the time when character is tested. Face to face with our own survival, we will not turn away from the family of Thurians here who need us to be all that we can. Upon this mountain, we are one – one family! To each I then say serve, give, share, love, shelter, be merciful, and hold to your sacred honor. Live you the rest of your life great or small, may you be always remembered for the good you did here. You walk from this place redeemed, with a purpose, and holding hope like a light against the darkness, because now, hope is yours again!"

Whoever was not weeping at such a powerful delivery was cheering frantically. Amyra looked over to Rahnahi and nodded. With a wave of her paws, she dismissed the assembly, and the crowd slowly started organizing after hugs and cheers. Buck Harlock stood beside Dania, who was blotting tears from her cheek fur. Amyra gave the PawLink to him and said quietly, "Please, please, change the ringer."

"Yes, Honored One." He waited until both matriarchs were out of the room before he yelled, "Everyone listen to me! If you have a WindStar PawLink, extra power cells, charger, or anything else, bring it to me! I'll be in this corner right here. Only WindStar, got it?!"

"Make sure you comply within the interval. We don't want to lose our only link to the outside world," Dania added, enforcing his order. As she saw movement in his direction, she whispered in his ear, "Quite impressive, Buck." He smiled, and pulled out his own data device to start recording numbers.

Time: 28.00 – 2 intervals before high night

"You've got to be kidding me!" Van exclaimed, still with tear-damp cheek fur, as she talked into the PawLink. "You don't have anything!?"

Tedarri was obviously as frustrated as she was. "Not for one thousand, plus, even if my hanger hadn't collapsed and crushed every flyer I had! The size of this – it's like a military operation!"

Sahni watched with inward pleasure as a thought obviously popped into Vanarra's head. "A military operation – wait a tick," she said as she dashed around to her book and started flipping pages. "I think … I have … there he is. Hey, can you make sure I get a call out?"

Tedarri was more than agreeable, if not a little curious. "We could conference you. We might even be able to configure the switch to let your PawLink operate normally."

Van's tone brooked no argument. "This first call is going to have to be private; I can't have anyone listening in."

"Sure, we'll set it up with the communications switch. You have someone that owes you a favor?"

"Just an old friend. Let's see what he can do. Give me a number he can call you at. He'll want to confirm what I tell him."

Marshall Terrat de Debonar of the Thuratani State Defense Force was "enjoying" a late, but quiet evening in bed. His shirtless gray back rested against the headboard, and his face scowled angrily at what he held. The fierce black accents along the side of his muzzle, above his eyes, and on the tops of his ears only seemed to underscore his intense displeasure. While his mate slept soundly beside him, he read through a series of status reports and operational plans concerning tomorrow morning's air lift exercise. The muscular Lupar rubbed his tired eyes and exhaled as he thought to himself, "I don't need this crap. What kind of idiot schedules a training exercise for four flyer wings on the same base at the same time?" His mind answered its own question. "Some furless, tailless, blunt-nosed, short-eared, neutered, mangy, parasite-infested fool in the force training command."

He had his teams running almost constantly trying to outfit the huge HVR-17's and the smaller HVR-9's, getting them serviced, kitted out, and fueled up. He had to cancel thirty-seven passes for time away (which had done loads for morale), and his logistics officers and seconds had been working double shifts to do the paperwork shuffle. All of this effort seemed only to have the purpose of proving they had enough emergency supplies and rations to blanket and cot everyone in a small town and feed them a meal.

To confuse matters further, an elite, all-Lupar troop of urban assault soldiers, known as the Storm Pack, had also been attached to his command; who knew why? He absently wondered if they were being punished for some prior infraction or mistake. Either it was that, or they all were being punished together for no good reason. In addition to the Storm Pack's liaison, his command center was already fully staffed, as if in time of war, going through the motions of collecting weather reports, scanning for intelligence, and checking communications – all preparations for yet another meaningless exercise.

His PawLink beeped quietly, and he grunted, slipped out of bed, and pressed the switch as he stepped into his study. "Terrat, go." The brief greeting standard came to his lips since he thought the call had to be from one of his crew.

"Terrat de Debonar?" It was a female voice he didn't recognize.

"That's *Marshall* Terrat. Who the mange is this?" he growled. It was much too late at night to suffer fools.

"My name is Vanarra Anasto," the female voice answered, as if she was expecting him to know.

"What unit are you in?"

"I'm not in a unit; I'm actually a caterer, sweetie."

Something in the way she spoke caused a memory from seasons ago to stir. "Do I know you?"

"Well, you may not remember me, but quite some time ago I kept you and a certain young Lupar female from being discovered at a most interesting, out-of-doors social event."

That got his attention. He had met his mate, Acillia, there, and he had won her there, too – claimed her on the field of battle. He vaguely remembered a young Anati who hid them afterwards when a defense force investigator came snooping around. The Marshall knew the fact he was at a Primal Dance and a winner of the same would almost certainly ruin him for future promotions; still, he wouldn't back down. "I won't be blackmailed."

"I'm not doing that, Marshall; I'm just making sure you remember me. Now, please, hear me out! What I'm about to ask for, I'm not asking for just myself. Do you know there has been a quake in the Yarvea Mountains?"

"I think I heard something from my staff. Seems like the local's have it well taken care of," he said, his voice still infused with annoyance.

"They've just discovered something that's completely beyond their ability. I'm really hoping it's in yours."

He sighed, relenting from his desire to slam the PawLink on the table. "I'm listening."

Time: 28.90 – 1.1 intervals before high night

After an interval of intense work, Buck Harlock was sitting in a small room off the main "war room" set up by the matriarchs and the dames to manage the situation. He had no less than ten communicators in front of him and three fresh power cells taken from hover bikes; obviously those vehicles were not going to help anyone stay warm. Two small candles lit the room, and he had his own little data device, too. He smiled to himself. It was as if he could actually feel the hope warming the air around him.

Vaguely, as he checked Arnat's communicator for the tenth or eleventh time, he realized that a meeting of some type was ending in the other room. When he set the device down, he received a surprise. Both grand matriarchs were standing directly in front of him, with Dania standing at the door. As he struggled to get up, Amyra motioned him to remain seated. "Please, Dania, ensure we're not disturbed." She nodded and closed the door as she left the room. As the two matriarchs sat down in the chairs on the other side of the small table, Buck felt a real twinge of fear.

"Vanarra Anasto," Rahnahi asked. "What can you tell us about her?"

Buck swallowed and said, "She's my friend, and she's been that for a long time. She's ... of mixed blood, and she runs a very successful business catering special events. Not all of the events would probably meet with your honors' approval, but most of them do. She is very competent, very customer-focused, and very discreet. She's had a very hard life, but she's kept a good heart."

Amyra leaned forward a little, and Buck began to see the discomfiture on her features. "What ... what can you tell me about her early life, her growing up?"

Just then, he remembered what Van had told him of her past, and the purpose of the matriarchs' questions became clear. "This may not be pleasant to hear, Honored Ones, but it is the truth, as best I know. Also, please understand that she doesn't really talk about this; she's only told me because we've known each other for so long. Vanarra's mother was a purebred de Gonari Faelnar. Her father was a disavowed Vulpi. Soon after Vanarra's birth, her father disappeared; he didn't leave – he disappeared. As a single mother, it was hard enough, but then the matriarch at that time—"

"Disavowed the young mother," Amyra supplied, obviously haunted.

"Yes. Yes she did, Honored One. By the time Vanarra was eight, her mother was destitute. When she went back to her family for help, several of the young de Gonari males beat her as Vanarra hid in the bushes. The males may not have meant to, but they critically injured her, and she died. Vanarra was on her own at eight seasons of age. The things she did just to stay alive and get educated – I really can't even talk about them.

Let's just say she endured more than anyone should ever have to." He had to stop for a moment; the memories of her confessions to him on a night long ago were still overwhelming.

They waited as he collected himself. After a deep breath, he asserted, "It would have been so easy for her to turn criminal, but she didn't. She's smart, strong, and a real beauty – inside and out. There are a lot of males that desire her, but they always leave her, and she believes they always will. Without anyone to support her, without a mate, without a family, she's always known she would have no place in this world unless she made one. So, she's worked hard, at first just trying to survive, but now Vanarra has made a legitimate life on her own. There is goodness in her that never sleeps."

Rahnahi's eyebrows raised, and she said, "I've never heard a better compliment."

Amyra was just shaking her head. She stood and walked to face the distant wall, with both of them looking at her. "I … I held her mother in my arms … as she died. All she asked for as she was breathing her last was that we would show mercy to her daughter. I told her we would. I told her … she could go to her great rest knowing that she was always loved and her daughter would be, too. We never found the child. We looked. Oh, how we looked! Sol after sol after sol, and against the wishes of the matriarch, until some of those same males tried to stop us. We turned them over to the authorities and testified against them in open court. Within a moon, our matriarch was deposed and removed from her position. Each of the males served no less than fifteen seasons. By the time of their release, I disavowed each and every one of them … in memory of … Vanarra and her mother."

Buck was stunned motionless, but Rahnahi stood, walked over, and placed her paws on Amyra's shoulders.

"I could hear it in her voice, you know? The moment I said my name, her tone completely changed. We—" The beeping tone of the PawLink alerted them. "Put her on speaker, but please, do not tell her we are here."

Buck nodded and pressed the speaker button. "Hello. Vanarra?"

"It's me. Are you alone? Can we talk?" Van's voice came through the speaker, both timid and afraid.

"Go ahead." He hated deceiving Van, but he was sure he couldn't go against the wishes of two grand matriarchs. Even his business wasn't that secure.

"Whew! Okay. I've got some bad news and some good news." Van's voice was now much more its normal tone.

"Bad news first, please," he said.

"Well, the local emergency management agency doesn't have any flyers available, and the paw-full they did have were crushed when their hanger collapsed during the quake. They were already having problems getting through the mountain of bureaucracy and other civilian needs to get replacements, and in the end, it wouldn't have been enough, anyway. However, then there's the good news!" Now, Van sounded absolutely chipper. "According to Marshall Terrat de Debonar of the Thuratani State Defense Force, one of the largest airlifts in seasons is gearing up at Harkstone Flyer Base, about three hundred courses away! He thinks he'll have his whole corps in the valley by mid-sol or afternoon, and that's only because he's got to fly around or over some of the bad weather that's coming our way. He's already coordinating with Tedarri to create landing zones and shelters in the valley for the evacuees!" The elation felt by the three sitting around that PawLink was positively electric.

"By Thuria, Van! How in the mange did you manage that!?!?" Buck accidently forgot his honored company in his excitement, and mouthed, "Sorry", which they both dismissed with a happy wave.

"Never you mind that. He's an acquaintance I met a long time ago, and I still had his contact info. I just had him make a call to Tedarri, and he explained how royally rape-mated we all are. That's all it took! Oh, and Marshall Terrat said that we were very fortunate; he's never had so many flyers under his command at one time. They were planning a big training exercise tomorrow, and now it's turned into the real thing!"

Buck was nearly on his hind paws cheering. "Van, you're amazing! That's totally incredible! Wait until I tell the matriarchs! You did an ace job kit!"

Again, Van's voice faltered. "Buck, look, I'm glad you know, but you can just tell them it was Tedarri who called the Marshall. Leave me out of it, okay? I … I just think it would be better. It's more what they would want to hear." Both matriarchs stopped their quiet celebration and just looked at the PawLink; Amyra with a truly saddened expression. "Hey, did you say 'matriarchs'? Who else is up there?"

Buck got a wicked twinkle in his eye as he looked at the accomplished poet. "No one really, just the Grand Matriarch Rahnahi de Dothnar."

"Buck! You have to be joking!" Van's voice was filled with unvarnished astonishment.

"Oh, you've heard of her?" he managed nonchalantly.

"Buck Harlock, stop teasing me! You know full well I've got a whole shelf of her books! I love her! Her stuff is what's kept me sane! Please tell me you're not playing with me! She's really there?" The wistful questions made Rahnahi smile and elbow her peer who gave her a dismissive wave and an accusing look.

"She sure is."

"Oh, Sahni, Buck Harlock just told me that Rahnahi de Dothnar is up there! Can you believe it? I think I have her latest book in my luggage. I'll give it to Sahni and perhaps she could get it signed for me."

"Why not just see her yourself?" Buck asked, already knowing the answer, but wanting the two Honored Ones before him to hear it for themselves.

There was a long pause, and Vanarra's voice was cautious. "I ... I'm just afraid, Buck, that's all. I've worked so hard; if I were to say one dumb thing, make one misstep ... I'd lose–" Now both matriarchs wore the same sad expression.

"Don't worry about it. Are you and Sahni alright?"

Van's tone relaxed again. "We're fine. It's getting cold up here, but not as bad as we expected. Terrat said he wouldn't have any report for at least three intervals. I was thinking about trying to catch a little sleep. How are you doing up there?"

"Well, I'm now officially in charge of communications, thanks to you; so I'm set up pretty well. Most of the work in the athletic field has been done, and they've got the young ones sleeping in nice, warm vehicles – thanks to your suggestion. Everyone else is making do, but what you just said is going to give them real hope. Awesome job, Van, and you're going to have to forgive me, but I am going to mention your part in this. You're saving lots of innocent lives, kit. Hey, and after all, if I were to lie to a matriarch and she found out, it could be my business."

"Then just tell them Sahni did it, please Buck. Please, please, please ... leave me out of it. I really don't want to be noticed."

"Alright, alright. I will. Don't think that they won't find out some other way."

"Perhaps that will be long after all this is over, and it won't matter," Van said, sounding resigned.

"Let me give you the numbers I collected, and then I'll let you go." Buck did so, and then said goodbye to Van, and pressed the control to end the call.

"She's got a good friend in you," Amyra observed. "I also know that, shall we say, you *leaned* a little in that conversation."

Buck bowed his head slightly. "I apologize if I offended your honors. I just wanted you to hear it from her."

"I'm not offended by anything other than by my own family," Amyra said in disgust. "There are a great number of us up here tonight that will probably be rescued thanks to her. I feel like I'm wearing disgrace," she said, rubbing her family emblem.

Rahnahi was also bereft. "For seasons, this child has held onto my words like a lifeline, and now she's too afraid to even speak with me? Amyra, we're going to do something about this."

"Tell me what! Tell me what I can do to fix *this*! Rahnahi, what words do I use? How do I even approach her?" Amyra was pacing and appeared to Buck genuinely distraught.

For a moment, Buck hesitated – the age and authority in that room powerful incentives to stay quiet. However, after both seemed at a loss, he offered, "If it pleases your honors, let her get through this ordeal first. Let her do what she does best, plan and organize, and work her contacts to help get us all off this mountain. When everyone is safe, bring her somewhere so you can talk to her face to face. No dames, no matrons, just one or two of you, and her and perhaps Sahni for support. Tell her what happened and what you did. Tell her what you're feeling right now. I know that both of you deserve great respect for everything you've done and all that you are, but I also know that underneath, both of you are Thurians like the rest of us. Convince her of that, and then ..."

He hesitated, but Rahnahi prompted, "Then?"

Buck knew he was way out on a frail branch, but still, he pressed ahead. "Find some way to make it right. You can start healing a wound this deep with just words, but it won't really get better unless something important happens. I don't know what that is, exactly—"

"I think we will know, Buck, when we see it, and when we see her." Rahnahi's words made Amyra nod.

Amyra smiled at him, voice still breaking. "We'll let you get some rest, too. I'll have Dania get a bed brought in here for you."

"Thank you, your honors," and he stood, head bowed. They, in turn, bowed to him and left the room.

Vanarra sat down in front of the fire that Sahnassa was tending and just stared into it. For several passes, she didn't move. "You okay, Van?"

It was difficult for Vanarra to pull herself out of her own thoughts, but after a moment, she answered, her soft voice nearly trembling. "I feel so messed up, not like fifth of fermentum messed up, but just really – I don't know. Here I am, still cowering like a little kit in front of the matriarchs, still terrified of them. My mom was always afraid. Now, to have ... that one, earlier, talking to me like she's an old friend. I just don't know." She was silent for a few moments longer, but finally confessed in a more certain voice, "I guess my view of the world has just been turned upside down a bit." She smiled weakly back at Sahnassa's concerned gaze.

"Well, you *are* saving all their lives," Sahni suggested softly, teasing a little.

Vanarra smirked back at her and took mock offence. "Stop it! Don't push all the credit to me! I can't even begin to compete with Sahni, the PawLink conjurer! She who can build a shelter that even that guy on VidStar who teaches survival would envy!" Sahnassa giggled as Van's smile broadened. "She who keeps her stupid chattering boss from walking over a cliff! She who carries enough *food* so that we could cater a pre-joining for all the small forest animals if we had to!"

Sahni was laughing now, walking over to their small tent, and said, "Yeah, but we sure couldn't charge them!"

"It would be hard to find napkins and cups in their size!" They both laughed for a moment, and Van turned around to face Sahni, who was starting to slide into the door of the shelter. "Sahni, you've met your own matriarch, haven't you? What do you think of her?"

"I like her, honestly. Even when I've gotten in trouble, she's always been very nurturing about it. I ... I actually look forward to seeing her. I miss her. We used to sit all around her and listen to her tell stories. She still does it, too, for the little ones."

"Doesn't sound like she has to get too harsh. Your family must be very well behaved." Van's tone was a little jealous, a little bitter, and a little admiring all at the same time.

"Not always, but those problems are managed in private. She's been forced, and I mean forced, to disavow one of my close relations. He kept hitting his mate and cub when he drank too much. What was nice about that was that we adopted his child and mate. Now, they're in our family, and he's not."

"Well, that sounds promising, at least."

"How much do you know of the current de Gonari matriarch?"

"Not anything, really. When I left, I left." Again, Van turned inward, and went silent, eyes almost glazing over. Catching herself, she said, "Oh, sorry. Can we talk about something else?"

"Sure," Sahni yawned. "How about sleep?"

"Don't start that—" Van demanded, but it was too late. She yawned so hard she yowled. "See what you made me do! Now, I have to wait out here by the fire while you sleep in there snug as you please."

"No, Van. It's survival. We sleep together for warmth," Sahnassa said, matter-of-factly.

Van was dubious. "How are we both going to sleep in there? We'll never fit."

"Completely ignore the concept of private space?" Sahni answered lightly. Just then, a cold wind with a little moisture blew through their camp.

"Oh, mange!" Van cursed through clenched teeth.

"It's warm in here," Sahni said with an air of satisfaction while snuggling down into the small, triangle shaped shelter.

"Sahni, I-I can't. I—" Another cold blast sailed through the camp. Van started to shake with the cold, her gut seized up, and she could barely move. She felt the end of her tail going numb, and her nose and ear-tips, too. "F-f-f-fine!" Van painfully made her way to the entrance of the shelter, knelt down, took off her paw shoes, and slid down in front of Sahni, who had moved to the back to give her room. As she finally settled into position, she was stiff; trying hard not to lean into her tent mate.

"Van, what are you doing?" Sahnassa asked, accusingly.

"What do you mean?" was Van's innocent sounding reply.

"What are you doing? You're like that log out there! You'll never sleep like that. Come on, relax! And I always thought I was the standoffish one."

"I've just never slept this close to ... another female," Van answered nervously.

"My sisters and I did it all the time when we were kits."

"I didn't have sisters. I've … I've been told that my tail … is … affectionate, when I sleep. Sometimes, the rest of me, too. I sometimes wake up and I'm–"

"Van, it will be fine. I promise. Come on now." Sahni put her arm around Van's midsection and slowly drew her close. Hesitantly, Van relented. "Now, slide down a bit, and put your tail between my legs."

"Between your–"

"Yes, between my legs. It has to go somewhere!" As reluctantly, she did, and she started to feel Sahni's warm body against her. The warmth and softness made her moan in pleasure. "There, that's more like it. Now listen, Van. I know you're my boss and all, but I want to tell you something, something really important. When the landslide happened, I thought I would lose you. It wasn't until then that I realized how much I care about you. You're closer to me than any friend has ever been. I don't know if it's because we're so alike in some ways or so different. All I know is that you're part of my family, and I love you like a sister." She squeezed her tight, embracing her. "Now, relax, close your eyes and get some rest, okay?"

Sahnassa could feel Van's body slowly lose its tension, but the Faelnar-Vulpi remained quiet for a long while. Finally, as Sahni listened to the wind blowing outside, Van confessed, "I … I love you, too, Sahni. I couldn't get through this without you." Van felt the arms that encircled her hugging her once again, and she hugged back, her eyes moist with tears. Finally, the time of night and stress caught up with both of them, and they fell asleep.

Chapter 7: Past as Present

Time: 01.14 – after high night

Sahni awoke to an odd tingling in her wrist. It took her a moment to remember, but then she slowly, carefully pulled her paw out from underneath Van, who only stirred a little bit. When she finally managed to get her watch to eye level, she smiled. The three colored circles were all glowing. The tingling stopped, and a message started to appear, one word at a time, on the time-piece's crystal.

"Tashar … calling … great … job … Sahni!"

"Thanks," she whispered quietly.

"Quake aftershock coming in eighty passes. No danger for you two, just a loud noise. Okay?"

"Okay," she whispered.

"Good," the watch flashed. "Please call den after and reassure them. Will happen again. This is the worst one. Gets smaller after this but no pattern. Got it?"

"Got it. Anything else?"

"Flyers getting ready to depart. Weather may slow them down. Tashar will help dampen storm letting them through. Until then, stay warm, stay safe, sweet Sahni."

"Thank you."

"Sahni?" A muffled voice came from in front of her. "You're talking in your sleep."

"Ha ha … Tashar … X-mit … ends!"

She could only smirk back at the watch as she feigned waking up. "Uh … what? Oh, sorry."

"S'okay. My tail hasn't felt you up yet, has it?" Van asked sleepily.

"No, you've been as well-mannered as a matron. Go back to sleep. I'll try to keep from talking to anyone in my dreams."

Van laughed quietly and then dozed back off. Soon, Sahni was asleep, too, after adjusting her watch to buzz her a short time before the aftershock.

Time: 01.90 – after high night

Van stirred after feeling some movement behind her, and she smiled happily. "Sahni," she remembered. "Sisters, like sisters." It hadn't been a long sleep, but it had been one of the most restful of her life. No male expectations to satisfy, no urges of her own to quench, no bad dreams, no fear, no sadness – it was just a wonder to her. She gently hugged Sahni's arms and leaned just a little more into her.

"Van?" Sahni's voice whispered behind her.

"Yes, oh, I'm sorry."

"Don't be. I think we need to get up. The bad weather's passed, and the fire needs some work."

"Just a little while longer?" Van asked like a small child, snuggling back into Sahnassa's warm body.

"Well, and I have to pee."

"Oh," Van said, leaning forward again. "Come to think of it, that doesn't sound half bad." Van slid out of the tent first, a little surprised that the temperature actually seemed somewhat milder. Looking up, she saw an astonishing number of stars in the large gaps between the slowly moving clouds. Sahni came out behind her. "It's amazing Sahni. It's so quiet, so beautiful."

"Yes, it is. Back in a moment." Sahni hugged her, and then stepped down the path to their agreed-upon place. As Sahni enjoyed a moment of relief, her wrist tingled. The circles were again glowing, and now the face showed a count-down. "30 … 29 … aftershock … 27 …" She finished quickly and headed back up the path. She didn't want Van to be alone. As she approached the camp, her timepiece returned to normal.

"Sahni? Sahni?" Van called, her voice tense.

"What is it?" she asked, running up beside her.

"Something's wrong," Van told her companion. "I … feel weird all of sudden … afraid—" Roaring, like thunder rolling away but in reverse, started gathering in their ears. Sahni reached over and took Van by the paw, squeezing tightly. As they listened, the trees began to rustle as if windblown, and the ground seemed to be alive underneath them. Van screamed in fear, "What's happening!?"

Sahni reached around and took her by the shoulder, looking her full in the face. She called back over the now dropping din of noise, "It's an aftershock! It's normal after a big quake! See, it's passing." Everything started to become still again as the noise died away. "You alright?"

"Oh, Sahni! I'm so thankful you're here! I would have gone crazy with panic if you hadn't told me!"

"I bet they've felt that up at the Meeting Den. You'd better call." Sahni took out the PawLink and offered it to her.

"Can you call? I … I have to go pee now. I want to check on the Racerra as well, see if any more of the hill came loose." Sahni nodded, squeezing Van's paw as she walked away.

Buck was awakened from a very comfortable doze by screaming. Then, he heard the roar and felt the slight movement of the building. "Oh, mange! Not again!" He tried to stand up, but instead, he fell back in his chair.

The matriarchs were taking turns sleeping, and it was Amyra who was startled awake by screams from the next room and loud banging as the building trembled all around her. Terrified, she clutched the edge of the cot. As the noise and motion died down, she got up as quick as she could and entered the room where the others were – some shouting, some crying, some ducked under the large conference table, and some simply silent. Then, she heard a beeping coming from Buck's room. In a moment, he walked in holding a PawLink on speaker, with Sahni's voice talking, but everyone else was chattering at the same time.

A loud shout of "QUIET!" from the poet matriarch silenced everyone. "Go ahead, Sahnassa, we can hear you now."

"I said it was an aftershock of the first quake, and it's completely normal," Sahni's voice emerged from the small speaker. "We'll have several others at random times, but the strength should diminish each time."

Amyra finally remembered, and exclaimed, "Of course! I heard about aftershocks following the Lirgate quake."

Rahnahi shook her head. "So did I, but it's quite different living through it! Dames, let's make sure we pass on what you just heard and check on everyone right now! We can't have a panic, and I don't want a tipped-over candle to burn us out of our home. Now, move! Let's get going! We've got a lot of terrified Thurians out there! Dania, get on our TransComs and pass all this along to the matrons, please."

"Yes, Matriarch," Dania said and pressed the talk control, calling out as she left the room.

The matriarchs both turned their attention to the PawLink in Buck's paw. Rahnahi asked, "Sahnassa, are you alright?"

"Yes, Honored One."

Amyra asked before Sahni could offer. "Dear, is Vanarra alright?"

Just outside of their camp, Van froze, hearing the matriarch's voice on the speaker.

"Yes, Honored One. She just stepped away to check on her vehicle. We were waking up to call you and to hear from Marshall Terrat when it hit."

"Hold on the line, a moment, please."

"Yes, Honored One."

Amyra motioned for Buck to give her the device, and then she stepped through the door into the next room, closing it behind her for privacy after a nod to the other matriarch. Quietly, clearly, Amyra asked, "Sahnassa, your matriarch is Selena de Orturu, is she not?"

"Yes, Honored One," Sahnassa answered respectfully.

Standing silently just outside the ring of low bushes surrounding their camp, Vanarra overheard the conversation. Her gut was wrenching as she realized this was where Sahni's happiness would come to an end. Van just knew the matriarch was going to get Sahnassa disavowed because she had dared to work for an Anati. She was about to ruin her best friend's life.

"She is my honored peerage, and our two houses have many bonds to one another. Now, in the name of that relationship and for the sake of honor, I am asking you, no I am pleading with you, to do something for me." If Vanarra didn't know better, she thought the matriarch sounded afraid.

Sahnassa must have picked up on it, too, because her next statement was said with a kind, reassuring confidence. "Anything, Honored One."

"For reasons I can't tell you, Vanarra is very precious to me. She's precious to our whole family, although not all of them know that. Take care of yourself, but please, also take care of her—" Amyra's voice began to break, and Van stepped out from the shadows to hear. "Watch over her please." It sounded like the matriarch was starting to cry.

Sahni smiled. "Oh, Honored One, she is my dearest friend, and I could never do any less."

Holding back sobs, Amyra continued, "If I do not make it, and you two do, make sure you make her known to Dame Kinnessa of my family, please."

Again, Sahni's tone offered comfort and reassurance. "If it was needed, Honored One, I would, but I have faith we will all leave the mountain safely."

Amyra took a deep breath and found she could take comfort in Sahnassa's words. "I hope so; I hope so. I really want to talk with Vanarra, just for a few moments alone, if she would be willing, once we're all safe."

The other PawLink started beeping, and Sahni said, "As you wish, Honored One. With your permission, the call from the Marshall is coming in. Would you like to listen in?"

"Yes, child, but how?"

"I have an idea," she said as she placed the two communicators a short distance apart and pressed the speaker button. "This is Sahnassa de Orturu, and I have Grand Matriarch Amyra de Gonari on the line as well."

"You're Van's friend?" the gruff male voice asked.

"Yes, sir." She smiled as she answered. He wouldn't know her, but she remembered him from when she and Theo visited "before."

As before, the Marshall's words were crisp and direct. "Marshall Terrat, here. I wanted to let you know we've made a lot of progress. All of the flyers are loaded, and the crews and pilots are getting their final instructions right now. We should be airborne in less than half an interval." She could tell he was moving around quickly, his breath a little ragged but not labored, and the sounds of different rooms drifted into and out of the background.

"I applaud you for your efforts, Marshall," Amyra said, "and please tell your soldiers how grateful and hopeful we are."

"Yes, Honored One. I'll pass that along. Word from Tedarri is that you just had another shake up. Everyone okay?"

"As far as we know, but we're still checking," the matriarch replied. "We were all scared out of our wits until Sahnassa let us know what was happening."

"Very good. Sahnassa, if you and Van keep this up, I'm going to draft you both. You're doing a great job managing communications for us up there. Hang tough, and we'll get there as fast as we can!" The Marshall's straight and level tone, as serious as confident, instilled even more hope in Amyra than Sahnassa's assurances.

A voice from the background yelled, "Sir, we have our approvals, and flight ops just gave us a break in the weather, but only if we leave right now!"

"Then what the mange are you waiting for? Get them off their tails and into the air, Chief! I'm right behind you. Time's up, Honored One, Sahnassa. I'll have Tedarri call you when we're in range. Sahnassa, one thing. Van told me you two were further down the mountain; I'm thinking you may be easier to spot. The weather officer is telling me the ceiling is really low up there. Have you and Van been up to this Meeting Den?" She could tell he was outside of the building, jogging with lots of others running around him.

Sahnassa spoke a little louder to compensate. "We have, Marshall! They're putting together a lighted landing zone using their vehicles. It should be about six hundred tracks by four hundred. If you pick us up first, we can guide you right to it, and you are correct, the visibility is a little rough up above us."

"Excellent, Sahnassa. Those numbers help. We'll be working out an evacuation landing pattern based on that info. Either the Chief or I will be in the lead HVR-9. We should be able to put that down or get close enough to pick you up. Be thinking of a signal – something big without burning the forest down." She heard the strapping of harnesses and the pulling tight of cords.

"I think I already know what you'll need. We'll have something ready by the time you arrive."

"Kit, if you were a soldier, I'd give you a promotion on the spot!" He clicked a button and talked into another device. "Marshall to all wing leaders! Get these ruttin' flyers up in the air, right now! Follow as instructed and keep good formations. (click) Alright, the thirty-first Air Recovery Wing is on the way! Terrat X-mit out!" The sound of engines spinning up abruptly cut out as the connection ended.

"What great news!" Amyra proclaimed. "Help is on the way, and I actually just heard it lift off!" It was clear that the matriarch had rejoined the others, based on the background noise Sahni heard which now included lots of cheering. Sahni smiled, and then felt a soft paw touch her shoulder. Van's face appeared beside her, and she motioned for her to not tell the matriarch she was there. "Very good, very good! You two have given us such great hope! Thank you, and please, thank Van for me, too. Now, get some rest. Can you call us in a couple of intervals?"

"Yes, Honored One. We will."

"Get some rest, and again thank you."

The connection went quiet, and Sahni looked at Van and asked, "You heard?" Van just nodded, with an odd look on her face. "Do you know what all of this is about?" Van sat on the long bench beside her and simply shook her head, leaned down, and then, unexpectedly, nudged Sahni to take her head into her lap.

"I'm … I'm really lost, Sahni," she admitted, looking into the dim fire.

"What I don't understand is why you're reacting this way," she said as she stroked Van's soft ear ridges. "You've actually served banquets to three matriarchs, at once! Remember your 'crowning glory' as we called it? Those weren't minor families, either. You were confident, polite, and dealt with that matriarch, you know, the crazy one—"

"de Caterra. It had to be that one," Van supplied, smiling despite herself. "There are VidStar performers who aren't as odd about their things as she and her dames were. Gosh she was tough!"

"But you stood your ground, even when one of them lost it and started calling you names, and you got them what they needed and everyone else as well." Sahnassa was proud of her boss for keeping her temper. She remembered how awful, how harsh, the de Caterra dame's verbal assault had been.

"I did, didn't I?" Van rolled over to look up into Sahni's eyes.

"And then there's Rahnahi de Dothnar, your creative inspiration. You put something from each of her works into every banquet you give, even in the primals and pre-joinings."

"And I can't believe, like, oh my gosh, she's actually up there! You have to get my book signed, Sahni, please? You know I can't approach her directly, I mean, since I have no status."

"Not everyone enforces that, you know. Only the raving lunatics like the de Caterra still do. This de Gonari matriarch – I mean she sounded rough at first, but now she's practically a sweet little kit. What's so different about this one? It's like she's got you by the tail and the scruff of the neck."

Van closed her eyes sadly and rolled off Sahni's lap, then sitting close beside her. After a few deep breaths, Van admitted, "de Gonari was my mother's family. When I was eight seasons, I watched three males of the de Gonari beat my mother to death while I hid in the bushes. After that, I was on my own."

Sahnassa was stunned. She had heard pieces and rumors, but this was awful. "Oh, Van! I'm so sorry. I never knew. What do you think it means?"

"I don't know," she said at a whisper. "I'm terrified to find out. Yes, I may be able to deal with other matriarchs, but I'm scared crapless at talking with this one. I don't know how de Gonari is now, but they actually *were* those 'raving lunatics' when I was a little kit. After we were disavowed and thrown out, mother told me never to hate them, and never to speak badly of them. She had made her own choices, and she always was so sad when we talked about it. I know she really loved my father, whoever he was. I can still remember when – I didn't even get to say goodbye and now," Van's voice broke as she held back a sob. "I did what she said, and I tried not to hate them; for seasons, I've just been pretending they don't exist. Now, for some strange reason, this new matriarch wants me protected, wants to speak with me – one on one. I don't have any idea what it means! Sahni, I don't want to talk to her. I want things like they were."

Sahni remembered something Theo had said to her while they were dining in one of the loveliest of cafés in Tapricia. She repeated it back to Vanarra now. "What we can see of our own past is so little. It's as if our eyes were always closed shut, even when we thought they were full open. Through muffled ears we think we've heard all music, and through hardened hearts we know we've felt all feelings. It is never so. If we know only of ourselves, the little we know is simply not enough."

The quote seemed to stir something in Vanarra's memory. "'Ignorance feeds fear' from Rahnahi de Dothnar. I used to quote that about others and how they responded to me. I never thought I would say it about myself. Yours was a pretty quote. Who's it from?"

"Oh, a space alien," Sahni answered with a wicked twinkle in her eyes.

"Sahni!" Van groaned, rolling her own eyes and looking back into the fire. "I'd almost forgotten about your space fiction fetish."

Sahni laughed a little sleepily, and then said, "Hey, there are some good writers in space fiction, too! Now, if you actually do decide to talk to the matriarch, I'll go with you, if it will help." Sahni moved back towards the shelter, taking off her paw shoes while Van thought it over.

Looking back at Sahnassa, she replied, "Maybe." Sahnassa's mouth was wide open in a deep yawn at that moment. Looking away, Van shut her eyes and tried to fight the impulse. "Oh, no Sahni, not again! Yowl!"

Recovering from her own yawning stretch, Sahni laughed as Van scowled at her for making her yawn. "Sorry! I was getting sleepy, and it started to feel a little cold."

Van didn't feel the same cringing chill she did last time, but looking at Sahni shuffling down into the shelter made her realize that she really wanted to be there. She stepped back over and was soon sliding down in front of her tent mate, placing herself with nearly practiced ease. She again felt Sahni draw her close, but this time, she relaxed freely into the embrace. "You know, I think I realized why I was so nervous earlier, at least one reason."

"Hmm? Why was that?" Sahnassa asked drowsily.

"My mom used to snuggle with me like this almost up until the very end. I've been with so many males; you would think I would have had my fill. It's just not the same. What's weird here is I'm supposed to be the boss, and you're *my* responsibility; I feel like this is just totally backwards, but it's so nice – wonderful, really. Thank you Sahni, so much. You've really … taken care of me."

"My pleasure; now, let's get a couple more intervals of sleep."

"Yes, ma'am," Van said, as a child might say to her mother. Sahni smiled, hugging her close.

Time: 03.75 – after high night

It was a horrible dream, one that had haunted her for so very long, as well as driven her. The scene again played in front of her; the vicious kicking, the vile laughter, and the cruel insults were all hurled at a poor defenseless mother laying on the hard stone steps and pleading for mercy.

Blood ran from mouth and nose, and once silken fur was splotched with blood. Looking up to a window above, she saw the matriarch, looking down with a fiendish type of glee, contesting with the males below for who could be more evil, more hateful. New dame though she was – watching this scene from the shadows – righteous anger burned inside of her, battling in chaos with fear. In those moments, indestructible purpose was forged within her very soul. This dame would wait, bide her time until the right moment, and then she would strike down the head of this house and end their alliance with the de Caterra.

The moments flashed forward, and she was holding the dying mother in her arms – a face she had known, now bruised, swollen, and bloodied. A voice she had heard sing so sweetly before was now gasping out every breath. "Protect … my daughter! Shelter her … please! She has no one … family cannot abandon—" The breath stopped. The eyes lost focus. The fight was over; death had won. Looking up to the window, she saw the matriarch scowling down at her, as if disapproving of the pity and mercy she showed the outcast at her last breath. Her dream faded into memories as she momentarily stirred.

After the mother's death, there were questions no one wanted to answer. Where was the child? Had she been left with someone? The fierce zealotry of the de Caterra and the de Gonari moved before her like a secret army, silencing all informants, quelling all information. Still, she kept going. Her mind's eye imagined a young kit, abused, rape-mated, and then found dead in the street. That image made her push on, fearlessly, for season upon season until one sol, the males who had murdered the poor mother started stalking her. At first, she was afraid, but by then she was far too wise and too well-connected for that emotion to keep her from her purpose.

It wasn't long before they trapped her in a blind alley and tried to beat her as she finally tricked them into admitting what they had done, right in front of a newly installed security camera that just happened to record very clear audio. The admission was complete moments before the authorities arrived – the right authorities. It was the perfect trap, because to the council of matrons, it did not appear like one. The de Caterra were so callous as to vote for acquittal, but they were alone. The matrons for de Gonari were of Amyra's cabal. Once they read their votes, the other houses fell in line. The verdict was guilty.

The jurists who sent the three away and assigned their punishment were hers, as well, and they sent the murderers to the harshest, most brutal imprisonment there was. True, they were released fifteen seasons later – only because the law required it. One was bedridden with a chronic disease; one had been crippled for life, and the other was so unstable he was permanently confined to a mental facility. There are worse punishments than death, and in the name of an innocent, dead mother and her lost child, she held back no fury.

Her last target, the matriarch, sensing the foundations cracking beneath her after the trial, tried in vain to distance herself from the event. However, after less than a moon of hard confinement, the three males knew help was not coming, and they started talking. Those confessions and revelations were recorded and found their way into just the right ears. The three received no favor for their belated honesty, and the matriarch caught all of the grief. On the eve of the time of feasting, the matrons of de Gonari voted unanimously: "no confidence." As if that disgrace were not enough, during the feast, in front of everyone, the de Gonari matriarch was literally stripped of her title by the vote of every dame in the family and by the bared claws of Amyra. Her purpose finally satisfied, she found herself unexpectedly caught up in the waves of relief and celebration. She was vaulted into the position of matriarch elect and then confirmed almost before the platters were clean. As the chief conspirator for the cause of justice, she didn't realize she had been placing herself at the top of a growing movement – the movement to reshape house de Gonari.

Once there, however, Amyra did not disappoint. The missing child and the dead mother were foremost in her mind, images kept close to her heart within an amulet she always wore. She became a matriarch of action. Rallying her family to help in famine, disease, oppression, and disasters became her passion. Because of their generosity and good example, de Gonari's star began to rise, and they formed alliances with de Orturu, de Dothnar, and de Debonar, just to name a few. Together, they had changed the matriarchy, at least in some quarters, ensuring that what happened to Vanarra and her mother would never happen again. Only in the last few seasons had she started to sleep easier.

However, tonight she stood weeping at the unmarked grave of the dead mother, with the female voice that had been on the communicator telling her that she had failed, that she hadn't kept her promise. She begged forgiveness, but the voice wouldn't stop.

"Amyra!" A voice called her back into reality. "Amyra, dear, wake up now." It was the voice of her friend, Rahnahi, who sounded worried. As Amyra sat up and came to, she felt a paw at her back supporting her and some warm, sweet drink being placed at her lips. She drank as Rahnahi said kindly, "That was some bad dream!"

"Awful," was all Amyra could say between sips; she was still trembling.

"Vanarra?" Amyra nodded. "You know, sometimes I really hate how we dream. Our sleeping dreams play upon our worst fears and doubts, and it's like they try to cancel out everything good and joyful. Let me tell both you and your subconscious something: That child is alive! Better still, she has friends, a livelihood, and a life! If it hadn't been for a few malcontents, she'd be holding a reward for her achievements right now, and if this rescue works out, she'll quite possibly be the way through which hundreds of lives are saved, including both of us! I don't know what you could do in eight short seasons to so prepare a child to live through hard times, but that young mother gave you both a great gift. Now, as Buck says, you have the opportunity to make it right! I see that as nothing but light, warmth, and hope!"

"Who could not love Rahnahi de Dothnar?" Amyra thought. Everyone should have a friend so capable of taking their worst depression and blowing it away like smoke. "Thank you. You're amazing, you know that?"

Her friend beamed with pride and said, quite self-satisfied, "I know! I *am* good, aren't I?"

"Now, tell me again what my contribution to this friendship is?"

"Hah! You've got a good cook!" Rahnahi did eat well when she was visiting, so the joke was well placed, and they both laughed. However, the poet matriarch's tone then changed to one of gentle sincerity. "Also, you've got a good heart, too. You've actually done all these wonderful things whereas I have only written about them. All the books in the world won't feed someone, won't clothe them, and they won't care for them. Those ideas need paws and a heart to make them real. That's you." They hugged tightly. "Now, the real reason I was coming to get you was that it's almost time for Sahni and Van to check in again."

"Sahni and Van?"

"Yes. Buck told me Vanarra likes to give her friends pet names. You didn't really think he was named 'Buck' did you? I have to say it's an improvement over Fanassaragatti."

"Damnable de Caterra and their crazy names. Buck it is, then!" she said, standing up as fast as her age would allow, her friend there for support. Together, they ⟨ornament⟩ and headed towards their erstwhile command center ⟨ornament⟩

))((

Time: 03.90 – after high night

As Dania saw the matriarchs enter, she knew they were not going to like what she had to report. She nodded a short bow before giving the paper to Amyra while Rahnahi read over the other matriarch's shoulder. The incident had been small, but it was the beginning of things to come. Although most were sleeping, the cold and stress kept many awake and active. Some of that activity was necessary – fire guards, volunteers checking on those sleeping in hovers, and matrons and dames doing their work. However, some activity was decidedly unproductive and had started to turn ugly.

A pair of Pantera males that worked for the Meeting Den – for security oddly enough – had been caught up in an altercation with an older Nephti named Leoniry de Nestanum when he found them hoarding a private stock of food. They verbally abused and threatened him, physically, if he told anyone. One of the matrons was nearly dragged to the scene by a Pantera female, who seemed to have a touch of Anati blood. It wasn't long before a mighty contingent of the matriarchy seized their full stock of food, weapons, and had even secured them in their own binders. They were under guard and under the threat of disavowal, as well, and that seemed to restore the peace.

"Not good," Rahnahi said shaking her head. "Not good at all."

"We're going to have more of this, you realize?" Amyra warned, a tone of certain experience in her aged voice.

"Any idea of what we do?" Rahnahi asked.

"At first light, we have the matrons announce the penalty for hoarding food, and we need to establish a plan by which food is distributed, especially to the medically needy – try to avoid someone getting desperate. In the meantime, we need to know if there are any weapons in this facility, and we need to get anything we find into the matrons' paws."

"Arm the matrons?" Dania asked, aghast.

Amyra's tone was enough to warn off any argument. "It may come to that. Certainly, as we get more and more hungry Thurians, we're going to have to protect this room and the remaining food stores. Things could get ugly very quickly; I've seen it happen before. We've started well by establishing a firm control on the situation, but we're going to have quite a job keeping that control."

The beeping tone in the adjoining room alerted the matriarchs to the call. "Let's go check on our lifeline, shall we?" Rahnahi offered.

"Yes. Dania see that those two Pantera receive only the barest water rations," Amyra ordered.

"Yes, Matriarch. For how long?"

"Until we say different." With that, the two matriarch's entered Buck's room and closed the door.

"I'm glad to hear it, Sahni," Buck was saying as they entered.

"How are you doing? Are things okay?" The PawLink was obviously not on speaker on Sahnassa's end, and she was almost whispering.

"Sahnassa, this is Matriarch Amyra. We are mostly doing well, but we've had our first episode of food hoarding. There was a small altercation, and we've got the two rascals fettered. However, I'm afraid we're going to have a lot more of this before too long. I would say that when we finally get off the mountain, there are going to be a lot of hungry Thurians who would have gone for most of a full sol without eating. When you speak with the head of rescue management – what was his name?"

"Tedarri," Buck supplied.

"Yes, Tedarri, tell him that he had better plan on feeding and housing the evacuees until such time as they can be transported to a major city. He should start working on it no later than first light, since finding food for fifteen hundred or so is not going to be an easy task."

"Yes, Honored One. I will call him immediately after we're done here."

"Is Van there?"

"Yes, Honored One, but she's sleeping. I ... I decided she needed the rest. This has been very stressful on her. Don't worry. I'm keeping watch over her."

Amyra smiled and said, "Thank you, Sahnassa, very, very much."

Rahnahi stepped forward. "Sahnassa, this is Matriarch Rahnahi. We should find out from Tedarri if he has notified any of the matriarchy. I believe both Amyra and I would appreciate a word in the ears of our seconds, just to let them know what's going on up here. They may be able to provide some help or at least let those who have loved ones up here know they are alive and awaiting rescue. Please, let us know what Tedarri says."

"I will call you immediately after I speak with him, Honored One."

"If you need to add our authority to your request, feel free to conference us as you did with Marshall Terrat," Amyra said earnestly.

"That could be a great help, Honored Ones. If that's needed, we'll find a way to make it work. Thank you."

Amyra couldn't help being struck by the realization of how strong and resourceful these two kits were. While matrons and dames had reported some terrified Thurians crying uncontrollably in fear, Sahnassa and Vanarra were carrying on as if this was normal business to them. "You are providing such magnificent assistance to us that it would be the least we could do."

"Amyra's right, dear," Rahnahi added. "You are our light in this darkness, and we can't thank you enough. We'll be awaiting your call."

"Yes, Honored Ones. We'll call you back as soon as we hear something."

"Thanks, Sahni!" Buck said and then disconnected the call.

"Excellent job, Buck," Rahnahi offered. "Amyra, if you don't mind, I would like to wait with Buck for that call." Buck swallowed hard, but caught the other matriarch's grin as she said "of course" and left the room.

She sat down at the table opposite him and asked, "Fanassaragatti de …?"

"Caterra," he supplied, a little embarrassed.

"Fanassaragatti de Caterra. Wow, that must have been a mouthful," the matriarch remarked.

"And there wasn't a short version of it that sounded good." They both started laughing, as being a poet and writer, Rahnahi mentally dissected his name nearly instantaneously and found no part that wouldn't bring the bearer much teasing.

"So, Buck, would you mind telling me what you did to get your last name lopped off?"

"Dania? Did she?"

"No, she hasn't said anything to me. You don't have to, you know, and I promise to keep it between us, but tell me only if you're going to be completely straight with me. Stick to the truth. Otherwise, let's not even go there. Okay?"

Buck considered for a moment and nodded. "What the mange?" he thought. "Why not?"

))((

Time: 04.05 – after high night

"Sahni? Where'd you—" Van poked her head out of the shelter, looking a little worried until she spotted Sahni by the fire.

"I'm here, Van. I'm sorry, did I wake you?"

"No, I just – did you make the call already?"

"Yes. I figured you would appreciate the rest."

"Thanks. I think I need to get up and drink something, maybe get a little snack." Van reluctantly got out of the shelter and joined Sahni by the rekindled fire.

Sahni passed her a drink with a meat bar and a sweet stick. "I'm feeling a little ashamed by our wealth of supplies," she admitted. "They've started to have some problems at the Meeting Den with food hoarding."

"That's not sounding good," Van observed, stopping in mid-chew.

"I was about to call Tedarri and pass on what the matriarchs wanted to ask."

"Sure, go ahead."

Sahni dialed the number for the Emergency Management Center. After a few rings, it was Tedarri who answered. "Van?"

"It's Sahni. Van's right here. We just had a conversation with the Meeting Den. They're already starting to have problems with food shortages that have turned ugly. They had an incident where they've actually had to confine someone."

"That's not sounding good," Tedarri said, and Van – still chewing – pointed and nodded based on the likeness of his answer to her own.

"They have things under control, for now, but they're asking about food and shelter after they are evacuated. What should I tell them?" Sahnassa asked, knowing already what the answer would be.

There was an audible, frustrated exhalation of air on the other end of the line, and Tedarri began slowly, "Please, understand what I'm about to tell you is the type of thing we are taught never to tell those awaiting rescue or evacuation. However, since you're our go-between to the matriarchs, I have to tell you. We're … we're still trying to work on that, and it's not going as well as we'd hoped. We've only been at this for a few intervals, so I'm hoping we can come up with something better, but here is how it stands right now. You may want to write this down."

"Van here, Tedarri. I'm ready." She had appeared beside Sahnassa during his last sentences, but Sahni only just noticed her.

"Let me give you the worst news first. We think the snow or ice storm we've been watching is going to hit here during or shortly after the evacuation ends. Word is already out through the emergency broadcast nets to the locals. First thing this morning, they're going to empty every supply store and food location for courses and courses around. It's what they always do, and the quake has made them even more anxious. We've got something of a back-stock, but not for fifteen hundred. With our normal emergency supplies, we have enough for about five hundred, but some of that is needed for fire, rescue, enforcement, and this office; so you can divide that by half. I'm hoping Terrat can make up the difference with what he's bringing, but right now, the picture is not good. Like I said, we're working on it."

Van's voice was shaky, but she answered, "I got it. What about shelter?"

"We're doing better there. I think we have actual beds for over one thousand. We're putting the specifics together, so we'll soon have an actual plan of what to do with the evacuees once they are down here. We don't want families getting split up because of some administrative oversight."

"Okay. I've got that. Wow, it's going to be tough telling this to those folks up there," Vanarra said, shaking her head.

"I know, I know. I'm open to any suggestions."

Sahnassa and Van just looked at each other for a moment, and then Sahni asked, "What about Shanandrae? Could they send supplies? Are they going to be hit by the storm, too?"

Tedarri's response was starting to betray his desperate frustration. "Yes, but they're going to catch only a piece of it, mostly cold rain. Shanandrae is on the plateau, perhaps even somewhat coastal. The bulk of the nasty stuff is actually going to hit here in the valley and in the mountains. As far as what they could send, no one's answering in their EMR center, and the messages we've left with enforcement haven't been returned. We just don't have relationships set up in advance for any of this, certainly not for anything this big. My troops have their paws full just trying to get power and basic services restored so the shelters have light and heat. We're a small staff, and the truth is we're maxed out. Still, we'll work on it somehow."

Van felt her insides knot up, and she became numb all over. She managed to ask, "Are … are the roads clear … between you and Shanandrae?"

"As a matter of fact, yes. I just got the report on my desk a few passes ago. The structural engineers just certified them, and we're about to open them up. We've got a pile of Thurians who want to get out of here and into hotels by the coast. Some of them want to duck this thing before it hits or camp out while they wait for their power to be restored after the quake. Why? What are you thinking Van?"

Sahni saw that Van was shaking, but not from the cold, and her eyes had a determined, yet fearful set. "Check with Terrat; find out what he has. Get back to me. I … I might have something." Sahni looked at Van, who seemed to be scared, unsure, and thoughtful all at once.

Tedarri was obviously intrigued. "Will do. We're trying to get through to the Marshall right now. Can I call you back in say, one interval? I should have some definite word on food and shelter by then."

"Alright," Sahni said, "we'll be waiting." She ended the call, and then sat by Van. Instantly, almost unaware of her presence, the Faelnar-Vulpi stood, went for her luggage, pulled out the UltraBright and several other small binders, and sat at the stone table. She immediately started doing some rapid calculations and research in her materials.

Sahni looked at her and started to ask something, but Vanarra raised her paw in warning. "I … I need a few passes, Sahni. Please, I'm sorry. I don't mean to be rude."

"It's okay. I'll go ahead and call the Meeting Den."

"Just don't put it on speaker, please. I really, really need to concentrate."

Chapter 8: Love as Actions

Time: 04.15 – after high night

Although tired, both Rahnahi and Buck were laughing. "Oh, Buck! That's funny and sad, all at the same time! I had no idea just how bad the de Caterra could be. I mean, I know they have a reputation and everything – I've even crossed them a few times myself, but really … and you're being totally straight with me?"

"Totally straight," Buck insisted good-naturedly. "Now, I'm sure the Matriarch de Caterra would be more than happy to tell a different story, and I have an obvious bias for my point of view, but my two siblings would be more than happy to back me up, plus a few friends, an enforcement officer, maybe a courier or two, and a fur-dresser. Like I said, it was kind of public. I could give you their names, if you want."

The elder matriarch laughed, but warned, "I may ask you to. If nothing else, I want to hear that story from more angles. It's one of the hazards you're likely to run into talking with a writer."

"Sure," he said, easily.

"And it doesn't bother you being disavowed?"

Buck's mood changed, and he seemed more thoughtful, careful of his words. "There are two questions there, Honored One. Do I mind being disavowed from de Caterra? No. The more I hear of them makes me think that it was the best thing that could have happened to me. Now, do I mind not having a family? I do, although it was worse in the past. I have a group of friends – well, we're a family of the outcast. We get together with a few others who either don't now or never did have a family. It's not what it could be I suppose, but it's better than nothing. We make the best of it."

"Is Vanarra a part of your family of the outcast?"

"She practically started it. She—" The tone from the PawLink ended that conversation, and he asked, "Forgive me, but are you here or are you not, Honored One?"

"I'm here, at least as far as I know."

Buck nodded and pressed the speaker button. "Hello?"

"Hi Buck; it's Sahni."

"Hi there. I've got Matriarch Rahnahi de Dothnar here with me. How are you two holding up?"

"We're doing okay, I guess. We've just had some news from the Emergency Management Center. They're trying to get everything ready for the evacuees once they are down in the valley. Tedarri says that as far as shelters are concerned, he's in fair shape. That's good, since the winter storm is going to hit sometime during the evacuation. He's working on a plan to break the population into groups of the correct size; keep families together and that sort of thing."

"Sounds good, but what's the bad news?" Rahnahi had heard it in Sahni's voice.

"Well, Honored One, there is a problem with adequate food."

"Oh, no," Buck groaned.

"I know," Sahni said with regret. "The problem is, in part, the winter storm. With so much already damaged and without power, the population of the valley is going to wake up and totally empty the food stores and warehouses in the towns. With the storm looming, the regular resupplies won't be coming either. Now, Tedarri can spare about two hundred and fifty meals from his own supplies, and he's checking with the Marshall to see what he's bringing, but it's not looking good."

"Forgive me for stating the obvious, but we're in a dire situation here. We've got the elderly, infants, and all sizes and shapes in-between," Buck exclaimed. "Unless the Marshall is flying up here with say, ten thousand or so meals, he's not going to make a dent in this! We'll have to get everyone out of town, back to Shanandrae."

"The roads from Shanandrae are clear, and they were checked out after the quake, but the timing is just not going to work for us. We won't be able to get everyone down the mountain and into some kind of transportation before the storm sets in. Maybe some, but not all."

"Sahni … oh, may I call you that, dear?"

"Yes, Honored One."

"Sahni, I don't mean to put you on the spot here, but you've already had some good information and ideas. Can you two offer anything more?"

"Well, Honored One, the moment Van heard about the food problems, she started feverishly working on something. I think she may have some ideas shortly. I'm going to let her work and try to collect any information from Tedarri and the Marshall."

"Very well. Will you please check back with us when you hear something else?"

"I will, Honored One. Thank you."

Buck pressed the end button. Rahnahi looked at Buck, who appeared deep in thought. He mumbled something like "could she actually be…"

"What are you thinking?" she asked.

Buck looked at her, thoughtfully, as if trying to piece something together in his head while he spoke. "Van's job is catering, right? She's done events of many different sizes, nothing this large, but she has all the right contacts. Food, transportation, and lodges in Shanandrae are things she works with all the time. It's just…"

"What?"

"I don't know if she can pull it off, Honored One. I can't even start to imagine what kind of money this will run into. I mean, she keeps excellent credit, and her business has deep pockets, but something like this?" He scratched his chin fur. "If she put everything out there, risked her lair, her business – I bet she actually could."

"She can set up all of that marooned on the side of a mountain?" Rahnahi found it impossible to believe.

"Honored One, you would just have to know her."

"I'll speak with Amyra, and we'll see what resources we can bring together to help."

Time: 04.50 – after high night

Sahni quietly walked back into camp, trying not to make too much noise. As she drew closer, she saw that Van really hadn't even noticed she was gone. Van sat at the table, flipping between binders, making notes, and keying into a math device at times. The fire was getting low, and Sahni thought she could see Van actually shivering as she worked. Quietly, she bent over and started to add more and more wood to the fire, growing it from nearly nothing into a blaze almost as tall as she. The heat radiated through the camp, and Van finally seemed to notice. "Thanks, kit. I was dying over here."

"I'll do better than that." Sahni walked over, took off her coat, and placed it around Van's shoulders. As the coldness started to penetrate through her fur and into her skin, Sahnassa walked back towards the fire.

"Oh, kit, you didn't have to do that!"

"Still taking care of you, I guess. What are you doing?"

Van shook her head as she went back to her work. "Trying to figure out how to feed everyone, if we need to. I just need a final number from—"

As if on cue, the PawLink beeped. Sahni quickly darted to the edge of the tent where she had left it the first time, but heard Van talking. She had obviously retrieved it when Sahni was gone, so Sahni returned to the fire. She also noticed that Van forgot to put the call on speaker.

"Go ahead, Tedarri. Yes? Oh, mange! That's not nearly enough! Fifteen hundred, and he has to keep back how many? So make it an even thousand then? Military rations only?" Van sighed deeply. "Yes. I know. Anything else likely to come our way in terms of food? No, I thought not. Tedarri, I … I think I might be able to help. Can you arrange an enforcement escort from the Keynote Center parking area in Shanandrae to your building? It's going to be at least six, maybe seven intervals before it's ready. No, they'll have to leave their cargo sections and turn tail before the storm hits. I don't know how big; it could be very big. Do you have any clearer picture of that storm's strike time here? How long it will last? Please, see if you can. That's going to have a huge part in this thing. Alright. I know. I'll call you when I have it figured out, and I'm going to need a few intervals of talk time. Okay? Got it. Bye."

Van pressed the button to end the call, and then just stared ahead blankly. Cold as Sahni was, she stepped over to Van and placed a paw on her shoulder. "Everything," Van was mouthing, almost silently.

"Everything." Sahni sat beside her, looking into her friend's blank stare in the warm firelight. "It will take everything..."

"Van, are you alright?"

She shook her head in complete distress. "I'm ... I'm ... oh Sahni, I don't know ... no, I don't know what to do! I ... it will wipe out everything I have! My company will go bankrupt if I feed and move all those up there. Everything I've worked for will ... will just..."

"Save hundreds from cold and hunger, and maybe even save some from death," Sahnassa said, putting her arm around her friend. "Cubs, kits, mothers, fathers, purebred, and ... Anati."

"But you'll be out of a job! I'll ... my lair ... everything ... I mean no one is going to pay me back! Oh mange, Sahni, I'll be out on the street!" Vanarra buried her head in her paws. "At least for awhile! When the creditors press charges, I'll be in jail! I'll be in jail for a very long time!"

"Surely the matriarchs would be grateful, Van? I'm sure mine will. Maybe even the government will help."

Vanarra wouldn't be consoled. "I'm Anati, remember – a mongrel bitch of no family!? No one's obligated to do anything for me! No one looks after me but me. It's the way it's always been. Everything I have, everyone who depends on me – oh, my gosh, and the orphans, they might lose the place!"

After a few moments of silence, Sahnassa reached around Van's waist and hugged her tightly. Van accepted the embrace, weakly, and just started crying into Sahni's neck. Sahni whispered, "I believe in you Vanarra Anasto. I believe you will do the right thing no matter how hard it is. It is what has made you a great business leader and a great friend. If only your mother could see you, I can only guess how proud she'd be. You have every reason to hate most of the Thurians up there on that mountain, but here you are considering giving up everything just to save them. For even considering it, you're a hero to me."

Van lifted her foot over the bench to face Sahni, and Sahni did the same. Van looked into her friend's loving eyes and hugged her. "Oh, what would I do without you? I love you, kit! I love you."

"I love you, too, Van."

Sniffling and trying to wipe cold tears off Sahni's shoulders, Van sat up. "Promise me you'll visit me in jail?" she asked, pathetically.

"I won't leave you, Van. You're my friend, and I'll stand by you, no matter what."

That broke up Vanarra once again, and she cried, hugging the only real female friend she'd ever had. After a moment, Sahni couldn't help but shiver. Van leaned up and said, "Oh, look at me! Here, take back your coat! I suppose we should start to get to work."

"First," Sahni demanded, "we tell the Meeting Den the truth, exactly, of what you're going to do, Van."

"I don't know," Vanarra sighed, shaking her head with her eyes closed and head downcast.

"Once you decide you have nothing to lose, it can be a very liberating thing, Van! Embrace it!" Sahni lifted her friend's chin up gently and looked her in the eye. "They should know who Vanarra really is, and what kind of incredible Thurian she can be!"

"Okay. Can you tell them? Perhaps it will just be Buck. That would make it easier."

Sahnassa looked her friend in the eyes and said, "I'll talk to them, but I want you beside me when we call."

Van nodded, and together, they walked toward the fire.

Time: 04.75 – after high night

"I don't care what some of my dames will think of the cost! What good is money going to do us if someone's baby kit dies?" Rahnahi quietly completed her argument with her friend in Buck's room. They were alone, as she had asked Buck to step out so they could have a private word.

"I agree. You know, the de Caterra would probably just stick her with the bill," Amyra answered.

"But we are not de Caterra, are we? Will you swear to her?"

"I can, but you know the law! Even *that* doesn't officially bind either of us. It won't convince her of anything. We can have a witness here, but would she believe that?"

Rahnahi thought for a moment, and then said, "We could do that, but wait! If we both swear to Sahnassa, she's de Orturu. That should carry some weight with Vanarra."

"Good, good. That just might work. Buck thinks she can really do this?"

Rahnahi nodded, answering, "He thinks she would throw everything into it, if we can somehow guarantee she won't be left out on the street. You know the kind of life she's led! She's got to be terrified, but we have fifteen hundred up here! We can't afford to have her feel like she can only do a half effort."

Amyra thought for a moment and said, "I think I know—"

The PawLink beeped, and she called for Buck. Buck came in, and Amyra called out through the open door, "Dania, please step in here, too. Buck, we're here for this one, understand? You start, though."

"Mange," Van said quietly, anxious to get this over with. "What's taking them so long to answer?" Just then, the call connected.

"Hello, Buck, are you there?"

"Yes. Yes it's me, Sahni."

"Hey, we just wanted to call to tell you that, between Tedarri and Terrat, we've only got 1,250 meals. Tedarri is having trouble getting the shelters up and running while trying to solve the food problem. Terrat has already loaded his, and he's only coming with military rations. Since we know that's not going to be enough, Vanarra is offering to do everything she can to make up the difference. We're going to start making calls as soon as we get off the link with you."

"Oh, Sahni, that's great! Is Van there?"

"Hi Buck; it's me." She sounded a little weak.

"Van, it's great for you to pitch in here, but what's this going to add up to?"

"Way more than I've got. I'm going to push every credit limit I have to the absolute max. They'll probably bury me under the poorhouse, if not the jail, but I've thought it through; I know what I'm risking, but … I couldn't live with myself if something happened to one of you – someone went hungry, someone got sick, someone…" She trailed off, leaving the worst things unsaid.

"Vanarra, you truly are amazing. That's not just generosity, dear kit; it's unconditional love."

For a moment, she didn't recognize the soft-spoken female voice, and there was a long silence. The voice she had heard earlier was so different. Even when it had moved from the commanding announcement of title and name into relieved conversation, it was never as tender as it was in that moment. Sahnassa reached around her and hugged her shoulder, and the gleam in her eyes confirmed Van's fear. "Honored One?"

"Yes. It's me. Is Sahnassa there? Are you both listening?" Her voice was still quiet, but firm.

"I am, and we are, Honored One," Sahni answered. Van didn't know what to think, and sat still, like a little child waiting for punishment.

"Sahnassa de Orturu, daughter of the honored house de Orturu of our peerage Selena, I, Matriarch Amyra de Gonari, pledge upon my sacred honor and that of my family that for every expense Vanarra Anasto spends on our behalf for this rescue, we will repay to her, in full and within the next ten sols. Have you heard and do you affirm my bond?"

Overwhelmed with an excitement that Van didn't quite understand, Sahni scrambled in her mind to remember the correct form of the response. "I … I do hear and do affirm your bond, with deepest gratitude."

"Sahnassa de Orturu, daughter of the honored house de Orturu of our peerage Selena, I, Matriarch Rahnahi de Dothnar, pledge upon my sacred honor and that of my family that for every expense Vanarra Anasto spends on our behalf for this rescue, we will repay to her, in full and within the next ten sols. Have you heard and do you affirm my bond?"

Sahni was now starting to cry with joy. "I do hear and do affirm your bond, with the deepest gratitude."

Amyra spoke once more. "Dania de Dothnar, honored dame of your house, do you hear and affirm these bonds?"

"With respect and honor, I have and I do."

As Amyra spoke the concluding forms of the promise, Vanarra reached over and pressed the mute button. "What does all this mean? They don't ever make promises to—"

"Their promise is to me, Van, and they have to keep it! You should thank them!"

After pressing the mute button again, Van heard Amyra say, "And so it will be done. Vanarra, you have every reason not to trust us, I know. However, Sahnassa knows that this promise I made to her on your behalf is not one I can break. You have such a good heart, and I couldn't stand the thought of abandoning you after what you're willing to do for us."

Still overwhelmed, sounding like a timid child, Vanarra said, "Honored Ones, I'm … I'm … thankful. I never thought – I will do absolutely everything I can. I will."

Buck added, "And coming from Van, that's a promise you can bet your life on."

"Of that I have no doubt," Amyra agreed with certainty. "What do you need of us?"

Vanarra took a deep breath before mustering the courage to give instructions to a Grand Matriarch. "Let us make our first calls and get things moving, Honored One. We'll call you back as soon as we set things in motion. I've done a lot of planning already. Depending on the time of the storm, we may actually be able to transport some of you into Shanandrae before it hits. I've got to start getting the transports moving, and I don't know how many I'll actually end up with. You should start trying to figure out who would be the first to leave. It would also help to know how many children of ages infant through four you have. My guess is that their food, diapers, and so forth are in short supply, and I need to know how much of that to include."

"Dania, see to anything Van needs in terms of information," Rahnahi told her. "In point of fact, help Buck with anything he needs from the communications side, as well. As soon as first light breaks, we're going to check over matters on our end, but please start now. Vanarra, Sahnassa – we can't thank you enough."

"And, you, Honored Ones. We'll be back in touch soon," Sahnassa said happily hugging her friend's shoulder.

Time: 09.25 – 5.75 intervals from mid sol

Despite the cold, the next five intervals were a frenzied blur of activity, with Van contacting charter companies, food preparation houses, and shipping companies, not to mention rousting everyone in her organization out of bed and getting them to help. The gathering of food she had left to Flint Bonar, her second in command back at the office, along with all of the account numbers and instructions he needed. She had even managed to contact the seconds of both of the grand matriarchs, and, after a little Sahnassa-arranged "conference," they believed Vanarra enough to lend their support. When light from the next sol started appearing on the horizon, a small army was assembling in Shanandrae to start pulling together a rescue convoy.

After organizing the food and transportation, she then focused on the more detailed logistical problems. With Sahni taking messages and cataloging what was turning into a sizable rescue force, Van was getting the final numbers from Dania and Buck regarding the sizes of the groups and who needed to go first.

"We've got an even fifteen hundred up here, if you count the staff," Buck noted, as he read off his data device. "Of that, we really need to get about one third of that out of here – families with kits, the elderly, the sick, and so forth. The rest could wait it out at a shelter for a couple of sols until transportation became available again."

"Got it, Buck," Van responded, taking notes. "That's going to work out just about perfect! I've got fourteen big charter transports heading your way. They should be leaving Shanandrae as soon as I can set up a place in Windston for them to meet. I'm talking with Tedarri the moment we get off this line. If we're efficient, that could get over six hundred and fifty out of here before the storm hits."

Dania responded with certainty, "Then we'll be efficient. I'll just go and start putting that together right now." Then, she briskly stepped out of the room.

When the door closed, Buck added quietly, "With everyone so tired and cold, the matrons and dames are really having to drive the herd up here, but they're working out a system to get the evacuees in the right order and moving without a break. That task is actually helping us keep order, because everyone has something to do. Oh, yeah. I almost forgot. We've got the landing field complete, at least as far as the vehicles that will be providing the lights, and Sahni's guess on the size of it was dead on, so no need to correct Terrat on that score. I walked out there and took a good look around, and I don't see anything, wires or trees, that will be a problem for the flyers."

"That's awesome news, Bucky! Alright, time for me to check in with Tedarri and Terrat, if we can get him. I'll call you back in half an interval?"

"Sure enough! Hey Van, you're my hero!"

Van smirked at the jab. "Hah! Just remember me for your next catering job, okay?"

"Sure thing. Talk to you soon!"

As she pushed the button to end the call, Vanarra looked over at Sahnassa who was sitting at the table with her, busily making notes from Van's conversation. "You get all that?"

"Yes, I did. You know my fear is that we'll get all of this organized up at the Meeting Den and down in Shanandrae, but actually getting the transportation and feeding and sheltering to work like it's supposed to in the valley might be a problem. Look at all of the vehicles we're bringing into one place: the flyers, the transports, the haulers. It could be a real tail knot down there!"

Vanarra hummed thoughtfully. "Yeah, and what I'm hearing from Tedarri isn't making me feel any better. We need to make sure he's got his end put together." Vanarra noticed that Sahni was looking at her watch … staring at it in fact. "What time is it?"

Sahnassa was a little startled, but answered, "9.30, perhaps we should call down early?"

"Yes, I think we should. We haven't heard squat from Tedarri, and his work is what this whole thing hinges on." Van picked up the PawLink and started dialing.

Time: 09.10 – 5.90 intervals from mid sol

Tedarri was rubbing the tops and sides of his brown muzzle, trying to wake up. He had too much to do to be this tired. Minus the Meeting Den, things were going well. The power crews were doing a fair job getting power restored, and the big prizes – the hospital, the schools, and the water treatment plants – were all back up and running. It would be a long while before the outlying areas were completely repowered, but the crews were spending extra time making sure the key facilities in town would survive the winter storm coming their way. Enforcement was doing a great job keeping both the traffic and any opportunistic crime in check.

"So other than the fifteen hundred on the mountain and the thirty-six flyers heading my way, everything's going as smooth as aster tree tea," the older Lupar thought to himself, darkly. He hadn't felt like this since he was in secondary; it was like he was a student taking a test, answering all of the easy questions first before starting to work on the hard, high-value problems. He knew, however, he was quickly running out of time on this test.

Just then, a paw he didn't recognize gave him some hot tea. "Looks like you could use this, sir."

"Thanks. You are?" he asked, looking up into the dark blue eyes of an adult Nephti who looked and sounded far more awake than Tedarri felt. The Nephti seemed to be a few seasons younger than he, and his coat was still solid black except for its white stripes.

"Theo de Allarrae. I was passing through and got knocked off my path by the quake – my vehicle's well, you know. I've done a little emergency planning, some communications work, and someone in the front office said you needed help in here. So, what's up?"

"What's up?" Tedarri asked in grim humor, leaning back in his creaking metal chair and placing his hind paws on the table. "I've got the whole mangy defense air force descending on me in less than three intervals to start a rescue of fifteen hundred or so up on one of our nearby mountains. I've never even thought of planning for something like this, and you?"

Theo seemed to jump right into the problem with ease. "You need to start with the traffic flow. That's the key. Now, do you have a map of this area? I'll need one with contour lines."

The Nephti's energy and attention spurred Tedarri out of his chair. He went to a file cabinet and found the appropriate map and laid it out on his desk. Without speaking, the Nephti studied it and then started pointing and writing a little on a small notepad he produced from his pocket. "Okay. Where are the fifteen hundred in relation to this here? Do you have anything that shows where they are in relation to where we are?"

"Yes. Just a tick." Tedarri was back digging through his filing cabinets, a little longer this time, but he finally produced just such a map. Again, after studying some more, the Nephti started pointing and writing notes.

"Okay. I think I have it worked out, or at least maybe a good start. How many flyers, and do you know what type?"

"Uh, yeah. Hold on." He went back to his notes and flipped through them. "Twenty-four HVR-9's and twelve HVR-17's. I have no idea what that means."

Theo whistled and then said, "Well, now that's an impressive fleet! They're going to need a very big plot of ground as a staging area, and that's where they'll need to land when they first get here. You don't have an airfield but … yes, look. Is that field still unused?"

Tedarri walked over and looked down at the spot where Theo was pointing. "I think some farmers use that as pasture-land, but it should be vacant right now."

"Alright, then that's where you start," the Nephti said as he scribbled down some numbers. "Someone will need to read this to the flyers when you contact them. It's the coordinates for the staging area. That should be large enough for them to set up an initial headquarters. Now, that's part one of the flow – the beginning. Presume that the flyers are landed and get established in the field. They're going to start making runs up the mountain and pulling groups off. The flyer pilots and their commanders will know how to keep things from bumping together in the air. However, you'll need a landing zone at the top of the mountain."

"Now, *that* we do have," Tedarri explained, sounding a little more confident. "We've got an athletic field up there, about six hundred by four hundred tracks."

"Hmm… That means they'll only get one HVR-17 or two HVR-9's down at a time. The 17's are about one hundred and seventy-five tracks long, and the 9's are about sixty tracks long. If they try to put anything more in that space, they could have a mid-air or put part of the flyer into the sidelines if they catch a good gust. How solid is the fifteen hundred number?"

"It's good."

The Nephti wrote for awhile and then stopped. "Destination? Where are you going to house the evacuees once you have them down here?"

The Lupar answered as he pointed on the local map, "We were thinking the schools, here and here, for starters. They're secondary and tertiary education centers, so they have a lot of space, and they're right across the road from one another."

"That's good. The athletic fields of the two schools – is either one lit?"

Tedarri drank down the last of his tea and thought for a moment. "Yes. The tertiary is. So is that a good place?"

"Not if we think they'll hit the light poles. It would be better to have the flyers set up their own landing zone here, at the secondary school if it's not lit."

"That's an open field. There is a fence here, and here, but you've still got … five hundred by five hundred tracks here to put down. It's pretty far away from the main buildings."

Theo avidly approved. "Excellent! So you can really start to establish a flow, now. Filter everyone through the secondary school, perhaps set up food and medical there. You'll be able to do some triage, give them access to a restroom, feed them, and get them sorted. Just lay it out like an assembly line, but it will have to be put together quickly." He went back to his calculations for another pass or two.

Tedarri looked at the Nephti bent over his desk quickly scribbling notes, and his curiosity started to spark. "Do you mind if I ask you a question?"

"No, go right ahead," Theo answered, not looking up from what he was doing.

"Where did you pick up all this information?"

The Nephti smiled. "I spent some time on a defense base recently, for my job. I've done some safety and research work for the government on contract. Made a good friend of the air chief, and he filled me in – even gave me and my assistant a ride. There, that has it! If they get organized quickly, then the flyers can get everyone off the mountain in about five intervals, maybe less."

Tedarri looked through a pile of papers on his desk and found the weather report. "That's going to be cutting it close. We've got a winter storm rolling in."

Theo stood up straight and looked him eye to eye. "If we try to compress the schedule, there could be a mid-air or ground collision, and then everything would stop. Besides, everything we're saying is just a suggestion. When the commander arrives, he'll make his own calls, and he'll probably want to see all of this. It would be a good idea to meet them in the field when they land. If you don't mind, I'd like to go along. You may also want to have someone with a camera there. These fellows are going to make quite an entrance when they arrive."

"Sure, Theo was it? Thanks, too, I was really running on empty," Tedarri gratefully offered. He now felt like he could possibly manage this, and the thought of seeing all those flyers landing at once injected a small element of "fun" into the equation. "Can you hang out awhile and help with the rest of the planning? Maybe communications? We've got a couple of civilians on the side of the mountain who are our only link to the Meeting Den where the fifteen hundred are. Terrat said he would call in a … well, about now," he said looking at his watch. "There are a few other things I need to get done if you can manage it."

"Sure, with my vehicle occupied, I'm not going anywhere."

Tedarri felt bad for leaving Theo alone with all this, but he had the sense that the Nephti could easily manage. Still, he asked, "Is it anything I can help with? I could get you a tow."

Theo was dismissive. "No, not right now. You need the help, and I have the time. It can stay where it is; there are more important things to do."

Tedarri nodded, grateful. "If you need me, I'll be in the next room." Theo nodded and watched as the Lupar stepped away.

The two communicators in front of Theo had two labels: mountain and air command. Air command, at that moment, rang. "Windston Emergency Management Center, Theo de Allarrae speaking."

An official-sounding male voice responded, "Theo, this is Rathnar tower. We have Marshall Terrat on the line for you. Please be advised that this is non-duplex communication. Please use 'end' and 'X-mit out' when done speaking."

"Very well, Rathnar tower, I understand. Please go ahead."

"Marshall Terrat, I have a Theo de Allarrae from Windston Emergency Management Center on the line. Please proceed."

There was an odd delay as the tower set up the circuit. Finally, a commanding voice crackled through the receiver, "Marshall Terrat here. We're about three intervals out, and we need to coordinate landing zones with you. End."

Waiting the appropriate half-tick, Theo shot back, "Understood, Marshall. I have selected an initial LZ and staging area for your group. Prepare to copy coordinates. End."

There was a moment's hesitation before the reply came. "Ready to … what's that? Hold one for Air Chief Tawnston." There was a rustling noise as the connection was passed to someone else.

"Theo? By Thuria, Theo is that you? End."

"Hi there, Chief! Long time no talk to! Glad to hear it's you who's coming our way. End."

The chief sounded truly thrilled, if not a little relieved. "Well you son of an Anati, I do not believe it! How the mange did you end up there?! End."

Theo had to laugh for a moment before he responded. "That quake pulled me off the path near here. I found this place looking for a tow and offered to pitch in. I think I've got a sweet LZ for you, when you're ready for it. End."

"Ready to copy!"

"Coordinates are 43-23-11-00 and 43-23-10-05 on the corners of the LZ. Repeat back as confirmation please. End."

"I repeat 43-23-11-00 by 43-23-10-05. What's the ground like, end?"

"Less than 2 percent gradual ascent, smooth, low grass, hard-pack. You should land facing north by north east. Even the 17's shouldn't have a problem landing level. End."

The chief responded, "Got it! Perfect! Any idea what we're looking at for our air control pattern and evacuation LZ's? End."

"You've got a standard hold and land, so you'll need to set up your air holds for the mountain and for the school athletic field where we'll have you drop your passengers. Coordinates follow when ready to copy. End." In a few moments, they had read and repeated the coordinates. After hearing the chief read back the final set of numbers, Theo confirmed, "You've got it, Chief! I have the sizes of the two LZ's as six hundred tracks by four hundred for pick-up, and five hundred by five hundred at the drop-off. Looks like you'll be limited to two 9's or one 17 for each landing on both LZ's. Please acknowledge. End."

"Got it. Two 9's, one 17 per landing. Wow, that's going to make it tight! Any hope of finding something better? End." The Chief was obviously not as pleased with this information.

"Negative, sorry about that. We dropped any of those sites out as LZ's because they're either too far away or have a problem with obstructions. They didn't have enough capacity, anyway. I really think this is the best we can do, Chief. End."

"You know me; I had to ask. Say, you going to meet up with us? End."

"I'll see you at the LZ when you land," Theo assured him. "I'll even try to get some visual aids to help you find the place if I can. What do you prefer? End."

"Smoke, if you have it. Wear an emergency vest and get some UltraBrights so my pilots can see you. As soon as our air controller group is on the ground, they'll take it. End."

Theo knew the Chief well enough to take the hint. "Understood. Once you're on the ground, it's your op." Theo had already been aware of Tedarri listening behind him. "Tedarri is running the show on the shelters, and for now, I've got communications. Can you drop me a TransCom when you land? That would help you keep in touch with the EMC down here. End."

"Sounds good. I'll get you one." There was a pause, as the Chief talked to someone off mike. "Marshall says we've got two civilians keeping the line open to the evacuees. What do you want to do with them? End."

"Wait one."

Theo looked back at Tedarri who asked, "Can he pick them up on his way? They've already done a lot for us, and they're familiar with the layout up there. Let's not leave them stranded any longer than we have to."

Theo nodded and then responded, "Chief, this is Theo. The request from Tedarri is that you pick up the two civilians on your first trip up the mountain. They may be able to provide assistance to aid in your landing. End."

"Understood, Theo. Will do. From what I've heard, it's only right that they be allowed to ride in with the cavalry. After all, they sent up the call. End."

"I'm sure they'll appreciate it. I'll coordinate details and ask for them to be ready for pickup in three and a half intervals. End."

"Got it. See you at the LZ, and I definitely owe you a pack for this one, if not a case! Here's the Marshall."

There was a pause, and then Terrat was back on. "Theo, good job, son. We'll contact you when we are half an interval out. Terrat X-mit out."

"Acknowledge, Windston EMC X-mit out."

"Well," Tedarri said appreciatively, "you sure know how to manage the comm. I'll get the enforcement guys to get you some smoke and lights for the landing. What else could you use?"

Theo thought for a moment and answered, "We need to protect the field from locals, so at least four enforcement units would be a great help. They could sit at the corners of the field with their emergency lights on, and help guide the fleet to the ground, as well as turn away the curious."

"That's a big area. Sure that four will be enough?" Tedarri asked, looking over the map.

"Once the defense force is on the ground, they'll provide their own security. All we have to do is get them landed."

"Thanks. Glad you're here, Theo!"

"Happy to help." The other communicator rang.

"That will be our two on the mountain, Van and Sahnassa. Can you fill them in? I want to check on the shelter work."

Theo nodded and Tedarri stepped away. The Nephti then answered the communicator, "Windston Emergency Management Center. Theo de Allarrae speaking. How may I help you?"

The voice on the other end was a little put off and annoyed. "Uh, hi. This is Van. Is Tedarri there? I really need to speak with him."

Theo was as polite as he was formal. "He is nearby ma'am, but he had to step away for just a moment. He did inform me of your situation. What can I do for you?"

Van was frustrated now, but pressed on, realizing that she couldn't realistically expect to monopolize all of Tedarri's time. Still, her tail twitched knowing that this conversation would likely not get her what she needed. "Listen, we have a large group of transports and haulers ready to head your way with relief supplies, but they won't leave until we can tell them exactly where they are going."

Courteous, came the reply. "I understand. I have that information for you. Do you have something to write with?"

"Right here." She sounded a little more frustrated than she knew she should.

The voice on the other end didn't show any sign of noticing her snippiness. "All transports are to be sent to the Windston Secondary Academy. That's at 18 BCT, Course Point 29. The first two food haulers are to go there, as well. We'll have someone ready and waiting to direct your convoy to the proper location when it arrives."

Van was startled and actually a little impressed, but asked, "What are you planning to do with the evacuees after they leave the Meeting Den?"

"We're going to land the flyers in the secondary school athletic field, put food into the evacuees' paws, and have a doctor or nurse give them a quick look to make sure they're fit enough for travel. Then, we'll get them on the road as soon as possible. It's all being prepared right now."

She raised an eyebrow; perhaps Tedarri had more of a clue than she thought. "What do you want me to do with the other haulers?"

"To make sure the transports can get in and out quickly and safely, the rest of the haulers will be directed to the parking lot of Windston Tertiary, which is just across the road. Those two schools are going to be the primary shelters for the evacuees until the storm passes. Just so you know, we may shelter some of the military there, as well."

Van was pleased and more than a little relieved by the confidence and professionalism she heard on the other end. She now started to feel like someone was working with her, and that she and Sahni weren't alone in trying to pull this together. "That's great! Any word from the flyers?"

"We just finished talking to them. We have notified them of their landing zones, and we're going to meet them in about three intervals – shortly after your convoy gets in, if my math is correct. You should expect them to be heading your direction in, say, three and a half intervals. We'll give you a call when it's time. Is there anything else you need, ma'am?"

"I think that's about it, sweetie! We'll call you back when our little rescue convoy is underway."

"That's great," Theo said. "We'll be watching and help them get in safely."

"Wonderful! They have an enforcement escort, from what I understand, so they should be moving pretty quick."

"Good," Theo asserted, and then dropped his professional manner. "Hey, I just wanted to let you know that we think you two are doing an amazing job up there! We're all pulling for you."

"Thanks darling! I look forward to talking to you again! I really appreciate what you have done down there, as well."

"You're welcome. Talk to you soon."

Van put down the PawLink and shouted, "Sahni, we're in luck! It looks like Tedarri actually has his act together!"

Sahni walked over as Van started dialing the charter company. "Who was that you were talking to? You seemed to warm up to him real fast. That wasn't Tedarri was it?"

"No, no! Someone named Theo de something or other – had a *very nice* voice – oh, hi! It's Van. I have your destination information and some instructions for when you arrive. Are you ready for it?" As she read off her instructions, Sahni quietly stepped away.

Looking down at her watch, she asked, "Was that you she was talking to?"

The watch answered, "Yes. Didn't expect me to just sit in the ship and miss out, did you? Besides, Tedarri needed help. By the way, I'm a Nephti now. Don't be surprised when we meet, okay?"

Without really meaning to say it out loud, she mused, "Just as long as that keen-looking Vulpi comes back sooner or later."

"He will, sweet Sahni. He will. Bye!" She smiled, trying to get her blush furs back down before she re-entered the camp.

When she arrived, she found Van dialing the PawLink again. "They're on the move! Finally!"

"Can you put that on speaker?" Sahni asked, a little timidly. She wanted to hear Theo's voice for herself.

"Sure."

She pressed the button, just as Theo's voice said, "Windston Emergency Management Center. Theo de Allarrae speaking. How can I help you?" Sahni smiled. It sounded exactly like him.

"Hey, sweetie, this is Van. Our convoy is on the way!"

"That's fantastic! I'll pass that along. Hey, I've got some evacuation information for you to pass up to the den. It involves how the flyers will come in, and how they'll need to move groups out. Are you ready?"

"Yes, sir! Go right ahead!" Van was cheekily falling in line with his almost military manner. Sahni just shook her head at her boss's outright flirtatiousness.

"The first flyer up the mountain will be a small one, an HVR-9 that will only seat about two or three more given all of the soldiers and cargo it will already have. That one will have the Air Chief aboard, and they'll be coming to get you two, first. From what I can see here, we have your approximate position, but have you given any thought to what your signal might be?"

"You're going to laugh at this, but I actually brought some fireworks up here."

"Now, that is funny!" Theo chuckled. "What on Thuria for?"

"I thought I might be doing a little celebrating; besides, some of my clients really like having a little surprise and sparkle in their evening, so I *always* try to please." Again, Sahni blushed her fur to full upright listening to Van almost instinctively seducing the male on the other end of the conversation.

"I think that will work great!" Theo exclaimed before dropping back into a more serious tone for the rest of the instructions. "Now, once they've got you, they'll need your help finding the athletic field. They know the position of the Meeting Den, but they've never actually seen it before. You two have. When you get on the ground, the matriarchs have to make sure they keep discipline. If fifteen hundred Thurians rush that first flyer, we're going to have a real mess! They need to divide the evacuation into groups of one hundred and four and then sixty and then one hundred and four and then sixty, over and over again until everyone is out. That's how many will safely fit in each round of the airlift. The first flyer, yours, will probably not stay on the ground for very long. Your first evacuation vehicle will be an HVR-17 that holds one hundred four. Make that the size of the first group. Do you understand?"

Van's tone was as serious as his, repeating back what she'd heard. "I've got it. First flyer picks us up, drops us off, heads back up, and then one hundred four and then sixty and over and over." Van slipped back into a slightly more seductive tone, adding, "See, I'm a *very* quick study!" Sahnassa just shook her head; Van was almost purring out her response.

"I can see that! Now Vanarra, there's something you've got to make clear to them, and the leadership up there may not want to hear it. Once the defense force is on the ground, *they* are in charge of the field – operations, security, everything. No one, regardless of their rank – matron, dame, or matriarch – can tell them what to do. They can give information and work with them, but Terrat and his soldiers *are in charge* of the airlift. Make sure that is well understood. If they ask why, tell them it's a safety thing – part of how they ensure evacuees don't overwhelm the flyers or get blown off the field accidently."

Van was more serious in her response this time, as she considered having to give these instructions to the matriarchs. "Makes sense. Although, this group up at the den seems to have things under control. I don't think it will be a problem."

"Be careful about that," Theo warned. "A stray rumor, hunger, cold, thirst, and some frayed nerves can do very bad things when mixed together, especially with a large group."

Van cocked an eyebrow as she thought to herself, "It might be a problem, at that." Aloud, she asked, "Any suggestions for them?"

"If there is any way they can broadcast this plan to the entire group or large portions of it, they should. From here forward, they should be practicing full disclosure. There will be suspicions enough without them actually hiding anything."

Sahni just couldn't keep quiet anymore. "Sounds like good advice. We'll pass it along."

"Hi there! You must be Sahnassa."

"That's right. It's so good to hear your voice!" She didn't really mean to say it, but there it was. Van looked at her with an odd expression. Thankfully, Theo's cover was smooth.

"I imagine so. It's got to be a little scary up there. How are you two holding up?"

Sahnassa stumbled a bit before answering, much to Vanarra's delight. "Yes, well, uh, we've been doing pretty well. I think we're both starting to get a little worn down though."

"Well, help is on the way," Theo offered confidently, "but I want both of you to listen to me on this, and I'm serious. Once you relay your information to the Meeting Den, there will literally be nothing for you to do except wait. I want you to eat plenty, drink plenty, and get some rest. If you can catch any sleep over the next two intervals, do so. I know you're both pretty revved up, but you don't want to drift off during the rescue, and it's going to be a long afternoon, evening, and night. I promise to call you if anything important comes up."

Vanarra jumped back in again. "Well aren't you the sweetest thing, Theo? You don't have to worry; Sahni has been taking good care of us up here. She's really the nurturing type." Van's smile caused Sahni to just shake her head again. "We'll look forward to hearing from *you*, Theo."

"That's great! Hopefully, I'll get a chance to meet up with you two at the shelters. Get some rest. We'll be back in touch soon."

The line went quiet, and Van looked at Sahni with a toothy smile. "Oh, I *like* him! You do, too. I can tell!"

"Stop it," Sahnassa said, in mock exasperation. "I've only just met him. You too, for that matter!"

"Hey, I've known someone to fall in love over a PawLink before. Besides, your muzzle says no, but your blush furs scream yes!"

Sahni placed her paws on the top of her cheeks and muzzle to force the furs down, which sent Vanarra into a laughing fit. "See! See!"

Sounding muffled and a little aggrieved, Sahni asked "Can we please just call the Meeting Den?" Van's laugh was so great, Sahnassa just had to smile and laugh some on her own. If only Van knew the truth, she thought.

Chapter 9: Readied

Time: 09:80 – 5.2 intervals from mid sol

Amyra was tired, so very tired. It was as if control of the situation was an actual rope in her paws, and she could feel it beginning to slip. As she had walked around the cold halls of the Meeting Den, the frightened faces, the screaming young, the coughing, the children asking their mothers for food they didn't have were all signs they would not have good discipline much longer. After so many intervals awake and active, even some of the matrons and dames were beginning to fade and grow lax.

Her mind kept going back to Vanarra; she couldn't fail Vanarra. If that lost kit who had survived the death of both parents wound up here, saving hundreds, Amyra knew she had to find the strength to keep going from somewhere. Rubbing her eyes with her paws, she sadly realized she could do this kind of thing so much more easily when she was younger. Now, she didn't just feel old or tired, she was actually starting to hurt inside. Rahnahi was on duty, and although Amyra knew she should be sleeping, she just couldn't. "Just a few more intervals," she thought in the cold, dark room. "We must keep control for just a few more intervals."

There was a tap at her door, and Dania opened it. "Matriarch?"

"I'm here."

Dania walked in with a candle. "You haven't slept?" Amyra coughed and teetered a little as she stood. "Matriarch?!" Dania's paw was there to steady her and provide support. The Nephti dame looked at her with anxious concern.

"Don't, don't worry about me. What's going on?"

"Van and Sahni have reported in, and everything is going well. Sahni, however, has a radical suggestion, and I think you should hear it."

"What does your matriarch think?" Amyra asked, trying to force strength back into her voice.

"She agrees with Sahni, Honored One, but trusts to your judgment in matters such as this. As she's fond of saying, poetry and reality do not always go paw in paw."

"Too true. Very well. I'll go with you."

"Take my arm, Honored One," Dania offered, obviously sensing Amyra's condition.

"No. I can't be seen as weak! There are too many watching. I will sit down as soon as we reach the room."

"Yes, Matriarch."

They walked together, albeit slowly, and they were soon in the communications room with Buck. He seemed genuinely excited and completely unflappable. She could understand why Rahnahi had taken a liking to him. Carefully, Amyra sat down, trying to ignore her friend's obvious stare. Rahnahi hadn't missed Amyra's condition either, but she waited until Dania shut the door before taking her own seat. "What is it?" she asked.

Buck suggested, "Sahni, why don't you explain?"

"We've received all of the information you'll need about the evacuation, but they strongly suggest we broadcast it to everyone, if there is any way to do that. Buck has the bulk of it, but we were just talking. Buck thinks either Van or I should say something to everyone before he starts reading it back to them."

"Full disclosure," Rahnahi said earnestly, "sounds like a good policy to me. Sahni or Van's word is going to carry a lot more weight than either of ours right now."

Amyra still was unsure. They were betting a lot on the words spoken by two who, while obviously brave and effective, were still quite young. A single misspoken word could bring disaster. "Sahnassa, we have a lot of frightened, cold, and hungry Thurians up here. Are you two *sure* you're ready to talk to them?"

"Yes, Matriarch."

"What will you say?"

"I'll simply describe what's going on – just the truth, just what we know. Van thinks I should do all the talking, for … certain reasons."

Amyra sighed. "As much as I hate to, I agree with her assessment. Are you ready now?"

"Yes, Honored One."

Amyra's decision had been made. She motioned to Dania for her communicator, took it, and pressed the priority call switch. After releasing it, she pressed "talk" and then spoke. "Attention, all dames and matrons, place the following message on speaker so that all may hear. I'll give you fifteen ticks." After the pause, she began, "This is the voice of the Grand Matriarch, Amyra de Gonari. Beside me is Grand Matriarch Rahnahi de Dothnar. We hope you know that many efforts are being made on your behalf. What you may not know is that our only link to the outside world is through two brave females who are marooned alone, five courses down the mountain. Without them, it is doubtful that anyone else would have even started to suspect our plight. One of them has asked to speak with you. Go ahead, Sahnassa, they are yours."

Vanarra watched as her friend stood, placed the communicator to her ear, and began speaking. "My name is Sahnassa de Orturu. I am here with my friend Vanarra Anasto. For the past fourteen intervals, all of us have been trapped here, on this mountain. None of us expected this to happen, and it's been very hard – I know. We're frightened, we're cold, we're hungry, but we're here. We can't wish that problem away; we have to face it. Thankfully, I can tell you that we don't have to face this alone or without hope. As I speak with you, thirty-six military flyers, fourteen large charter transports, and seventeen cargo haulers are coming to rescue us. Literally hundreds of Thurians from every station and family have banded together to save us and provide us with shelter and food once we're off the mountain." Sahnassa gave that a moment to sink in, but Vanarra was astonished. Sahni seemed transfigured as she spoke.

"Now, comes our part. Everything they've been preparing, everything they are doing will only work if *we* make it work. In less than four intervals, it's going to be up to each of us. If we don't follow instructions, act with patience, and help in every way we can, the rescue will take too long, and a winter storm will trap many of us here. I know how you feel. We're all tired, and we've all had to endure so much, and we've all wondered what's going to happen to us. Now, we can tell you. It's a plan that's been created by the Emergency Management Center, the Defense Force, by your matriarchs, and Vanarra all working together. This plan can't succeed unless each of us understands it and helps make it happen. Buck Harlock is going to read the plan for you now and once again shortly before the first flyers arrive. All of you will hear the same plan, our only plan for escaping what's to come. We hope to see you soon. May we all do our best. Buck, if you would, please."

Sahni placed the communicator on mute as she listened to Buck begin to read through the details of the evacuation plan. "Well, I hope that helped." Glancing over at Van, she found her friend looking at her with a wide-eyed stare. "What?!"

"I ... well, that was like ... just amazing, Sahni! Wow! You're so going to announce all the events we cater from now on! I had no idea you could do that!"

"No way! You know how much I hate public speaking."

"Public speaking? Sahni, that was like fifteen hundred Thurians! That's bigger than any group I've ever talked to! And it was amazing – you said exactly what they needed to hear! I don't even think the matriarchs could have done better, but just don't tell Rahnahi de Dothnar I said that."

"Don't be silly, Van. You're embarrassing me!" Sahni complained, sitting down beside her. "I just had one image in my mind when I was talking – a little cub and his mother. I was talking just to them. That made it easier."

Van put her paw around Sahni's shoulder and hugged her gently. "I'm so glad you're here."

"You, too."

They listened for a few more passes until Buck had explained everything. Finally, he concluded, but surprised them both by asking, "Sahnassa, is there anything I've left out or that you'd like to say?"

Again, Sahni stood as she pressed the control. "Buck, you've done a great job relaying the plan. For the rest of us, my wish is that we would be brave and look to the welfare of others first. To all the children, please, I know this is very hard and that you don't understand everything. Don't be afraid; we will do everything we can to get you home safely. Listen to the adults; stay close to your parents or those who are caring for you and obey them. They won't let you down. Vanarra and I look forward to seeing all of you when we arrive on the first flyer. We will stay until everyone else is off the mountain. Until then, be well, stay safe, and take care of one another. Matriarch?"

Amyra's voice came over the speaker. "You've heard Sahnassa, and you've heard the plan. It's up to us, now. Your matrons and dames will start organizing you soon. Until then, may we all be as Sahnassa wishes us to be. Thank you all for what we, together, are about to do." Amyra motioned Dania to close the broadcast.

"Sahnassa, my dear, that was simply wonderful," Rahnahi said, appreciation in her voice. "I don't think I could have said it better myself."

"I agree," Amyra offered gratefully. "That may have just pulled us back from the brink! Tempers were starting to flare up here. You may be assured that Selena is going to hear from me on this."

"You're very kind, Honored Ones. Van's much better at public speaking. I learned from listening to her. I just hope I didn't say anything I shouldn't have."

"You did fine, Sahni, just fine," Rahnahi offered. "Now, what are you two going to do next?"

"We'll call back down and confirm that you know the plan, but then we're probably going to get some rest. It's going to be a very long sol."

"There are some of us here who are going to get some rest, as well," Rahnahi demanded, looking pointedly in Amyra's direction.

Shaking her head wearily, eyes rolled up in resignation, Amyra sighed, "We'll wait to hear from you, dears. Talk to you soon."

"Talk to you soon, Honored Ones. Thank you, too, Buck. Great job."

Sahni closed the channel and looked up into the cold, gray sky. She felt Van come up behind her. She expected to hear something like "See, I told you so," but there was only silence. Sahnassa turned around, and saw Van – standing still, just staring at her – a tear rolling down her cheek fur. "What now, Van? What's wrong?"

Vanarra slowly shook her head in disbelief and amazement as she looked at the young Nephti before her. "I … I can hardly put this into words. You're just … so much … more than – there's so much more to you than I ever thought. It's like I've known you, but not really until now. Everything that's happened to us has just – I can't."

Van stopped for a moment and stepped close to Sahnassa, holding back tears as she spoke. "Sahni, not since my mother has there been anyone else in my life like you. You mention my name and yours together without as much as a pause in front of everyone up there – matriarchs and all. I've lived my whole life with images of how wonderful it would be to have a family and be purebred, accepted, and fully avowed. I was never going to have anything like that … I knew it, but with you … with you I do." Sahni started crying to match Van's sobs, and for a few moments, they just embraced.

Finally, Sahni managed to say, "You're as much my family as anyone is. Don't even start telling me how great I am when it's you who has pulled this whole thing together! I will say to my last breath that it's because of you anyone gets out of this!" The two friends held each other for a few moments longer.

Tedarri walked back into the communications office and found Theo there, talking with the Weather Bureau. "And how many degrees again? At what time? Okay. Sorry, it's just a bad connection or a lot of noise in the background. No, you're alright. Are all your warnings out? Great! No, it's true. No, that's not true. No, well, I don't know, honestly. Yeah, me, too. Alright Matreal, take care now. Thanks!"

"So what's the weather department say?" Tedarri asked, drinking some more tea.

Theo's tone was cautiously optimistic. "The storm might give us a little break getting here later than we first thought, but it's going to hammer us when it does. Still, we've got a good shot at getting everyone down. According to Sahni and Van, it looks like everyone on the mountain will be ready; how's it looking down here?"

"Better and better, actually," Tedarri offered, seeming more certain of success than before. "Word has started to spread about what's happened up there amongst the townsfolk, and they're actually offering to pitch in during set-up." Suddenly, the ground rattled as if a heavy vehicle had pulled right up next to the building. It completely died away after about half a pass. "Aftershock?"

"Yep. Aftershock. Not so bad this time. We've probably seen the last of them. Everything else may be too minor to feel."

"That's a relief. I've been puzzling a little about what to do with Terrat's folks when the storm comes. Some of them may be able to get out of here, but certainly not all of them."

Theo thought for a moment before answering. "You know, they still may be useful. Can we bunk them in the shelters? Create an area just for them?"

"I suppose so, if we get everyone we possibly can out on the transports. What are you thinking?" Tedarri queried, taking another sip.

"Well, they certainly can't fly during an ice storm, and it's going to take awhile to get the flyers, especially the big ones, clear enough of ice to take off. However, the smaller ones might be able to serve as air ambulances or recon, once things do settle down. We may need that in the next couple of sols."

"Sounds good. Talk with Terrat and see if he's game."

"You got it boss!"

Tedarri crumpled his cup and tossed it in the trash. "I'm going to keep checking on our shelters. I think I'm going to have a drive out there, see it myself again. I'll be back in time to take you to the landing zone. Just call me if anything comes up, okay?"

"Will do."

Tedarri left the room just as the communicator rang. "Windston Emergency–"

"Theo, please!" Sahni's voice came through. "I think by now we know it's you."

He chuckled. "I guess you do. How did it go?"

"She did amazing, Theo!" Van shouted. "You should have heard her!"

"That's great! Well, everything else is tracking here, too. According to enforcement, your convoy is burning up the road getting to Windston, and the flyers just called in with an update. They are right on schedule. The shelters keep looking better and better. There's a down note on the weather, though. We're going to get an interval or two longer to get everyone out, but when it does hit …"

"… it's going to be bad," Van completed. "Isn't it?"

"Yes. I'll be very glad to get you all off the mountain and down into some nice, warm shelters to ride this out. It's not the best accommodations, but it does have beds, a cafeteria, a gym, and a library. Speaking of beds, are you two going to finally get some rest now?"

"I –" A yawning yowl interrupted the sentence from Sahni.

"Sahni, no! I—" Van's yowling cut her off as well. "You're always doing that to me!"

"I think that answers the question," Theo said with a wry smile. "You two bed down, and we'll call you soon."

"Great, Theo. Thanks!"

Van pressed the control that ended the call and looked over at Sahni, who once again was in her place in the shelter. Without any argument, Van walked over and slipped into her spot, and let Sahni's arms wrap around her. She felt more at home in this tiny shelter in the woods than she ever could remember feeling. Soon, both of them were soundly asleep.

Time: 12:03 – 2.97 intervals from mid sol

Van was standing in their camp, alone, and she didn't know where Sahni was. Overhead, a loud, dark flyer hovered over her, lowering a small, thin, smooth rope. It was slick; she knew she was supposed to tie it around her, but it was almost impossible. The rope started pulling her up, but she wasn't ready. She held on for dear life, but she saw it slipping through her paws as she dangled in the air. Just as shadowy forms reached down to grab her, she realized who the faces were – the three who beat her mother. Laughing, they cut the cord, leaving her screaming as she fell to the rocks below.

"Van! Van! It's alright! Ow!" Sahni struggled to hold onto her friend as she wildly thrashed about, and now Van's tail had popped her in a very sensitive place. Through gritted teeth, she yelled, "It's just a dream, Van! Come on, wake up!"

Finally, Van snapped out of her dream and back into reality. "Sahni?"

"Yes," she managed, eyes watering and teeth clenched.

"Oh, what an awful dream! Hey, what's wrong?"

"Your tail," Sahni grunted a complaint.

"Oh, no, did I?"

"I wouldn't exactly call it affectionate! Well, not unless you think getting hit between the legs with a game stick is affectionate."

"Oh, I'm so sorry, kit! I … I had no idea."

"I'll be alright in a pass," Sahni said, a little more softly as Van slid out of the shelter.

"I am so sorry, and this … this may be a good time to tell you something. I … don't … really like … flying. I kind of … avoid it. I think my dream was about that, well, kind of. Falling. There was some of that, too." Vanarra bowed her head in embarrassment.

"You'll be fine. Besides, my guess is that the flyer will at least be warm," the Nephti said, rubbing her leg discreetly.

"Warm would be nice. It's gotten colder," Vanarra observed, putting her paw shoes and coat back on. Sahni got out of the shelter and moved a little stiffly, causing Van to gasp. "Oh, no, Sahni! I am so, so sorry!"

"It's going to be alright. It was my thigh that took the brunt of it." Sahni looked at her watch. "We needed to get up anyway. We need to start thinking about breaking camp. What do we take, and what do we leave behind?"

"Let's take care of our private business, first. Then, let's get some food and find that UltraBright and those fireworks."

"I want to take all the food with us. There will probably be some very hungry kits and cubs when we get to the top."

"Yes. Good idea. You sure you're okay?" Sahnassa nodded, and they both started walking around looking for things to pack. After a pause, Van looked around their little camp and sighed. "You know, I'm really kind of sad."

"Why?"

"Because this place has been our home, and I've … I've gotten so much closer to you here."

"I understand. Me, too, Van. Me, too."

Dressed in cold weather gear, Tedarri and an old Vulpi farmer stood beside Theo in a large, flat pasture surrounded by a mix of evergreens and bare trees in the distance. Theo surveyed the field and spotted the four enforcement units, each in a corner with their lights flashing. The sky was gray and seemed lower than it had just a few intervals before, but the wind was thankfully still. "Shouldn't be long now," Theo said. The PawLink in his pocket beeped. He pulled it out and listened for a moment, eyes tightening. "Got it, Chief! Popping smoke now – purple and green! X-mit out." He pressed the end button and then placed the device back in his pocket. "Alright, it's time."

Tedarri and the farmer took their respective canisters to a pair of upended stone blocks, lit their fuses, and dropped them on top. A loud hiss began to come from each cylinder as green smoke from one and purple smoke from the other began to froth out and loft upward. Walking forward into the field, Theo reached into his pockets and pulled out two big UltraBrights, switched them on, and then waited. Almost at the exact moment he stopped, they started to hear the pulsed humming of vehicles overhead. It grew louder, and slowly, forms began to appear in the cloudbanks above. "By all Thuria," the stunned farmer uttered.

"You got that right," Tedarri agreed. Almost as a unit, forty aerial vehicles slipped under the silvery gray cloudbanks as if they had descended into clear water. The sound was now penetrating, almost deafening, and Tedarri shouted, "That's louder than the last aftershock!"

Several of the smaller craft spread out to the left and right of the formation as it came to a hover, about a thousand tracks in the air. The lead vehicle, one of the smaller HVR-9's, dropped down and hovered right in front of Theo, wearing his bright orange vest.

Tedarri watched as the Nephti stood like a statue, clothes being viciously blown about by the down thrust of the vehicle. Theo gave it landing instructions – both arms raised, arms up and crossed, motioning to the left, and then arms crossed and down. The vehicle with its stubby, down-swept wings and forked-V tail slowly settled onto the pasture, its extensible skids dropping out at what seemed like the last tick. Theo made a cutting motion across his throat, and the HVR-9's engines powered down and rotated to face aft. It was only a slight reduction in noise given the clamor above them.

Tedarri saw almost a dozen soldiers exit the side doors of the HVR-9 in each direction. Some had vests like Theo's, and it was clear they were going out to land the other vehicles. Some had weapons and were beginning to establish security. Three of the figures paced steadily towards Theo, and Tedarri walked forward to meet them. All four of them arrived at the same time, with the large Lupar's uniform rank instantly marking him as the leader. "I'm Regional EMC Manager Tedarri de Bosnar. Welcome to Windston, Marshall! Glad you could come!" Tedarri shouted reaching out to grasp Terrat's paw.

"Happy to do it! After we've got the vehicles down, checked, and refueled, we can start the first flights! Figure on about half an interval! You manage communications with the Meeting Den until we get to the top, and we'll take over from there!"

Tedarri nodded. "Got it! Thanks to Theo, I know the score! We'll stay out of your path, Marshall!"

"Many thanks! That makes our job easier! Theo! The Chief has a little present for you!" The Air Chief motioned to a big soldier beside him who gave Theo a heavy backpack. Theo settled the pack on his back easily, and then he just smiled. The golden brown Faelnar Chief, who had been smiling if not smirking, now stood stunned, his yellow eyes open wide in disbelief.

"Cut the clowning, Chief! You've had your fun!" the Marshall said, shaking his head.

The Chief looked embarrassed, and his tail dropped to the ground as he admitted, "It's full of power packs!"

"No wonder!" Theo shouted.

"Couldn't resist!" The Chief offered a small TransCom to Theo who already had the pack in one paw. Theo all but tossed the pack back to the Chief. "Mange! Do you work out?"

"You might say that!" Theo shouted, but the noise around them was already starting to relent as the large shapes moved to the ground in groups and cut their engines.

Terrat looked at the Chief and said, "I think you owe me a case."

Theo chuckled. "After that backpack, I think I'm calling in a marker, as well." They all laughed. "Marshall, it's good to see you got the three ORF-35's. You might need them."

"They're fully loaded, too, so we have plenty of fuel. We also attached one medical transport. We'll put it down near the shelters when everyone is off the mountain."

"Sounds great!" Tedarri answered. "All of the ground transportation and food haulers just pulled in, and they're setting up their operations. We've got the party ready; all we need are the guests!"

"Chief, you want to ride up with me and get the lay of the ground?" Theo asked.

"Sir, I do want to get a visual on that evacuation LZ, if you don't mind."

"Go ahead, Chief. Just don't take too long. You know when your ship leaves," the Marshall warned.

Tedarri stepped up. "Hey, if you drop me off at the station, I'll give you the hover, and you can swing by the schools on the way back."

"Sounds like a plan!" With that, the three headed back up to the road and the waiting hover. As they walked up, Theo was talking on his PawLink. "Yep, Sahni, you heard right. They're on the ground. Give it about three quarters of an interval, and your ride should be there. Alright? Good-bye." He hopped in just as Tedarri started the engine.

A few passes later, Theo was driving the Chief into the Tertiary school parking lot. "By Shasta's pouch, would you look at that?!" The parking lots of both schools were abuzz with activity, and big transports and haulers were either getting in line or settling their loads. "Whew! I'd swear *this* is the military operation!"

"You wouldn't be far off. The landing field is around back."

"I don't know about these maps, though," the Chief complained, looking over what had been provided to him by Theo. "The last time the region around the Meeting Den was surveyed appears to have been more than ten seasons ago. Why the heck is that?"

"I bet the coordinate diagrams of the best beaches on Ricia aren't exactly up to date, either. No one ever thought a resort area required a military grade aviation or navigation map. It's all private areas and preserves up there."

"Do you think your civilians up on the mountain can eyeball us to the target?"

"Sahnassa de Orturu is going to be your navigator. She's got some charting experience she picked up fairly recently, and she knows the ground. You find her, and you've got your map to the Den."

"Sweet deal," the Chief agreed, putting the map away. In a few ticks, Theo had them parked, and they were walking towards the large open sports field.

The Chief was pleased as he quickly surveyed the area. "We can do this! Sure, even with the 17's. I'll put my controllers down here, get some beacons up here and here. You're right, this is a sweet set-up! I owe you another one."

"Speaking of that," Theo said, broaching the subject carefully, "remember I said I was calling in a marker?"

"Uh, yeah," the Faelnar answered warily, nervously rubbing where his brown fur turned gold under his chin. "Like what?"

"The two you're picking up first going up the mountain – one's purebred, but the other is a mixed blood named Vanarra Anasto – 'Van' for short. I want you to treat her with the utmost respect and kindness. I expect for you and your troops to show her every courtesy up to and including protecting her from assaults, verbal and physical. Assign her a bodyguard, too – and an effective one at that."

"You are asking a lot," the Chief growled out in a measured, nearly spiteful tone.

In an equal tone, Theo responded, "I am doing you a monstrous favor." Theo softened his voice and explained. "Van is now highly favored by both of the matriarchs you're going to be saving – as hard as that may be for you to believe. Don't create problems for yourself and your soldiers by screwing this up and letting something bad happen. Saving your unit's tail on an inspection is going to pale in comparison to this one."

The Chief was not convinced, and he stewed angrily for a moment before asking, almost belligerently, "Answer me this, oh he who can hold his own weight in power packs, why should I? I was taught that Anati are Anati because someone broke the rules! Their parents, if that's what you call them, left them in this state, and now they become the sob stories we're all supposed to feel sorry for? Tell me, what did her parents do, or even what did she do to merit equal or even special treatment?"

"You see all the transports and haulers full of food here?" Theo asked, calmly indicating the large group of vehicles and their attendants.

"Yes."

"Do you see yourself and all your soldiers here now as opposed to five intervals from now?"

"Yes."

Theo spoke in a tone of absolute and unshakable certainty. "Vanarra Anasto, your so-called Anati, pulled all of this together. If she didn't act when she did, you'd be showing up several intervals too late, if at all. Best case, you would be saving only a fraction of the evacuees, and you would be moving them from a place where they would be freezing to dcath to one where they would starve. You'd leave well over half of the rest to die on that mountain, and you'd crash a lot of your HVR's trying to valiantly fly in an ice storm. She's responsible for saving the lives of everyone up on that mountain, at least as much as you or I."

"How the heck do you know that?" the Faelnar chief asked, still not believing what he was hearing.

"I caught wind of it monitoring the communications."

"You know, I hate you. You saved my tail for sure last time, but now you're going to make it so old kit de Caterra skins my hide instead!"

A wry smile crossed Theo's face. "If she heard you saying 'old kit', you'd lose more than your skin. Been thinking of picking up a creative last name, recently?"

"You wouldn't?"

The mischievous twinkle in Theo's eyes was unmistakable. "Now, how heavy was that bag?"

The Chief groaned. "Okay, okay! I'll get the word out. I'll make it happen."

"Chief, regardless of her checkered parentage, she's a good soul who's made her own way without much help from others; I picked that up from her camp-mate. Like I said, I may be doing you a big favor."

"Alright, already. I'll do it. Let's go," growled the Chief, throwing his arms in the air and walking back to the hover with Theo.

"And Chief?"

"Oh now what?" the Faelnar said with unvarnished frustration.

"Just a simple thing. Van's afraid of flying, so actually land the flyer to pick them up – no sling extractions. Besides, they have some food cargo you're going to want up top."

"Can do," the Chief sighed in defeat as he got back into the vehicle. "You want the keys to my hover, as well?"

"Have a little faith in me, Tawny," Theo said, "I haven't steered you wrong yet."

Time: 12:85 – 2.15 intervals from mid sol

Rahnahi paced back and forth. Buck watched her as matrons and dames came in and out of the communications room almost constantly. With the report that the flyers were in the valley and the shelters were ready for them, the matriarch's demeanor had changed. The last three and a half intervals were a blur to both of them, and had, without question, been difficult.

Someone had raided the stores of the small dining area in the main building, or tried to, only to find that all of the food had been removed earlier. Upon finding nothing, the thieves turned to vandals and smashed several of the fixtures before someone saw them, and they fled. Such an act so close to the matriarch's command center was disturbing proof that matters were starting to slip out of control.

The Grand Matriarch of house de Dothnar also found it a monumental challenge to sort through the entire population of fifteen hundred and select who would be first to evacuate, and, conversely, who would be the last. A few of the dames who came to report to Rahnahi complained angrily that some of the more influential business leaders were feigning sickness to get prioritized ahead of everyone else. Without question, no one wanted to be last. Even the dames showed their nervousness at the prospects of being left behind.

As the last dame left, Buck ventured quietly, "Honored One, you're wearing a path in the floor. I think you've done everything you can."

"This isn't going as smoothly as I hoped." Her words were curt. "I had hoped that Sahni's pep-talk would have gotten them to think a little less of themselves and more of everyone else!"

"With all respect, I think it did, Honored One. You've got that ten percent of the population that, no matter what you tell them, are going to screw things up. I live with that in every project, and in fact, I plan for it." The elder poet came and sat on the edge of the table listening to him. "Look, Sahni helped you get the general population in the right frame of mind. It may have been a real pain to do it, but you've got them organized the way they need to be. Considering the number of hungry and scared and all of the litigators, especially," Buck opined in a teasing manner that brought a smile to the matriarch's muzzle, "that's monumental. You know, we could have easily been looking at a riot or a take-over or some tail-for-brains telling everyone to climb down the mountain. Or even worse, we could have been served ten cease and desist letters written on Meeting Den wipe paper!"

"Oh, please! Anything but that!" She laughed a little before becoming introspective again. "It's hard, Buck. This is the hardest thing I've ever done – deciding who may end up living and who may end up dying. Oh speaking of which, Amyra's going to kill me when she wakes up. I'm sure she'll berate me for not leaving this in her expert paws."

"I think you've done very well, Honored One; besides, she needed the rest. You said it yourself."

"Well after this, Buck, we're both going to need a long vacation."

The PawLink beeped, and he pressed the speaker button. "Hello?"

"Buck, it's Sahni! We've just been told that the first flyers are headed up the mountain and will be picking us up in about ten passes." He heard movement, straps tightening, and a couple of comments to Van before she resumed talking to him. "We're breaking camp and heading up to the road with our signals. When we're ready to take off, I'll try to call you one last time to let you know we're on the way. You may have a hard time hearing me, though. Have someone turn on the lights around the field then get well back when I call. Are you ready up there?"

"Sahni, this is Matriarch Rahnahi. We've got everyone organized. I think we're as ready as we're going to be."

"Great, Honored One! Do everything you can, though, to keep them from rushing the field."

"I think we've got that one covered, Sahni," Buck answered. "We've got the various groups staged on different floors with guards posted. Other than a few of us, there should be no one in your way."

"Great! I'll talk to you soon. Sahni, X-mit out!"

"Now *that* is one incredible Nephti," Rahnahi confessed, to Buck's nodding approval.

Chapter 10: Landing Zone

Time: 13:04 – 1.96 intervals from mid sol

Sahni and Van placed their gear on the side of the road as they walked onto it. Sahnassa pointed to a large area where the small, two-lane road broadened into the larger overlook. The main area of the overlook had been decimated by the landslide, but there was still a large, flat section of road that would hopefully serve well as a landing spot. The wind blew light but very cold and misty, and thick clouds seemed to be right above them, only a few tracks above the tree line. Inwardly, Sahni was very glad they had a fire in their camp. She saw Van peering down the hillside into the valley below. Although somewhat covered by clouds, the ground in the distance was still visible. "Sahni, did I mention that I don't like flying?"

Sahnassa patted her friend on the shoulder and reassured her. "Yes, Van, you did. I'm sure it will be fine."

The PawLink in her pocket beeped, and she pulled it out. "Sahni, this is Theo. Your flyer is coming up the mountain. Get your signal ready, and light it when I tell you."

"Come on!" Sahni called, and they ran over to the bundle of fireworks and opened it up.

As she pulled one out of the package, Vanarra commented, "You think they would tell you something useful, like this one's a giant flare or something?"

"Yes, 'Screaming Meanie' isn't much of a description. Let's just pull them all out."

"Mange, why not?" Van agreed, ripping apart the package. Van and Sahni made quick work of pulling the round tubes out and placing them on the even pavement. "Hey, what are these?" Van asked, looking at several long tubes that obviously weren't meant to stand up on their own.

Sahnassa's eyes lit up with excitement. "Oh, I've played with these before – 'Shooting Spirits!' They send out colored balls of light for a good ways, actually, but we have to hold onto them, the tubes I mean." With two "Shooting Spirits" each and the eight large cylinders on the ground, Sahni thought, hopefully, that would be enough for the flyer to home in on.

Just as they finished getting ready, Theo called to them. "Alright, light them now! When you see the flyer, tell me."

"Okay, Theo! Here we go!" Sahni pressed the control on her torch, and it lit the first time. A quick stop at each of the tubes on the ground had all the fuses lit, and Sahni touched off one "Shooting Spirit" for each of them.

The display that erupted before them was impressive. Blazing rockets of light sailed and screamed into the gray sky, disappearing and flashing in the clouds above. The crack of explosions as the fireworks burst in mid-air sounded like echoing gunfire. "There's no way they won't see this, even with the fog!" Van thought proudly.

In the flyer, the Chief scanned the foggy banks in front of him as the pilot rotated the craft slowly left and right. A series of bright flashes in multiple colors above him and to ship's right caused him to key the TransCom talk button. "Alpha One to EMC Control. I believe we have a visual on the signal. Moving in. Stand by."

Over the whizzing and popping and banging, Sahni started to hear something, another sound, an engine sound! "Van! I think they've found us!"

Van turned and tried to pick out where the sound was coming from. Downhill, towards the valley was her best bet. She motioned to Sahni and had her light her two remaining "Shooting Spirit" tubes, and she angled them to go over the dirt and mangled ground of the landslide. A pair of bright green and orange balls shot out and sailed down the mountain like missiles.

"What the—" The Chief felt his body press to the floor as the pilot rapidly lifted the craft to avoid two projectiles coming from the hillside above. Watching the next salvo pass beneath them, it was easy to track their path back towards the launch point. Almost laughing, the Chief called over the TransCom, "Alpha One to EMC Control, please advise parties on the ground to cease and desist signaling! I repeat, cease and desist signaling! We have their location but cannot approach – until they stop shooting at us! End!"

Theo laughed a little as he acknowledged and called up to them. "Alright you two, the goal is to signal the flyer, not to blow it out of the sky! They've seen you. Point whatever you've got left at any solid rock you can see. I think you've given them enough help."

Embarrassed, Van turned her barrage towards the slide itself, and the burning orbs of light bounced into the dirt and fell harmlessly to the road. "Alright. We've stopped," Sahni said apologetically into the PawLink. The two looked at each other and at the same time whispered, "Oops!"

Laughing, Theo's voice over the communicator acknowledged and told them to clear the road. From nearby, the humming sound started to grow louder, slowly turning into a roar sailing up the contours of the landslide. The greenish-brown vehicle suddenly appeared like a great predatory flyer soaring on a strong thermal, lifting itself effortlessly from the edge of the road and angling back towards them. Van had never seen a military flyer except on VidStar; it seemed huge, at least the size of a charter transport in length with half again the wingspan.

Jumping up and down, Sahnassa whooped and shouted triumphantly, "They're here, Van! They're actually here!"

Vanarra returned a smile but wasn't as elated. She was starting to feel overcome with fear as she watched the craft shift back and forth in the misty, overcast sky like some kind of hunter sizing them up. Then, two long skids extended from its sides and came to rest right below a large sliding door that was now opening. The vehicle settled into a perfect hover as two black ropes trailed out of bags dropped to the ground. Instantly the fears of her earlier dream overtook her, and she started to panic inside. "Oh, no! No! Please no! I can't do that!" The words weren't loud enough for Sahni to hear, and still amazed by the sight in front of her, she hadn't looked back at Van.

Then, both of them saw two uniformed and helmeted soldiers step out onto the skids. After a brief moment to nod at one another, they both quickly repelled to the ground. "Oh, wow!" Sahni shouted. "That looks like fun!"

"You're crazy!" Van managed to say loud enough for her to hear, which only made Sahni laugh, despite the fact she was almost bouncing up and down. The two soldiers unhooked from the ropes, did something to the bags, and the bags and ropes were smartly reeled back up into the craft which then broke from its hover for a slightly higher position. One soldier pulled landing signals from his pockets and started to move to the far side of the overlook, near the debris. The other walked right up to Sahni and Van.

"Air Chief Tawnston de Caterra," he shouted as he raised a paw in greeting. "Heard you two need a lift! So you are Sahnassa, and you are Vanarra, right?"

"Right! How did you know?"

"Easy, ma'am," he replied to Sahni's shouted question. "We have a mutual friend – Theo de Allarrae! He sends his compliments! Now, don't worry about this at all! My Air Sergeant is going to guide our HVR-9 to the ground, and we're going to shut down the engines so you can board nice and easy!"

Instantly, Van felt tremendous relief. "Oh, thank you, thank you, thank you!" she shouted back at him, almost crying. "I thought you'd have us dangling at the end of a rope!"

Looking directly at Van, he patted her on the shoulder and said, "Not unless you want to! Right now, I wouldn't advise it. Hey, according to Theo, you've done great things up here! You both have! There's a lot of folks—" He had to stop because the flyer was now landing, and they were all forced to turn away from the windblown debris and noise. As the craft settled down and the engines throttled back, he continued, "There are a lot of folks that are going to live and have some good hot meals thanks to you. That's pretty amazing, and we're going to take good care of you both. Now, is that bag all you're bringing?"

Sahni answered, "Yes. We have some extra food we're going to give out when we land!"

"That's top rank! We brought a few rations as well, but the goal is to get everyone down as quick as we can. Our medics are going to look for who really needs it – who's desperate. Everyone else will need to wait until they get to the valley." The engines started to fully wind down, and the Chief was now able to talk in a normal voice. "Now, Sahnassa, Theo tapped you as our navigator, so you're going to be up in the front with the pilots. Are you good with that?"

"Yes, Chief! I'll be happy to help."

"Vanarra, I've got you a great middle seat in the back, well away from the door. You'll have a strong five-point harness on and two of my best soldiers looking out for you. That sound doable?"

Van was now completely relieved, and she couldn't believe how nice he was being to her. She wondered if she had heard his name right. "He can't be de Caterra," she thought. "That's great! I can't thank you enough! I'm a little afraid of flying," she admitted.

"I'll ask the pilots to make it a smooth flight. Now, if you're both ready, we'll get aboard." The Chief grabbed their bag and started at a good stride towards the craft.

Sahnassa took Van's paw and said, "Well, here we go! You okay?"

"I'll manage. Sahni, thanks for everything." As they walked towards the craft, Van hugged her friend about the shoulder.

"Thank you! I guess I'd better call the Meeting Den now. You go ahead and get aboard." Sahni stood outside as the Chief led Van in through the doorway.

Sahni popped her communicator out of her pocket and dialed. "Meeting Den, Buck here. Sahni, please tell me you have good news!"

"Light up the landing area, Buck! We're on the way!"

"Alright! I'll let them know! See you soon!"

"See you Buck!"

As she finished the call, the Chief's head popped back out. "Everything good at the landing site?" he asked, now offering a paw to her.

"Yes. They'll be ready!" she stated, hopping in. Looking through the darkened interior of the craft, she saw Van settling down in a row of seats behind several crates of strapped-down cargo. Soldiers lined the opposite wall of the craft from the door, and as promised, Van was getting help from two big Lupar.

"They're my field medics," the Chief told her. "They'll be good to her. Come on. Your seat's up front." He led her up a short access way where two helmeted pilots turned to look at her. "This is Captain Keel on your left and Lieutenant Crastor on your right."

Sahnassa nodded to the two flight-suited Perratti. "Nice to meet you!"

"You, too, ma'am," the Captain said, nodding. "Chief, get her set up with a headset, if you would." He pointed his charcoal colored paw at a compartment above their heads.

"Yes, sir." Fishing in her pockets while the Chief located the device, she slipped her sunglasses on. They were a pair she had specially ordered that covered even the sides of her eyes completely; however, no one would believe exactly how special they were now.

The Chief turned back to her and looked at her a little curiously. "Cuts down on the glare. Can I just hold on here?"

"Uh, sure, after we get airborne. Here you go." He gave her the heavy headset, and she placed it on her head, adjusting and moving the mouthpiece in front of her muzzle.

"Can you hear me alright, ma'am?" the voice of the Captain sounded in her ear.

"Yes sir, I can. Don't worry about the ma'am; just call me Sahni, okay?"

"Very good. Just give us a moment, and we'll get through our preflight checklist. You'll want to flip the seat – oh, I see the Chief has it for you already." She looked back and saw the Chief holding down a fold-out seat with a built-in harness. She'd only be able to view the take off by looking to her right, but she would still be able to see. Without hesitation, she found the small cut-out for her tail and took her seat. The Chief strapped her in and gave her a nod.

"I'm going to go back where Van is and get plugged in. I'll let you know how she's doing."

"Thank you, Chief!" she said gratefully, covering the mouthpiece. He nodded and was away.

As she listened to the pilots go through the checklist, she began to see lights flash and take form as shapes before her eyes. As if on a giant screen, she saw a message appear in front of her. "Interlink with Tashar complete. Greetings, Sahnassa. This is Haloizar. Answer by nodding slightly if you are seeing this message clearly."

She nodded, and Haloizar answered back. "Very good. Once airborne, I'll enhance your vision and give you a map to your destination. Remember to act as if you're doing this from memory. I'll display items in green that you actually can see, items in orange that a Thurian with the highest visual acuity might be able to see, and items in red that are impossible for you to see. Do you understand?" Again, she nodded discreetly.

"Sahni, we're done with our checklist. I'm going to check with the Chief, and if all's well, we can get underway. Once we're airborne and in a good hover, I'll let you know when you can unstrap and stand for a better view."

"Thank you, Captain."

"Chief, this is Cap; is everything settled back there?"

"We're good, Captain. Please keep it smooth though; we've got a nervous VIP back here."

"Will do. Alright LT, here we go. Ground clear? Panels green? Start APU's." Under her hind paws, the craft began to hum, and the lights grew brighter. "Start thrusters one and two." The winding up of the engines seemed a little far away beneath the heavy earpieces, but the sound was rapidly growing, as was the gentle buzzing in the deck plates. "Thrusters up to power. Start three and four." The additional wind-up noises and vibrations made the ship seem to course with energy. Sahnassa was smiling and almost giddy with excitement; the feeling of the flyer coming to life was thrilling. "All thrusters up to power. Ready for liftoff."

At a nod from the co-pilot, the captain gently pulled back on the controls, and the scenery outside the window started to drop away. There really wasn't much feeling of flying, more like what she experienced in a building lift. They gracefully glided away from the face of the mountain and slowly came to a stop just underneath the clouds. "Alright, Sahni, we're in a good hover if you want to get up."

"Yes, sir." She unstrapped, stood and folded the seat up. Holding the silver grab rails on either side of her, she looked down over the pilots' shoulders; their large, transparent enclosure provided good visibility, even without Haloizar's help. Looking at the heading indicator, she suggested, "Sir, I believe you should start by proceeding along the road, making your heading zero degrees. We're going to want to be careful about three courses ahead. The road goes into a tunnel."

"Alright, here we go." The nose of the craft pitched forward gently, and they started to pick up speed. "Mange, would you look at that!" The downed bridge was now in full view beneath them, and it looked just as bad from this altitude as it had right at its edge. "You two are definitely lucky to be alive."

"Yes, sir. We should make our heading now roughly one-five-zero following the ridgeline to ship's right."

"Turning to one-five-zero," the Captain said, with a sideways glance to his copilot. "Where'd you pick up your skills, Sahni?"

"I have a close friend who flies for his job. He explained a lot of this to me, and he's even taken me up a few times." Smiling to herself, she thought, "If they only knew what, exactly, Theo had taken me up in wouldn't they be surprised!"

The Captain admitted, "It's a big help. I thought we were going to have to deal with someone telling us to go a little more left and a little less down." They all laughed.

Afterwards, they flew in silence for a few moments, and then Sahni started to see the outline of the mountain in red directly in front of them. "Sir, I suggest we reduce speed. I believe we're coming to the tunnel area. I would guess we're less than half a course from it."

"Got it. Visibility is really dropping. This is going to get really touch and go, if we're not careful." The Captain's normally confident voice started to betray his concern.

Haloizar responded instantly. "At the mountain, take them up one thousand tracks. Visibility improves at that level and some of the topographical landmarks are still visible."

As the mountain started to drift into the orange, Sahni said, "Sir, I think we've got the mountain ahead."

"The sounder has got it, too, I think," the co-pilot uttered, sounding tense. "The reflection is pretty mangled."

"No, wait. I see it," the pilot said, relieved. "Good eyes, Sahni! Now what?"

"Let's hover and go up about a thousand – see if the top is clear."

"That sounds good." With the elevator-like grace he showed before, the Captain brought the HVR-9 into the cloudbank, and everything went gray around them. At about nine hundred and fifty tracks higher, they broke through another layer into clearer air. "Excellent call; this looks much better! Can you still direct us from here?"

"I think so. I remember the hilltops near the den. See that one with the forest tower? Head in that direction, about bearing zero seven five," Sahnassa said, pointing.

"Turning to zero seven five, increasing speed to 25 CPI." The tower advanced on them steadily, and Sahni could now see, albeit in red, the entire landing area less than two courses away. They came to a hover about five hundred tracks away from the tower. "Any ideas now?"

"Gosh, this looks like soup below us," the co-pilot interjected, again sounding tense. "I can't see a thing."

"Give me a pass. I have to put a couple of things together in my head," Sahni requested. For a moment she was silent, but then said, "If my memory is right, we should turn to bearing eight zero zero for about one and a half courses. That should put us very close to the den. We could then try a slow descent and look for their lights. They've got an athletic field ringed with vehicles, all with headlights on and marker lights flashing. Hopefully, we'll be able to see it, even through this."

"Turning to eight zero zero, marking off one point five courses at 25 CPI." The tower drifted away to their right, and in a few moments, they were again still. "Alright, let's keep our eyes on alert. LT, keep an eye on that collision sensor. I'm dropping the skids, but I'm not going to hit our lights just yet. That would only blind us in this mess." They all felt the whirring, popping, and clunking as the skids dropped into place.

In her glasses, Sahni could see that they were not far away from the field, which was just off and to their right, about nine hundred tracks below them. The pilot started letting the HVR-9 drift downward back into the thick cloudbank. Sahni watched as the field drifted and sparkled from red to red with flashes of orange. "Captain," the LT piped up. "I've got a large bank of flashing lights at bearing one zero zero in a rectangular pattern, Sir!"

As the Captain reoriented the flyer, the lights started to become plainly visible. "Excellent job everyone. Sahni, you especially; I think we'll let you fly us home. LT, when we get this thing down, get on the TransCom to the Marshall. Until we're sure that those instrument beacons we brought with us are going to be enough, tell him we're going to have to post ourselves up in that clear layer and direct everyone else in above the mountains. That way, the others can avoid the terrain altogether. Okay, I'm firing up the landing lights. Chief, get your crew ready to dismount; we're about to touch down."

Time: 13:20 – 1.96 intervals from mid sol

For the last ten passes, Dania, Buck, and Rahnahi were the only ones standing at the edge of the field. The twenty volunteers who had turned on all of the vehicles' lights had retreated back into the buildings, as directed. Rahnahi had hated to tell Amyra that she couldn't come out and wait in the cold with them, but she was concerned her fellow matriarch was starting to fall seriously ill. It troubled her even more that her friend agreed without much of a fight. Now, the elder poet just shook her head, looking at the mist swirling all around them. "How are they going to find us in all of this?" Rahnahi asked, sounding a little doubtful.

"Hopefully, the lights will make this area glow in the fog. That may be all they need," Buck replied.

"Listen," Dania whispered, her ears perked up to full attention. "I think … I hear something." It was hard to make out, since the vehicles all around her were humming as well, but this sound had more bass to it, and the direction was different, even if somewhat muffled. "You hear it too?"

Buck furrowed his brow in concentration and nodded. "Above us? Getting closer, slowly?"

"Yeah," Dania breathed, ears rotating, head slowly turning around, trying to locate the source.

Inwardly cursing her age, Rahnahi couldn't pick out what they were hearing, so she looked up, trusting to her eyesight which had always been good. Tiny, faint flashes in the pale mist above were the only hint that anything was there, but Rahnahi smiled – there was definitely something coming towards them. "Up there!"

The moment they turned to look, that portion of the sky went ablaze with a shaft of light pointing in their direction. Buck shouted, "Yeah! Alright! They've done it! By Thuria, they've done it!" Rahnahi was amazed and fascinated at the way the brilliant light cut through the gloom around them. She knew, amongst a hundred other experiences in the last few sols, that she would have to write about this, just so she remembered it in all its wonder for seasons to come. Looking away, she found herself catching Dania and Buck who had embraced, much as siblings would. That could work well for her plan, too, she thought. "Buck's service definitely warrants some consideration by Amyra's house when this is over, and having Dania as an advocate for him would certainly carry some weight."

They started to feel the downdraft from the engines course around them, banishing the fog in streams and swirls like some kind of magic spell. From behind her, even with her modest hearing, even over the growing roar of the descending flyer, she thought she could hear cheering. Looking behind her, she saw hundreds of heads, reaching out of the buildings' windows that faced towards the athletic field. There were arms waving, and some pillow covers were flying back and forth as if they were flags.

As elated as she was, she grabbed Dania. "Make sure they keep control!" she ordered firmly, and Dania's glee broke back into duty, and she started shouting into her TransCom.

Looking almost otherworldly, the vehicle now touched its skids to the soft grass in front of them and came to rest. For a moment, the vehicle stayed just so, and then the engines started to wind down. Thankfully, the pilot had parked the craft with its nose pointing directly at them, which prevented most of the down blast from reaching them. Bright lights shone in their direction, so it wasn't possible to see anything beyond them. A rare feeling of excitement mingled with impatience permeated Rahnahi, as she said to the others, "Alright, you two. Let's go meet our rescuers." With Buck and Dania joining her on her left and right, they all stepped forward together.

Walking a little to the side, they were soon out of the blinding light coming from the front of the craft, and they were amazed by the amount of activity already taking place. Dozens of soldiers had poured out of the vehicle and were starting to run here and there, with most fanning out in a circle. One jogging towards them aggressively carried his firearm in both paws and shouted, "Hold it right there, please!"

They stopped, and as he came closer, they saw this strong and very fierce-looking Faelnar's golden eyes grow wide when he saw the matriarchal emblem shimmering on top of Rahnahi's shoulder. Looking at the other two, he also noted the dame's emblem Dania wore. Looking a bit less intimidating now, he apologized. "Sorry, Honored Ones! I couldn't see who you were. Tactical Sergeant Agari de Gonari, at your service. It's a real honor to finally meet you."

"We're very glad to see you, too, and believe me Sergeant, the honor is all ours! Dania here is my second and is in touch with all of the dames and matrons organizing the evacuees. Buck is in charge of communications with the outside world. Your matriarch is inside, too, but she's not feeling well. If you can manage it, I would like her on the first transport out of here."

A tinge of worry crossed his brown face, almost in time with the movement of his close-cut facial fur lightly blowing in the cold breeze. "I'll see what I can do, Honored Ones. We've got a couple of our field medics aboard; I can send one of them out to check on her. Once he's had a look, he'll work out something with the Chief. One tick, excuse me," he apologized as he clicked the TransCom control on his chest harness and said, "Chief, I've got your VIP's right here at eight zero zero. Yes, and we need our field medics. The de Gonari matriarch is down ill and requesting first transport. I'll tell them. Yes. Yes, Chief. X-mit out." He released the control and explained, "The Chief's going to send out his medics right now; we just need someone to lead them back. What kind of situation is it, Honored One? Do they need an armed escort? Do we think we'll have a problem with civilians rushing the field?"

Dania looked straight at him and answered, "No. I just heard from the dames and matrons. They have good control. You shouldn't have any problem."

Agari looked relieved. "That's great! The Chief wants you to come over, but they're unloading equipment. It will be just a pass or two." Two big Lupar medics carrying bags and heavy backpacks jogged over to them. "Ah, here are the field medics."

"Buck, can you please take them to Amyra? I want to keep Dania with me for communications."

"Sure enough. Come on guys, let's go!" Buck headed towards the buildings at a jog with the two Lupar right behind him.

Agari couldn't contain his concern any longer. "How ... how bad is she, Honored One? If I may ask?"

"Bad enough that I don't want her getting any worse. She's weak, feels a little nauseous, although she'd exhaust herself leading this whole operation if someone wasn't here to keep her from doing so. I think she'll be fine, with the right care." Again, they heard cheering erupt from the buildings behind them.

Dania laughed. "It's Buck and the medics," she said. "They're getting cheered just for entering the building."

"Uh ... yes, Chief? Alright I'll let them know. X-mit out." Rahnahi realized that the Sergeant was getting more instructions over his earpiece. "Honored Ones, the Chief asked me to bring you to the vehicle. Please stay right beside me."

"Delta three nine, you listening? Good. Now, you can bring our VIP's over to the flyer. I've got two heroes here I'm sure they'll want to meet!" Sahni and Van listened to the Chief call out to the guard holding the Matriarch Rahnahi and her dame, Dania, at the periphery while the cargo was unloaded. Looking into Van's eyes as they waited inside the flyer, Sahnassa could tell that what was about to happen terrified Vanarra more than the flyer had. Sahni was grateful to hear that her friend had actually done quite well during the flight, and might have even been accused of flirting a little with the two "rather keen" Lupar assigned to keep her company. "Alright, it's not good form to keep matriarchs waiting any longer than we have to. Let's go!"

Chapter 11: Revelations in Rescue

W alking up to the craft was, in itself, an amazing experience for Rahnahi. She had never really been around military aircraft, and looking at this one, she would have sworn it had actual teeth somewhere. Approaching an open door on its side, she saw three figures, one in uniform stepping out ahead of the others and giving them a paw down to the ground. At almost the exact moment that their group reached the craft, the uniformed one spoke crisply and boldly. "Air Chief Tawnston de Caterra, at your service, Honored Ones." Rahnahi and Dania both nodded, and he dropped his salute to introduce his companions. "May I present Sahnassa de Orturu and Vanarra Anasto."

Sahnassa's eyes greeted her, keen and snapping with excitement, but Van's eyes were downcast, her head nodding only slightly at the mention of her name. With a commanding air, the matriarch ordered, "Step forward, you two." They did, although Van required a bit of a push from the Chief. Smiling broadly, Rahnahi walked forward and wrapped her arms around both of them and drew them into as heartfelt an embrace as she knew how. "Oh, you sweet dears, what would we have ever done without you? I can't thank you enough!"

Van was stunned and hugged back as carefully and respectfully as she could. "You are so welcome, Honored One!" she heard Sahnassa say happily. As they released, Sahni added, "and we're happy to keep on helping in any way we can!"

"Well, you're going to have to, sweet child! Since your little speech, all of the kits and cubs in this complex want to see you, so I'm told. The matrons are pretty worried about getting the young ones on the transports. You may be able to help convince them it's safe."

"I'd love to help with that, Honored One."

Rahnahi seemed well-pleased. "Wonderful! When we go back in, Dania will set you up with the matrons managing those sections. Chief, when will you need the first group for loading?"

"No more than twenty-five passes, Honored One. The transport is already in the air. Your first group of one hundred and four ready?"

The matriarch nodded, answering, "They are. Do you want them at the field's edge when it lands?"

"No ma'am. Can you stage them behind that small building? It's close enough, and we shouldn't have any down blast issues there."

"We'll do that. Dania?"

"I can have them there in fifteen passes, Chief. Will that do? I don't want them in the cold longer than that."

He gave her a curt, soldierly nod. "I can work with that. If you all will excuse me, I have beacons to set up, and I have to get this flyer back up in the air to act as a guide."

"Very well. Thank you, Chief. We'll do our best to make this work smoothly," Rahnahi offered.

"Thank you, Honored One. It looks like you've already done a great job." He saluted her, and she bowed slightly in answer. He again nodded, dropped the salute, and walked quickly towards where one of the large cargo boxes was being unloaded.

"Let's get back inside, dearest kits." The group turned and started walking towards the building, but Vanarra stood still. Noticing the absence, the matriarch looked behind her at the fearful female, eyes downcast, paws folded in front of her. Sahni was already turning around to reach for her when the matriarch said, "Vanarra, you are to accompany us as well, unless you have an objection?"

"Yes, I mean no, I … uh, I will, Honored One." Feeling the terror in her friend, Sahni took Van's paw in hers and walked with her.

As they walked past the line of vehicles, Rahnahi wondered why Vanarra hadn't thought herself included in the invitation to go inside. "All I said was let's get back inside – oh, 'dearest kits' is what I said," she thought to herself. "That's something she's probably used to hearing addressed to *others*, especially if it's coming from a matriarch." Glancing behind herself and Dania, she saw Sahni dutifully holding the paw of her friend, who walked – in as much as was possible – with head and eyes down. "Vanarra," she called over her shoulder. "I've heard you've read some of my work."

"Uh, yes, Honored One," Vanarra responded, surprised.

"What's the title of my second book?"

"*Eyes Up and Forward*, Honored One." Her response was immediate. Rahnahi smiled inwardly; so she was a true fan.

"Then, Vanarra, you do that, right now. Eyes up and forward!"

"Yes, Honored One." Vanarra, with some effort, obeyed.

Glancing back again to see the beautiful mixed Faelnar-Vulpi's golden eyes, Rahnahi said smiling, "There. That's better." Timidly, Van smiled back.

As he watched the four heading out of the landing area, the Chief felt a moment of tense panic – remembering Theo's requested favor. "Mange, mange, mange!" he said to himself as he jogged over to where Agari had again taken up his perimeter position. "Agari! You're relieved from this post. I want you to follow Vanarra. You're her bodyguard until I tell you different. Stick with her and make sure that none of the evacuees do anything to harm her. Stay in the background, but help her out where you can. Simply put, if she gets in trouble, it's our can! Get a move on, Sarge! Hit it!"

"You got it, Chief!" With that, Agari was away at a fast jog, slinging his weapon over his shoulder as he went.

By the time he had almost caught up with them, they were already under the assault of cheers and now shouts of "Sahnassa! Sahnassa!" and about to disappear into the building. He felt all the eyes in the balconies above turn on him, and, suddenly, a flash of inspiration struck him from his seasons as an all-star defensive charger on his tertiary school team. He stopped and gave them all a very forceful double claws up – a sign of victory – bringing on cheers all the more. Snapping a salute in return, he smiled, and charged towards the doors that were now swinging shut.

While not fresh, the smell within the building was not as bad as he thought it might be. Through several buildings, he trailed behind them inconspicuously, getting a little closer each time. When they entered the main building of the Meeting Den, it took him a moment in the crowded hallway to catch sight of the group of four ascending a nearby staircase. He had completely caught up with them by the time they reached the top of the stairs. The matrons standing guard there passed him in without a second glance, and he homed in on Vanarra. However, as they entered what must be the command center, one of the elder de Dothnar dames raised her paw. "We have no need for a guard here," she said imperiously.

"With all respect Honored One, I'm not here to guard you." Without asking further permission, he dodged past her into the room. She was about to follow when he was recognized by his academy class sister, now a matron, who ran over and hugged him. "Oh, Saletta, by Thuria, it's so good to see you!" he exclaimed, returning the embrace of the petite matron and lifting her fully off the floor. Seeing this reunion, the haughty door guard returned to her post. Gently, he sat her back down again, looked into her smiling eyes and golden-brown face, and quietly asked, "How is she?"

She smiled tenderly as she saw his expression tinged with real concern, for there was no doubting who he meant. "She's fair, Agari. I think it's an infection; it's probably minor, but we'd better not take chances at her age."

"Everyone, everyone!" Rahnahi was calling the room to order. "I want your attention." As the busy room grew silent, a nearby door opened, and Amyra stiffly walked into the room followed by one of the Lupar medics and, somewhat painfully even with his assistance, took a seat in the back. Once her friend was settled, Rahnahi spoke. "We don't have long. The first group has to be out and ready in less than ten passes, but I just had to introduce you to the beautiful faces that go along with the voices that have given us all so much hope. May I present to you, in honor, Sahnassa de Orturu and Vanarra Anasto!"

Both bowed their heads as all assembled cheered, "In honor!"

"Thank you. Honor to you, as well," Sahnassa responded, but Agari noticed that Vanarra didn't raise her eyes, and looked for all the world like a small, embarrassed kit in a room full of adults. He had the oddest feeling that he should know her, but he couldn't place her in his memory.

"Now everyone, let's get to our duties and make sure this goes quickly!" The group nodded and started to get back to their tasks. He saw Sahnassa being led out the doorway by Saletta, but before he knew what had happened, Vanarra was being ushered into a nearby room with just the de Dothnar matriarch. As he approached, the dame he met on the landing field, Dania, was closing the door.

"That the only way in or out?" he asked.

A little confused, she responded, "Yes. Yes it is. May I ask what you're doing?"

"Following orders, Honored Dame, same as you. Just following orders." He took a guard's stance beside the door to her right.

"Oh, in that case, can you make sure no one gets in? They're not to be disturbed."

"I'll take care of that."

"Thank you." Still a little bemused, the dame left her post and moved to other duties.

Agari shifted his weight a little bit left and right to get his "paws into the floor," a little tradition he had made up when taking over a guard post. While doing this, he didn't see the small figure making her way slowly towards him. It wasn't until he saw the medic looming behind her that he made the connection. Looking down, he saw the smiling muzzle of his own matriarch looking up at him. "Agari," she said warmly, and he gently embraced her.

"Yes … yes, Honored One! Oh, it's so good to see you! I'm so sorry you're sick. Our medics are top rate; they'll take good care of you!"

"I've already seen that," she replied, smiling. "If it wouldn't both offend our house doctor and deprive the military of a valuable resource, I'd keep him on full time."

"Can she travel, Bal?" he asked over her shoulder to the medic waiting a discreet distance away.

The Lupar stepped closer and spoke softly. "Yeah, but I want her out of here soon. We'll need to wrap her up good, and I want to carry her out no matter what she says. If we get her down to the shelters, and I can get one of the docs to start some antibiotics, she'll be in good shape."

Agari looked back down at his matriarch, who obviously was not fully pleased with the medic's opinion. In a cautious tone, he whispered, "I agree with him, Honored One. Please, let us take care of you. It will be alright; I promise. We'll make sure the evacuation runs smoothly, and everyone gets out safe."

"I know you will," Amyra said, obviously not fully convinced, but then changed the subject. "So, why are you standing guard here? I thought Dania was…"

He wasn't sure exactly what to say, but knowing his matriarch, the truth was the only right answer. "My Chief gave me very clear instructions to protect Vanarra, Honored One. I'm to stay with her and protect her until I'm relieved."

The look in her wise green eyes grew very focused and sincere. "Sahnassa's work, no doubt. I'm glad of it. Agari, listen to me carefully; take very good care of her. She's very important to our family … and to me."

"You can count on me, Honored One."

"I know I can." She smiled and brushed the fur on the side of his muzzle as a mother would a young cub. He smiled back.

The medic leaned over and cleared his throat. "I need for her to lie down and rest. We're having a stretcher sent up." Again, she grimaced.

He patted her shoulder and warned, "Bal can be kind of a pain. Best to humor him, Honored One."

She chuckled and nodded, saying, "Alright, if you insist. Thank you, Agari." He nodded, and then the medic offered her an arm, and she slowly left with him. Looking at her go, Agari wondered, sadly, how much longer she would be around.

Vanarra was somewhere between excited and terrified, drifting in a dream-like state as she was led in for a private audience with the Grand Matriarch Rahnahi de Dothnar. She had entered a room that had no other doors save the one they entered. There were a few small windows, a small table, a few chairs, and several PawLinks and chargers against the wall.

The elder matriarch pulled the door closed and sighed, "Finally. We're alone." Vanarra's eyes were downcast, and she stood at almost rigid attention, feeling like she might pass out at any moment. She saw the lower half of her literary idol walk across the floor and take a seat on one of the chairs. Van heard her sigh again and then speak. "Dear, I don't know of any other good way to say this, so I'm just going to say it. Sit down, relax, and look at me. I'm not going to bite you, and in case you are wondering, I'm not going back on my promise, either."

A little reluctantly and very carefully, Van did what she was told, and saw, with her own eyes, the warm, dark, compassionate face she had seen only in the inside of book covers. The bluish purple of the poet's eyes seemed to gaze into her soul, but not in an unkind or invasive way. "My dear, you have me at a disadvantage, you know?"

"Honored One?"

"Use that term once we've escaped this place. Here, it's simply Rahnahi."

Vanarra's mind reeled; to be on a first name basis with a matriarch was implausible in her world, not to mention a dangerous affront. Nevertheless, she was following the order of a matriarch. "Yes ... Rahnahi."

"You've read a lot of what I've written, so I've been told. How much?"

Vanarra blurted out, "Everything you've published, although I haven't finished your book that was released ten sols ago!"

Rahnahi's eyebrow fur rose in surprise. "Then you know far more about me than I know about you. Although, please understand, that your friends here, Buck, for one, have given me a very positive report! Not to say that you might occasionally provide services for some rather interesting events, such as, let's say ... a primal?"

Ashamed, Vanarra looked away. "Don't be embarrassed. If you promise not to tell anyone, I'll tell you a secret. I've been to three." Vanarra looked back at her, genuinely shocked. "Now, don't look so surprised! I went in disguise, and I was a little younger then, but a poet can't do her job without first experiencing life. I didn't participate in the games or the shedding, but I got a good look at the goings on. Afterwards, I felt I understood a portion of our population a little better. It's helped me to write to them in my books, ask them to question what they do, but also to force others to question their opposition. As long as someone innocent isn't injured badly or someone doesn't create a new life without taking into consideration the consequences, I'll hold my peace. I've been around long enough to realize that primals aren't the only place in our society where risky behaviors occur. So, why do you do business with them? Come on, answer me honestly now."

"I ... I guess because they're kind of ... outcasts, like me. They are loyal customers and very appreciative. They've never behaved badly to me, well, most of the time. They can have a very surprising guest list, actually. It's ... it's a good place to network."

Rahnahi nodded with understanding. "I take your first answer with a lot of weight, and that, my dear, is what I wanted to talk with you about. Amyra de Gonari has been my dearest friend for a very long time. I've always believed that she, alone, was responsible for turning house de Gonari away from its parochial and fiercely traditional roots to a more open and compassionate family. It wasn't until I was here with her, in this very room, that she told me that it hadn't been her alone. Sure, there were many members of her house that helped, but there was someone who inspired her to become all that she is now, and that someone is ... you."

The elder poet gave the point a moment to sink in, and Vanarra shook her head. "I've ... I've never met her."

"Nor has she met you or even seen you until tonight. Understand, though, that she knew and loved your mother. When your mother died, she knew you were out there somewhere, and she did what she could to find you, for seasons in fact, and at some risk to herself, but to no avail. Since that sol, she's kept the thought of your mother and you in her mind, and it has driven her to do everything she could to change her house and make sure that what happened to you and your mother never happens again in house de Gonari."

Vanarra was looking at the floor, breathing heavily, trembling, and bathed in memories she always tried to keep buried.

Rahnahi continued. "It changed her world forever, for the better, to know you're not only alive, not only doing well, but that you ... are ... good." The poet's paws reached across the corner of the table and grasped Van's right paw gently. "You have every reason, I know, to want harm to come to us, we so-called purebreds, but you were willing to sacrifice everything you have for us."

Van heard the poet's voice break, and she looked up and saw the soft graying fur on the face of her artistic idol lined with tears. She grasped back with both of her paws and felt the tears in her eyes, as well. "You know, I've heard stories ... over the seasons. Those three, who beat your mother ... they've been put away. The matriarch who encouraged them, she was deposed, replaced, disgraced, and is now long dead, laid in a common grave. There are still some in that house who hold old views, but they are in a small minority. Amyra wanted you to know all of this, in case something happened, Vanarra; she really wanted you to know. You made a difference in her life – and because of her, in thousands of other lives ... and in mine, too."

"How ... how can this be true?" Vanarra did not let go, but shook her head. "By rights I shouldn't even be talking to you; I ... I have no family, no status! Now, you tell me that I've been the inspiration for a matriarch!? I've spent my whole life hiding from the de Gonari – pretending they didn't exist. I've tried—" Van swallowed hard. "I've tried so hard to keep from hating them, like my mother pled with me to do, but deep inside ... sometimes ... I did."

"But you know," Rahnahi admonished her gently, "that all of those without a 'de' something or other on their last name are not all the same, right? Your friend Buck, for instance? You should also know that all of the voices inside house de Gonari, in fact inside any house, are not all the same. You suffered greatly; I've heard what I'm sure is just the bare surface of it, but what happened to you was the catalyst for all this change! It was the key event that turned that house around, and finally, finally made them something to be proud of!"

Vanarra was still stunned. "I don't know. I just don't know. It's too incredible to be true. Just too incredible…"

Rahnahi let her go and leaned back up. "I understand. I know it must seem that way, but Amyra did give me one small token of proof that I can give to you. It's something she's always carried with her, and now she wants you to have it." From within her robes, she drew out a jeweled locket on a golden chain.

"Oh by Thuria, I can't accept that!" She shook her head; the piece of jewelry now being offered to her was worth at least two or three seasons of her own pay.

"You must, because it's not its outside that has the most value. It's what's on the inside that matters, much like me, much like you, and much like Amyra."

With trembling paws she accepted the locket, and with a gentle claw tip she opened it. In the grayish-gold light from the windows and the flickering candles, she saw an image within she never thought she would see again. "Mommy!" Vanarra burst into heart-rending sobs as she held the locket close to her chest. The matriarch moved her chair alongside of the crying Van and sat, placed her paw around her shoulder, and simply cried with her.

After a few passes, Van could halfway control herself and looked into the locket again, stroking the image on one side with tender affection. "I thought I'd never see her face again," she uttered in a rough whisper as she looked into the eyes of the young, proud Faelnar image. It was her mother, but so different than the beaten down, sorrowful one burned in her memory. "Oh, my soul, how I've missed you."

Rahnahi sniffed and suggested, "And look on the other side."

Looking into the other half of the locket, she saw a small bundled kit with a face peering out. "It's … it's me, isn't it?"

"Yes. According to Amyra, it's the only picture anyone was able to find of you – the only one that exists in the whole family. That picture of your mother was one Amyra hid away. There are a few others that Amyra has been able to find and gather over the seasons."

Van sighed raggedly before speaking again. "I guess it's true then. Why … why didn't Amyra… come, herself?"

"Finding you has shaken her to her core. What you're holding there she looked at thousands of times. It motivated her to keep going and try to change things when she ran out of hope, energy, or both. It emboldened her when she should have been cowering in fear. When I saw the state she was working herself into, I ... I told her I would talk with you first. She's a dear friend, and as I've told her recently, she's actually done great things where all I do is write about them."

"But the action needs a thought, and the thought needs an inspiration," Vanarra said, smiling back at the poet matriarch.

Rahnahi looked at her in mock admonishment. "No fair using my own words against me!"

Vanarra chuckled slightly. "I'm sorry, but I really have read and reread every one of your books. Oh, and before I get all muddled and forget to say something—" Her voice dropped to a whisper. "Thank you for what you've written. You kept me sane. You guided me. You helped me go on. You kept me alive."

The poet's eyes welled up again, and she stood, drawing Vanarra into an embrace. "You're so, so welcome. Now, let me thank you. You've helped to keep us alive. You've given all of us the chance to keep on living. Like it or not, Vanarra Anasto, you've got a new friend – lots of new friends." They hugged again, but Rahnahi's timepiece chimed. "I have to go now. They should be ready to start loading the first transport. Perhaps you should spend a few quiet moments in here, finding your center again. Come out when you're ready. Once everyone's out of here and settled in the valley, I would appreciate it if you could just talk, once, with Amyra – for me."

"How could I not?" Vanarra asked, looking at the locket once more before closing it and placing it around her neck.

Sahnassa had been led away from the meeting room by one of the younger matrons and had just caught a glimpse of the grand matriarch and Vanarra going into a room together. "Oh, I hope that works out," she thought as she went down the hallway back towards the staircase.

The petite Faelnar with golden brown fur and smiling golden eyes looked back at her and explained, "I've been instructed to take you to the first group that's evacuating. We're hoping you could help calm them. They are very excited to meet you."

"I'll do my best," Sahnassa answered. "What's your name?"

"I'm Saletta, matron of house de Gonari."

"Sahnassa de—"

"I *know!*" the young matron teased, smiling. "Everyone here knows *you!*" Saletta's playful tone turned to one of genuine awe as they exited the stairway and pushed through the doors into the cold air. "That was some speech you gave! Gosh, it helped us more than you can know!"

"I don't understand." They pushed back into another building and down a long, cold hallway full of closed doors.

"As you can guess, we've got a lot of very nervous parents and children. There are two buildings full – over five hundred! Since you spoke to them, ensured everyone knows the plan, you're all they can talk about! I've been with them the whole time, you see? You're just going to love seeing this! Parents have been drilling their kits and cubs in the plan, and it's made the children feel so much more secure. We've got the first batch just ahead. Thankfully building eight at the end didn't take as much damage on the first floor since it was the laundry. We've cleared away as much of the work area as we can, and we're going to use it to assemble each flight out. We can see the field from the far doorway, and it's double wide which means we can move our groups out quickly." They pushed out again into the cold and were soon back inside again.

Sahnassa couldn't help but smile at the matron's excitement. "That's great work planning! You've been thinking about this a lot."

"Matriarch Amyra is completely amazing! She's about worked herself into a coma organizing all of this, but she's really done it right. Do you know we've actually done drills with nearly all of the groups to practice leaving quickly?"

"Oh, you're so good!"

"Hey, you don't get to be a matron in our house unless you can think on your hind paws," Saletta observed.

They exited building one and traversed a paved pathway leading past the southern end of building eight. After entering a door halfway along the length of the building, the matron stated, "Okay, we're almost there." Saletta halted their progress in a very plain entranceway marked with a sign that said "Associates only." In the light of a few candles set outside the door, she looked at Sahni very intently and said, "Now, Sahnassa, let me tell you something. I don't know much about you, I admit, but I hope you understand how much a sign of hope you are to everyone here. If you're sure they're going to do well, they'll pick up on it, and they will do well," she explained, indicating the closed door ahead and with it, the Thurians beyond. "They need for you to be brimming with confidence. Do you think you can do that?"

"Oh, yes. I know that everyone is going to make it," Sahnassa answered with a quiet certainty that stunned the young matron.

"How do you know?" she asked, at a whisper. "For sure, I mean?"

Smiling slightly, Sahnassa explained. "Let's just say that since this started, I've sensed ... a presence watching over us – just making things go right. I know this sounds a little ... alien or strange, but I just know this. It's going to be fine, Saletta. It really is." Sahni put her paw on the young matron's shoulder. Saletta clearly didn't understand, but she smiled and her long tail lifted a bit, Sahni's reassurance buoying her up, as well.

"Thank you. Come on in, and let me introduce you!" They pushed through double doors into a dimly lit area which smelled of detergent and children and many other things both good and ill. The place where the laundry was normally sorted had been cleared out to create a large open space where kits and cubs ran around amongst a varied collection of folding and portable chairs. Parents were trying to keep their children under control, feeding their young with supplies from Sahni's bag, or just holding them while they dozed.

"Everyone! Everyone! May I have your attention?" The din of noise in the room dampened considerably, although it did not dissipate completely. "I have someone I'd like you to meet. This is Sahnassa de Orturu who spoke to you earlier and told you all about the plan." Now, everything went silent, and Sahnassa was acutely aware of all of the eyes – young and old – that were turned on her.

"Hello there," she said in as strong and warm a voice as she could manage. She imagined Theo's tone when he comforted her and felt herself fall into that same soothing manner. "It's so good to see all of you and finally get to meet you! In just a few passes, you're all going to get aboard a big flyer and go down into the valley. In the valley, there is a nice warm school with hot food and lots of new friends who are just waiting to help you. Some nice doctors and nurses are going to take a quick look at you, and then you'll get into some warm transports so you can start your trip home! Now, when it's time, we're going to leave quickly and stay together. We don't want anyone to get lost or left behind, so I want you children to hold onto your parent's or an adult's paw nice and tight until you're all aboard the flyer. Can you all do that?"

The children nodded and said yes, and Sahni felt the strange rush as if she had magically been transformed into a primary school director before a student assembly. "That's great! Now, all of you parents and adults, I have a job for you, too. Make sure that everyone is wrapped up nice and warm and that everyone stays together. Don't send anyone away to go get something. Keep your families close together no matter what from this point on. Everything you'll need has already been provided for you in the valley. It's so important to keep your families and groups together. Parents and adults, can you do that?"

The adults, catching on easily to Sahni's tactic for reassuring the children and re-enforcing the need to stay together, all eagerly and vocally agreed. At the other end of the UltraBright lit room, a soldier emerged from between rows of cleaning machines. "Excuse me. Is this the assembly area for the evacuees?"

"It is," Saletta answered.

"I'm going to be sitting just inside the doors back here, and I'll give you a warning when we're ready for your group to head outside. I've also got a TransCom for … Buddy? Was that his name?"

Saletta corrected him. "I think you mean Buck. I'll take that and make sure it gets to him."

As the gray-furred soldier gave over the device, Sahnassa asked him, "Sergeant, what's your name?" He told her, and she asked, "Would you mind if I introduced you to the children? It will take just a pass."

Looking a little stunned, the well-muscled Perratti answered, "No ma'am."

"Everyone, this is Sergeant Korick de Mastif. He's one of the soldiers who are helping to get you home. Wouldn't you like to say thank you to him?"

The younger children said thank you, but the adults and older children cheered and waved their paws; some even saluted. As the cheering continued for almost a full pass, Sahni noticed that the sergeant had broken into a smile, and even seemed to get a little misty eyed. He waved back and nodded in response to the adulation. Saletta raised her paws and lowered them slowly – a gesture which caused everyone to get quiet. "Now, Sergeant Korick has a lot of work to do, so we're going to let him go do it. Say goodbye to him."

"Goodbye!" the group said, nearly in unison, and again he waved and thanked them as he headed back down the rows of machines and out of sight.

"Now, we'll be letting you know it's time to leave in just a few passes, so let's do what we can now to get ready, okay?" With that, the group seemed to return to their prior activities, although some parents were now starting to organize the small bags and coats around them. "Wow, you are good at this!" Saletta whispered to Sahni with unvarnished admiration. "Would you like to stay with them and see them onto the flyer?"

"Oh, I'd love to!" It was only then that Sahni saw her, sitting quietly in a corner, nearly out of sight, looking sullen and bereft. Leaving Saletta talking into her communicator, Sahnassa walked over to the young Nephti kit and asked, "What's your name?"

"I'm Cari," she answered in a voice that clearly told Sahni she was heartbroken.

"Sweetie, what's wrong?"

"Nothing. No one wants to hear it," the child replied sadly.

"That's so not true. I do, really." Sahni looked earnestly into the cheerless purple eyes, and placed her paws on the young kit's shoulders.

"I ... I saw two—" Then, she started to actually cry. "They were in the fire; nobody believed me. Now the building is—" Cari leaned over, hugging herself and crying.

It was clear that the young kit was completely traumatized by what she had seen. It took just a quick moment for Sahnassa to reach her decision. "Oh, I see. Do you mean Celeste and Theo?"

Cari sat up quickly, stopped crying and was wide-eyed with amazement. "Yes!"

"They are safe, sweet one. Really!" Sahnassa was at her most calming and convincing.

"They can't be! I saw them!" Cari protested, stunned though she was that Sahnassa had spoken the right names. She had been given false assurances before by adults who just seemed to want her to be quiet.

"Now, you listen to me. I know Theo and Celeste. Theo probably didn't tell you he was a conjurer, did he?" She looked at Cari slyly.

"Yes! Yes he did!" Cari knew she hadn't told anyone that detail, and she looked up into Sahni's eyes with complete astonishment.

"Well, he told me all about the little disappearing act he did when the quake happened. The container fell, right? It caught fire and then boom, it exploded. He did a little trick and got them out the back way just in time. Celeste was really surprised, as well, but it's the kind of trick Theo does all the time. He really didn't mean to frighten you, Cari."

"They're okay?!" Cari was hanging on every word.

"They're fine sweetie; they really are," Sahni said, gently stroking the side of Cari's muzzle.

"But I haven't seen them! I've looked all around! I looked ... until they told me not to."

"The Meeting Den is a big place, and the matrons and dames were just trying to keep you safe. I'm sure you just barely missed them. They've been going lots of places and helping, and, yes, I have seen them myself. Maybe we can arrange for you to talk to them once you get down to the valley. Would that make you feel better?"

"Oh, thank you, thank you, thank you!" Cari shouted jumping into Sahni's embrace, hugging her tightly. Sahni hugged her back. After a moment, Cari let go and demanded crossly, "If you see Theo before then, tell him he was bad for tricking me! I was so scared and sad! Tell him I'm going to tell my grandama on him if he ever does anything like that again!" the little Nephti scolded officiously.

"I will Cari, but I'm sure he didn't mean anything by it. He's actually very nice."

"Yeah, I suppose so. Celeste was real pretty too, and she was nice to me."

"Thank you," Sahni caught herself saying, but then she thought of a great cover. "That's so sweet. She's very close to me, I'm sure she'll be happy to hear that you think well of her. Now, there's just one important thing. If you want to see Theo and Celeste again, you have to make me a promise. I want you to keep them a secret. They could both get in bad trouble for their little trick, and that wouldn't be fair since they didn't mean any harm. Can you do that?"

"I can. Oh, thank you Sahnassa! I'm so glad you're here!" They hugged again.

"Now, you stay out of trouble. You're going to like being on the flyer. It's fun! I've already done it. Now, why don't you go wait with the others?"

"Yes ma'am!" With that, she was happily away.

"Would you stop that?" Saletta asked coming up behind her.

"Stop what?"

"Stop working minor miracles! You're going to get a reputation, you know? I've tried for intervals to calm her down. What did you say to her?"

"Just enough to ease her fears," Sahnassa said, shrugging.

"You are so not going to tell me, are you? A conjurer never reveals her secrets?"

"I'm just a new voice. Sometimes it's easier to believe a stranger than someone you know."

"Alright, so don't tell me," Saletta grumped, finally relenting. "Can you spend some time with the others? There are a whole lot of miracles needed in this group."

"Sure." With that, Sahnassa spent several passes with different kits and cubs (and even a few adults) reassuring them about what was happening.

Finally, Saletta was at her side. "It's time. We have to start moving them out. Do you want to tell them?"

"I'll do it." Sahnassa stood and took a spot where the rows of cleaning machines began. "Everyone, please listen to me! It's time for us to go! We're going to walk together to a waiting place while the flyer lands. Then, when we're told to, we're going to get onboard the flyer for our trip to the valley!" Everyone quickly gathered clothes, bags, and children and started to walk towards her. She called out, "Alright everyone, follow me! We're going to start slowly to make sure we have everyone! Saletta, can you make sure we don't leave anyone behind?"

"I'll make sure!" she called back.

Walking at a very slow pace, she guided the group down to the large double doors, one of which was already propped open by the sergeant. "Four passes, ma'am, until touchdown. It will be two more passes before you can start loading."

"Got it! Has Buck got his TransCom?"

"Yes, he just called in. The matrons are moving the next group into the space you just left."

"Very good. I'll come back to help with the next group." He nodded, and with that, he pulled open the second door, and the group walked out into the cold.

Walking slowly until the path turned and she could see the end of their group leave the laundry, Sahnassa started to pick up the pace as she led them towards the athletic field. A warm, small paw grasped her own. Looking down, she saw Cari and smiled, squeezing the paw gently in return. Looking then to her right, she noticed Van coming down a parallel path and bearing a stretcher with a soldier holding the other end. Behind them, at a distance, were two other stretchers and their bearers, as well. "Hi there!"

"Hi yourself!" Van shouted back. "I see you've been busy!"

"You, too!" Their path wandered away from Van's a little bit before rejoining near the field house, so Sahni decided to hold off on any further conversation until they were closer. She knew the questions she really wanted answered would have to wait until they were alone.

"I'm NOT going out on the first transport!" Amyra argued with the medic. "It will send the wrong message!"

The frustrated Lupar was still insistent. "Honored One, I'm very worried about you, and I don't think having you fall gravely ill a few intervals from now and not being able to evacuate you because of that fact is going to send a good message, either. This could be minor, but it may not be."

Dania walked into the room and closed the door. "Tell him I shouldn't go on the first transport," Amyra demanded sternly.

As apologetically as she could, Dania answered, "I ... I can't really do that, Honored One. I think we should get you out now, too. My own matriarch agrees and sent me here to make sure you go."

Amyra was exasperated. "But what kind of a message is that going to send when the matriarch gets evacuated first?"

"I understand your concern, Honored One, but your life is at risk, potentially at serious risk," Dania tried to explain.

Amyra grunted, and there was an uncomfortable silence between them all for a moment. The medic's big, Lupar brow then wrinkled slightly. "How ... exactly ... would anyone know it was you?"

"Well, for one thing there's all this," Amyra said, pointing to the elaborate jewelry on her shoulder. "Let's not forget about the dames and matrons who are always around."

"What if they weren't?" Dania suggested. "What if we dressed you in other clothes?"

"Don't be silly," Amyra answered, dismissively.

The medic retorted, "No, no, ma'am! It could work! I've put a lot of Thurians on stretchers. We can wrap you up nice and tight; mix you in with some of the others being evacuated. No one would really know." Amyra still looked at the medic shaking her head "no." "We've got to do something! I'm sure you've got a lot to look forward to. We have to get you off this mountain and into a doctor's care, now. I've done all I can for you, Honored One!"

Amyra was deeply conflicted. There was a big part of her that really did want to escape, ensure her own survival. There was also a part that wanted to make sure she lived long enough to have the chance to talk with Vanarra. Duty and sickness, honor and weakness rolled back and forth in her thoughts. Finally, a tense pain in her groin and back prodded her decision. "Alright. If you can find me something to wear with a big hood and make *sure* no one knows, I'll go."

"Good." The medic was relieved that his patient was cooperating, finally. "Now, you lie down here, on the bed, and we'll get everything taken care of." The medic and Dania both left the room and closed the door.

It was with guilt-tinged relief that Amyra finally laid down.

Vanarra was grateful that the matriarch had given her a few moments alone, understanding that Van needed time to find her center again after such powerful revelations. Slowly, she stood and walked towards the closed door and opened it, only to find herself staring at the back of a military uniform. "Excuse me?"

"Yes, ma'am," the soldier answered, turning around. "I was on the flyer with you earlier. I'm Tactical Sergeant Agari de Gonari. The Chief assigned me to you."

"Assigned you … to me?" she asked, trying to understand.

"He wanted to make sure you stayed safe," the burly Faelnar explained with a calm, matter-of-fact demeanor, as if he did this kind of thing all the time.

"I'm not like under arrest or something, am I?" Van queried, eyebrow fur raised.

"No ma'am! Certainly not. You're free to go where you want to. I'll just be there to accompany you and watch your back."

She really didn't understand it, but "then again," she thought, "my whole world is flipped upside down right now, so why not?" She shrugged, saying, "Okay with me, I guess. I just don't know what I'm supposed to do."

"Agari!" One of the Lupar medics she met in the flyer walked over. "Agari! I need someone for stretcher duty; can you help and find someone else for me?"

"I'm sorry, Bal, I've got orders."

Van stepped out from behind him. "To stay with me. What if we both did it? I mean I want to be useful, not just sit here like a lump with you guarding me."

Agari thought for a moment and said, "That's very good of you ma'am. Okay, Bal, you got your litter crew. Where's your patient?"

"I'll have three out in the hallway in a tick. Find one you can manage, and head towards the athletic field."

"Will do!" Vanarra exclaimed, happy to actually be doing something useful.

As the Lupar walked quickly away, Agari asked, "Are you sure you can manage? It's a long way and a lot of steps."

Almost smirking back at him, she retorted, "Try carrying a night's worth of fermentum up fifteen flights of stairs because they won't let you use the elevator. I'll manage, sweetie. I'm stronger than I look." Her can-do, almost soldierly, attitude struck a positive chord with Agari, and he smiled.

Chapter 12: Uplifted

Amyra felt "weird," and even the use of that word in her mind was strange. Despite being wrapped up in heavy blankets almost like a swaddled kit, she felt somewhat naked without the heavy jeweled piece on her shoulder. The robes and ornamentation, rings, bracelets, and so forth were all gone, and she was left only wearing soft, modest nightclothes – clean, thankfully enough – rescued from Dania's own luggage. Laying still, on the stretcher, on the floor, and in a hallway next to two others in similar condition was simply surreal.

Now, much to her embarrassment, she didn't feel all that bad. Sure, she thought, what the medic had given her just as she laid down probably helped, but now, she was awake, not in any real pain, and in full control of her mental faculties. She half thought about getting up and proclaiming she didn't need to be evacuated or sneaking back into the command center, but there was the constant passing of soldiers, dames, matrons, and regular Thurians. It was just impossible to do such a thing without creating an incident. She hated feeling this way: utterly helpless.

"Out here?" a female voice she knew she should recognize sounded near her, but her ears were wrapped up in the hood, slightly muffling the sound. "Oh, yes. How about this one?"

"It's okay with me. You want the front?"

"Oh, no," she thought, having heard a male now speak. That was Agari's voice. She closed her eyes and turned her head to the side. Hopefully, he wouldn't recognize her. In her thoughts, she cursed all manner of things and Thurians for bringing her to this "weird" state.

"Yes, let's take her hind-paws first," the female directed, and Amyra immediately presumed this was someone else from Agari's unit. A moment later, she could feel them grasping the poles.

"Sounds good. Is she awake?" Agari asked more quietly.

The medic, Bal, stepped around the corner and said, "I gave her some stuff. She's pretty knocked out. Be very gentle with her and just let her rest. I wouldn't bother her unless she asks for something." The medic's face appeared in front of her as the two lifted her up. "It's going to be alright ma'am. These two will take good care of you."

"Thanks," she whispered, although she really wanted to yell at him for putting her in this position. He nodded, winked, and left her.

Agari asked quietly, "You good with the weight?"

The female chuckled. "She's light as a leaf. I'll be fine. We'll just go slow down the stairs, but we'll make good time on the ground, I promise you. You don't get meals to three different joining receptions on the same sol on time by dragging your tail."

"Oh by Thuria!" Amyra's eyes went wide as the realization came together in her mind. "It's Vanarra! It's Vanarra who's carrying me!" She was flooded with thoughts and fears and amazement. The impulse for running away fought with that of hiding, speaking with silently listening, crying with cheering, and so many others at the same time that she felt consciousness slipping away. With great effort, she calmed her mind and struggled to breathe again, realizing that she almost caused herself to pass out.

As she considered what a fool she had just been, the voice of one of her old philosophy teachers came back to her. "There are times when you should take no action or you simply can't. Then, just do what you can do – watch, taste, smell, feel, experience but most of all … listen." With that thought fixed in her mind, she finally started to focus.

By then, they had reached the stairway, and Van headed straight down without stopping, smoothly lifting the long poles higher and higher to keep Amyra level. Agari, to his credit, noticed the ease with which she dealt with this somewhat uncommon situation. "Well, that was kind of instinctual. You carry a lot of stretchers?"

With a light, airy tone, Vanarra retorted, "Fully loaded banquet tray, four flights of stairs at least, three times this season, so far."

Agari chuckled, "Really? What can't you learn from catering?"

As they reached the landing and Vanarra and Agari readjusted, Van replied honestly, "You know, I am not really sure, so I can't tell you.

I keep finding there are new things to learn. I mean, take the last sol. Escaping with your tail in one piece from a buried vehicle, building a shelter from the junk in your luggage, sleeping with absolutely NO concept of private space at all, starting a campfire using a blow torch and wipe paper–"

As they started moving again, Agari was laughing more and more at each item she ticked off her list. "Oh, and then there's how to go pee in the woods, how to get on a flyer when you really, really hate flying, how to fasten one of those fifteen point harnesses or rather how to get two *nice* looking medics to do that *for you*. How to chat up those keen-looking Lupar so well you don't even notice you've taken off and landed, not to mention finding out which one was single and which one wasn't—"

Agari was still laughing, but now begged her, "Stop, stop! I'm not going to hold up my end if you keep going on like that!" Amyra was also trying not to laugh, but managed to keep her amusement to a well-hidden smile.

"Alright, I'll behave. I'm just teasing, anyway. Your medics were really very nice to me. Let's change the subject. How long have you been in the service?"

"About ten seasons."

"Do you like it?"

"Love it. Although after hearing you talk, I'm thinking about changing to catering command!"

Vanarra laughed, and Amyra heard a nice warmness in that voice – a very pleasant sound, she thought. "Oh, stop! Now *you're* doing it! So what made you want to enlist?"

"My matriarch," he said proudly.

"Really? She told you to?" Vanarra asked, cautiously.

Agari's response was openly and honestly delivered. "No, it wasn't like that at all. When I was growing up, we had a terrible matriarch – just awful. Then, and I'm still not straight on all the story, but suddenly she's out, and our current matriarch is in. My father thought nothing would change, but was he totally wrong! Suddenly, things we were taught on a regular basis were just … gone. We started actually seeing and speaking to dames and matrons, getting to know them and all about our family. Our house changed our motto, our rules, our outlook – it's like that one Faelnar just altered our whole world. We started doing volunteer work, including missions way overseas and in disaster areas. We even started volunteering and donating to orphanages – something our old matriarch would never have allowed. I was on one of those volunteer trips when I got to see the military come in and save everyone. I was hooked right then and there!"

They were now out of the buildings and well down the path. Van was about to ask another question, but she heard "Hi there!" coming from somewhere at her left. It was Sahni's voice! Looking over, she saw her friend at the head of a large group of children and adults streaming down a path nearby.

"Hi yourself!" Van shouted back. "I see you've been busy!"

"You, too!" Both had to stop the conversation there because the paths diverged somewhat. "That's an amazing story," Van remarked thoughtfully over her shoulder. Amyra was crying, quietly; her hot tears almost steaming in the cold air beyond her muzzle. She always had this reaction when she heard someone say that she had inspired them. What's more, she knew Agari's endorsement was honest. "What do you think of her now?"

"She's slowed down a bit; getting older, you know? She's still a force to be reckoned with. The de Caterra matriarch hates her; that's pretty evident."

"Hates her, why?" Vanarra asked, seemingly perplexed.

"Well, you know de Caterra is one of the last Faelnar families still holding to the old traditions. The Chief told me all about it, although he doesn't hold a grudge himself. Almost everywhere they are now, I mean where they live now, they're isolated. That's a far cry from where they were not even fifteen seasons ago. Males from that family are finding it almost impossible to find Faelnar females from another family to join with. We're starting to wonder if they'll just die out."

Vanarra said what Amyra thought, almost exactly. "We should be so lucky, although your Chief is an exception to that." Now, they were at the small building, and the paths were meeting.

Sahni walked up beside her and seeing her load asked, "Why don't you put your stretchers down on that paved patio on the other side? I'll keep my group away from them, and we'll let you board first."

"That sounds great, Sahni. Thanks! You're the best." Sahni gave her a quick hug at the shoulder and then darted back to her group.

It took them just a moment to navigate around the small concession building and find a space where they could set down. When Van and Agari started to lower her, for just a moment, Amyra's hind legs were higher than her head, and something in her throat began to tickle. By the time she was on the ground, she was coughing. "Hey, are you okay?"

Agari asked, standing over her. Thankfully, it was dark, and he couldn't make her out.

"No, Agari; she's not! Here, let me sit her up." Agari stepped back, and Amyra soon felt strong, soft paws at her back and head gently lifting her up. Vanarra settled into a sitting position beside the stretcher so she could keep supporting her. "There, there, is that better? Can I get you something?"

"Something … (cough) … something to drink?" Amyra rasped.

"I've got something. It's juice, and it's a little warm, but hopefully, it'll do the trick." There wasn't more than a moment of shuffling before Amyra felt the rim of a container at her muzzle. "Drink slowly now. Try not to make it worse."

The juice, warm though it was, was slightly sweet and very smooth, and it went a long way towards ending the coughing fit. "Thank … you," Amyra whispered as the container was taken away.

"I'm going to find out when that transport's coming," Agari said. "Have you got her?"

"Yes. I think we'll be fine," Vanarra replied, kindly.

"Good. Be right back!"

As she saw Agari's muscular form disappear into the misty, gray darkness, Amyra tried to look at Vanarra's features. The light was so poor where they were, she could barely see anything more than the reflection in her eyes. A cough shook her body again, although others didn't follow immediately. "I have something else that may help. Just a moment." Vanarra did some more fishing around in her pockets and came up with several small lozenges. Unwrapping one, she offered it to Amyra saying, "These really work well for me when I get choked up. They're aster tree tea flavored. Want to try it?" Amyra nodded and took the offering from Van's paw. After a moment, Van asked, "Is that better?"

Amyra nodded and said in a whisper, "Yes, thank you. You're … very well prepared."

"Working in catering will do that for you," Vanarra responded, and although she couldn't see it, Amyra could tell Van was smiling.

"Now why's that?"

"It doesn't matter why an event fails, even if it's not your fault. So if the speaker starts to cough his way through a speech, it's better for everyone if I can just take care of it."

Agari returned and jumped back into his carrying position, saying, "They want us closer, since we're going in first. We're to come right up to the gap in the parked vehicles. I just told Sahni that she's to start her group moving the moment they see the ramp hit the ground. That's when we'll be walking up it!"

"I'm going to lay you down now so we can move you," Van explained kindly, and gently lowered the elderly female. "Is that good?"

"Yes," she said, still whispering. Even in the dim light, Amyra could see Van smiling at her. After a moment, they were moving again. As they rounded the corner, the lights from the field came into view, and it was clear that the military had made some adjustments. What was a perfect rectangle before was now as close to a circle as they could manage. The vehicles which had been closest were moved away, most likely for safety, Amyra thought. Several tall, flashing beacons had been arrayed around the field, and looking over her shoulder, she saw that some type of shelter had been erected on top of the building they were just near – presumably to act as ground control.

It wasn't very long before another voice told them to wait at the top of a little rise at the edge of the field. "Who do you have there, Agari?"

Amyra's guts congealed inside of her, but again she was saved by Agari's kindness. "We've got the sweetest kit, Chief! She's been a perfect passenger."

"I'm glad to hear it! The first of the 17's is on final, and should be on the ground in less than a pass. All of you carrying stretchers secure them in the forward section! The loadmaster or Sergeant Agari here will show you how. We've got staff at the LZ to unload, so you don't have to ride down if you're still needed up here. I'll be back in a moment to call you onto the vehicle."

As he spoke, Amyra could hear the whine of engines above them, growing closer and closer. She turned her head and could just see the landing area to the right of Van's body. Above them, lights manifested in the low-hanging clouds and a great, dark shape started to appear.

"Wow!" Van exclaimed, loud enough for Amyra to hear it over the engines. The craft was all the more amazing to view now as it was fully below the clouds and shifting gracefully into position to begin its final descent. Its long, dark green body looked almost like a flattened hexagon, and two long wing-like pylons swept down and back from its forward third, paired with another shorter set of the same near the tail. Those were mounted just below the tall, V-shaped tail fins. The great craft slowly turned to face away from them, starting to bring its massive bulk to the ground. Large landing skids appeared from underneath its surface as the HVR-17 started to drift straight down.

The noise was intense, but not so intense that Amyra couldn't hear the Chief yelling. "As soon as the pilot throttles the engines down, you two go, got it?!"

"Got it!" Agari and Van both shouted back.

It was just a moment longer, and the great hulk was settled on the ground, and the pitch of the engines started to drop. With good speed, Amyra's stretcher started moving forward, past the line of vehicles and right up to the back of the craft. Over the idling engines, she heard a higher pitched mechanical sound and barely could see a large payload ramp and door assembly opening ahead of them.

Van looked up at the widening opening, not really knowing what to expect, but being stunned all the same. Riding the payload door down was clearly the Thurian in charge. Helmeted, he held up his paw in a warning gesture as the ramp descended the last couple of tracks to the ground. The bay beyond was sparse, utilitarian, and looked to Vanarra like the inside of a steel can. Long metal poles met in multiple T-junctions halfway up its inner height, forming the supports for four long rows of seats made from metal pipe and red webbing. As ramp and ground finally met, Van was surprised again as the *female* soldier ordered loudly, "Up and in, up and in, as fast as you can safely manage! All the way to the back along the right side! Secure your stretchers in the racks!"

Moving as quickly as she could, Van walked up the metal ramp which, thankfully, was coated with sections of a rough black material that formed a walkway. Small, pinpoint lights shone very brightly down on the seating area, but Van found herself having to walk carefully to avoid banging her hind paws on the poles. "Close in here, a little bit," she said, struggling to keep moving forward at a decent speed.

"Has to be," Agari answered. "That's the only way we can get one hundred and four inside. It's a short ride; they should do alright." They made it past the seats back into a small section of the open bay, and Van shot a glance over her right shoulder as other noises, Sahni's voice for one, came to her ears. Looking back, she saw her friend guiding a large group of families and children up the ramp right behind them. "Keep going. They're two stretchers behind us!"

She moved forward and rounded a partition to see six support rails facing her. "We'll put her on that middle set, ship's right," Agari instructed. Van turned around to face Agari as he slid his poles onto the rails and into two locking clamps that held the stretcher securely. She imitated what he did, and looking back at him for approval, she was met with his smiling face. "You got it right! Now we can help the others." With that, they assisted in the task of getting the other stretchers installed on ship's left.

Once all the stretchers were in, Agari picked up a series of padded straps from the wall. "Now, we belt them in," he instructed the small group. "Not too tight. Make sure they can breathe! We just don't want them to slide off if we shift during flight."

"How many?" Van asked reaching out for the straps in his paws.

"Three," he said, giving her that same number. "Ankles, hips, and under the arms. Can you manage her while I help them?"

"Okay," she stated, looking somewhat uneasily at the straps, but soon found they were no more complicated than normal clothing belts. Leaning over the face of the elderly female she had been carrying, she found the Faelnar awake and alert.

"How are you doing?" Amyra asked, and although Van couldn't easily hear, she made the words out nonetheless.

Van smiled back at her. Although it took some effort to talk over the din of noise coming from beyond the partition, she replied, "I was just about to ask you the same thing! Are you okay?" Closing her eyes and nodding, somewhat gravely, her charge responded. "Wonderful. I'm going to strap you in now, dear. I'll be as gentle as I can."

Van carefully placed each strap and tightened it just enough. Unwrapping the female's blankets exposed the night clothes of a common, middle class Thurian – nothing remarkable.

"No, no, no!" Agari shouted angrily at her side. He was fussing with the other two stretchers to her left. "He's a burn case! You have to look where the burns are and put the straps in other places. Hang on buddy; we'll get you fixed. You good, Van?" he asked turning to her, clearly hoping she was.

"Don't mind us kits; we're doing fine!" As he turned back to his work, she leaned over and asked, "You are fine, aren't you? Not too tight?"

"It's okay. I'm just a little cold." It only took Van a moment to bundle the elderly female as snuggly as she had been before. However, upon reaching her face, Vanarra stopped and looked hard into the green eyes of the Faelnar in front of her.

"What's your name?"

Although she meant to say her name clearly, it came out as "Uh …
Myra …"

"Myra? Now, Myra, answer me honestly." Amyra just knew she
was going to give herself away. She couldn't lie; that would ruin her
credibility later, and she really needed that with Vanarra. "Are you afraid
of flying?"

With a relieved expression, she mouthed the truth, "Yes. I don't
like it."

Van smiled broadly, "Me, too. Hang on a moment." She turned
and called over her shoulder, "Agari?"

His attention was still on his other patients. "That goes there, and
that goes there! Got it? Now hurry up! We'll lift off in a pass or two.
What do you need, ma'am?"

"Can we ride down with them? We'll come back up afterwards."
She saw his confused expression, but Van leaned over to him and
whispered, "She's old, she's sick, and she hates flying – she's scared!"

"Oh, oh I see," the big Faelnar said nodding. "I'm good with it.
I'll go down and help the loadmaster get the rest of this crowd settled. She
might even be grateful for the extra help. I'm also going to get those other
guys out of here so we can take off. Please, double check what they did
and make sure you think it's right. The one on top has burns, so make sure
nothing's rubbing on his wounds."

"You bet!" He stepped away, and Van leaned over her charge and
said gently, "Myra, sweetie, I'm going to ride down with you, alright?" A
surprisingly strong paw reached from the stretcher and grabbed her own,
squeezing it in thanks. "I'll make sure you're taken care of. I also want to
see how things are going down there, anyway. Now, I'll be back in a
moment." With a smile, she was off.

Vanarra stepped to her left and looked at the top stretcher. She
carefully examined the strapping of the "burn case." He was a male Anati,
something between a Perratti and a Vulpi. "Hi there," she said sweetly.

"Hi," he replied, obviously in pain, but he still managed to smile.
She could tell he found her attractive; she could always tell with males.

"I won't trouble you long; I just want to make sure none of the
straps are bothering you."

"No, you're no trouble. They fixed it. They just didn't know."

She put her paw on his forehead and stroked his fur gently. "The
way you're wrapped up; I can understand. Is there anything I can get you?"

"No. The medics took good care of me. I just want to get into a nice hospital bed."

"Alright, if you're sure?" Van asked.

"Thanks. I'm fine," he said gratefully.

She smiled back at him and ducked down to check on the last stretcher case. Her eyes went wide with astonishment. "Arnat?!?" He was equally as stunned and horrified to be looking into her face, but said nothing. "You little sneak! You had better have lost a paw or something to be going out on the first flyer!"

"I don't have to explain myself to the likes of you!" he growled out through gritted teeth.

"Oh, really? Anati above me! Anati to the side of me! We're all around you now. You know I'm pretty tight with these military types, and I don't think they like self-serving little fakers very much. They can probably do some really bad things to those who play sick to get the first ride out!"

He groaned, although she had a hard time telling if it was from pain, fear, anger, or embarrassment. "I'm not *playing* sick, you rape-mated little tramp—"

"Oh, yeah? What the mange is wrong with you? Couldn't be your conscience for getting us shafted and kicked out of the Meeting Den, could it?"

"No, and I'd do it again, too." He groaned in pain. "I'm … I'm … they think I've got … a knot in my intestines, swelling. I've been retching my guts out for the last ten intervals!"

Van stepped out from behind her anger and took a cold, hard look at him. The smell on his breath was testimony enough. His blood-shot eyes and whitish tongue and gums, too, were evidence. He was clutching an area he couldn't fully reach under one of the tie-down straps that looked just a little too snug. "Oh, there's a big part of me that says you deserve that much." She grabbed the strap he was trying to move and released its grip. "But still, I'll help you, regardless of how worthless I think you are."

Despite himself, he sighed with relief. "Thank—" He didn't allow himself to complete the sentence before clamping his jaw shut.

Van refused to let that go. "Oh, you are so very welcome! I ask only one thing in payment, and you sure as mange owe it to me. Why? Why did you do that to me? Why rape-mate poor little Vanarra like that in front of everyone? I'm no threat to you!"

He clearly didn't want to tell her, but he forced himself – whether out of pride or honor, she couldn't tell. "You know about my … primal." His voice was a whisper. "You know what happened and how I was – how I lost. If you became well-connected with the association, they might actually start – you might tell someone. Ruin us. Ruin our reputation."

She laughed at him. "If you hadn't noticed, sweet cakes, I already have a lot of friends, inside and outside of the association, and I've made a career based on keeping quiet." She pointed a clawed finger at him. "If you had actually bothered to get to know me, even though I'm just a stinking Anati, you would have figured that out! Have a nice flight."

She abruptly stood up and walked away. She stormed around the partition, and what she saw instantly melted her anger. There was Sahni, shuffling up the rows, checking on everyone, making sure their straps were secure, and comforting children and parents alike. As she reached the end of the row, Vanarra called, "Hey kit!"

Sahni looked up and smiled, but then got a curious expression on her face. "You're not leaving, are you?"

"I'm going to ride down with one of the ones we brought out, have a look down there, and come back up on an empty transport, I think."

"As much as you hate flying?"

Van was about to answer, but a loud, female voice cut her off. "All right! We're just about ready to go! Everyone off right now unless you're coming with us!" The loadmaster's voice carried well throughout the bay, even though she was standing at the far end.

"By Thuria, she's loud!" Van marveled.

"That's why she's the loadmaster!" Agari said, coming back up the other row. Looking at Sahnassa he warned, "You'd better *run* if you want out! She'll close the door on you. She's done it to me!"

"Got to go!" Sahni hugged Van and kissed her on the cheek, and then Sahni quickly worked her way down the rows. "Stay safe!" Sahnassa shouted over her shoulder.

"You, too," Van called back. Sahni quickly jumped off the ramp as it started lifting off the ground.

"Get your tail off this field, missy! Run, run, run, run, run!" The loadmaster shouted after her. "Come on, hurry it up! We'll blow you right off this mountain if you're too slow!"

Sahni ran as hard as she could for the line of vehicles in front of her. As the engines roared to life, she felt the down thrust kick at her heels and back. Looking behind her, she saw the large vehicle already lifting off the ground, although the rear door was still only half closed. She had to smile as she saw the silhouette of the loadmaster snap her a quick salute before disappearing from sight. Another short sprint put her well out of harm's way, but she mentally chastised herself. "I'll have to be quicker next time."

Chapter 13: Colors of Mercy

V anarra watched Sahni jump off the loading ramp just before she felt Agari's paw on her shoulder. "We gotta strap in! Here!" He pointed to an inboard seat at the head of Amyra's stretcher. Van sat quickly and pulled the lap belt across her waist, snapping it shut.

"Thank you," Van said, looking over at Agari who was now belting himself in. Almost instinctively, her paw found its place upon the elder female's shoulder, offering comfort and support. Feeling the touch of Myra's paw upon her own, she leaned over and assured her, "It's going to be okay."

The engines now roared to life, and the sound grew loud in the cargo bay – much louder than in the commercial flyers she'd flown. Both females' paws holding tight, they felt the craft lift up into the air and tilt slightly forward. They were shocked to hear cheering and applause pouring over the partition from where the families were sitting. Van couldn't help herself, she started laughing and cheering and crying, almost at the same time. Agari joined in, loudly whooping as well.

The loadmaster appeared at the edge of the partition, her visor finally up, revealing a pretty Vulpi with burnt orange fur. A huge smile graced her muzzle as she listened to the exclamations of relief and joy. As the cheering died down, she pressed a button on the side of her helmet. "You brass-tails in the cockpit hear that? Good, so can you make it a smooth flight – for once?" Van could easily tell she was teasing the pilots by the mischievous look in her silver gray eyes. "Sirs, with all due respect, I've flown with you too much to believe that! Yes sir, sure. In a little bit,

I'll get our passengers spun up for dismount. Wait for my signal prior to T.O.; they won't all be sprinters like that last one. Fillie out."

She released the button and walked over. "How's everyone enjoying their trip aboard my fine flyer?" While she had to yell the question over the engine sounds, it was clearly a volume she was used to. Van's talent for assessing character clicked in, telling her that "pretty she may be, but she's as tough as cold steel fasteners." Even though the Vulpi's teeth were smiling sharply, almost bared, Vanarra decided instantly that she liked her. Here was someone with the same confident attitude that had served her on so many occasions.

"I think we're okay," Van answered loudly, but motioned to Myra. "I want to stand up and check. Is that alright?"

"Sure, here," the Vulpi said as she walked over, and clicked Van's belt release. "Just keep a firm paw on her stretcher, and whatever you do, don't yack on my deck!"

"Mange, Fillie! Didn't anyone ever teach you how to act?" Agari shouted in a half laugh as he undid his own belt.

"Lot of 'em tried, Broke Tail! A lot of 'em tried!"

"Oh, let's not start that again," Agari groaned, clearly aggrieved.

Responding to Agari's remark, however, the loadmaster did temper her warning. "All I'm saying is that if you feel sick, sit down, got it? I'm just hoping to get through the night without it smelling like a barf barn back here!"

Van tried to think of an answer, but simply nodded and stood slowly. The feeling of the deck moving under her hind paws was disconcerting and odd, but not unmanageable. Scared though she was, she tried to put on a brave face for Myra. As she looked over, fear turned to concern as she saw the tear marks streaking the eye fur going back towards the back of the head. "Hey, sweetie, Myra? Are you okay? What's wrong?" she tried to ask as nicely as she could without shouting, and she bent down low over the Faelnar's face.

"I'm … happy, dear. That's all," she said, although Van had to strain to hear it.

"Much happier when we're on the ground, I'd bet!"

Amyra's eyes opened, and she nodded. Just as she was grasping Myra's paw, a male's scream of pain pierced the air. Looking over, she saw Arnat involuntarily straining against the straps, his features twisted in agony. "Arnat! I'll be back in a moment, Myra!" She worked her way over, somewhat unbalanced, to the lower stretcher on ship's left. Agari and the loadmaster were already there.

"It'll be just a little while, and we'll be on the ground, okay? You gotta tough it out until then." Agari was trying to be encouraging, but it was clear to Van that Arnat was well beyond that.

"Arnat!" Van shouted, grasping his head and turning it towards her. "What's wrong?"

"Straps! Straps!" Instantly, Van popped the release on the ankle and midriff straps.

"What the mange are you doing!?" the loadmaster demanded fiercely.

With equal intensity, Van shouted back, "Stringing him out like this is killing him! We've got to let him lie on his side – curl up if that will help! We'll just have to strap him down again once he's turned! Please, I've had friends die like this!"

Looking doubtful, the loadmaster released the strap under Arnat's armpits, and he curled up into a ball on his side. Carefully, Van tightened the straps around him again. "Do you feel better Arnat?"

"Yes!" he cried.

Gently, she started rubbing his back. She felt his muscles tighten and knew that if he had one grain of fight left in him, he would have shooed her away. He didn't. She could feel him starting to shake. "Agari, can we get a blanket?"

"I'll look!" the burly soldier answered, turning back towards the rear of the craft.

Turning to face the loadmaster and looking her dead in the eyes, Van shouted, "This is serious! We've got to get him on the ground and into an ambulance quickly! If this is what I think it is, we don't have a tick to spare; his insides are ripping open! We've got to speed up – he's going into shock! If we take too long …"

The loadmaster nodded and pressed the control on her helmet. "Cap! We've got a serious medical concern back here! One adult male, bad abdominal pains and signs of shock; might have internal injuries! We're going to have to pick up the pace and get down there as quick as we can! Yes, declare a medical and get an evac unit ready for us when we land."

"Hang on, Arnat! We'll get you down. We'll get you help," Van comforted, rubbing his quaking back as Agari threw a rough blanket across him.

In the headmaster's office of the secondary school that was now acting as their command center, Theo called Tedarri over to the military TransCom they were monitoring. "Boss, I think you'll want to hear this."

"What's up?"

"HVR Six One to Control." The voice that came through the speaker was obviously from one of the flyers, based on the engine sounds ramping up in the background.

"Control, go ahead," the air controllers down the hall replied.

"Control, this is HVR Six One; we're declaring a medical emergency. End."

"HVR Six One, understand you are declaring a medical emergency, please specify. End."

"One adult male, severe abdominal pain, possible internal injuries with signs of shock. Request clearance to increase speed to four five zero with rapid descent and landing. End."

There was a slight pause as the air controllers checked their boards. "HVR Six One, increase speed to four five zero. You have a clear pattern ahead, rapid descent and landing procedures are authorized. End."

"Control, this is HVR Six One. Acknowledge four five zero, clear pattern, RDL authorized. Request you have medical evacuation at LZ for immediate transfer to hospital. End."

"Understood, Six One. Local authorities are monitoring and will coordinate. End."

Theo looked up at Tedarri. "Can you get an ambulance here? I don't think we're going to need triage on this one."

"I've got two on stand-by. Can you meet them at the front and show them where to go?"

"Sure. Give me one of those flashers and tell them I have it, will you? It'll make me easier to spot," Theo requested as he stood, pointing to a table beside the Lupar.

Tedarri reached over and tossed him the cylindrical device. "There you go!" He then called out the doorway, "Ace, get in here and monitor the TransComs; I've got to send Theo out for an ambulance." With that, Theo nodded and was out the door heading to the front of the school. As Tedarri popped open his communicator and dialed the EMC, the Perratti from the adjoining office came in and took over.

As Theo jogged down the hall, one of the soldiers yelled from a far doorway, "Hey, did you guys hear about the medical emergency?! Marshall wants to make sure you did!"

"We've got it! We'll meet you on the right side of the field with an ambulance!" Theo shouted back and got a high sign from the soldier. Shoving his way through the door into the cold gray afternoon, he saw the ambulance moving fast down the road to meet him.

Moments later, Theo stood beside Marshall Terrat, two other soldiers, and the medics a few dozen tracks from the waiting ambulance, its back doors wide open. As the HVR-17 appeared above them and started to quickly descend, Terrat shouted, "Wait for the engine sounds to drop, and then haul tail to the ship's right forward hatch! All of the other evacuees are coming out the back, but we're going right to where they have the patient. We'll escort you and keep you safe. Stay with us! Got it?"

"Got it." They all acknowledged in some fashion.

"Glad you're here Theo! Didn't know you had a medical background?"

"Picked it up on another job travelling with a doctor. She was a specialist in internal medicine."

Terrat nodded, replacing a suggestive comment he would have said in other circumstances with a slight smile. Looking to the flyer, he recognized its readiness to land. "Alright, let's go!"

Van was trembling, but she was still holding fast to the stretcher with one paw, and rubbing the back of a largely placid Arnat with the other. Everything she feared about flying had been poured into the last few passes: the noises, the drops that send your stomach halfway up your throat, and the feeling that the craft you're flying in is actually out of control and spiraling to the ground. Agari was helping to keep Arnat on the stretcher largely by holding under his arm pit where the straps had been loosened.

The loadmaster had gone to the other side of the partition to explain what was happening to the frightened group of evacuees. Now, she stuck her head back around it to yell, "Ten ticks to touchdown! Hang on; we're almost there!"

"Won't be long now, Arnat," Van reassured. "You feeling any better?"

"Yes, some," he replied weakly, and even though it was hard to hear his voice over all the noise, there was no mistaking the tone of utter humiliation and defeat wrapped around the two simple words that followed. "Thank you."

The entire cargo bay resonated with loud popping and whirring noises. Agari explained, "That's the landing struts!" Less than two ticks later, a strong shake and a feeling of downward motion abruptly stopping prompted Agari to say, "And that's the ground! We're down!" Agari jumped up and ran to the hatch at ship's right. Vanarra's legs ached from keeping her odd position for so long, and it took her a moment to stand. Soon, however, she searched for and found the releases for the stretcher, just as a blast of fresh air and natural light flooded into the compartment from the opening hatch.

Agari turned around and nodded at Van's efficiency. "Perfect, let's go!" They carefully lifted the stretcher and walked it the short distance to the hatch, squatted down, and fed it out carefully to the pair of medics waiting just below.

"Get him down on the ground so I can check. Careful now! No jarring," ordered a Nephti with a voice that sounded familiar to Van. The two medics holding the stretcher obeyed. After a moment or two of quiet questions and placing his ear to Arnat's midsection, the Nephti raised his head and said, "Acute bowel obstruction. Probably some tearing already. It's safe to transport him, but get him right into the operating room with your best gastro-doc as soon as you get there. No delays; no paperwork! You don't have a moment to lose; now get going!" The medics took up the stretcher at the Nephti's command and quickly moved towards the waiting ambulance.

Van's eyes drifted back towards the Nephti, and she gave him a quick yet thorough appraisal as he watched the medics load Arnat into the waiting ambulance. A slight smile crossed her muzzle until a cough from nearby got her attention. It was only then that Van noticed the big Lupar bedecked with rank standing to the right of that rather keen looking Nephti. "Take the other two out through the back," the Lupar ordered, his eyes fixed on Agari standing just to her right side. "That will put you closer to where the rest of the docs are. Do you need help with the other stretchers?"

"Just one of the two, Marshall," Agari answered. "We've got the other one."

"I'll help," the Nephti offered turning towards Van and smiling before reaching for the ladder release under the hatchway.

The Marshall agreed, "Alright. You," he added, tapping one of the two soldiers beside him, "jump in there, as well. I want this flyer back in the air in no more than ten passes! You there!"

Van was startled because the Marshall was now looking straight at her. "Yes, sir?"

"You Vanarra Anasto?"

She nodded and said, "Yes, sir."

"Soldiers! Salute!" With that, all of the military soldiers, even Agari, turned and saluted her, paws up, claws sheathed. Embarrassed and uncertain, she returned the gesture as best she could, and then they lowered the salute. "You did one heck of a job up there, ma'am! Drop by my command center when you get the chance!"

"Thank you, Marshall. I will." As he turned away, she turned back to Myra, who, propped up on her elbows, had been watching everything transpire with a rather sentimental looking smile. "You alright, darling?" Van asked concerned, walking back over to her. "Oh, no. The chest straps slipped! I'm sorry to leave you like that, but Arnat he—"

"It's alright. It's alright. You did the right thing," she responded in a whisper, and Van helped the elderly Faelnar gently ease herself back down.

"I'm afraid you had a rough flight, too." It was then that Van noticed Agari, standing on the other side of the bay with an odd look on his face, like he had seen someone he knew but couldn't remember their name.

By this time, the Nephti was in the flyer with them, and he introduced himself. "Vanarra Anasto, so very nice to meet you! I'm Theo de Allarrae."

"Theo!" she burst out ecstatically, and she gave him a giant, enthusiastic hug, which he happily returned, laughing. "Oh, it's so good to see you, finally, and you're every bit as cute as I thought you'd be!"

"Hey, now! Don't you get me into trouble!" he warned with a smile, as they released.

"Oh, no! I want to get you a *date*, with Sahnassa! You'll have to get into trouble all on your own!"

He laughed heartily at her forwardness. "Every bit as charming and lovely as I thought you'd be," he offered kindly, but then he gave her an appraising eye. "Hmm ... not too much the worse for wear, either. Now, I think we can start moving out of here. Mind if I help you?"

"No problem. That okay with you, Agari?"

"Yeah ... oh yeah, sure. We'll get this one." Van was curious. Agari was clearly distracted, but she couldn't place why.

Van motioned to Myra, and said, "Now, Theo, let me introduce you to the lovely one you'll be carrying. Myra, meet Theo! Theo, this is Myra!"

"My *honored* pleasure." Theo smiled at her and bowed. Seeing the loadmaster stick her head around the partition out of the corner of his eye, Theo turned right to her and asked, "You ready for us?"

A little stunned by his quick change of focus, the loadmaster managed, "Uh ... yes. They're almost all out."

"Then we'll be right behind them," Theo asserted, motioning Van to take her place at the head of the stretcher. He expertly released the straps and locks, took his end and directed, "Lift. Now shift off the rails. Very good. Let's go!"

A few short moments later, they were walking down the ramp. It wasn't until Van's hind paws touched the dry grass of the field that it really hit home. She was safe. Looking at the groups being herded into the school ahead of her, she could easily see and hear their relief. Some wept; some jumped up and down. Some knelt for a moment with their paws raised skyward, and others just walked close together paw-in-paw. The sight of this caused tears to stream out of Vanarra's eyes and down her cheek fur. Seeming to sense her emotions, Theo observed, "You can almost see the joy shining right out from them, like it was a light. It's incredible, Van, isn't it?"

"Yeah," Vanarra sniffed and swallowed.

"Just wait until you see what your hard work has helped to bring all these Thurians." Van wanted to speak, but her emotions were so overwhelming, she just couldn't.

Smiling volunteers who looked to be from the local fire suppression squad opened the doors and directed them into the warm school building. Other volunteers led them down the hallway towards a triage unit that had been set up in one of the small classrooms. Someone opened a door for them, and a full team of nurses came out and took the stretcher. "We'll take good care of her," one of them said. "The doctor will be in as soon as he's finished looking at the burn case."

"Can I say goodbye?" Vanarra asked, still a little teary eyed.

"Sure. Just a moment." Vanarra and Theo watched from the doorway as they worked around Myra, taking vitals and making sure she was comfortable. "Okay, you can come in now." They both walked in to see the elder Faelnar comfortably resting on a hospital bed which had been brought to the school. The Lupar nurse admonished them, "Please keep your visit short; the doctor will be here in a moment."

They walked up to Myra, and she smiled up at them. "This is so nice," she said in a whisper.

"You going to be okay?" Van asked, taking her paw.

"I will; I'm sure of it. Thank you ever so much. Please, come back to see me later?" For a moment, they stopped talking as the sound of thruster noise outside alerted them to the departure of the flyer.

"I'll do that. You get some rest and feel better, okay?" Vanarra bade, wishing she could stay just a little while longer.

"I will, and thank you for everything, dear." Van hugged Myra gently and then turned to leave. Vanarra exited first, affording Theo a moment to look back into the elder Faelnar's face and wink. Amyra had to wonder if she had been recognized.

Less than a pass later, she knew she truly was. One of her young matrons burst into the room carrying a pink envelope; the young Faelnar looked terrified and confused and worried. She had obviously received the note that had been secreted with one of the other passengers. For a moment, Amyra thought she'd have to share her new bed when this one fell unconscious on the floor. "Don't be afraid my dear," she said in a clear voice. "I'm not in death's claws just yet."

After spending some time in a real bathroom, Van emerged into the hallway of the school to see Theo chatting with a young female Perratti. "Yes, and make sure each evacuee has food and drink in their paws *before* they step onto the charter out of here, understood?" As the young female nodded and dashed away, Theo explained, "One of the many volunteers who rode the transports up here. Are you feeling a little better now?"

"It's been a sol since I've seen a real bathroom. That was nice, although I could still use a shower."

"You're fine," he assured her, smiling. "Now, would you like to look at everything you helped put together?" Gallantly, he offered her his arm, and a little bemused, she took it. As they started to walk down the long hallway, he explained, "It's not only young volunteers like that kit who came. Several ranked females from various families are here, as well. News of your little rescue convoy spread rather quickly and drew quite a crowd of Thurians and organizations willing to help."

"Did anyone from my company come with them?" she asked.

"They were going to, but no. There was more than enough help, titled or otherwise, and they actually had a couple of events crucial to your business they wanted to make sure happened. The last thing they wanted was for your business to suffer during all of this."

Vanarra was somewhere between grateful and furious. "But … but how are they paying for it? There's nothing left!"

"Well, that's exactly it. They're paying for it, out of their own pockets – well with a generous donation from an interested party." They turned a corner and approached a long line of Thurian evacuees. "Your employees really care about you, you know?"

"I know, but to risk their own money," she said, shaking her head. "Who made the donation?"

"Ah, now here is the first station – medical," Theo responded, clearly deciding not to answer her. She looked and saw several doctors and nurses talking to families, giving them various medicines, and answering questions. "The local hospitals of three cities in the valley contributed to this." They walked past more of the waiting evacuees into another hallway. "Now, here are the gymnasium restrooms – they can accommodate a lot quickly, so it just seemed to make sense. The entire custodial staff of the school piled into an all-terrain hovercraft just to come here and keep these clean."

As they walked further down the long line, they saw the young female volunteer with several others giving each evacuee a large bag. "Now, here is obviously where they get food and drink. Everyone!" Theo announced in a loud voice, getting their attention. "This is Vanarra Anasto. It was her company that provided all of this good food; isn't there something you'd like to say?"

A grateful cheer and applause came from the group within earshot, and Vanarra wanted to just die. She ducked her head, smiling, and said quietly, "I'm going to get you for this, Theo!"

"Highly doubtful," he shot back in a whisper. "Now, wave and say you're welcome, and we'll move on."

She did, albeit under duress, and then they walked ahead. "And here, a little further down, is the special needs station. All of the diapers, formula, medicine, and so forth you so thoughtfully provided are being distributed here. Everyone! This is Vanarra Anasto! She made sure you would have all of these wonderful things. Isn't that nice? Isn't there something you would like to say?" All but one Faelnar family cheered and yelled "Thank you" many times over.

As Vanarra meekly accepted their gratitude, she felt like strangling Theo. As he led her down the hallway towards the front of the school, she grabbed his arm hard – finding it surprisingly muscular. In a whispered growl, she demanded, "Will you *please* stop doing that?"

Without a flinch or any other indication of how hard she had grabbed him, he airily said, "I don't have a choice, now do I? No one else has made it this far, yet."

"Are you always this—"

The words she couldn't find, he did. "Am I always this intent on making sure that someone who did so much for so many, despite their lack of title or family or breeding, gets a little bit of face-to-face recognition? Oh, in a word, yes!"

Again, she was almost growling at him. "It isn't recognition I did this for!"

Now that they were out of earshot of everyone else, he stopped and faced her. Theo's manner and tone had become quite serious. "No, but the recognition is coming no matter what, my dear Van, and you've got to think about how to manage it. You can't just shrink back, hide, and pretend this never happened; you know that, don't you?"

Van dropped her gaze and only now, released his arm. "I know," she answered quietly. "I've been trying not to think about it; I don't like some of the thoughts I'm having. I mean, I've been a little shameless, from time to time, in promoting my business or … flirting with someone, but I … I don't know what to do with this. It seems … too important for that. What my instincts tell me to do, I mean."

Theo agreed. "You're dead right on that score! A lot of those smiling, thankful faces, even the ones that weren't so thankful, would be frozen corpses in a paw-full of intervals had things gone differently. Now, think about how much pain and grief comes from losing someone you love. Multiply that, conservatively, a thousand fold. That's the misery you have saved not only these, but their communities, their friends, their children, their mothers, their fathers … and their matrons, dames, and matriarchs."

Theo gently lifted her muzzle until it was level with his own and looked her in the eye. "Once the evacuees are back home, everyone I just named will have time to think of all they might have lost. Parents will look into the eyes of their children and see in loving horror what might have been, and then they'll think of you. Children will hear stories of how Vanarra and Sahnassa brought help to hundreds even though they were marooned on the side of a mountain. Whole houses will know you two saved the lives of their matrons, their dames, and their matriarchs. Are you ready to cope with that level of gratitude, that level of admiration, that level of ... *hero worship*?" The stunned look in her eyes spoke volumes. "I thought not. Becoming a hero can truly ruin your life, Vanarra."

"I ... I need to sit down," Vanarra said weakly. Theo ushered her into the teachers' lounge, sat her down on a soft couch, and brought her a cup of water from the nearby dispenser. She drank it as another pair of flyers made their presence known overhead. As the sound faded, she looked up at him helplessly. "Oh, mange, Theo! You're right. I didn't want to think about it like that, but ... oh Theo, what do I do?"

"Consider this piece of wisdom," he offered, and then repeated a quote from memory.

Would you call me a hero? This frail and failing soul that sins and schemes and sleeps as any other? Try to call me a hero, and I will lift up all those upon whose shoulders you would dare place me; I will call them by name and laud them with honor. If you believe, still, what I have done to be the work of a hero, remember me not for any exceptional skill, quality of spirit, or righteousness. Remember one who simply acted with all of these others standing beside me. Do nothing to honor me, but honor us all by acting when your time comes. Prepare for it, expect it, and it will come. Heroes are only for a moment, then they once again are what they never ceased being – one of us.

He gave that a moment to sink in. "Rahnahi de Dothnar, book six, chapter three, *Reflections on the Hero Matriarch*. Written in honor of Amyra de Gonari, unless I'm much mistaken. They are good words to hear, to think about, and to repeat ... or paraphrase ... or live out. That's how to deal with what's coming, Van. For both you and Sahnassa." He sat down on the couch opposite of her.

She shook her head, pleading, "I ... I need more, Theo. I need something plain, step-by-step, simple! What do I do, for example, when someone does what you just did?"

He leaned forward and held her paws in his. "With real humility and grace, accept and give thanks for a reasonable compliment. If it's unreasonable, gently correct it, but still be grateful to the speaker. The compliment is a gift; be gracious and polite. Then, and this is the most important part, acknowledge what they have done that deserves praise. A young mother is brave because she kept her children's hope alive when her own was failing. An old bureaucrat is generous because he offered his talents where they were sorely needed to manage food. A young cub with a bag of diapers in his paw is merciful when he gives that as a gift to someone who really needs it. They're none of them heroes, but all of them are good, just like you. Everyone loves heroes because we all want to be one. We only start tearing them down when we think we never will. When you take their admiration, acknowledge it as a gift, and then give it back, you're not a hero any more. You're a friend! That's far better, and that's something you can live with."

He released her paws, giving her a thoughtful look, and spoke his next words slowly. "Here's a moment to practice. Can you think of anyone to whom you would least like to give credit, but in your heart, you know deserves just a little?"

She thought for a moment and grudgingly admitted, "Arnat de Gonari."

"And if he were to proclaim you a hero, what could you say about him in return?"

Vanarra was thinking hard, brow furrowed, and still trying to keep down her anger. "He may be a self-serving pain in the tail, but at least he had the sense to keep his PawLink on. Without him, it may have been intervals before we were able to talk to the Meeting Den." She looked into Theo's strangely wise eyes as the light dawned inside of her. "And he told me the truth, even when he didn't have to."

He nodded back at her. "Yep. That small bit of empathy can change everything. Now, if you were speaking to him directly I might expect you to be a little … gentler, but still you're getting the idea. Now, do you think you could do it for real?" Van nodded, and Theo took her by the paw, guiding her out of the lounge.

"Where are we going?"

"To the front of the school. All of the drivers and a small group of starry-eyed teen volunteers from the local orphanage are waiting there for the evacuees."

"You've got to be kidding!"

"It's time to think on your hind legs! Come on! You can do this," he stated in such a confident tone that she truly started to think she could. Still, Van's mind was racing as the door opened in front of her, and she stepped through.

A teenaged Vulpi saw her first and asked shyly, "Are … are you one of the other volunteers?"

"No, sweetie," she answered gently, "I'm one of the ones they brought down from the mountain."

His eyes went wide, and he turned to the rest of the group and yelled excitedly, "They're here! They're here!" Suddenly, the group that had been talking over warm drinks was all staring at her.

One of the older drivers asked kindly, "Ma'am, didn't they give you any food inside?" Then, he saw Theo step out from behind her. "Oh, Theo, is she with you?"

"Yes, she is. Please, allow me the honor of introducing Vanarra Anasto. She is one of the two I told you about earlier."

There was an awed silence, and the driver who had spoken first placed his drink on the top of a flat trash bin. Looking at her, smiling, he started clapping. The others followed suit - enthusiastically. More than a little embarrassed, Van nodded and smiled at them. After a moment or two she raised her paws to silence them.

"Thank you; you're so very kind! Now, on behalf of everyone coming off that mountain, please let me thank all of you! When those Thurians who thought they were going to freeze or starve to death get a bag of food from you or see your nice, warm transport waiting to take them home, it will just be the most amazing gift they've ever received! You're really doing such a wonderful thing, and you are all going to make a huge difference in their lives tonight. You know, they'll probably remember your kind face, your vehicle, and that bag of food for the rest of their lives! So again, on behalf of all of us you're going to help tonight, thank you! You're our heroes." With that, she applauded them, and they in return, smiling broadly, joined her.

Theo whispered in her ear, "Well done, Van." Then, he said louder for the group, "Alright, it's time! Your first group of families is just a few ticks from that door. Let's get them loaded as safely and quickly as we can. Good chance to you, and like Vanarra said, great job!"

The doors behind them opened, and the faces of the first timid Faelnar family, holding two small children, neither more than three seasons old, appeared hesitantly in the doorway. "It's okay. You're in the right place," the skinny young Vulpi said. "Here, can I help you to the transport?" Taking bags of food from them, he walked them to the door of the vehicle that the driver was now opening.

"Come on in! You can change the little ones on the back seat if you need to. We're going to keep that one clear if we can." The driver patted the mother on the back and offered her a paw as she stepped up.

"Oh, bless you, bless you!" the mother said to the driver and the young volunteer, her tear-stained cheek fur again tracked by tears of joy and relief. "Bless you all!" she cried, turning back to the group.

"Yes, thank you, so much," the father managed – voice breaking – before turning back to board the transport.

Theo had his arm around Vanarra at the shoulder and gave her a gentle hug. "You see? You said it, and it's true. They'll always remember the face of everyone who helps them tonight."

"I … I just got so choked up looking at her. The mother—" Everything about her own mother's struggles and painful death rushed back into her thoughts. Van felt herself emotionally unraveling, but quietly managed, "Theo, can we please go back inside … another way?"

Seeming to sense her distress almost immediately, he quietly agreed. "Yes. Let's go." Theo took her at the shoulder and gently walked her towards the doors at the other end of the covered porch. He guided her through and into a quiet hallway. "Are you going to be alright, Vanarra?"

"It's … it's just been so much, so quickly – too much. There's a lot in my past not many know about." She was struggling, unsuccessfully, to keep her tears in check. "This brings it all back!" She leaned forward into him seeking his comfort, feeling no hesitation for some strange reason, although some part of her knew there should be.

He slowly wrapped his arms around her and embraced her gently, and then her tears and sobs came full force. As the emotional release washed over her, Van wondered if this was what it felt like to have a father. Unlike others in her past, he said nothing; he didn't try to console or fix her. He simply held her, patted her back gently, and let his presence comfort her.

After a few passes, Vanarra was spent and breathing quietly. Slowly reawakening to Theo's patient presence, she whispered, "Thank you."

"You're welcome. After everything that's happened, you are entitled, and believe me when I say, I do understand a little. My past is a secret to almost everyone I've ever met. Not everything that's happened to me is something I can talk about. Very few would understand."

Van looked up into his eyes, and she saw a little sadness in his gentle expression. "It makes it hard sometimes, doesn't it?"

He nodded. "We're stronger for it. After all, what choice do we have?" She leaned into him again, and nodded. "You know, we could arrange to get you out of here. There are a few seats on the last transport that aren't–"

She pulled away from him immediately and exclaimed, "Oh, no! I'm not going to do that! I'm going back up there and help Sahni! I'm not going to have any kind of peace until she's down here and safe – until they all are."

Bracing herself for an argument, she was relieved to see him smile and give her a simple nod of agreement. "Very well. Now, there's a bathroom right over there. Why don't you go get cleaned up, and then go to the cafeteria for a hot meal – and no, that is NOT an arguable point. Then, we'll get you back up there."

"Hey," Agari's voice boomed from the end of the hallway. "Is everything alright here?" His words were a warning, if not a threat, directed at Theo, and that was evident in his eyes and manner as he quickly strode up.

"It's okay, Agari, really! Theo was being very kind to me. Now, I'll be back in a tick. I'm going to go clean up."

When the restroom door had shut behind her, Theo said to Agari, "You're doing a good job watching over her. Thank you."

It took a moment for Agari to register the import of that comment. "It was you?"

"Yes. I asked the Chief to detail someone he could trust to protect her. Vanarra is very important," Theo asserted firmly.

"It certainly appears so," Agari offered, but then looked as if he regretted saying anything - as one accidently betraying a confidence.

"Well, so now you've got *two* good reasons to keep an eye on her." Theo turned to smile at Agari's stunned expression. "Don't ask how I know. Just stay with her. She wants to go back up the mountain and help out. Can you get her to the cafeteria and get both of you some warm chow, while I make the arrangements? When I've got everything set, I'll come and get you."

"Are you sure they need us; that they'll let us back up? I mean the point is to get everyone off the mountain, right?" Agari asked, unsure.

"Very true, and I'd be the first to concede there's no logical reason for her to go back up there – that we know of right now. However, after everything Vanarra and Sahnassa have managed to do, I think these two deserve a little leeway. Besides, they've already proved far more useful than your average civilian. That's something I think both Tedarri and Terrat can grasp."

"We'll see. Ah, here she is." A much more composed Vanarra walked over to them.

"You didn't like hurt him or anything?" she asked Agari, in mock sternness.

"Only a mild beating," Theo replied on his behalf, smirking. "Hey, Agari's taking you to get some food, and I'm going to see about your ride. I'll meet back up with you in the cafeteria. Alright?"

"Okay and … thank you." She gently kissed the side of his muzzle.

"You're very welcome. Now, off with you two. I'll be along in a little while."

Less than half an interval later, Vanarra was standing quietly at the grassy edge of the school's landing zone, looking up into the dark gray sky, waiting for the next flyer to land. The worry that something might happen to Sahnassa while she was away made her tail swish back and forth impatiently. Van also thought about all of the children and families she had seen pouring through the school – how tired and worn they all looked. "What about the rest of them? Is everything still going okay?" she silently wondered. She also wondered about Amyra, the matriarch, and what she would be like and if she had already been brought down or not. Absent mindedly, Van found herself rubbing the center of her chest as if expecting to find an object there.

"Missing something?" Agari asked, noticing her preoccupation.

Vanarra stopped and smiled at him. "A locket. I left it with one of your dames, to keep it safe. I couldn't stand the thought of losing it, now that we're going back…" and she pointed up to complete the sentence.

"Probably a good idea," Agari said thoughtfully, matching her gaze. "I have to admit I'm surprised they're letting us back up there."

Vanarra shook her head, looking into the gray sky. "I'm grateful they are. It's killing me being down here and not knowing what's happening to all of them."

"Your good friend Theo must be pretty persuasive," he observed, his statement obvious cover for his curiosity about the mysterious Nephti.

Van shrugged, answering, "You know, as for Theo, he's really not my friend – more of a recent acquaintance. I just met him, but it's odd. He's been so kind to me. It's like we're—"

"Kindred spirits?"

She thought about that for a moment, but the words didn't seem a perfect fit. "Perhaps. It's more like he's a relative or part of a family I didn't know I had. Just like what you're doing; he's watching out for me. Sahnassa did that, too, when we were stuck up there. Thurians like me don't get that very much. I don't know what I've done to deserve it, but still I'm thankful for it, for all of you."

"It's good duty, and I'm happy to do it, ma'am," he said, matching her skyward gaze, his smile genuinely kind. The whine of engines high above them signaled the next flyer's approach.

"Only two more times, only two more times," Van chanted quietly through gritted teeth.

"Ma'am?" Agari asked, looking back at her again.

"I only have to ride one of these things two more times, and then I'll be done," Van explained, closing her eyes in fearful resignation.

"Aw, come on!" he teased, "You did really well last time. You looked like you were a real pro up there!"

She smiled nervously and chuckled, "Thank you! I must be doing an excellent job pretending I'm not absolutely scared to death!" They both laughed, and then all speech was drowned out by the final descent of the big flyer. As before, at almost the exact moment of touchdown, the ramp lowered. As they walked forward, Van started to see tired Thurians stream out of the back of the vehicle onto the cold ground below, all visibly grateful for being rescued. Van and Agari waited a few steps away as the evacuees were directed into the school by eager volunteers who had also emerged at the flyer's arrival.

As the last few walked down the ramp, Van and Agari walked up, only to face the Vulpi loadmaster from their first flight. "What the – Fillie, not you again!" Agari complained, almost swearing.

With a very self-satisfied smile, the female Vulpi asked, "Agari, when are you going to realize you can't escape from me? Hey, the marshal said you'd be making one more round trip. Wait here, and we'll go up to the front." She was obviously watching to see when the last group was clear of the thruster down-blast zone.

"Do you know how the evacuation is going?" Vanarra asked her.

"We've got about a third off the mountain, mostly families, the sick, and the elderly. But the weather up there is in serious danger of going to crap. This could get a lot harder. Ah, there we are." Fillie pressed a button on her headset. "Cap, we're clear." She pressed the ramp control as she listened to his response, and Vanarra grasped for the metal bars holding the seats in place as she heard the engines power up again. With near horror, she felt the craft move and saw the ground disappearing beneath them through the slowly closing doorway. "Let's go forward," the Vulpi shouted. "It's more comfortable up there!" With great effort, Vanarra led the way through the rows of seats back to the front.

"Only two more times," she told herself. The rocking motion was disconcerting enough, but the feeling of the floor dropping out from under her made Vanarra yelp in surprise.

The loadmaster, following right behind, yelled over the engine noise, "Sorry about that! We're starting to get more of that as the weather gets worse!"

"How about I just sit here?" Vanarra asked loudly, voice breaking.

"Suits me! You're getting off when we land, right?"

"That's the plan," Agari answered from behind them.

"Yeah. Go ahead and sit here! You can get to the ramp quicker!" Fillie directed her, gently guiding Van into a seat. Vanarra was unspeakably grateful to sit down and strap in, but as the loadmaster settled into a seat across the row, Agari looked like he was going to try to ride it out standing up. The loadmaster's scowl showed she would have none of that. "You, too, Broke Tail! We'll get our back-sides bounced around pretty good when we get up to altitude! I don't want to have to think up a new name for you, like busted butt!"

Grimacing again at the nick-name, Agari sat down and strapped in. "How bad is the turbulence at the mountain LZ?"

"It's not bad so far! We've got five waves landed and—" She seemed distracted as she listened to the TransCom chatter in her helmet. "Yes, and we now have five in the air. The last one left just now. They're all reporting smooth air getting into and out of the LZ, but the ride up to altitude is definitely getting rougher!" A small bounce punctuated her statement. "Good news is, I think we'll be the ones taking off with the last of the families! So only the adults are going to have to live with a rough ride!"

As a jarring lift and drop shook the whole craft, Vanarra could only manage, "That's good, I guess!" Van knew that if there was more conversation, the nausea that was starting to suggest itself to her might actually take hold. She closed her eyes and thought, "Only one more time. Only one more time."

Chapter 14: Clarity in Service

For the fifth time, Sahnassa stood at the head of a large group of children and families walking down the path towards the athletic field. This was the last with children, and about half of this group was adults. However, it did include someone she was pleased to "meet." Walking behind her was Leoniry de Nestanum, the older Nephti business owner she and Theo met when visiting the Meeting Den before the quake. He, like several others, had been judged as not tolerating the cold very well, perhaps because the cold was now truly making itself felt. She could swear it was already freezing, and the light, variable wind did nothing to improve matters.

Regardless how cold she was on the outside, Sahnassa felt like she was warmly glowing on the inside. All of the children looked at her with a sense of awe, respect, and affection. Even the de Caterra families were friendly and grateful. She had hugged and comforted more than a hundred children in the last few intervals, she guessed. Sahnassa found it very hard to think about so many of those beautiful young faces in such dire peril. "Oh Theo, thank you!" she whispered to herself as she watched the HVR-17 descend from the darkening sky.

Again, it settled slowly down, but unlike the three HVR-17's that had landed previously, the ramp doors started opening before the craft had even touched down, and Sahni saw the loadmaster riding the ramp down as before. She immediately knew it was the one who had her sprinting away after the first airlift. Smiling, she called back to Saletta, "Let's get moving!" With a few quick gestures and encouragements, Sahni easily had the group following her, moving in good order. As they approached the ramp, she got an even better surprise. Looking a little out of sorts, but well nonetheless, Vanarra stood with Agari holding her arm. "Hi there! Are you okay?"

Vanarra shouted back. "I still don't like flying ... even more, but yes! Are you going down with this load?"

"I'm staying until the last transport," she said, walking up the ramp. "They still need lots of help."

"You heard her, Agari! If she's staying, I'm staying, too! Let's go," Vanarra ordered, starting to move down the ramp.

"Hey, before that, can you help me get them strapped in, please?" Sahnassa asked, touching her friend's arm.

Vanarra nodded, smiling. "Sure, just so long as I don't have to ride in one of these things again for a few passes."

As the evacuees walked into the flyer's cargo bay, the loadmaster counted everyone into rows. Sahni, Van, Saletta, and Agari went up and down the aisles, helping the nervous group get strapped into their seats. Amused, Van watched as a young Perratti cub carefully closed the buckle on his safety strap, pulled it tight, and then looked back up at her with an adorably proud smile. She nodded approvingly, unable to keep herself from ruffling the fur on his head, which made him giggle. "Good job, sport!"

However, when Vanarra moved to the next seat in line, she was halted by a female's paw thrust forbiddingly in her way, preventing her from helping a young, frightened Faelnar kit. Looking up, she saw the stern yellow eyes of the mother, and around her neck, the family crest of the de Caterra.

"I'll get that one," Agari offered, seeing her dilemma.

"Suit yourself," Van huffed as she moved several seats down to the next family. "May I help you strap in?" she asked a young Nephti female, just out of her teens, who had her head down and was fumbling nervously with the straps.

"P-p-please. I hate flying," admitted the young female, who then stared up into Van's reddish-brown face and golden eyes with an expression of both surprise and dismay.

Looking carefully into the Nephti's silvery-grey eyes, Van could see real terror, and she pushed past her own feelings of rejection. "Hey, don't worry so. It may be a little bumpy, but you're going to a really nice place! I just got back from having a look around down there." Vanarra made a show of checking the straps while the Nephti's arms were spread apart; whether she was trying to give Van access or keep from touching an Anati, Van couldn't tell. "What's your name?"

"Alatta … de Orturu." The Nephti's response betrayed the traditional discomfort purebreds seemed to have around those of her kind, but given Alatta's obvious fears, Van let it slide.

Gently tugging the straps tight, she answered, "I'm Vanarra Anasto, nice to meet you. Hey, are you from Sahni's, I mean Sahnassa's, family?"

Embarrassed by the realization that this was the very same "Anati" from Sahnassa's speech, Alatta immediately dropped any pretense of restraint or distance. "Oh, yes, I am! We're distant relations, though. I … I don't think I've ever met her before, honestly, but I'm really impressed." Alatta wriggled a little under the straps. "Are you sure they're okay?"

Vanarra nodded, smiling. "They'll be fine, and so will you. Sorry if they're a bit snug, kit. As I said, it's a little bouncy up there right now, but at least it's a short flight. You'll soon be on the ground, toasty warm and well fed. That's a nice thought, huh?"

"The best!" Alatta answered, smiling up at her in genuine gratitude. "Thank you, for everything."

Seeing the de Caterra male beside Alatta look positively ill at the Nephti's friendly interaction with her was truly the best revenge. "You are so very welcome, Alatta! Take care."

In a few passes, Sahnassa, Vanarra, Agari, and Saletta were all gasping for breath at the edge of the field, watching the HVR-17's bulk disappear into the clouds.

"She certainly believes in promptness!" Saletta observed, trying to put what she really felt in the kindest possible terms.

"And seeing us run like frightened kits and cubs," Agari complained, grimly. "I think she gets a kick out of it."

"She certainly gets the job done," Vanarra interjected, her respect for the loadmaster undiminished.

"Yep, she does at that," Sahnassa admitted, smiling. "Now, that's all the children, right?"

"Yes," Saletta answered, finally starting to breathe normally but also starting to shiver because of the cold.

"Let's get back under cover," Agari suggested, and no one had any objection.

"Been keeping busy, I see," Van said to Sahni as she reached over and grasped her paw.

"I've really enjoyed it. The families are just so grateful. Did you have a look around in the valley?"

"Oh, yes. They're set up very well. The first transport pulled out while I was there, and the second was nearly loaded. They've got food and doctors and – well, we had an incident on the way down I'll have to tell you about later. Oh, and I got to meet Theo!" Van exclaimed brightly.

"What's he like?" Sahnassa asked, a light smile touching her muzzle.

Vanarra bit her lower lip and smiled broadly. "He met us when we landed, showed me all around. I really liked him, Sahni. He was so very kind and understanding. Oh, and he's very nice looking – pretty blue eyes, athletic build, really quite keen!" She leaned over to Sahnassa and whispered loudly, "Nice, and I do mean a really nice butt!"

"Alright, you two," Agari grumbled, sounding much aggrieved.

"Who are you talking about?" Saletta asked with barely contained interest. The rest of them couldn't help but laugh at her question as they entered the laundry room. The next group of evacuees was filing in from the other direction, mostly older business owners with some companions.

The Chief strode up alongside them, shouting instructions. "All of you coming in, move all the way down, and fill up every seat! Each seat in here is a seat in the flyer, so make sure they are all full!" As the tired group meekly complied to the Chief's satisfaction, he walked back over to them. "Sahnassa, Korick told me what you've been doing in here for the children and their families. That's great, but I think my soldiers can take care of the rest of this lot. Vanarra, you too. I got word from Theo on what you've been up to. Did you like what you saw? Did our soldiers impress you?"

"They're the best, Chief! I have to say, though, you've got one loadmaster who is just amazing! Agari and I have ridden with her twice now."

The Chief looked to Agari, who shamefacedly admitted, "It's Fillie, Chief."

The mischievous twinkle in his eyes and momentary pause told Vanarra all she needed to know. Innocently she queried, "Does this explain the whole 'Broke Tail' thing?"

With that, the Chief burst into laughter while Agari moaned. When Tawnston recovered enough to speak, he exclaimed, "Mange Agari! If you ever run into good luck, would you kindly ask what you did to piss it off? Ma'am, I hope I haven't saddled you with a hopeless bad luck charm! So you rode on her ship twice, eh, Agari? Twice? And do you still have all your parts?"

"Yes, Chief," Agari answered in the tone of someone who knew he just had to tolerate the teasing.

"Now, now," Vanarra cut in. "Agari's been an enormous help, and he's done a great job keeping an eye on me."

"Well, carry on, then," the Chief said with a smile, still chuckling. "I've got word the Grand Matriarch in charge would like a word with you two. Especially Vanarra, since you've been down to the schools."

"I received that word, as well," Saletta agreed.

"Great. We'll catch up with you in a little while and–"

Korick's booming voice echoed from the far end of the room. "Chief! Next two flyers are on final! We need to move this group out now!"

"Alright Air Sergeant!" he replied. "Okay. I'll see all of you very soon. Wow, twice," he chuckled as he walked away.

As they started walking forward, Sahnassa asked, "Eh, did I miss something?"

Vanarra shrugged. "When we were on the flyer, this 'Fillie' kept calling Agari 'Broke Tail'. I figured it was because she'd shut the door on his tail or something."

"Well, she might want to," Agari explained, "but if she did that, I really wouldn't have much of a tail left." Sahnassa recalled in horrifying detail the memory of her own injuries after the landslide, and Sahnassa stayed silent, but the other two laughed a little.

"So fess up, Agari!" Vanarra demanded. "What did she do to you?"

"She stamped my tail under her boot, as hard as she could," Agari answered, humiliation coloring his voice. "Broke it in two places."

"Ouch!" Saletta cried in sympathy. The females all held their tails in their paws for just a moment. "What did you ever do to deserve that?"

"Let's say I ... made a rude comment, and leave it at that." Agari was trying very hard to bury this subject, but Saletta would have none of it.

"You're not getting off that easily, Agari. You're family. Come on, tell us what you said."

"Can we just drop this, Saletta, please? It's not like *you* don't have embarrassing secrets."

"Oh, I do, that's for sure, but you don't actually *know* any of them, do you?" Agari thought desperately as they walked between buildings. As they finally entered the southern doorway of building one and walked through another hallway, she repeated the question. "Well? Do you?"

Defeated, Agari gave in. "No. Okay, I made a silly comment about Vulpi mating drives. It was a stereotype thing; I never should have said it."

Sahnassa's own dreams about Theo surfaced again. Oh, how she hoped her own Vulpi might live up to the legends. "I've ... I've heard rumors about that."

Vanarra's tone was unforgiving. "I have, too, and sometimes said in a very cruel way."

"Well, I haven't," Saletta said slyly. "I must lead a rather mothered life, Agari. What, exactly, did you say?"

He was really squirming now, but managed to explain. "We were all joking around with each other, when she made a hard dig on me. I dug her back by asking her if she was sure she was a Vulpi, because the only thing she ever got really passionate about was a secure tie down in a cargo hold."

As she thought about it, Vanarra had to cut him a little leeway on that one. "Well, she does seem a little over zealous about her position."

"Every sol, every interval, every pass. She never turns it off. I shouldn't have said it. I apparently struck a nerve."

"Yes," Saletta offered, amused, "and so did she, 'Broke Tail'!"

"Great!" he said, exasperated, and they all had a good laugh at his expense.

Now in the main building, their laughter echoed down the dark corridor, and Sahnassa started to sense how desolate the Meeting Den was becoming. The evacuation was literally draining away its life, making it feel empty and forsaken. Looking at the paneled walls, the beautiful ceilings, the doors to elegant parlors and banquet halls, she felt sorry for the place. Someone, long ago, wanted this built, went through all of the effort, made it successful, and now, it would be completely abandoned in no more than a few intervals' time. Then, the buildings would be covered by snow and ice, inaccessible for who knows how long. "Will animals live in the buildings? What about all of the possessions that get left? What happens to them?" she wondered. Her mind was instantly drawn back to how horrible things might have been were there no Theo, no Vanarra, and no rescue.

Sahnassa reached out and clutched Vanarra's paw. "I'm so glad you're okay," she said quietly as Saletta and Agari walked ahead. "You could have stayed down there, you know, in the valley?"

Van looked at her fearfully. "I couldn't do that! After all that's happened to us, after all you've come to mean to me – I just couldn't take the chance. I'm not leaving until you leave, and I don't think either of us wants to leave until this is really over. Do you?"

"No. I want to stay until everyone else is out. It just seems like what we should do. And, Van, I feel the same way."

Vanarra nodded and squeezed Sahni's paw once again, smiling.

In a few short moments, they were opening the door to a command center that seemed far busier than when they had left it the last time. There were matrons and dames almost pushing each other down to get into and out of the room.

"This doesn't look good," Vanarra said to no one in particular.

As they managed to find an empty wall to stand against, Saletta explained, "I think this comes from our problems with the family TransCom systems. We've been using them for a full sol, and some of the power packs have started to run dry. We have to rely on written messages and runners to keep the evacuation going. It looks like … it's created some real confusion."

"I'd say so," Agari agreed, looking at the swirl and having to almost yell over the din. "That's why the military took over in the laundry. Anyone whose TransCom is still working is needed elsewhere, and—"

"Saletta! You're here!" A dame on the far side of the room shouted to her. "Is yours still working?"

"Yes!"

"We've cleared buildings four and five! I need you to go to building six, third level! They're second in line to go, and no one has started moving them yet! You've got a quarter of an interval before they must be seated in the laundry! Remember you need exactly sixty of them!"

"Yes, sixty from building six, third level!" With that, Saletta told them "bye" and rushed out the door.

Vanarra looked to her left and noticed the door to the communications room had opened, and Matriarch Rahnahi de Dothnar stepped out. Seeing them standing there, she motioned for them to come over. They worked their way around the busy room towards the door, and Vanarra swallowed hard, wondering if this was when she'd finally meet the de Gonari matriarch. Instead, as she entered the room, she got a much better surprise. "Buck!" Immediately she rushed over and hugged him as he stood.

"By Thuria, kit, it's good to see you!" he exclaimed as he hugged her back, unashamed. They let go, and he held her back to look at her. "You look fabulous! I'd never guess you were rolled down a hill and forced to survive in the woods!"

"You don't look so bad yourself!" she offered, with a slight tilt of the head. She'd forgotten how cute he could be sometimes.

"Oh, if I only looked as tired as I felt, then you would weep indeed," he said, rubbing the sides of his head with his paws.

"That's starting to be a real problem for us," Rahnahi interjected as she closed the door. "We're getting tired, and we're making mistakes. We almost didn't have the last group sat when the transport landed, and they had to nearly run to the laundry. Now, we've got family communications breaking down, power-packs going dead—"

"Honored One?" Sahnassa asked, timidly. "May I make a suggestion? What kind of power packs do the TransComs take?"

"Hold on a tick," Buck said as he sat down and turned over a crescent shaped device on the table. "Looks like A14. Commonly available at any corner store, if we actually had a corner store."

"Doesn't this place have a gift shop?" Vanarra asked, a little apologetically. There was a long, blank stare between Buck and Rahnahi. "I mean, they would need to have some to sell to the guests, right?"

"I think I saw a display in the shop when we were here for the conference. If someone can get a key, I can go get them and run them around to all your dames and matrons," Sahnassa offered.

"Like I said," Rahnahi sighed, "we're not thinking straight." She walked over to the door, called for Dania, and then explained. "Dania, go and get that Perratti who ran this place. I'm going to send Sahnassa with him over to the gift shop to scrounge for power packs. Once they find some, Sahni said she would take them to anyone who needs them."

"Oh, mange!" Dania exhaled, exasperated. "Why didn't I think of that?! Come on, Sahnassa. That will really help! You get to save us all, yet again!"

"Don't be silly," Sahni responded as she followed Dania out the door, "It's you all who are—" and the closing door cut off the rest of the conversation. However, Vanarra nodded in approval at her friend's response, remembering Theo's advice.

"Oh, will that ever help!" Buck exclaimed, standing up again. "I can't believe we didn't think of it! Like I said, we're all tired."

There was a knock at the door, and a medic opened it. "Agari, we've got one down because of exposure. I need another paw on a stretcher. This guy's big, too."

Agari looked at Van, who said, "You go. I'll be perfectly fine here. I won't go anywhere until you get back, okay?"

"Just you do that." Then, looking straight at Buck, he warned, "I'm coming after you if something happens to her, just so you know."

"I'll keep an eye on her, don't worry." Buck put his arm around her and squeezed her shoulder, Van not protesting in the slightest.

Agari had to smile back at him, seeing that there was an obvious friendship there and perhaps, something more. "Thanks. Okay, Bal, let's go!"

"He's such a good guy," Vanarra commented when the door was closed again. "May I ask, Honored One," she queried, her voice still colored by the respect she felt due the matriarch in her company, "have you heard anything of Matriarch Amyra or Arnat?"

Rahnahi looked at her sternly, but raised her paws in frustrated acceptance. "Not 'Honored One', Vanarra, please! I can't blame you, I suppose."

Van's blush furs actually raised a little – a rare occurrence. "I'm sorry, Rahnahi, it's all still so new. I never imagined being on a first name basis with you."

Buck jumped in, as he could see Vanarra's discomfiture. "The word on Arnat's pretty serious. He's been in surgery almost from the moment he got to the hospital. It was really close, but they said he got good care on the way down. You were with him?"

Van nodded grimly. "Yeah, he was bad off – really bad off. I haven't seen anyone like that since … well, since I was a kit. How long before we know for sure?"

"Some time yet," Buck answered. "Theo said he would let us know."

"Now, there's someone who has a good head and heart, and he quoted you far better than even I could," she told Rahnahi, who seemed surprised.

"He did seem exceptionally competent when we talked with him earlier," Rahnahi mused. "What did you say his name was again?"

"Theo de Allarrae, I believe. A Nephti."

"de Allarrae … de Allarrae?" The matriarch was obviously searching her memory. "You know, I'm not familiar with that one. It could be from a small family or from a remote area," Rahnahi mused, but still seemed doubtful. "Vanarra, what else can you tell me about him? What does he do?"

Van cocked her head to one side trying to remember. "He's real bright, level-headed, and pretty good looking, too. I guess he works for Tedarri. He seemed to have some medical background. He diagnosed Arnat right on the spot! Other than that, I can only tell you he was very kind to me, and treated me … well, he treated me like family, I suppose."

"What do you mean?" Buck asked, and clearly Rahnahi was also interested in the answer.

Shrugging, she explained, "I've kind of learned how to pick up on how others feel about me. I can almost hear what they're thinking. Some just look at me and see 'the mix-up.' Others, well, the males, they look at me like I'm their next hunt. Theo … Theo just looked at me like … like a father would. I got the feeling … or the sense from him that he was just the kindest fellow. He didn't want anything. He just wanted to help."

Buck nodded his head in understanding. "I guess he's got the right job then. Sounds like he's perfect for emergency management."

"It would seem so. Now, what about Amyra?" Van asked.

"She's fine. I've talked to her already," Rahnahi answered, smiling. "She's cursing me for sending her down there; although, strictly speaking, it wasn't all me. The medics said she needed to go, too. Theo let us know the doctors put her on a strong antibiotic and gave her fluids by needle, so they obviously thought she was in need, as well. She said that she actually—"

Again, a knock on the door interrupted them. Dania opened the door when bade to and said, "With apologies, Honored One. We've got an odd report from the matrons in building six. They counted heads intervals ago, but now their counts are coming up twenty or so short. Communications broke off right after they reported."

Rahnahi sighed and stood. "None of us are going to ever sleep well again if we think we left someone up here. Alright, let me see what I can do to help. I'll leave you two to talk for awhile?" They both nodded, and soon, they were alone.

Buck looked at her as she stared at the closed door, obviously lost for a moment in her own thoughts. As tired and hungry as he might be, Buck couldn't help admiring her and smiling. For him, it wasn't just her looks, which were stunning to say the least; more than anything he admired her strength and heart, proven beyond all doubt by her selfless actions over the last sol. He was so lost in these musings that he barely noticed she had started speaking. "This is all just so strange, Buck. I'm on a first name basis with a matriarch? I don't know what to make of any of it," she admitted shaking her head, but then turned to see him staring at her. "What? I don't look that bad, do I?"

Buck's reply was gently sincere. "No, not hardly. You are actually very good to look at … anytime, but especially now." His tone grew more earnest. "I was really worried something bad happened to you, you know?"

Smiling back at him wryly, she countered with a little sarcasm. "I think something bad has happened to all of us, Buck!"

"No," he countered quietly, seriously. "I thought we had lost you. Until the moment you called, I just knew that you and Sahni … were gone. Either you had driven off a bridge or been buried by a landslide or swerved off the road or so many other horrible things. I mean, I was mad enough at what happened to you here, when they threw you out. I searched through the lot for your hover, but the valet said you were ordered to leave the premises. Then the quake hit us. I was standing outside talking to him when it happened. We actually heard the bridge go, the one right outside the gates. I ran down there … looking for you."

Vanarra laughed a little ruefully. "Well, I was so mad, I must have broken the speed limit until Sahnassa asked me to pull over. We were long gone from here, thankfully. It was close, though. We ended up not that far away from another collapsed bridge, and we were actually hit by a landslide. We caught the edge of that, but not too badly." She paused for a moment, and she could tell he meant what he said. "It's really sweet of you to be worried for us."

"Dania will tell you how worried I was," he confessed, looking away. "I can't tell you how relieved I was when I actually heard your voice."

"It was great to hear your voice, too," she whispered, reaching over to stroke the side of his muzzle, gently bringing his gaze back to her own.

He smiled into her eyes, shaking his head. "You know, we're always so busy, this is the first time I think we've ever had a moment just to talk. I was afraid I'd never have the chance again."

She took his paws in hers. "I'm sorry I worried you so. It's like I'm just waking up after all these seasons and realizing that there are a few kind souls out there who actually care about me. I haven't seen it until now."

"You're right, and I'm one of them." Leaning forward, he kissed the side of her muzzle and reached his arms around her, and she returned his gentle embrace. "When we get back, I want to buy you a dinner – a real, big, wonderful, expensive, lavish, eat till you fall down and have to be carried out dinner where we can just talk and talk and—" Just then, his stomach gurgled, almost sounding angry.

Vanarra broke the embrace in laughter. "I felt that! I actually felt that!"

He laughed as well, but then, embarrassed, added, "I guess my stomach's a little upset with me for talking about food when it hasn't had any in awhile."

"Oh well then, I guess you're lucky I'm a caterer." She reached inside of her coat and pulled out two meat bars.

"You've got to be joking!" he gasped, wide-eyed.

"Sahni loaded up for the trip, luckily enough. Go ahead, enjoy!"

"They'll disavow anyone they find hoarding food." She gave him a long and knowing look. Realizing that neither he nor Vanarra were avowed in the first place, he shamed-facedly sighed, "Oh, never mind." With that, he opened the wrapper and dug in. "Oh, gosh, Van – oh, that's good."

In moments, the first bar was gone, and he was halfway through the next when there was a knock on the door. Buck almost choked in surprise, and then tried to swallow quickly as the door was opened.

The matriarch walked in, smiling. "Just wanted to let you know Sahnassa's come through for us again! That Perratti returned and said they found a whole box of power packs and – hey are you eating something?" she asked the last in a hoarse whisper.

"Well, I … I uh," Buck stammered, but Van reached into her coat and pulled out two fruit bars. Grinning, she held them up in the direction of Rahnahi. With a knowing smile, the matriarch quietly closed the door behind her.

"Look, I know you're tired. You don't have to come with me; I can manage these, really," Sahni reassured Siflin, a Perratti, that he could return to his place in the last evacuation building. Although sent along to help, he had actually slowed her efforts, and it had been difficult not to grow impatient with him. It was remarkable how much his pathetic demeanor varied from his haughty disposition when he ejected them from the premises earlier.

Even though Sahnassa had been angry with him for that curtly delivered speech, he was just too pitiful now to even consider holding a grudge; time had already paid him back more than adequately. It was clear from his frightened mutterings that he fully expected all blame for the Meeting Den tragedies to be laid upon his back. He had already refused several suggestions and entreaties to let Sahnassa proceed on her own, fearful that someone would cite that as yet another one of his failings. After listening to his anxious twittering about the bridge collapse, Sahni finally had to say something. "Come on; they can't blame you for a ground quake or construction that happened well before you were even born!"

"They'll try," he said nervously. "They will say we should have had the bridges inspected more frequently, that we should … have done … something." Again, he was staring, paralyzed by his fears.

Sahnassa's lips slipped above her teeth for a moment in anger. Frustrated, she thought to herself, "There's a whole evacuation that's falling apart, and all you can do is feel sorry for yourself!" She decided to take a firmer paw and spoke as she'd heard dames do when they gave orders. "Siflin, take this bag of power packs to the matriarch, and then go back to your building. You need to rest."

That snapped him out of his stupor. "Are you sure? In case someone asks, you told me to go back. Still, if I come back alone, they'll think I didn't do anything to help you."

Before he could descend again into self-pity, she thrust the bag into his paws. "You are helping! You're taking a whole bag of power packs to the matriarch and dames and telling them what we've found, while I take the rest to the other buildings. Go on now," Sahni bade, half-disgusted with him, but almost unable to contain her desire to be alone for just a few moments – alone so she could talk with Theo or Haloizar. She knew she'd need their help to get the packs distributed quickly.

"Yes, yes. I'll go, if you insist," he said, barely moving away.

"I do," she almost shouted at him. It was with great relief that she saw his hindquarters disappear through a doorway. She waited until she actually heard the door at the end of the next hall close before she reached into her pocket and took out her sunglasses.

Once they were securely on her face, a message appeared. "Interlink with Tashar complete." Then, "Greetings, Sahnassa. This is Haloizar. Sensors show no one in range capable of hearing or seeing you. Speak freely."

"Hey there," she said as she stepped into an empty room carrying her three heavy bags. "Can I ask a favor? Can you please point out the dames and matrons whose power packs are low?"

"Certainly." Sahni had to sit down as a three dimensional map of the Meeting Den swirled in front of her eyes. "Red indicates no power. Orange indicates a device that may run out of power prior to complete evacuation, and green indicates devices where power will likely last until the evacuation is complete, based on predicted usage patterns."

"Buildings three, six, and eight seem to be the worst," Sahnassa observed, noting the distribution of symbols on the floating map in front of her. "If I hit those first, can you scan again?"

"Yes, I can. However, Theo wants to alert you to a concern. We're starting to detect a pattern amongst some of the evacuees, purposefully shifting themselves to the end of or even out of the evacuation schedule. Also, we've detected another family network in operation. Observe. These are transmissions within the last interval."

Her glasses showed communications coming out of building eight which housed the laundry and was closest to the athletic field, and buildings four and five which were the greatest distance away and, supposedly, had already been cleared. "I see it. What are they up to? Who is it?"

"Scans indicate members of the de Caterra familial grouping, for the most part. There is only one individual in building eight involved in these communications. So far, twenty-three individuals are now located in building five, within a large suite. It appears they've posted lookouts in other rooms."

"What are they talking about? Can you tap into their TransComs?"

"I have. Most of the transmissions have been short queries of status and replies from the building lookouts. There has only been one substantial exchange, directing a Faelnar in building eight to divert de Caterra staging for evacuation to building five. Other than a demonstrated willingness to disobey the instructions of the matriarchs, dames, and matrons, we cannot as yet determine their true intent. We suggest you use the southernmost entrances of the buildings you intend to visit to reduce the possibility of contact with these individuals in buildings four and five. The Tashar will continue to monitor in order to determine what threat they pose and what coordinated plan they may have. At this point, neither has been established."

"Should I tell anyone?"

"Not as yet. The most critical task is to re-establish communications. Succeeding in that may make it difficult for the de Caterra to continue their actions. It may even convince them to abandon their present activities."

"Okay. I'm off to building three then," Sahnassa said, standing.

"Very good. Tashar X-mit out."

Sahnassa removed her glasses, folded them neatly into her coat pocket, picked up the heavy bags, and walked towards the north entrance of the main building towards building three. Even though the main building felt chilly, it wasn't anything compared to the blowing cold between the buildings. As quickly as she could, Sahni covered the short distance and entered building three through its southern door.

Within, it was almost completely dark; the stairwell echoed her footsteps and the shutting of the outer door. She groped forward for the inner door and finding the knob, pulled. A foul, stale smell hit her nose. It was like the combination of a sweaty locker room and a sewage pit. Walking forward slowly, glass crunched under her paw-shoes, and she heard mumbled conversations, coughing, and soft weeping. A layer of cold air circulated around her ankles, passing in from underneath the doors on the right side of the hallway. "What an awful place to be in, and had things gone differently, to die in," she thought. It was a smell and a place she knew she would never forget.

"Matron? Dame?" she called out. A figure slowly and carefully crunched over the glass and finally reached her.

"Yes. Who are you?" A female Nephti approached her, cautiously.

"I'm Sahnassa. I have power packs for your communicator." She set the bags down and pulled out one of the sealed packages.

"Oh, bless you! I don't have any light. I'm not sure I can install this."

"I'll help. We can use my PawLink's light." It was a few passes work to get the packs installed, but as soon as it was done, the matron, Delease de Dothnar, did a communications check to the main building.

"Oh, thank you! That's great! I can take four more packs to the matrons and dames that are here."

Sahnassa pulled out the packs and gave them to the matron, but asked, "The other buildings, the laundry I mean, didn't seem so bad. All of this glass and that smell – what happened here?"

"The laundry doesn't have windows facing the dining hall, and this did. All of the windows blew out on that side, and broken glass was sent flying through the doors that were left propped open; some was even blown under the doors! As for the smell, there's nowhere else to go, not without freezing. Hey, if you have a few more spares, I think we might be able to power a couple of small UltraBrights."

Sahnassa gave one of her three bags to the matron. "I think this would be quickest. I need to go to two other buildings as soon as I can."

"Alright. Thank you, Sahnassa. It's a great honor to finally meet you."

"You, too," she replied and lightly hugged the matron.

As the matron stepped away, Sahni shifted her remaining load to get ready for the hike to buildings six and eight. A young female voice ahead of her asked timidly, "Excuse me … are you Sahnassa de Orturu?"

"Yes, I'm Sahnassa." Another Nephti stepped forward, and in the dim light, Sahni couldn't make out much more. "Who are you?"

"My name's Illesea de Fantar. Are … are we … really going to be rescued?" The voice was so frail, beaten down, and hopeless that Sahnassa could almost feel the Nephti's fear and despair. "We haven't heard anything in so long."

"Don't worry, Illesea. Everyone's getting out, and that includes you, too," Sahnassa replied with absolute assurance. She hugged the almost painfully thin young female gently and said, "The matrons needed new power packs for their communicators, and I'm bringing those around. You should start to hear something very soon, okay? I've already seen hundreds evacuated, and I'm not leaving until everyone else is safe – you included."

Sahni could almost sense Illesea's spirit brighten as she tightened the embrace. "Thank you! Thank you so much." They released, but Sahnassa patted Illesea on the shoulder one more time before turning and leaving through the southern door. This time, stepping out into the almost generous light of the darkened, overcast evening was a joy. Smelling the fresh, if terribly cold, air was an almost blissful relief. She took several deep, slow breaths to clear the stench from her lungs.

The pause gave her a moment to assess her situation. Looking down the path to her right, she saw crumbled wreckage from the dining facility strewn between the buildings. The pit where the building had once stood still smoldered, and whiffs of smoke continued to waft up from its depths. As far as she could tell in the dim light, debris was everywhere on the paths, but looking up, she could see the bulky outlines of buildings six, seven, and eight on the opposite side – where she needed to go. The path was far too dangerous to attempt without an UltraBright, and doing so would make her visible to the de Caterra in buildings four and five. Shifting both bags to her right paw, she reached into her coat with her left and drew out her sunglasses.

Once they were securely on her face, again, the message appeared. "Interlink with Tashar complete. Greetings, Sahnassa, this is Haloizar. Sensors show no one capable of hearing you in range, but you can be observed. Speak discreetly."

She put the bags down and pulled up the hood of her coat and unrolled its edging so it covered most of her face and muzzle. "Hi there. Can you guide me through all this to building six? It will take me a long time to work my way around, since I can't go through buildings four and five."

"Certainly. Just remember to remove the sunglasses prior to entering building six." In front of her left eye, the darkened ground grew light as if the sun had been pulled above her and the clouds swept away. Slight shadows and red outlines helped highlight all the dangerous debris on the ground. In her right eye, a darker display mapped a route through one of the pool areas, past what had been the back of the dining facility, then through a garden gazebo and into the southern entrance of building six. A message from Haloizar also read, "The enhanced imaging of the ground in front of you will only appear in your left eye. This will preserve the night vision in your right eye. You may proceed forward."

The message and route in her right eye disappeared, and she started making her way forward after picking up the bags. It took a little getting used to, although after a few moments, Sahni found she was able to make good progress. As she walked carefully by the paddling pool, she saw the discarded buckets that had been used by the fire squads earlier. The water was down a couple of tracks and filled with floating debris. There were also several sun shades missing, torn away, or ripped. One or two were burned, as were several tables and chairs which were either in pieces or damaged. Clearly, they didn't belong near the pool, and then she realized they had been blown here by the force of the explosion.

She started to sense the burnt smell of the building much stronger now as she approached, and it wasn't more than a pass before she stood near the edge of the gaping hole that had once been the dining facility. Turning towards it, the enhanced view in her left eye showed her the amazing devastation. Some charred wood, pieces of tables and equipment, a few rows of metal chairs melted together, and what appeared to be the base of the flamgas tank were all that remained.

"I'm glad we got Cari out of here, Theo. This is awful," she said aloud.

"Me, too." The message softly appeared in front of her right eye and then faded. Turning away sadly, she resumed her progress towards building six. As she made her next careful forward steps, Sahnassa turned to her left and looked at buildings four and five. A chill not caused entirely by the cold passed through her.

"Ah, Theo?" she whispered. "I'm feeling a little ... exposed out here. Can you tell if the de Caterra have ... weapons of any sort?"

The message in her sunglasses answered, "Yes, they do: several short-range weapons and ammunition. However, do not be afraid. They cannot see you. I am actively preventing that. In fact, stop and look at those buildings for a moment."

Just as she did, one of the flyers lifted off from the athletic field, and its bright landing lights cut through the southern gap in the buildings, illuminating where she knew the de Caterra were hiding. For just an instant, Sahnassa could see two sets of reflective eyes peering through the shattered windows in the upper and lower corners of building five. As the light faded, the display in her right eye magnified and enhanced what she had seen. Two big, dark Faelnar were visible to her. One appeared to be holding something shiny, perhaps a weapon. The images persisted for a moment, and then faded away. "Now that you've seen someone in building five, you have a plausible excuse for bringing it to someone's attention, if that is needed. You're now free to proceed."

She turned and started walking again. "Have the matrons in building three made use of what I gave them?"

"Yes. They have restored almost every communicator, and they have at least two UltraBrights per floor. That's fast work. Impressive."

"It is. Everything else going okay with the evacuation?" Sahnassa asked quietly, stepping over a mangled chair.

"Yes. All is occurring as planned, and we're still able to moderate the weather, discreetly."

"What's Vanarra up to?"

"It looks like she's having a good discussion with Buck and the matriarch. She's fine. Time for the glasses to come off. Talk with you again soon. Theo, X-mit out."

"Thank you," she whispered as the display went dark. Sahnassa shifted the sacks, carefully put away the glasses, and stepped towards the southern door of building six. Once in the hallway, the same smells and sounds assailed her as before, and she again called for the matron.

Chapter 15: Foundations

Theo walked through the halls of the secondary school, looking at the long lines of tired Thurians waiting for food. Most of the transports were gone now, and that was good, because weather reports had identified a large swath of freezing rain moving towards the Shanandrae evacuation route. So most in this line now, he knew, would have to weather the storm in the shelters. His PawLink beeped, and he pulled it from its holster. "Theo, word from the hospital. Looks like Arnat's out of danger," Tedarri said. "He's going to make it. The doctor said it was close, too close, and that every bit of care he got made the difference. Think his next of kin's still up on the mountain?"

"I'd be almost certain of it. From the description I received, his sire shouldn't have been on these first few flights. I'll call up; I'm more or less done looking around out here."

"How does it look? Everything moving smoothly?"

"It looks like the evacuation to Shanandrae is working itself out to a clean finish, but we need to start transitioning over to shelter mode. You may want to send someone through the front and start redirecting the part of the line that's staying. Right now, it's all just one line," Theo warned.

"That's not good. Okay, I'll get a couple of my staff down there to start directing traffic across the street to where we've got the bunks set up."

"I'll call up to the den and let them try to pass the word to Arnat's sire. I'll try to get a status from them, as well. Theo, X-mit out."

))((

"I … I could write six poems and a small essay about how *good* that tasted!" Rahnahi drawled, and Buck and Vanarra both laughed. "Got any more?"

"I have a few left. Let me see," Vanarra answered as she searched in her pockets. "Four more meat bars and two more fruits."

"Then, if you don't mind, could you save some for Dania? She's been working her tail off."

"I will. She seems a very nice sort," Vanarra commented.

Rahnahi gave a cautionary laugh. "Nice she may seem, but her teeth are long and sharp. Be careful to stay on her good side. She's real–"

The beeping of the military TransCom drew their attention. "Uh, oh. Let's see what this is about," Buck said, keying the speaker button on the device. "Meeting Den, please go ahead."

"Buck! It's Theo again. How are you doing up there?"

"I think we're starting to put things back together again. We were having family TransCom problems, but Sahnassa was able to scrounge up some power packs. We should be able to pass messages back and forth normally in half an interval or so."

"Sounds great. I've got word on Arnat. He made it out of surgery, and he's recovering. Is Vanarra there?"

"I'm right here, Theo," she answered.

"The doctor said that the care you gave Arnat on the way down helped save his life. If he had been kept strapped down, he would have gone into shock, had muscle spasms, and possibly ripped himself inside more than he already was. You did very well, Vanarra."

Van rubbed a tear from her eye. "Okay … okay thanks, Theo. I know everyone down there did a good – helped him get through it, too. That's nice to hear."

"Yes, it is," Theo agreed, and Rahnahi noted how thoughtful his voice sounded.

"Theo, this is Matriarch Rahnahi de Dothnar."

"Yes, Honored One?"

"How are our evacuees doing?"

"Very well, in fact, Honored One." Theo's tone was upbeat. "As of this moment, we've actually put five hundred and sixty-four on the road, and the last two transports will leave in less than half an interval. That's going to work out well, because if it had taken any longer, a line of ice showers would start making the road to Shanandrae very dangerous. As you are aware, we've had eight medical cases so far, two of which are at hospital. The rest are being treated here and are recovering. Food is getting to where it needs to go, and we're going to start sending everyone else over to the shelters to get some rest."

"Are there any danger signs for the rest of the evacuation?"

"No real dangers, just concerns, Honored One. The military has just brought in its second group of flyers to take over while the first refuels and cleans up. So far, we haven't had any close calls or accidents, and the weather, while it's a very iffy thing, is still holding in our favor. There is one item from my prior experience that you may want to consider." Theo's voice was now sounding more serious.

"What's that?"

"There are those, Honored One, who, even in the face of real danger, will want to stay behind – tuff out the storm. Call them crazy, but they believe they have a point to make or something to prove, perhaps something to gain or to protect. It's generally not a big portion of the population of any evacuation, but it's been seen before."

Rahnahi nodded at the warning and mused, "Now that you mention it, I remember Amyra saying something – a local chieftain whose village was at the edge of a volcano. They knew it was going to erupt and evacuated everyone, except him. No matter what she did, she couldn't convince him to leave. He died there."

"Exactly," Theo responded. "Now that you're getting your communications back in order, you may want to ask the military's help to go through and lock down the buildings and sweep the parking lots. Prevent anyone from intentionally backtracking or accidentally missing their ride. Make sure every head gets counted onto those transports; no matter what."

"What do we do if someone … doesn't want to go?" Buck asked.

The silence in the room, telling though it was, lasted only a moment. Theo decided to answer, "I'll give you my belief. If you look at the desire to suicide as a form of mental illness, then you don't leave the weak or the sick behind. Talk them down if you can, but in the end, get them on that flyer. Stun-shock them if you have to, because there's a whole family somewhere who wants that Thurian alive, even if he or she doesn't seem to care at that moment. They may be off their medication or simply scared or confused. All of those are temporary conditions. Death is not."

The silence in the room hung longer this time; Theo's final sentence was a hard reminder of their situation. "Thank you, Theo," Rahnahi said. "We'll take steps right away."

"Very well, Honored One. You should know we have mental health professionals on the shelter staff, so anyone you bring down who needs that kind of help, we can help. Is there anything else you need?"

"No, Theo. Thank you. I do look forward to meeting you face to face," Rahnahi said, a curious tone in her voice.

Theo quoted her own work back to her. "'And when that warm meeting comes, it will be us old friends who shared heart to heart before we ever looked eye in eye or placed paw in paw.' I will be honored, Grand Matriarch; I will truly be honored. Theo X-mit out."

Rahnahi looked at Vanarra with a little astonishment, and Van shrugged saying, "I told you he had everything you'd ever written memorized!"

"You told me he quoted me well, but – you'll have to forgive me. I'm just surprised sometimes by what happens once I've written something."

At that moment, Agari knocked on the door while opening it. Looking at Vanarra first, he then turned back to Buck and said, "Good. You get to live."

Buck sighed, a little uneasily, but Vanarra chuckled appreciatively and asked, "You done with the 'big guy'?"

"Yes," Agari answered, sounding pained. "I won't need to do charge thrusts for moons!"

They all laughed at his expression. "Hey, I've got an idea," Vanarra offered. "Why don't Agari and I take a casual stroll around and see if there is anyone who wants to ride out the storm?"

"What? What do you mean?"

Buck answered Agari, "We don't want anyone left behind."

"And there have been some miscounts as we've moved the evacuees out. Theo's right. I want to make absolutely sure we haven't left anyone," Rahnahi asserted.

"Can we get the keys from – what was his name, the Perratti? Siflin?" Vanarra asked. "We could lock up the empty buildings as we go along. If we find someone where they're not supposed to be, we can call it in."

"Yes," Rahnahi agreed. "Agari, if you would, please call Dania in here." As he turned away, Vanarra stood and placed a fruit bar and a meat bar in Rahnahi's paws. "Thank you," she whispered to Vanarra, who smiled happily back at her.

"Oh, Sahnassa, you're an absolute miracle!" Saletta exclaimed as she eyed the bag of power packs. "My communicator just started going dead, and no one else here has one that works!"

"Oh, you're welcome. Well, here, let me give these to you," Sahni said as she offered Saletta the bag.

"We'll get these passed around quickly! We managed to get our last group out on time, but now we're waiting as they're pulling evacuees from building three. You've already been there?"

"Yes. All of their communicators are working again." Just then, Sahni's wrist beneath her watch began to tingle – very insistently.

"Oh, this is great! Can you stay with us for awhile? I'd love the chance to talk with you some."

She would have liked to have said yes, but knew she had to get somewhere private, and fast. "I've got this other bag, and you'll have enough to do getting those installed. I'll come back, okay?"

"Okay," Saletta replied, sounding disappointed. Sahnassa knew she liked Saletta and hoped their budding friendship would carry on after all of this was over, but smiling and wishing Saletta good chance, she left and headed towards the stairwell. Unfortunately, she found the stairwell wasn't empty as she reached the bottom floor.

"Are you Sahnassa de Orturu?" a haughty female voice asked. The ensuing conversation with Dame Prattura de Gonari lasted several passes, with the dame wanting to know any updates on the condition of her own matriarch, how the evacuation was going, and what she thought the weather would do. The older dame deserved respect, but Sahnassa still struggled to get away, finally using the power pack delivery to building eight as an excuse.

That only served to prolong her delay as the dame insisted on walking with her and continuing the conversation. Finally, at the southern door of building six, the dame held her for another pass or two talking about the de Caterra. With as much politeness as she could manage in the cold air between the buildings, she excused herself and was forced to walk into building seven's north entrance, the dame "seeing that she made it safely." Grateful that no one was there, she looked at her watch in the darkness.

"Prepare for–" the message read, but she had to look away as a nearby door opened.

"You're not supposed to be in here," an older and very proper Faelnar male addressed her. She couldn't make out his features in the darkness of the hallway.

Not sure what she was supposed to prepare for, Sahnassa was careful. "Who are you?"

"I should ask you that, young kit."

"I'm Sahnassa de Orturu, and you are?"

There was a pause, and he cleared his throat. "I'm Arkest de Gonari. What are you doing here?"

Sahnassa wondered how convincing she could be. "I'm delivering power packs to building eight, but I need to get back to building six. Can you possibly take these to one of the dames or matrons?"

"I … I'm sorry, but I was heading to – someone said there was a working communicator in building five. I – it's my son, you see? He was very ill, and they evacuated him. I didn't – I haven't heard anything." She could hear the genuine worry in his voice, and then his name clicked in her head.

"Oh, are you Arnat's sire?"

"Yes, yes I am."

"These power packs are for the family communicators. If you take them and back-track to building eight, one of the matrons is sure to let you call in for a status on how he's doing. Who told you there was a communicator in building five? That building's been cleared already."

"I'd better not say. I'll take the power packs for you. Thank you."

Earnestly, she offered, "I hope your son is okay."

"Thank you," he said softly as he took the bag from her and left through the door.

As soon as the door was closed, Sahnassa was blinded by bright light and surrounded by warm, clean, comfortable air. "Sorry, Sahnassa, I couldn't wait anymore. I had to bring you back aboard." As her eyes adjusted, Sahni realized where she was, standing again on the raised dais.

"The Tashar!?" Turning around she saw Theo, a Vulpi now, and excitedly she embraced him. "I'm really here, right?"

"Yes. And we're in temporal hover again."

"Hover?" she asked, letting him go. "What's wrong?"

"Vanarra. She and Agari volunteered to lock up the empty buildings and look for stragglers, and they entered building five. Both have been stunned unconscious and captured by the de Caterra."

"Why would the de Caterra do that?" Sahni asked, horrified.

"I think they don't want to participate in a rescue which was largely organized by…"

"…an Anati!" Sahnassa was angry, as she finished his thought. "But, couldn't you stop them?" She looked at Theo in hopelessness and disbelief.

Speaking softly and kindly, he explained. "The physical me is still in the valley below, so no I couldn't just appear and tell them not to go in there. It's doubtful they would have listened had I appeared as someone they didn't know, and the only ones they would have listened to – you, the chief, the matriarchs, and so forth – were already someplace else; I couldn't credibly take their place without someone knowing. Besides, there are … other rules. Up until now, the de Caterra have taken no action against those I've chosen to protect. That's no longer true. As strange as this sounds, I can do far more now that they have been attacked and captured than I could before."

"What do you mean? What kinds of things can you do?"

Looking at Sahnassa's hopeful expression, he answered, "The kinds of things from which the future is borne."

Sanratatarrae de Caterra, known as Sanrat to those of the de Caterra "blood," shivered from more than cold when he looked at the two bodies laying in front of him. One, an Anati female in conventional dress, gave him little pause. The big Faelnar male in military garb shoved splinters of pure terror into his scholarly heart. In his head, a voice unbidden told him "It's over" – he swore he could hear it in his head like it was spoken. "They'll find us. They won't leave without him." It was a chilling thought that penetrated his normally calm reserve and stoic detachment.

"Cur!" he finally called out in a voice that sounded more like a call of panic than his usual haughty, professorial one. "Cur! Come here, now!"

Ocurattiaster de Caterra didn't like being summoned, especially by some thin-necked, light-weight "academic", and his displeasure was blatantly obvious on his features as he stalked up. "What, Sanrat? And keep your mangy voice down!" he growled in a hoarse whisper as he towered over the pale yellow-furred professor.

"What is the meaning of this? Who did this? Now it's over, Cur. It's over!" Sanrat bleated, motioning to the unconscious bodies, his golden eyes wide with horror.

"Shut your muzzle, you fool! I'll knock you out cold and throw you face down into a paddling pool if you keep this up! It's not over until we say it is, and this changes nothing!" Cur raised himself to his full height, his dark golden-brown fur and black stripes along his arms made him seem all the more imposing.

"How can you say that? What reasonable argument can you make that explains how this doesn't change anything?" Sanrat was still too wound up by his own fears to catch onto the overbearing threat in the green-gold eyes of the big, muscular Faelnar.

"I don't have to make an argument! I only have to take care of the problem. The Anati skank is no problem," he growled, his tail twitching with displeasure.

"Obviously! What about him?!" Sanrat's voice slipped again into a near shriek.

"I said shut your yip!" Cur grabbed a thin shoulder hard and shook Sanrat. "There's a lot we can do. We can hold onto him, douse him in fermentum and leave him in the watering hole for them to find. We could shove him into a paddling pool or throw him into the debris, head first. Mange, we could even send one of us out with him and tell the military that this piece of Anati excrement blind-sided him. We've got options, you hopeless twit! Someone with your education should actually try thinking for a change instead of screaming like a scared little kit!"

Hard stares, in particular from the piercing green eyes of Dame Katuratatallenar de Caterra (Katur to those of the blood), enforced Cur's point that Sanrat should calm himself. "I'm … I'm sorry, Cur. I just – I'm not used to thinking … like you do." Sanrat cursed himself inwardly for ever leaving the safety and security of his academy office. All of those high-minded Foundationalist ideals about genetic purity and a saved society died under the crushing weight of a single realization: he was associated now with a group which seemed to have no qualms about ending a life – even that of a purebred.

Before Cur could come back at him, Katur's yellow-brown face – frosted somewhat white with age – was at Sanrat's nose-tip. "You had best start thinking and stop acting like a frightened child. We are adults with a purpose and a plan; we are soldiers in a war against those who would corrupt our society. This is a fight to the death, and you had best be prepared for that kind of fight. Are you, Sanrat? Are you?"

He nodded and backed away. "Now what?"

Talnar de Gonari, one of the few non de Caterra in the group, slithered into the conversation. "Separate them. Confine them in separate rooms. The last thing you want is for them to talk to one another. Besides, it could be more fun to play one off the other, later."

Cur looked eye-to-eye with the yellow-brown Faelnar and nodded. "Yes. Good thinking, Talnar. Tana, you and Sanrat take the Anati up to the third level. Tie her in the closet. Keep her quiet. I don't want any noise. Talnar and I will take the soldier. We'll tie him out on the bed and make sure he's kept dosed up so he doesn't cause trouble. Then, we'll figure out what's next." Cur stepped away, obviously done with the conversation.

Sanrat couldn't help but ask one more question, "What … what if they come looking for him … sooner, rather than later? Has anyone thought of that?"

Cur and Katur looked at each other in a way that made Sanrat distinctly uncomfortable. Katur answered, "You had best leave the thinking to us for awhile Sanrat, until you can control your cowardly streak. Now go!"

"There's no hope. They're not even thinking straight. Will they kill me, too?" Sanrat's newly vocal dark side whispered into his mind again, and it took a step forward by Cur and a threatening snarl to get him moving on his task. Waiting impatiently, the golden Tana was already standing beside the unconscious Anati.

As he mimicked Tana's movement, reaching under the Anati's shoulders, he realized this was yet another first. He'd never touched an Anati, just as he'd never worked with killers before, either. He tried not to think of what he was lifting as a Thurian, rather just a mistake, but the muscles and fur and warmth that his paws felt seemed to penetrate him as if he was touching her directly, not through her thick clothing.

He watched as Tana wrapped their victim's arm around her neck, and he then did the same. As they walked down the hallway, he tried not to think about how this was as close to a female as he had been in a very long time. "...in particular a female whose scent is so ... nice." He tried to look at her – her face, her chest. His thoughts started to wander. "She's attractive, even exotic. I wonder if she has enough Vulpi blood in her to—"

Tana instantly caught onto what he was doing. "Would you really soil yourself so?" she asked in a loud whisper.

He straightened somewhat, but his pride – horribly wounded by the previous encounter – felt prodded to answer the initiate matron, many seasons his junior. "Foundationalist teachings do not prohibit such things. In fact, it would be a kindness to her – I mean it – to be so favored."

Perhaps another initiate matron would have agreed, but Tanassadurini de Caterra had been forced to fight off a rape-mating from within her own family, and not that long ago. In some ways, she wondered if her recent title of matron wasn't a type of blackmail to keep her silent and in the fold or worse, keep her well-watched. "You can't hunt in the wild, so you'll hunt in a pen? I doubt whatever its tastes are, it won't consider itself much favored. Females usually like their males to have a bit more—"

"Bold words for an *initiate* matron!" he scoffed. "You're not a matriarch yet, Tana, nor will you be with that level of impudence. Don't think that males of merit and position have no say in who becomes a dame."

They pushed open a door and were now in an enclosed stairway, and they turned on their UltraBrights the moment the door shut. As they started to trudge up the stairs with their charge, Tana grunted, "This has nothing to do with merit or position, other than the rape-mating position, maybe. This has to do with ... hypocrisy!"

As they reached the first landing, Sanrat was foolish enough to ask, "Please, oh learned *initiate* matron, how is this hypocrisy? It's allowed in the tenets of Foundationalism, expressly."

Tana's reply was matter-of-fact. "You say Anati aren't true Thurians, right? You say they're not fit to be anything more than slaves. They're genetic mistakes; am I correct?"

"Yes. That's fair."

Now, Tana's voice turned scornful. "Then why would you want to put your purebred little – why would you want to get anywhere near them?

Aren't you afraid they'll contaminate you? They're supposed to be carriers of genetic mutations, even diseases. They're supposed to be devious, treacherous, and murderous."

"She ... she might not be."

"Well, then, she's a poor specimen of Anati, isn't she? And, if this Anati is really not as bad as some say, then, you may actually come to like her. Oh, and then you may actually develop feelings for her." The mocking tone in her voice was unmistakable.

"That would never happen." His denial was flat, but weak.

"You may be an academy teacher, but I know males. You're driven by instinct. Sex turns into love, even for males – especially for some males. Suppose you fall for her; then what? Would you start treating her as an equal? A friend? A lover? A mate? I can't imagine the grand matriarch would like that very much."

"I think that's quite enough!" he said angrily as they started to go up to the third floor.

"Hush! See, that's just the point," the golden-eyed Tana countered quietly. "I've struck my quarry, haven't I? You can't look at these things as sub-Thurian and still want to mate one. You can't commit to deep intimacy with something you say is so vile, can you? I don't care what the Foundationalist tenets say. You can't both hate and love these things. You've got to pick. If you won't pick, then you're a hypocrite."

Whether it was from her stinging remarks or the three story climb, he was unable to make a reply, and any conquests he had hoped for now held no interest for him, at least for the moment. As they turned off their lights and stepped into the dim hall on the third level, he also knew she was right. He was a hypocrite.

About half-way down, they turned left into a room with its door propped open. A small candle burned, providing pitiful light, but Sanrat could see the room had a bathroom near the door, and then a sitting room, and then a bedroom with a deep wall closet facing the outer windows. These were still intact, having been on the outside of the complex facing away from the dining hall.

"Lay her on the bed for a pass or two," Tana directed, "until we're ready." Sanrat was trying to slip out from under the Anati's arm, but Tana stopped him. "No, not like that. Turn around. No, turn HER around! Now, we'll sit on the bed and lower her down." With Sanrat finally understanding, they both sat down with the Anati between them, and then gently laid her back, her legs dangling open slightly off the edge of the bed.

They both stood and looked down at her. Dressed in moderately nice clothes, the odd mix of Faelnar and Vulpi didn't look exactly ugly, Tana mused. Its chest was slowly rising and falling, and its figure, even lying down, was enviable. She could understand, although not forgive, Sanrat's interest. Looking at Sanrat, she could almost swear he was drooling again, so she elbowed him saying, "Come on." Tana took the candle holder and shone the dim light into the closet. A single, solid bar traversed from left to right. Tana reached in and shook it. "That will do. It's solid enough. So, do you have some rope? A belt, something to tie her with?"

"Uh, I don't think so."

Tana's eyes rolled in disgust as she reached into an inner coat pocket. She drew out a black, metallic bar about two tracks long and gave it to Sanrat. "Shock prod. Guard her until I get back. I'm going to find something to tie her up with."

"I've … I've never used one of these before," he admitted, ashamed.

Again, Tana was growing impatient with Sanrat. "It's a simple concept; even an academy *initiate* should be able to operate it. If she moves, shove the end into her midsection, press the black button, and watch the Anati dance before she passes out again. It disables with electroshock before administering a strong sedative three ticks later. She'll sleep for about an interval."

"Why, why do you have this? I mean, none of us were planning for this to happen."

"I was caught unprepared once, and I don't ever intend to be caught that way again. And, that's not the only little toy I've got, so don't think of starting anything. Just remember, you'd never wake up from my other toys." Tana put the candle on the table and left the room. Sanrat listened as she stepped down the hallway, the door finally closing behind her.

Almost in rebellion to Tana's impudence and effrontery, he walked around, sat down on the bed beside the Anati, and pushed the stun prod into her mid-section. With his free paw, he turned her muzzle to face his and looked at it intently. She was beautiful. She was exotic. Her breath was regular and sweet. Above all, she was completely and utterly helpless – at his mercy. After all, he, for now, was the only one here. "So what if Tana doesn't approve," he thought. "She's only an initiate matron, when all is sifted." Perhaps he could get up, lock the door, and delay Tana until he had what he wanted.

It was only then that the first chill hit him. With his expensive coat and fine dress gloves, it hadn't been hard to stay relatively comfortable despite the cold, but now, they seemed to be losing any ability to keep him warm. He half wondered if he could lay with the Anati for heat, but he didn't think he could exactly shock her if they were touching should something happen. Besides, the Anati might grab the shock prod and use it on him. His trembling paw made one last attempt to reach for the slowly rising and falling chest of the female. Just as he was about to touch, his whole body shivered violently. He was forced to shove both paws into his own pockets to try to stay warm.

Standing up, he walked to the window, half expecting to find it open, but it was securely shut. He drew the curtains tighter closed, and rooted around in the front closet for a moment, looking for a coat. There was nothing, not even a spare blanket. Going from drawer to drawer, he found nothing helpful as the cold ate into his bones. Frustrated and shaking, he sat down in a chair near the bed, wondering what was taking Tana so long. Finally, he heard the door open down the hall.

As she stepped into the room holding a set of metal binders and small lengths of rope, she glanced at him and sneered, "I thought you'd have her clothes off before I got back." She walked towards the closet and was obviously testing to see if the binders would work.

"D-d-don't be preposterous. The thought never entered m-m-my mind."

Turning to face him from the closet doorway, the Faelnar's flashing golden eyes gave him a curious look. "What's wrong with you?"

"I'm just … a little cold. Don't you feel it?"

Slowly, she replied, "Yes. It's cold, but not THAT cold."

"It's freezing in here." As he said that, they heard a groan coming from the Anati lying on the bed. It was faint, but it could also mean she would awaken soon.

"Come on, get up. I can't do this alone." As he was struggling to do so, she grabbed a collapsible luggage stand and snapped it open inside the closet. A strong click indicated it had locked into place. Since none of the chairs in the room would fit through the small doorway, Tana realized the luggage stand would have to do; with its two metal bars spanned by straps of crisscrossing soft material, it made a passable seat. Placing it under the sturdy wooden clothes bar that ran across the back of the closet, she returned to the room and found Sanrat sitting, facing away from the Anati, just where he should be. She took her place, and they carefully lifted the female up again.

It was only the work of a few moments before they had her paws stretched high above her, with her bottom resting on the luggage stand. Small lengths of rope bound the Anati's ankles to the stand and reinforced the binders that held her wrists. The Anati's long furry tail stuck out to the side, but probably wouldn't cause her much pain, if any, Tana mused. As she stood back and admired their work, she nodded approvingly; it was secure without being harmful to the creature.

Sanrat had backed up onto the bed and started wrapping up in the covers, trying to get warm. "I have to go back downstairs. Dame Katur wants you to guard the Anati. Can you … manage it?"

"Yes … yes I think so," he answered, not entirely sure, but knowing he didn't want to go down and face either the Dame or Cur. "I'll be fine. I just … just caught a chill, that's all."

"Well, if she gives you any trouble, don't think twice. Use the prod." With that, she turned and left him.

Vanarra felt completely warm, relaxed, and at peace. As she became aware of the sensations around her, a wide smile graced her muzzle. Softly lapping water just beneath her was the loudest sound she could hear, momentarily punctuated by wild flyer calls echoing in the distance. No electronic devices, no traffic, nor anyone else's words assailed her; it was truly restful.

Opening her eyes slowly, she stared up into a late evening sky dappled with soft pink and orange clouds hovering at the edge of her vision. That sky was now starting to glisten with stars and planets – for she could already see Cassius and Bonari – and a stray streak of light above her, a flame star, added just the right touch of magic to the scene. Leaning her head to the side, she saw the distant outline of trees on the far side of what had to be a lake. Again, the flyer calls from the small flocks hovering at the water's edge added just the right seasoning to this perfect moment. Without much concern about where she was or why she was there, she simply stared and sighed.

"It is lovely, isn't it?" a male voice, a familiar one, asked softly beside her.

"Yes," she said wistfully back. "I could stay here forever. I've never been anywhere so peaceful. I feel like I'm living in a Rahnahi poem." Vanarra sighed dreamily.

"In a way, that's truer than you know, Vanarra."

With that, Van's mind started trying to place the voice. With curious interest, she looked to her right. A keen-looking Nephti was reclining in a long hammock right next to her own. "Theo?" she asked incredulously.

He smiled back at her. "You could say this place comes as close to Rahnahi's vision of perfect harmony as any around. It's called Reston Lake; it's in the foothills of the Yarvea range. It's not that hard to find, if you know the name. Kind of a cute word play, too. Rest – on?"

Van laughed a little, but then sat up. "Theo, you've got to forgive me, but I'm not really sure how I got here."

Looking over at her, his face took on a serious expression. "Yes, and that's something we have to talk about."

"How I got here? You didn't like … abduct me, did you?"

"No. I didn't, but someone else did." He leaned up and sat facing her. "What's the last thing you remember?"

She furrowed her brow in concentration. "I … I was at the Meeting Den with Agari. I was, we were … checking the buildings. And then—"

"And then you stumbled into something someone didn't want you to see. They stunned you and Agari, drugged you, and took you prisoner."

"I … I don't understand, Theo. I am here, and I am talking to you. I'm awake, aren't I?"

Theo smiled and shook his head. "If you mean here, at Reston Lake, well, no. If you mean here, in building five, tied up in a closet, then the answer is sadly yes. Agari's tied up a floor below."

Van sat up and faced him now. "Theo, if I'm not here, then what are you? What is this?" she asked, pointing to the scenery all around her.

He seemed to understand how afraid she was becoming as the memory of being attacked slipped back into her thoughts. His tone was calm and kind. "Do you remember how we talked earlier? Do you remember what you felt when we talked?"

"I … wondered if you were – if talking to you was like what it meant to have … a father."

"Oh, and why's that?" he asked, curious.

"You didn't want anything; you just wanted to help, and … you cared."

He smiled at that before saying, "Then perhaps I'm just something inside you that wants to help. Perhaps, I'm a guide that you need to listen to. Perhaps all of your experience, subconscious thought, and instinct are coming to the surface, taking form, and giving voice to what you need to hear."

"And what do I need to hear?" she asked, uncertain.

"That you're in the paws of a group called the Foundationalists, and they are very, and I do mean very, dangerous." Vanarra's guts ran cold. "You've heard of them?"

"Yes! What are they doing here?!" Her fearful voice was almost a whisper.

"Trying their best NOT to be rescued by an Anati. They haven't discovered that the Anati responsible for the rescue is actually you, and if I were you, I would keep it that way."

"What … what are they going to do with me?"

Theo closed his eyes and shook his head, sighing. "If they have their way, you won't make if off this mountain alive. You can also bet that your last moments of life will not be enjoyable, either. They think of you as, at best, diversion and entertainment, and at worst … completely disposable." He paused a moment for that to sink in, before continuing in a brighter tone, "You've got a few things in your favor, though!"

"Such as?"

"Sahnassa, for one, and everyone else who isn't going to abandon you, regardless of your parentage. Your friends will find you," Theo said with absolute certainty.

"How can you know that? How can I know? Is any of this real?" She was still trying to grasp what he and everything else around her actually was – reality, vision, or mindless delusion.

He stood, walked to the edge of the platform, and faced away from her. "You remember when I said I might be something from inside of you that's found a way to speak? Well, consider another possibility, Van. It's one you're going to find difficult to understand or believe, but one in which you need to try to have some faith. The very same Theo who talked to you in the valley is who is speaking with you right now." He turned to face her. "So, let's be clear about this. I can't tell you anything you already know to prove I'm really Theo, talking to you in your own head when you are, for all practical purposes, drugged and completely unconscious."

"Uh … yeah," Vanarra responded warily, shaking her head and trying to understand. "If you're just a drugged-out fantasy in my mind, there's no way for me to know if that's even … like possible. So how do you prove that you are the real Theo and not some weird dream?"

He sat back down on the hammock opposite her and placed his paw gently on the side of her head, much as a father would adoring his child. "Simple. I tell you things you don't know and have no way of knowing right now, but that you will discover are true – soon enough. I'm going to tell you about your captors and how to deal with each of them. That way, even if you still don't believe me," he said drawing back his paw, "at least the information will help keep you alive until we can get help to you."

Van thought about it for a moment and cocked her head to one side. "As crazy as this sounds, that kind of makes sense. I guess I'll take any help I can get, even from a hallucination!"

In response to her plain-spoken acceptance, he nodded. "Very well, then. There are five who are the main actors in this conspiracy. Four of them are truly bad news, and you would be wise to play the humblest, quietest, most obedient, self-effacing little Anati they've ever seen."

Vanarra felt real anger boil up inside of her. "I … don't know if I can do that."

"You will," Theo demanded sternly, "if you have any illusions about staying alive. In one form or another, this quartet would be more than happy to slit your throat to prove their point. Give them no reason to do so. Your main goal now is to buy us time. Got it?"

"Okay," she accepted, earnestly.

"Very well. Cur is a young male, and physically he's very intimidating. He's their brute strength. However, he's more likely to dismiss you as unimportant than actually try to harm you; just stay out of his way. Sanrat is an academy professor; he's an intellectual regarding Foundationalist philosophy, but for an attractive Anati, he may be tempted to put those theories of 'rightful dominance' into practice. Dame – and I did say 'Dame' – Katur of the de Caterra is old and bitter about her house shrinking and losing prestige. She thinks this little drama is a way to change that, and her title gives her solid clout with the others. Talnar is a real piece of work. He's a male from the de Gonari; he's been working to subvert Amyra ever since the old matriarch was deposed. He's a killer, Van, and he enjoys doing it. He'll try to get you to talk and then use anything you say to pry out your secrets. Don't let him inside the real you. Compliant little Anati are always respectful. Yes sir, no sir, very short answer, or silence, if you can get away with it. It will deny him his pleasure and keep him tamped down."

Van shook her head. "Now that's one heck of a crew! So, it's Cur, Sanrat, Dame Katur, and Talnar – wait, that's only four. Who's the fifth?"

"Her name is Tana. She's gold on gold, eyes and fur. I have a feeling that she'll be alone watching you at some point. Of all of them, she's the least in tune with what the others are doing. You should talk to her, respectfully and humbly to be sure, but I think you'll find she can be turned into an ally, and she can help protect you until help arrives. The truth is, she already has. Sanrat found your unconscious body rather appealing and was starting to make a list of everything he wanted to do with you or … to you. Tana sensed what he was thinking and called him a hypocrite to his face for wanting to get intimate with someone he thinks is a genetic mistake."

"That only sounds *so* positive," Van offered, doubtfully.

"Don't discount it. She may have used that argument, but I sense there's a reason she stood up for you. It's something special about her – something profound." Van noticed that all around them, it was starting to get genuinely dark. Theo followed her glance and nodded. "Yes. It's almost time. You're only a few passes from waking up. Give me your paws." She offered her paws to him, and he held them in his. Looking into his eyes, she heard his voice in her head. "Have faith Vanarra. I'll make this as easy as I can for you. Be brave and be wise, and above all, be patient. Help will come. Just buy us time."

"Thank you," she heard herself say in her thoughts. He smiled and nodded, and then darkness wrapped around her like a blanket, leaving her insensible to the world.

Chapter 16: Playing in Wait

Slowly, Vanarra felt again. She was drowsy, still waking up, but the vivid dream-like experience she just had caused her to be careful. It took only a moment to realize that her body was at an odd angle, not lying down. Her head was tilted forward, and her arms were above her. Very gently and only slightly, she tried lowering her arms. Her wrists were pressed together, and together they felt the strain of ropes and metal binding them. "Theo! He was right," she thought to herself. She then noticed how foggy she felt, and Van remembered his warnings. "Ah yes. Drugged." She also knew, if everything else was true, she was being watched.

Vanarra thought for a moment about what to do next. The phrase "Buy us time" kept replaying in her mind. "Well, they don't have to know I'm awake. I'll just play at being asleep, and I'll listen." She figured that strategy would work, at least for a little while. Besides, she needed time for her head to clear and time to think about everything else Theo had said.

Sanrat blinked and ⬡⬡⬡⬡⬡ lf up. He thought she had just moved, but now, she was still again. The cold was mercilessly penetrating him, and he wondered if he was running a high fever. He felt his nose, and the moment he moved, he was gripped by another chill. He tried to remember how long the drugs in the stun prod were supposed to last, but that depended on how much was administered. "Cur was the one to do the dosing; perhaps he would know. Mange, it's cold up here! Why are they leaving me alone for so long?" he quietly complained, looking at his timepiece. Disappointed, he sighed. It had only been half an interval since Tana left.

Vanarra listened with a little amusement at her apparently reluctant captor. She was becoming more aware, and the sluggishness brought on by the drugs was almost gone. He was obviously freezing cold; she could hear that in his voice. The rustling of what sounded like covers on a nearby bed also seemed to confirm his discomfort. "Who is it?" she wondered, thinking through the names Theo had told her. The voice, even under duress, had a scholarly touch to it. "What was that one's name? Sanrat. That was it." As she listened, she could almost hear him shivering aloud.

Considering her captor's apparent discomfort, Vanarra realized she hadn't really been paying much attention to how she felt, which she supposed was a good thing. Happily, Van didn't feel like she was injured in any way. Still, she took a quick mental inventory and was actually quite surprised. As trussed up as she was, she should have been in all sorts of pain around her wrists and ankles, but there just wasn't any. She was simply unable to move. She wasn't really hungry or thirsty, and she didn't feel any other urgent needs requiring relief, either. For that, she was grateful. Finally, she was amazed that she wasn't actually cold. To her, the air was comfortable, and it didn't even really smell bad.

It took her a few moments of thinking it through, but she realized that she *shouldn't* be feeling so good. After all, she had walked through most of the Meeting Den prior, and its cold, dank hallways were still a very pungent memory. This place didn't seem to have any odor. In fact, the only thing she could smell was a faint trace of her own perfume, mixed with a little of her own scent – strong enough for her to notice since she hadn't been able to bathe in awhile.

Theo's voice played in her mind again, "I'll make this as easy as I can for you."

"Could he actually be doing something to make this easier? How could he do that?" she wondered, idly.

At that moment, she heard what sounded like the distant opening of a door; it sounded like the heavy fire doors at the end of the Meeting Den hallways. Her captor heard it, too, and he started moving around. She heard him shuffle off the bed and step in front of her. Then, his steps moved away, and the sound of a piece of furniture, perhaps a chair being dragged across the floor towards her, met Van's ears. Muffled curses condemning the cold were whispered as Sanrat took his seat again, it seemed, only a few tracks in front of her.

There were paw steps now, heavy paw steps near the door of the room and then entering. They came to rest nearby, and Vanarra could feel a new set of eyes on her. "Has it moved yet?"

"J-just a l-little, a few passes ago. Then nothing."

"She should be awake. She's probably just shamming you. I thought academy professors were smarter than that." Suddenly, a powerful paw grabbed her under the neck and lifted her head up. Vanarra was dazed, not by the rough pawing, but because at the moment he touched her, her whole body had gone completely limp. "Hello, little Anati bitch! Hello! Oh, mange," her captor groaned, disgusted. Vanarra felt her mouth open and her tongue fall limply out one side of her muzzle, covered in drool. "Great, just great!" She then felt a paw finger roughly try to lift open one of her eyelids. She didn't offer any resistance, even instinctual. For some reason, she just couldn't. "Nasty creatures. We should rid the planet of them."

"So, is it f-faking?"

"No. No, it's not. It's still out. I've dosed lots of these things before, and all of them have woken up by now. They kick, they scream – oh, great! They don't just hang there and fricking drool!" With that, he released her head, and she felt it fall limply forward. "Rape-mating little vermin!" From the sound, he was obviously wiping himself off.

Voice still shaking, Sanrat offered, "Maybe it's just physiology, Cur. Perhaps, it has a substandard resistance to drugs. Can't clear such things from its system."

"If you're so interested, we can cut it up later, and you can study it. In the meantime, make sure it doesn't escape and beat in that academy skull of yours. Katur says you do a good job putting our message out to prospects, even if you're kind of lacking as a guard."

"Yes," Sanrat said, his voice finding some strength and getting testy with the buff, young male. "About that. When is someone going to come and relieve me? I do not want to stay up here all alone with this ... thing."

Cur chuckled. "I don't know, Sanny; it kind of suits you. Shouldn't you be asking us to leave you two alone for a little while, not trying to get away from it? Perhaps its genetic mix has made it better to bed, even if it's unconscious and drooling. Mange, maybe that would wake it up."

"Cur, I can't stay up here another interval," Sanrat admitted, and his voice dropped, embarrassed. "I think I've come down with something. I need some time down stairs ... where it's warm."

"Don't make your type out of solid stuff, do they? Alright, I'll send Talnar or one of the others up here in a little while, but not until we have our other guest taken care of. Sit tight, and do your job. If it gives you any problem, shove the prod into its gut and shock it till it pukes. Try to keep it alive; we'll need some entertainment later, but don't try too hard." The heavy footsteps started to leave, but Cur turned around and added, "And if it doesn't wake up in a quarter interval, then buzz it a little anyway. That should help bring it around." The heavy footsteps faded down the hall, and finally, the door sound triggered an audible sigh of relief from Sanrat who started making his way back to the warmth of the bed.

Inwardly, Van breathed her own sigh of relief. The strange, limp feeling was gone, and she felt like she could open her eyes if she wanted to. The question was just picking the right moment. The little exchange between her captors had given her so much to think about, Van felt she needed to play unconscious a little while longer just to work out everything in her head: what she was going to do, what she was going to say, and how she was going to act. "Theo was right," she thought to herself. "I'm not even a *she* with them. I'm an *it*! I don't know how you did it Theo, but thanks." There was a weird echo in her thoughts, like she could almost sense him for a moment, and then it faded away. Still, she was glad she didn't feel completely alone.

Sahnassa entered the command center, carefully trying to keep herself under control. She felt an almost unconquerable urge to run in screaming "They have Vanarra", but as Theo had told her, she couldn't. She didn't "know" that Van had been taken hostage, and revealing too much information would create suspicion, confusion, and/or apprehension that could prove harmful to herself, but moreover, deadly to Vanarra. So, in the strongest test of her will yet, she tried to walk in as if nothing was wrong. After all, as far as she was supposed to know, she had just finished her rounds delivering power packs, bringing back up the de Gonari and de Dothnar communications nets.

She surveyed the room and saw Rahnahi, Buck, the Chief, one of the medics, Dania, and a host of other matrons and dames. Walking over towards Buck and the Chief, she smiled her best. "It's done."

"Yes, we can tell," Buck said appreciatively. "The whole network is back up and running, now. You should have seen Dania; she was positively glowing!"

Upon hearing her name, Dania stepped over. "So there you are! Everyone is so relieved now that the communications are back up! Sahnassa, thank you! I really think we'll make it through this alright!"

Sahnassa could hold back no longer. "You're welcome, but is the evacuation not going well?"

All three looked at her curiously, and the Chief answered, "No. It's actually going to plan. Why do you ask?"

"I was walking outside between the buildings, and, through the windows, I saw a few still waiting in building five. I thought that was supposed to be empty."

Dania blinked. "It was. I don't understand. Sahnassa, are you sure?"

"Yes. I saw them very clearly when one of the flyers took off. The light hit the building, and I saw several of them standing at the window, holding something in their paws."

The Chief's interest was now piqued. "Sahnassa, this is very important. Could you make out exactly *what* they were holding?"

Sahnassa continued her act. "Short, black, maybe shiny. I couldn't see much more than that."

A grimace crossed the Chief's face, and he stepped back a pace or two. Pressing a control near his shoulder, he spoke, "Delta three nine, cross call." He waited, and there was no response. "Delta three nine, cross call." Again he waited, and again, there was nothing. "All units, Lambda three nine, Frost delta two, ultra. Confirm on two." Releasing the control, he looked at them and asked, "May we step into the other room?"

Quietly and discreetly, the group entered the small room that had been Buck's communication center. Rahnahi saw them and followed, as well. "What's going on?" she asked as the Chief closed the door behind her.

"We have a problem, Honored One. Agari is not responding to TransCom calls, even one with an urgent priority. That's not like him. What's concerning me is that Sahnassa clearly saw some number of individuals looking out the windows of building five—"

"Which we thought we'd already cleared," Dania added, worry now invading her voice.

The Chief finished the picture. "She saw them holding what might be considered weapons. If I remember, someone said that Agari and Vanarra had gone around locking up empty buildings. It's possible they ran into something."

"Chief, what exactly do you think that something is?" Rahnahi asked.

"I won't know until I have a look, Honored One. Sahnassa, I need for you to come with me. I want to get a closer look at building five, perhaps from the roof of this building."

"I noticed a roof access at the top of one of the stairwells when I was here earlier. I can show you where it is," Sahnassa offered, her long tail twitching with impatience.

"Excellent. Now, let me emphasize that we don't know what's happened. It could be a bad communicator, but I'm sensing it's more than that," the Chief warned.

"What should we do?" Dania asked.

"It's important that no one sees any change in our operations. We don't want to tip our paw that we know something is wrong. Just keep doing what you're doing, and find clever ways to keep anyone from going to building five or any of the other abandoned buildings."

"We'll take care of it, Chief," Dania said, nodding.

"With your leave, Honored One?"

"Certainly Chief, and you both be careful," Rahnahi ordered.

"We will. Thank you. Sahnassa?" With that, they both left the room.

As the two maneuvered their way out of the control center, Sahnassa wanted to run, and the Chief sensed it. "Not yet," he ordered quietly. "Wait until we're out of sight. Walk slowly, keep your eyes open, and pretend everything is normal. It's the best thing you can do when you don't want an enemy to know they've been spotted."

She nodded and even feigned a smile as she passed the dour old matron guarding the door. It was only a few paces until they reached a stairwell, and soon they were both inside. Sahni was sprinting to the top, having pulled out a small UltraBright from her pocket. The Chief pounded up behind her. As she neared the top, her wrist tingled. Looking at the watch, she saw a lock symbol, and then saw it open. The image disappeared as the Chief stood beside her. She pointed her light up. A small ladder led to a hatch, a hatch that appeared securely locked. The Chief, disappointed, growled, "We'd need cutters. We have to find another way. This will take too long."

"One moment, Chief," Sahni bade, climbing the ladder. As she got to the top, she looked at the lock closely. Reaching around it, she gave it a good pull. The bottom part of the lock detached and swung open. "It wasn't locked. It was just closed." She pulled out the lock, removed the restraining bolt, and then pushed the release to open the small hatch.

"I am so going to enlist you," the Chief said appreciatively as he followed her up onto the roof. As he emerged, he saw Sahni's silhouette standing against the gray sky. "Lie down, Sahnassa! All the way!" She did as she was told, which was fortunate. A flyer departing the landing field briefly lit their general area with its lights. "Wait here, while I scout ahead."

She nodded, again feeling the bite of the cold air. She was grateful she had a moment aboard the Tashar to warm up. The Chief crawled by her quickly and disappeared out of sight a few moments later. Sahni watched ahead, but placed her wrist in front of her. "Thanks," she said quietly.

The watch replied in printed words. "You're welcome. Van is awake, but playing asleep. So far, so good. Watch your step. Go slow." She looked over her watch, and saw the Chief signaling her to come forward. Trying to crawl like he did, and using a little of what Theo had taught her, she joined him. He helped her over a thin ledge onto another section of the roof.

"Over there," he whispered. "Behind that. If we crawl up carefully, we can peek over the top with the night vision scope and have ourselves a good look. Remember, keep your tail down and tucked. It's the first thing someone would notice." She nodded, and the Chief crouched down and began to crawl.

As she fell in behind him, she started to wonder. "He's de Caterra. What if he sees someone he knows? Will he turn them in? Will he dismiss it? Hopefully he's a soldier first and a de Caterra second." As she arrived at the two-track tall edge barrier, he was already peering through the night vision lenses at building five, off to their left. She just waited behind him patiently, the same questions and answers rolling around in her mind.

"Well shave my ass and break my tail – oh, sorry about that," the Chief said quietly, looking down from his viewer, his apologetic expression a little ghostly in the projected light from the scope.

"It's alright. You should hear some of the things Vanarra says from time to time." He nodded appreciatively.

"Yes, I think we have a problem," he breathed, returning to the viewer. "What I'm seeing doesn't look like half-wits who want to wait out a storm. This looks a little like a well organized—" He paused, fiddling with the eyepiece. "No, no, no, no!" he growled softly, but she could hear the regret mounting in his voice.

"What is it?" she asked, knowing full well what he was probably seeing and, likewise, knowing that now was the time when he had to choose. Less than a track from the edge of a building's roof several stories in the air, she hoped he chose well. He rolled onto his back, so his head was slightly propped against the wall.

"See for yourself," he said grimly. "Look at building five ... in the corners." She took the scope and edged her way up to where she could see. Although the view was nothing close to the clarity she saw through her Tashar-enhanced eyewear, it was still possible to see the Faelnar guards holding weapons, keeping a careful watch out the windows.

"I see them. What are they doing?" He didn't answer her, and she lowered the device. She looked down at him, and he was staring blankly ahead. "Chief?"

"I know them Sahnassa. They're from my own family. They're de Caterra, like me." She reached out her paw and held his shoulder. He patted it, and opened his paw for the viewer. In a moment, he was again watching the guards in building five with Sahnassa ducked behind the low wall. "What in the name of all Thuria do you think you're doing?" he asked softly, intensely, as if he were right there, confronting them. "What is this going to accomplish?" He sounded not only disappointed, but heartbroken. "What the crap will this prove, you rape-mating idiots?" Now, he was starting to get angry.

"What do you think they're doing?" she asked quietly, hoping to calm him down.

"I don't know," he answered, a little more softly. "They're hiding from the evacuation, but it's like they want to get left behind! Why starve and freeze to death up here?"

"When everyone's gone," Sahni offered, "they could make better use of whatever food is left and burn whatever scrap wood they need to stay warm. They could still survive, I suppose."

The Chief shook his head, still unable to grasp the motives of his fellow de Caterra in the viewfinder. "But why? They'll just have to be rescued by someone else, later."

"Perhaps there's something about *this* rescue they don't like," she suggested, as delicately as she could.

He looked down at her in stunned amazement. "Dammit, I think you're right! Could they know that the rescue was organized by—" He didn't have to supply Vanarra's name for Sahnassa to nod, grimly. "Mange, and now they have her!"

"They may not know who she is, but, without a doubt, they'll know what she is."

He shook his head. "Her life won't be worth a rotten stack of creele, if this is who I think it is."

"Who?"

The Chief lowered the viewer and looked at her, embarrassed. "Something de Caterra are not supposed to talk about to those not of the blood, but something all of us have heard about – at least a little. There's supposedly a group in our family that quietly 'takes care' of any Anati-related issues that crop up in our house. It's the kind of thing parents warn their children of when they get too friendly with those of another species, especially an Anati. Lately, my relatives have been telling me the group has come out of the shadows, and they've started gaining members from other families, too. They call themselves Foundationalists. Every problem in Thurian society, so they say, comes from the Anati or those tendencies which cause others to create them. Now, unlike some who just *talk* against the Anati, they – apparently – *do*. What, exactly, no one's said. That part is still rumor. I never suspected anything like this!"

She could tell from his expression that he earnestly meant it. "What do we do now?"

He closed his eyes, was still for a moment, and then shook his head slightly. "We stop them, and we get back Agari and Vanarra. I'll probably be disavowed, but funny enough, I'd rather keep my honor. Right now, seeing those … fools at the windows, I think I'll take that over my family name, anytime. Come on. We've got a rescue to plan."

Vanarra knew she was running out of time to play the sleeper. She thought she could hear Sanrat looking down at his timepiece almost every pass, so it seemed, and she didn't want the clock to run out on her. What was frustrating her now was that she had to actually decide how to wake up, something she normally did without thinking. As Theo had alluded, she was now playing a role, since being Vanarra Anasto around these "Foundationalists" would be far too dangerous. She had thought of a name, had a good back-story, and had even decided how to talk and act, largely based on Theo's advice. However, waking up was worrisome. If she was too placid, Sanrat would know she had been faking. If she woke up too violently and pulled at her restraints in shock and fear, she might just get a prod stun for her trouble – hardly the accolade she was hoping for. Finally, a light tickle at the back of her throat gave her an idea.

Sanrat looked at his timepiece again; six passes had fallen without so much as a twitch from the Anati. He looked at the stun prod and tried to imagine himself shoving it into the limp female in front of him. Unlike some of those downstairs, Sanrat knew he lacked a sadistic disposition, although he had nothing but contempt for Anati. True, he believed that all Anati were a genetic mistake, and they should be controlled, sterilized, and thoughtfully managed until they simply died out. Yet, try as he might, he could not believe those who said things like, "They don't feel pain; it's instinct" or "They don't really think; they just react." As much as he hated to admit it, he knew that wasn't true.

His somewhat overly progressive academy had hired an assistant instructor who just happened to be of "mixed ancestry" – a term used by those who thought the term "Anati" was offensive. Although there were some protests and reports of cruel jokes and even assaults, the Anati male had persevered. Even when several academy donors threatened to pull their funding, still more came offering a replacement for those funds. What turned both his stomach and his reason end-over-end was when he had overheard students speak of this Anati with grudging respect. Some even spoke with admiration about him. He never heard his own students talking about "Sanny" that way; it was almost too depressing to think about how he was envious of an Anati.

Chilled to the bone and lost in this melancholy line of thought, Sanrat was startled by a rough cough in front of him. He felt his chair beginning to tip back, and quite clumsily he tried righting himself, accidently throwing the prod half way across the room as he clawed for both dresser and bed.

Finally stable, he looked at the Anati. Although its head still hung forward, it now wasn't limp with unconsciousness; it was tossing slowly back and forth like someone waking up from a bad dream. Ruefully he thought, "Waking up *into* a bad dream." He wondered what she was feeling, and then instantly he chided himself on two points. He shouldn't call it a "she," not even in his thoughts, and he shouldn't care what *it* was feeling. After all, he couldn't give Tana the satisfaction of being right; he couldn't let himself become "attached" to this Anati in any way.

The legs, torso, and arms began to shift around, as if each was independently trying to understand where it was. It took several more passes, but slowly the Anati started to move and breathe as if it were awake. He could see its eyes were open, though still glazed over, looking down at the floor. He saw it pull hesitantly against the restraints and then, to his amazement, he heard it softly sobbing. Tears dropped to the cold wooden floor, and the cry was muffled, as if someone had already yelled at her to be quiet.

He caught himself a second time thinking of it as a she, but it was such a hard thought to fight. He closed his eyes, and he didn't hear an Anati. He heard a female crying, and every dormant instinct in his body and mind was now coming to life, urging him to rush to her rescue. A soft voice in his mind dragged him to the next thought. "Rescue her from whom? Rescue her from *you*." He shook his head trying to get the thought out of his mind, but it would not leave him. "Why is she crying? Why won't she stop? She's afraid of you, terrified, and in pain. You're not an accomplished academic, are you now? No, you're just a common thug."

"Please," he bade her quietly, "please stop crying. The others—" That was right; he had to tell himself, convince himself he wasn't a thug like the others. "The others won't like it. If you're quiet, if you behave, they—" He wanted to promise her everything would be okay. Just then, he realized he had given up all pretense of being detached, of calling her an it. "They'll leave you alone, at least for awhile."

She looked up at him, and her tearing eyes ripped him like bared claws. With effort, she quieted, and then she nodded, dropping her gaze before she again let her head sink forward. "What's your name?"

"Alliana is my name," she answered in a whisper that, while still sad, was as feminine as any bedroom mating talk he could imagine.

"Alliana," he acknowledged. "That's pretty. Is that it? Just Alliana?" She nodded. He knew most Anati gave themselves last names, even if they had no family. He wondered if, perhaps, she was already someone's kept Anati, as the tenets of Foundationalism directed. "Why were you with that soldier?"

"Soldier taking me back" was the humble response.

"Back to who?"

"Taking me to Master."

So, she was kept. That meant that somewhere, there was an owner who was going to be displeased his property had disappeared. "What happened to your master?"

"Could not find him," she said sadly.

"What is your master's name?"

"Master is his name," she replied softly, obediently. He shook his head in resignation. There wasn't anything threatening here, just an already compliant slave, and a poorly educated one at that.

"How did you lose your Master?"

"Turned, he was … gone." She couldn't keep from sobbing this time, and he knew she was horribly afraid of being away from him. He had a vague memory of hearing the mothers of small children talk about losing sight of their kits or cubs for just an instant, and being terrified. Had her owner abandoned her? Had they just gotten separated in the dark confusion of the Meeting Den?

"Did he tell you anything about what to do if you got lost?"

"Lost. Never lost before," she said, and her crying overtook her again.

"There, now. Perhaps—" and he realized he was again about to try to promise something he couldn't deliver. "Maybe something will work out. Perhaps your master will find us. Just don't cry. Be quiet and behave, can you do that?" Again, with effort, she obeyed him and nodded. "Just rest for now."

She nodded again and leaned forward, closing her eyes. Quietly, he stood, and with the chills still buffeting him, he retrieved the prod and sat, making himself as comfortable as he could. He looked at the cowering figure and then at the metal prod, which he silently placed on the bed. He knew, now, he would have no immediate need for it.

Vanarra had to nearly bite her own tongue in two to keep from laughing when she startled Sanrat, and he had believed every suggestion of her being a kept Anati. Although the thought was thoroughly revolting to her, she had seen and even met a very few Anati who had been kept and were smuggled away from their owners. She took several of the young kits she knew at the orphanage and wove them into this Alliana. With some regret, she remembered the true bearer of that name: a kept Anati teen who was abducted into freedom, only to commit suicide in grief at being away from her master. Alliana would live again, just this once, and buy Vanarra the time Theo said her friends needed.

Sahnassa stood beside the Chief, providing him some moral support as they waited for Dania and Rahnahi to enter the small communications room off the command center. Buck walked in, and when Sahni saw the Chief start to raise a paw motioning him to leave, she placed her own on his shoulder and said, "Of anyone, Chief, he'll understand."

"Alright," he conceded, sitting down on the desk. Waiting for a nod, Buck moved forward and closed the door. "Jam a towel underneath. This can't be overheard ... what I've got to say." Buck reached down and did what was asked.

Dania and Rahnahi both saw how stricken the Chief looked, and instantly feared the worst. "Is he ... are they dead?" Dania asked.

"We don't know," Sahni answered quietly.

"What we do know," the Chief admitted raggedly, "is that members of my ... of the de Caterra family are armed and appear now to be occupying building five." He paused, for he was obviously struggling to get this out. "I can only hope they haven't been stupid enough to harm either Vanarra or Agari, but the fact Agari is not responding is a pretty good indication that something bad has happened to both of them."

Dania's teeth were almost instinctively baring, and Buck was simply dumbstruck, mouth hanging open. "So Chief, what next? We're ready to follow your advice." The matriarch's simple statement did much to bolster the faltering soldier.

"Even though I'm—"

She stepped forward and looked him in the eye. "What right have I, even as a matriarch, to doubt your honor, now? I think that's evident to all of us."

For a moment, he bowed, but finally, he looked up and said, "Now, I know why they call you Honored One, and that *you* truly deserve to be called that."

Rahnahi nodded, answering, "And I know why they call you Chief, and why your soldiers follow you." The look that passed between them, the elder poet-matriarch and the life-long soldier, was a crystallized moment of understanding. Sahnassa's heart was beating in her throat, and she watched them embrace through tear-filled eyes. They finally separated, and the matriarch nodded, asking "So what are we to do?"

He nodded and stepped back, bowing again to her slightly as he did. "We make doubly sure, Honored One, that building five gets no more visitors, accidental or purposeful. This message has to be passed muzzle to ear, and discreetly. It can't be passed over open channels, even over your family nets. As for me, I have to call down to the Marshall and request a special strike team."

"What kind of a strike team?" Dania asked, worry in her voice.

"We came prepared in case things were out of control when we arrived. They're not normally a part of our unit, but for the exercise we were originally planning, before all of this started, they were along for the ride."

"Who?" Buck asked, and the answer caused his jaw to drop open once again.

Marshall Terrat de Debonar was walking away from the serving line where the evacuees were gladly receiving their first hot meal in many intervals. He had to chuckle to himself at the wild mix of circumstances that caused some of the most elite urban assault troops ever trained to be serving under his command, and serving as kitchen help. He had been honored at the time, if not a little confused, when the training division had placed their troop with his for the exercise. When the exercise turned into a real mission, he was grateful. Having some defense force all-stars along for the ride had made them all feel a little bit better about what would happen if the situation on the mountain was bad when they arrived.

Thankfully, that fear hadn't materialized. Left with nothing but a soft creele evacuation, for the most part, the famous "Storm Pack" had taken to helping in other ways. What's more, they seemed to be enjoying themselves. They had also been a morale boost to the evacuees, many of whom knew of their amazing service record.

"Marshall?" called a familiar voice from behind.

"Yes, Theo?"

"About an interval ago, one of Tawnston's soldiers dropped comms, and the Chief flipped the ops frequencies. Now, your command center has a priority signal from the Chief. He's requesting you."

Turning on his heels and rapidly walking back with Theo towards the command center, Terrat was furious. "Theo, would you please tell me why I'm hearing this a full interval after it happened?! And why in Thuria's name it's you who's delivering this message?"

Answering honestly, Theo explained, "As for the delay, I'd have some pointed words with your ops officer. As for my part, your soldiers are pretty strung out with the evacuees moving between the buildings; I was the only free paw."

As they turned the corner, they saw Tedarri finishing a conversation, and Terrat called, "Tedarri, could you please join me in the command center?" It was phrased as a question, but it was an unmistakable order.

Tedarri, being Lupar as well, had no problem picking up on the urgency in the Marshall's body language. The tail alone was enough of a warning, down and flat. "What's happened?" he asked in a low whisper as he came up alongside them.

"We're about to find out," he growled, pushing open the door to the classroom that was his command center.

In less than a quarter interval, Theo guided a new group of volunteers into the kitchen. Comprised of members of the valley neighborhood association, they were a pleasant assortment of young to elderly adults who, after finding their own lairs in good order after the quake, heard about the evacuees. "Storm Pack," Theo announced as he entered, "your relief force has arrived." A little surprised, the soldiers turned as the new volunteers entered and started talking with them, introducing themselves and thanking them for doing such good work.

A large presence loomed up behind Theo. "I didn't get orders we were being relieved." It was said loud enough that all conversations in the immediate area ceased.

Theo turned in a near military about face, which brought him right up into the eyes of a very stern looking sergeant. Staring fearlessly up into the menacing face and steely grey eyes, Theo explained quietly, "I'm sorry you weren't told, sergeant, but your *talents* are needed ... someplace else. They seem to need help with some *heavy lifting*."

"You?"

Theo was pleased to see the black eyebrow fur lift. "Yep."

Just seeing the Nephti standing in front of him, someone he trusted, was more than enough motivation. "Get ready to move out, Storm Pack! Cappy, Scraps, Buzzer, get them formed up out back in five passes."

Conversations resumed, albeit a little hastened as Theo and Cutter, the sergeant in charge, stepped down the short hall to the outside door. As the door closed, Cutter said, "Didn't expect to see you here. Thought you civilian supply—" and he omitted an obvious pejorative term at the last moment. "Well, I thought your type always stuck close to the desk."

"You know me better than that."

"That I do," Cutter admitted, remembering the ill-considered contest he had with Theo back at his base earlier in the season. He had half-heartedly challenged the somewhat mild-mannered Nephti contractor to run the assault course against him, for a bit of sport. To his surprise, the Nephti had readily agreed. The whole troop turned out of their barracks to watch the competition.

Then, they were both off, charging over obstacles, picking up weapons, knocking down targets, swinging on ropes over pits, and all other manner of high pressure activities. In some phases of the course, Cutter was ahead, but in others, Theo passed him by. At the end, it was a dead tie. Theo conceded that he thought he came in just a bit behind Cutter, but it was clear that, minus their all-Lupar tradition, Theo was easily their equal. After that, Cutter had assigned extra soldiers to help with the inventory, and a good night was spent by all at the local post establishment drinking fermentum and telling Theo all their war stories.

"It's just not the normal way I get my instructions."

"Terrat thought sending me with a bunch of replacement volunteers would make it look more like you were going somewhere else down here as opposed to what you'll read in this." He presented him with a printed sheet of orders.

Cutter took it, read it, and then read it again. "And you're coming with us?"

"You'll need bait – someone to divert their attention when you're moving in. A dopey-looking Nephti plodding around with an UltraBright is going to be far more believable than a Lupar who has obviously spent his life in the vaunted Storm Pack."

"What do we know about the hostiles?" Cutter asked, his demeanor now all business.

"About twenty-eight, mostly de Caterra, lightly armed, but dedicated and desperate."

"Hostages?"

"Two hostages – one civilian Anati female and one Faelnar defense force male. They were ambushed. Both are extremely high value. You should be able to spot them easily on thermal."

The door beside them opened, and Lupar started pouring out, stepping down the stairs of the loading dock onto the pavement below, and getting into formation by habit.

Cutter looked down at his orders and pointed at the phrase "Capture hostiles alive, if possible."

Theo clarified flatly, "Within reason, of course. If it points a weapon at you, feel free to blow its tail clean off." Cutter laughed quietly. "We've got a transport coming around that will take us to the assembly area. You'll gear up and depart via HVR-9 from there. We don't want to let the evacuees know anything is wrong, either here or on the mountain."

"You know the lay?"

"Yeah. I'll draw it all out for you. I went up there last season. You'll have a good avenue of approach and easy entry."

Looking down at the group forming up on the pavement below them, Cutter answered, "Yeah, we like it that way." They heard the sound of a vehicle coming around the side of the school, so Cutter called the group to attention.

A fair amount of time had passed in silence, Vanarra quietly playing "Alliana", while Sanrat played the role of guard. She wondered if she could break free, pull the rod from the closet, knock him out, and then escape. There were a lot of "ifs" in that line of thinking, and she knew it. All of those ifs had bad alternatives. If she couldn't break free when she tried, he'd know she was a threat, and he would know the character she had built was a lie. Even if she was successful, she had no way of knowing who was waiting down the hall or in the stairwell. No, that wasn't buying time and, although it was counter to her nature to just "stay put," that strange experience with Theo kept hovering in her mind. After a few passes, she decided it would be better to think through Alliana's life, try to invent details, and make sure she was ready for new questions.

Van thought she had most of Alliana's characteristics pretty well figured out by the time she heard the door at the end of the hallway open. Vanarra listened carefully, and thought she heard muffled conversation for a few moments. Sanrat reacted too, but he didn't leave his blanket-filled chair. He simply listened and waited, and it sounded like he shed a blanket or two.

Then, a smooth and masculine voice from the doorway startled them both. "Well, Sanratatarrae, haven't frozen to death yet, have you?" Vanarra liked the sexy voice, and wondered if the speaker was as wonderfully keen as he sounded.

"No, Talnar, I have not."

A chill shook Vanarra back to reality, and she instantly remembered Theo's words. "Talnar is a real piece of work. He's a killer, Van, and he enjoys doing it." She now knew she had to hide who she really was, at all costs. Mentally, Van thanked Theo again. If she hadn't known what Talnar was, she knew her normal "tendencies" would have been to try to warm up to him.

Very light paw steps betrayed that he had walked closer. "So, what do we have here?"

"I … I think she's kept," Sanrat offered.

"What do you mean kept, like a pet?" Talnar's tone was incredulous, but with an undercurrent of hopefulness that sickened Vanarra.

"Something like that. I think she's someone's … slave."

"Really? I've heard of that before, but I've never actually seen it!" Now, he was excited, like a cub with a new toy, and Van hoped fervently Theo's advice would work on this monster in Faelnar fur. "Our family seems a little reluctant to engage in such practices. Shabby thinking, if you ask me. That's especially true if slaves can be as hot looking as this fine piece."

Sanrat's tone betrayed some level of disgust at Talnar's interest. "I met a Foundationalist a long time ago who tried to keep one as a slave, but it was just too difficult. He ended up putting the beast down. He told me he would never do it again. Too impractical. Too risky."

"Oh, but perhaps he just lacked the right … touch," Talnar countered, obviously fascinated with the possibilities tied up in front of him. "Now, why don't you go downstairs and warm up a bit? I'll keep an eye on this lovely creature for awhile. Perhaps, we'll get to know each other. I've never met a live slave before."

Without so much as another word, she heard Sanrat get up and walk out. The silence which followed was completely unnerving, and she could feel his eyes looking her over.

"So, having a good night?" he asked, chuckling to himself. "Bet you didn't think this was how your life would turn out, did you?" When she didn't answer, he seemed to grow impatient. "Now, now, stupid creature that you are, I know you know how to speak. There's no way Sanrat could believe all that crap about you being a kept Anati unless you could speak. So what's your name?"

He grabbed her muzzle hard with his paw and lifted it up to look into his face. Her stomach turned as her eyes met his. He was so keen, so nice looking, but now that she was searching for it, the cruelty and ugliness was evident just below the surface. "Speak to me, dammit!"

"I obey your command!" she exclaimed as if completely relieved to finally be speaking.

Talnar was confused for a moment. "What? I was asking you questions; wasn't that good enough for you to know you had to speak to me?"

"He ordered me silent." It was said as apologetically as she could manage, eyes pleading for forgiveness.

"He? Your master? Oh, Sanrat. Don't tell him I used his short name; it pisses him off because I'm not 'of the blood'. So, tell me your name."

"My name is Alliana."

"Alliana? That's it?" She nodded. "What's your master's name?"

"His name is master."

Suddenly, he appeared to notice something. "I obey your command. He ordered me silent. My name is Alliana. His name is master. Every response is exactly four words long! Did your master train you to do that?"

"Yes, my master did."

"There, you did it again! This must make you quite the conversationalist at parties! So, do you know why your master trained you to talk this way?" She nodded. "Tell me then ... in four words."

She thought for a moment and said, "Slaves need few words."

"Slaves need few words, huh? Did he say why? No, tell me why slaves need few words."

"Slaves listen, not talk."

"Unless asked a direct question or ordered to give a response. Very smooth, very smooth! I noticed you delayed a moment ago before answering. Is this something he told you to start doing just recently?" She shook her head no. "Well, then you're not very good at it. I guess you're not very smart, are you?" Again, head now bowed, she shook her head no. "So, what does your master look like?"

"He has gold fur."

"Well, that 'narrows it down' doesn't it?" he asked mockingly, pacing slowly back and forth in front of her like a house inquisitor. "What else can you tell me? What does his face look like?"

"I do not know," Vanarra answered as she feigned shame, turning her head away.

The answer stopped Talnar cold. "You don't know what your own master's face looks like? Now, now, you're stretching this just too far. Or are you? Why don't you know what your master's face looks like?"

"I always look down."

"All the time?" She shook her head no. "Only in his presence?" She nodded yes, still not looking up at him. "That must make it *very* interesting when he beds you. He does bed you, doesn't he?" She nodded, slowly. "Do you like it when he beds you?" Again, she nodded. "Why?"

"He is so kind," she answered in a most warm and appreciative voice.

Vanarra heard a grunt of dissatisfaction from across the room, and the questions stopped for a moment. Again, she had to smile, if only inwardly. She couldn't be totally quiet, but at only four words an answer, he was going to have to wait a very long time to draw any details out of her. He was obviously thinking, strategizing, by the humming sounds he was making. After another long pause, he tried again.

"Why are you here? More specifically, why would your master bring you to the Meeting Den?"

"He wanted me shown."

"Shown? Shown to whom?"

"I do not know."

"Oh of course you 'do not know'!" She could almost hear the eye roll. "So, you know we could set you free? You wouldn't have to listen to or obey your master anymore. Wouldn't you like that?" With that, she started to cry. "I'll take that as a no. So you *like* being a slave?" She nodded, still sobbing. "Would you like being someone else's?"

For a full interval he probed her history, and what her "master" made her do. Vanarra was grateful for Theo's warning and the time she had earlier to prepare. Knowing what Talnar had done, she tried very hard to remember any names he dropped casually. Sometimes, he told stories as a part of asking a question, and the subjects of those stores – Liniana, Dorithra, Asuala, Daken – were Anati he had known; her heart told her, they were Anati he had also killed.

When she, in four-word answers, explained that her master assigned exercises to keep her proficient at pleasing him, Talnar finally stopped asking questions and simply laughed. "Oh, this is wonderful, Alliana! I can't figure out who your master is, but whoever he is, I want to be him! He's got you trained to treat! I bet he even has others that you don't even know about. I wonder if he'd be the sort who'd be willing to—"

They both heard the door at the end of the hallway open, and Talnar stopped his questioning. Quick, light steps came towards the room. "They told me you were up here," a young, female voice uttered from the doorway.

"Yes, Tana, I'm here," he sighed with some degree of frustration, as if she had interrupted him during his favorite VidStar program or near the end of his favorite book.

The female nearly spat at him in anger. "That's Tanassadurini de Caterra you de Gonari—"

He interrupted her with a condescending sneer. "Now, now. Manners, manners, 'Tanassadurini de Caterra'. Young matrons should never use foul language. It sets such a bad example for everyone else." He looked up at her and could see she was still incensed. "Oh, what stubbornness you have about your high and mighty names! If this little adventure goes badly and the shooting starts, I'll make sure to pronounce your name completely and properly before I tell you to duck the weapon pointed at your head. Now, what do you want? I'm busy."

"The Dame is coming up. She thought someone should relieve you, if indeed there was anything left alive up here to guard. I have to say I'm surprised; it appears to still be breathing. You're obviously not living up to your reputation, Talnar." Now, it was Tana's chance to snipe back.

He dismissively waved a paw in her direction as he stood to stretch. "Now, now. I am always selective about how and when I take my prize. Besides, it's been *so* interesting. She's a kept Anati!"

"Sanrat told me that, but I didn't believe it," said Tana in a voice that was unashamedly skeptical. "I thought he was thinking closer to his tail than he ought to be. Maybe, you're guilty of doing the same?"

"Oh, no, I think it's actually true! We've been having the nicest conversation, and I've been finding out all kinds of wonderful things. Do you know she only speaks when spoken to, and when she finally does say something, every response is only four words long? I've tried as hard as I can to trip her up, and it's ingrained in her. Not five words, not three, not one, not ten, only four words come out of her mouth before she goes silent again, and you have to ask another question. In some ways," he said, pacing back and forth between Tana and his captive, "it's maddening how she talks, but in some ways, it's amazing! Oh, and you have to hear how he has her trained in the bed!"

"I'd rather not," she groaned, looking down at the pathetic female Anati.

"No, it's amazing! I bet that lucky purebred mates her three times a sol! Anytime he wants, he's got hot tail just ready and waiting!" He was almost giggling with excitement.

Tana swallowed quietly, memories of her own experience returning, unwanted, to her thoughts. "She doesn't fight back? Ever? She just rolls over?"

"I think he's got her so well in her rightful place that she's grateful for the attention. You know, I think after we're done here, I'll try to get me one, train it up secretly. I could start with a young one like her; she was taken while she was very young. Shape and mould her – what fun that would be!"

Tana was now thoroughly disgusted, and said, "Well, now, you just head downstairs and work that out. Sounds like a wonderful idea."

"I was really hoping to stay a little longer," he complained snidely.

"Too bad," Tana retorted. "Dame Katuratatallenar de Caterra orders you to come downstairs and look at the communicator we took off the soldier. It seems to be broken – either that or Sanrat fouled it up. Your expertise is required, now." She said it in such a manner that he knew he had no choice.

Reluctantly, Talnar acquiesced. "Oh, very well. When all of the other evacuees are away and we have some time to ourselves, I'll be continuing this conversation. Mange, I may even pick up some good training tips. Here's the prod."

"Ow!" Tana screamed in pain as a slight shock passed through her arm. He had obviously keyed the trigger for an instant while giving it to her, either by mistake or on purpose. "Watch it you idiot!"

"Of course, matron! My mistake, matron! Apologies, matron," he drawled in his sickeningly charming way. With that, he was away.

For a moment, Vanarra thought she had been left alone because she heard Tana's steps exit just a few ticks after Talnar's. The door close at the end of the hall, and the audible sigh from the doorway that followed it spoke volumes. Tana was looking to make sure he actually exited, which made Van wonder if Tana knew any details of his "reputation." She heard steps return in her direction, so Vanarra again played silent.

Chapter 17: Disavowed to Honor

Immediately after he jolted her, Tana wanted to shove the prod right up Talnar's backside and squeeze the trigger until the power pack died or he fried. Thankfully, she hadn't gotten any of the toxin it carried. She was content to just let him go, of course making sure the sneaky Talnar was actually going to do what he was supposed to. There was no way to trust anyone who had so much blood on his paws. What she had heard this evening, even when placed in the most conservative light, was utterly chilling. "What a horror to be at his mercy," she thought. Her abusive, rape-mating family member was a thoughtful soul next to Talnar. "Better to have just a little empathy and mercy in one's tormenter, than to be cursed with one having absolutely none at all."

Walking back into the room, Tana took a deep breath. She was relieved to be free of the others, if only for a moment. Looking at the disheveled room, she groaned, "Males." The Dame wouldn't come up here expecting to see the room in such a state. It looked like there had already been a fight. If she had learned one thing about Dame Katur, it was that appearances mattered to her, regardless. So, Tana started walking around, picking up, making the bed, and moving furniture back to where it was supposed to be. She was pleased and actually felt more at peace when the room was back in an orderly condition.

Taking one last look around, she almost stumbled over the tied Anati, its head bowed low. Stunned, Tana realized that she had actually forgotten about her prisoner in the closet for several passes. The sight of the pathetic female affected her strongly, as did her blithe dismissal of its existence from the room. Realizing she had completely let down her guard was part of it; while "cleaning up," she could have easily been blindsided had it gotten free. However, what really turned her guts was what had happened to this Anati, long before it had the misfortune of being captured here. Sitting down on the side of the neatly made bed, she looked at the female for awhile, remembering.

Before becoming a matron, before she was almost rape-mated, Tana had worked in an office. Although she liked the work and most of her peers (who seemed to forgive her being de Caterra), there were several Anati who were employed there, as well. That had been a source of friction and something that had gotten her into trouble. She made, what for a de Caterra, was considered a mild observation about her Anati coworkers to the wrong group, and she found herself in front of the Thurian resources review board less than a sol later.

It seemed the Anati in question had made themselves almost invaluable by having a certain technical skill, something involving internetwork security. This skill made them "far more valuable than a junior clerk, regardless of their parentage." She had been reprimanded, forced to write a letter of apology, and told to keep her muzzle shut on that subject ever after. It took a long time before those in the office forgave her, and work was quite difficult for awhile.

The experience, although painful, was the first time that an authority figure insisted that, against everything she was brought up to believe, Anati must be treated with respect. To her manager, those Anati had a value far higher than her own. The lesson was enforced when a massive contract landed on her desk, and an insanely tight deadline made her think they wanted her to quit. Without being asked, another one of the clerks, an Anati mix of Lupar and Perratti, offered to help her. After thinking she couldn't refuse without telling her why, she relented.

The Anati worked as hard as she to complete the assignment, and Tana found herself returning the favor sometime later. She actually got to know Asuala pretty well, and had even come to like her, consider her as a friend. Then, one sol, Asuala was gone, and no one knew where. There was no trace, and far too many things pointed to an abduction. Several of the Anati in the office quit after that, and much to Tana's surprise, she found herself grieving the loss like it was a family member.

She looked down at the pitiful figure before her. "Was that or something like it what happened to her?" Tana was shaking as she asked the chained female "Are … are you awake?"

"Yes, I am awake," the response came softly, without the head being raised or eyes opened.

"Look at me." Obediently, the mix that appeared to be Faelnar and Vulpi looked up at her. Golden eyes, not unlike her own, returned her gaze. Strangely, they were not tinged with fear or glazed over with submission as she had expected. The eyes now fixed upon her seemed to be searching her out, attempting to look inside Tana's soul. There was a strange thought that came unbidden to her mind, "I hope I'm worthy." In the de Caterra, she had hardly ever experienced true friendship, but at that moment, some kind of shared suffering clicked into a bond between them. "Do you need water?"

"I am thirsty, yes."

"Here," Tana said, pulling a bottle from the sling pack around her waist. She opened it and held it to the Anati's lips. Without any hesitation, Tana helped her drink. When she was finished, Tana took the bottle away asking, "Did you have enough?"

"Yes, I did. Thanks."

"Are, are you in any pain? Can I loosen anything for you?" Tana caught herself. She couldn't believe she had just asked that.

"No, I am fine."

Shaking her head trying to break the spell that had come over her, Tana sneered, "If you think this is fine, I wouldn't want to see what bad looks like. Although, you might just get that in a moment. The Dame is coming up. She hates Anati, and she doesn't mind hurting them. Be as respectful as you can, and do what she tells you to. It may be just enough to keep you in one piece. Do you understand?"

"Yes, I do. Thanks." The tenderly grateful expression of the Anati further melted Tana's heart, but the sound of the door opening at the end of the hall almost made it stop.

"Head down, eyes closed," Tana ordered, and the Anati obeyed. Trying to school her expression and demeanor, she picked up the prod. It was only a few ticks before Dame Katur entered, followed by Cur.

"I hear that it's awake, finally," Cur said with some disgust, "and talking."

"It's awake," Tana replied dispassionately.

"It is the talking that has me concerned," the Dame growled, angrily. "I hear it's supposed to be a kept Anati. That can't be!"

"Why not?" Tana asked. "It certainly seemed to convince Talnar."

"And Sanrat, too, but all of the Foundationalist pack are to tell me what Anati they're keeping, which ones they're putting down, and how they're disposing of them. No one's said anything about keeping one like this."

"Perhaps someone has a hobby," Tana offered, slyly indicating fragmentation in the Foundationalist ranks and diverting from the thought the captive might be faking.

"If they do, then they'll be paying for it. The only way we can continue to win in this war is by being careful," confided the Dame.

"Should you be saying things like this, in front of it?" Cur asked, concerned.

"Oh, it won't be leaving here alive, so it's not exactly going to be a problem. Even if it is what it seems to be, I want that owner to learn a lesson!" The dame looked at Cur and Tana with an almost admonitory gaze. "You don't hide things like this! One misstep and we might completely lose our ability to act when prudence requires."

"Like now?" Tana asked.

"Yes. We've a new target in mind. Once we have survived the storm and been rescued, I want this Vanarra Anasto they are so enamored with. Nothing makes Anati seem less like an abomination than when they pretend to help others, or in this case, as I'm sure, are made to look that way." Katur's tone clearly indicated a dubious conspiracy. "Doubtless that old hag Amyra or that senseless poet Rahnahi is manipulating this situation to their own ends."

"Mange, I just love it! Praise be, an Anati caterer of all things, comes to our rescue!" Cur laughed sarcastically. "Whoever this Sahnassa is, she's either in on it or the grand matriarch of all idiots!"

"We may have to take her down also," the dame mused, stepping around for another look at their prisoner. "Perhaps we could take them together. We'll just have to observe them for awhile. It should be easy to find a good time."

Cur scratched his chin as he mulled over the possibilities. "So, who does the deed? I think Talnar wanted to, but both he and Sanrat wanted to play around with it a little, first."

"I don't know if it's worth the risk," the dame said, unconvinced. "Keeping this … thing alive any longer could be too much of a hazard to our plans."

"It's not a risk; it's pathetic!" Tana exclaimed, shaking her head. "Haven't they told you how simpleminded it is? It just heard you talking about killing it, but it continues to sit there quietly. Whoever trained it did a great job, and I mean it's not like it's getting out." Katur seemed to take a step back and consider, so Tana continued on that tack. "After everyone else flies down the mountain, it's going to get pretty boring up here. We'd better have something to keep Talnar entertained, and who knows, I haven't fully calibrated this prod yet," Tana chuckled as she lifted up the prod and keyed the trigger, sending a brief electric crackle echoing through the small room. Tana was trying very hard to hide the part of her that wanted them both to just leave.

Dame Katur stepped up to the Anati and demanded, "Look at me then, pathetic beast!" Seeing the fearful gold eyes staring back at her visibly repulsed the dame. "An abomination indeed – it makes me sick! Seeing gold eyes stare out of Vulpi fur makes one see why such things should be put down." Katur pulled the long de Caterra family pin out of her blouse and aimed its sharp point directly in the Anati's face. "I would like so very much to put out those eyes, so no one ever has to see the horror of such a misshapen creature again!"

Tana's paw rested softly on the arm of the dame. "If you do that, then we won't be able to find out who disobeyed you. Sanrat and Talnar will also be … disappointed. Sanrat we can manage, but Talnar—" The dame shook off Tana's grasp.

"I can manage him," Cur said, and the dame drew her needle-like pin closer to the Anati's eyes.

The dame was going to strike, but then a soft gurgle punctuated the silence. She suddenly had a distracted expression and appeared uncertain. She tried to focus again, but this time, a little louder gurgle sounded in the room. Tana was certain that it had come from the dame. Slowly, as if trying to save face, she straightened. As she did, there was a metallic "clink" sound, and the pin fell apart in her paw. The long metal piece that was pointed at the Anati's eyes rolled between the floorboards and disappeared. Katur was horrified, and she looked at what remained of the pin as if it were her own child broken in pieces before her. "No! No! That pin has been in my family for—" The dame went silent, overcome by the horror of her loss.

"Oh, no, I'm so sorry!" Tana offered, sympathetically. "I'll stay up here. There's not much to guarding this one. I'll take a candle and search for the pin. I'll pull up the floorboards if I have to!"

"We could just kill it, and then look for the pin," Cur argued dispassionately.

"Best not move more than we have to, if we want to find it. If you both step out carefully, I'll have the best chance. I will find it for you, Dame."

"I … I would appreciate it … more than you know." Carefully, Katur back-tracked out of the room. "Come, Cur."

"Close and lock the door behind you, Cur. If one of those other dolts comes in here, I'll never find this thing."

"Yes, good thinking. Let's go Cur, now!" Tana didn't know why Katur was so insistent, but she was still grateful. Almost too fast for reality, the door was closing and locking, leaving her and her Anati captive alone. Fast footsteps, well muffled by the door, trotted away to be punctuated a few ticks later by the door at the end of the hall opening and closing. After waiting a moment, Tana stepped towards the door, unlocked it, and looked up and down the hall. Seeing everyone gone, she closed it and secured all of the locks. For good measure, she shoved a towel beneath the door to prevent anyone from easily overhearing.

When she finally reached the room, she found her Anati captive looking right up at her, a large smile gracing her face, a face that Tana had to admit was pretty. A face that Tana also realized had completely transformed. "You did great, kit! I can't thank you enough for that save," the chained Anati said.

Tana was utterly stunned by how conversationally and confidently the words came from her captive. "You – that's more than four – you were pretending the whole time?!"

"That I'm a kept Anati, yes. I told them I was Alliana, but that's not my real name. The real Alliana was a sad little Anati teen that someone kept as a prize slave until some friends of mine rescued her. It was too late, though. She was so dependent on her old master that she committed suicide."

With no trace of hate or cruelty, Tana asked her captive, "Who … who are you really?"

"I'm Vanarra Anasto."

Tana almost fell back on the bed, but still, albeit ungracefully, managed to sit. "You're the one they want to go after! What … what makes you think I won't turn you in?!"

"Instinct, mostly, and watching you just now. You see, I think you're worth it, and from what I can tell, your paws are still clean. Are they?" Tana, dumbstruck, nodded yes. "That's good, because I have friends coming, and they are going to rescue us. When they get here, well, let's just say that it would be safer for you to be in here with me."

"How, how do they know you're gone? I mean, no one seems to care. We've not seen signs that anyone's noticed you're missing."

Vanarra chuckled. "Oh, you don't know Sahnassa! That kit can do almost anything, and she's sure to have missed me by now. The fact that you haven't captured her means that she's managed to convince someone else to take her concerns seriously. Otherwise, I would expect her to try to rescue me single-pawed. Oh, and that soldier you took captive? His buddies are going to tear this place apart, and they won't leave until they find him. Also, for reasons I don't totally understand," Vanarra confessed, her head shaking, "both matriarchs seem to want me kept safe."

"Did ... did you put all of this together? The rescue?"

"I did, with a lot of help from Sahnassa and others."

Some of her prejudice slipped back into her next question. "How could an Anati do all of this?" she asked, motioning to the window, where the low thrusting sound of a passing flyer reverberated, accentuated by its light slipping in past the edges of the closed curtains.

Vanarra laughed, quietly. "I know. I'm still amazed at it, myself! You see, I'm just a lowly 'Anati' caterer. I have a simple celebrations business. However, over the seasons I've gained a few friends. Some work for me, and some I do business with. Some I barely know, and others, well, they are my friends for life. When I called, they came – some in the defense force, one with a transport company, another with a hauling company, and someone who could quickly pull together huge amounts of food. They all worked together, regardless of who was pureblood and who wasn't. It meant more to them that I was their friend and business partner than the fact I'm an Anati."

Tana was shaking. Only in her old office had she not felt alone, and only when Asuala had been kind to her did she ever feel as if she had a friend. Here, before her, was an Anati who confidently claimed to have not just one friend, but many. In her whole life, Tana had never felt poorer than at this moment, or more envious. It was envy, mixed with a grudging respect. Tana tried not to admit what she was feeling, but even admiration sang a quiet song in the recesses of her soul.

Into that long silence, Vanarra answered quietly and tenderly the question of "why" that was written so plainly on Tana's features. "I've risked a lot providing all of this, literally all I have, but I had no choice. My anger and my desire for revenge could never be worth the suffering of so many. I never could have lived with myself if I hadn't done everything I could to save those who were stranded up here on this mountain."

Tana leaned forward and spoke in a whisper. "But, they're purebloods … like me. You've every reason to fear them and … to hate them for what they do to ones like you."

Vanarra whispered back, her tone intense. "Oh no, kit. You don't understand; *it was me* they did it to. My father disappeared because someone took him; he didn't leave us – he was stolen from us. We never saw him again. I barely have any memory of him. Later, after letting us live in squalor for seasons, my mother's family murdered her right in front of my eyes. I was on my own as just a kit. I've never had it easy. I was at the mercy of almost everyone. They violated me in every way imaginable, and I was so angry. I hated all of you. Then I met purebloods who accepted me, mostly those cast out of their own families. I found that they, too, like my mother, had suffered. In time, I met fully avowed, true purebloods like Sahnassa who had everything, or so I thought. Still, in time, I came to understand not all of you are alike."

"Just like all … Anati are not alike. I'd never had friends … only family, and then I met – I had a friend too … who was an Anati. She just disappeared—" Tana had to stop; her emotions were too close to spilling over.

"I understand. Now, listen to me. I have just one question, Tanassadurini de Caterra; will you let me rescue you?"

"I … I don't know," Tana answered, turning away.

Vanarra's tone was gently pleading. "Don't you want to be free? Don't you want to have friends who love you for who you are?"

"Yes."

"Then help me. Take everything you know and help me. After this is over, I will take care of you and give you a home. I've done it for others. Please, let me do it for you."

Tana fell to her knees, and now she was eye to eye with Vanarra. "That would mean leaving my family." A look of fear and sad desperation was on her face. "Forever."

"And gaining a new one. Long names don't make anyone truly love you. You can make a new life for yourself; make your own choices about what's right and what's wrong. You can avoid all the horrors, like what we're going through now."

"It … sounds too good, too good to be true?"

"No, you and I know there will be a cost. It won't be easy, but I'll help you, and I probably won't be the only one." Vanarra looked away, sadness in her own eyes. "I've spent a lot of my adult life moving from one male to another, just happy of the company, I guess. I didn't realize until all of this happened, until I was almost killed, that there are those who truly love me. Maybe someone in particular. Even though he is an outcast and I'm an Anati, if we choose to, we can be together. Can *you* say that? I know what's happening to not only the males but the females of your house."

Tana's head bowed, and her eyes closed as she confessed. "No one outside of our family wants any part of us."

"But you, kit, you're different! You are absolutely beautiful, and it's not just the outside! If you lose your family name, become an outcast, you'll be free to love, to find someone. I … I do a lot of reading, and in the back of one of my books is a true story about a female who was an outcast. She was redeemed into a new family. She found her love because of that family. There are no guarantees, but you should think about that."

Her captor was silent for a long time, and then Vanarra noticed pools of tears appearing on the floor. Van could tell from her body language that no more words were needed, and after awhile, in a whispered voice, Tana agreed, "Yes."

After hearing no response, Tana looked up and saw that Van was crying, too. Nervously, she laughed a little and hugged the neck of the tied Anati. Van leaned forward, returning as much of the hug as she could.

When their embrace broke, Tana chuckled and said, "I suppose I should untie you."

As she reached for the knots, Van warned, "No, not yet! We need to wait until the very last tick. The others could still come up here at any time. If they found me untied, it would be bad for both of us. Now look at me! No matter what happens to me, I want you to live. If something bad is going to happen to me, just let it happen. There may be consequences after, but then at least you'll be alive, and you can leave your family … sometime in the future."

"No. I – Vanarra … I couldn't." She reached her paw to the side of Vanarra's muzzle in entreaty. It struck Tana to the heart to think that this Anati stranger would actually be willing to give up her own life to keep Tanassadurini de Caterra, a member of a murderous family, alive.

Vanarra's direct stare and forceful tone allowed no dispute. "Promise me, kit! If rescuing you means it's all over for me, then so be it!

Understood?" Meekly, Tana nodded. "Now, let's stop this arguing and start thinking. Can you peek out the window? How high up are we?"

"We're on the third level," Tana answered, trying to control herself. Standing, she walked to the window and looked out. "It's nearly full dark, and I think it's straight down outside. We can open the windows, at least."

"That's good, but leave them closed for now. What's in those drawers? Let's see what we've got to work with."

"Okay," Tana agreed, stepping away from the window, and she started searching through the drawers.

As Van looked at her, her vision seemed to go fuzzy for a moment, and then she thought she heard a voice whispering in her ears. "Vanarra. It's time, Vanarra. Soldiers are about to break through the windows. Stay in the closet where you are, cover yourself with a blanket, and tell the one with you to do so. Do it now."

"... and I suppose we could always use the old standby of tying sheets together. We could hide that quickly if they came up again. But what would we anchor it to?"

Van regained her senses and was finally able to speak in an urgent whisper. "Tana! Oh my gosh! Please, stop! Grab a blanket off the bed and come get over by me, quickly!"

Tana looked at her with a confused expression. "I ... I don't understand."

"Trust me kit! We're ticks away from rescue! Come over here, get me loose, and let's both get covered by the blanket. It'll protect us from flying glass."

Still not fully understanding why, Tana moved quickly nonetheless. "How, how do you know?" she asked as she opened the binders.

"I don't know how I know, Tana; it's just a sense I have. Every one of these warnings in my head since I was captured has been dead on. Oh, gosh that feels good!" Van rubbed her wrists as Tana sliced the ropes holding Van's other limbs with her belt knife. Then, Van was free. She stood, stretched for just a moment, and threw the luggage rack out of the closet. "Okay, back in as far as we can go and cover up." They did and waited, Tana wondering if Vanarra was crazy or unstable.

Just as she was about to ask, "How long do you think it will take?" the windows of the room exploded sending countless pieces of glass falling around them. Tana screamed, and Vanarra held her tight. With a loud thud, two huge soldiers swung into the room on ropes, weapons drawn, their UltraBrights mounted atop.

"Stay where you are!" one shouted as the light from his weapon found its mark. Another pair of Lupar soldiers swung in and charged to the door. On the floors beneath them, they heard other explosions, weapons fire, screams, and crashing around. Four more soldiers swung in and rushed out into the hallway.

Vanarra felt relief and joy, but glancing at Tana, she could see the terror in her eyes. "It'll be okay," she whispered.

"Put the blanket down, now!" Vanarra did as ordered. "Put your paws where I can see them, and come out one at a time!" Again, Van and Tana did as commanded, and as one soldier held them at gunpoint, another moved towards them.

"You," the huge dark furred Lupar said to Tana. "Face down on the bed, now!"

"No!" Vanarra demanded sternly and with surprising authority. "There's glass on the bed; don't you dare hurt her!"

The soldier seemed confused. "Alright, up against the wall then!" One quick moment after she complied, Tana was pushed against the wall and searched. Several knives and a short stunner were removed from her clothes. "Anything else?"

"No … no sir," Tana said, looking into Vanarra's eyes in helpless terror.

"Good, back into the closet! Paws up front! Move!"

A soldier returned from the hallway. "You good in here?" the Lupar asked.

"Yes, Sergeant!"

Reaching for his communicator, the Lupar sergeant reported, "Cutter here. Hostage one secured, appears to be in good condition. One prisoner."

"Roger that," the Chief's voice crackled back through the speaker. "The rest of the building is secured, and we've got Agari. We've got one casualty among the hostage takers. It's a Faelnar. We're questioning the rest to find out who it was."

"Roger, Chief. X-mit out." Looking at Vanarra, he asked, "Are you alright ma'am? Can you walk?"

"Not without my friend. She helped me, and she's not going to be a prisoner." Vanarra's statement was calm and firm, and obviously surprised the sergeant.

"She's … de Caterra, isn't she?" The large Lupar sergeant was not letting down his guard.

"She was," Vanarra answered, walking to the closet and offering the frightened Tana her paw. "Now, she's part of my family." Trembling, Tana stood, still conscious of the weapons pointed at her.

"I still have to restrain her," the Lupar stated flatly.

"Perhaps that won't be necessary, Cutter," a familiar male voice said from the doorway.

"How the mange did you get up here so quick?!" Cutter was shocked and his mouth dropped open.

"I'm almost as fast as you are on the assault course, remember? I followed the Chief in, met your crew in the hallway, and they gave me a pass to come up."

Vanarra couldn't contain herself anymore. "Theo? Is that you!?!" She almost pounced on him as he walked out of the entrance hall into the bedroom.

"Good job, good job, kit! It looks like you did alright in here!" he exclaimed happily as they embraced.

She pulled away and looked at him, his seemingly normal appearance so out of tune with the visions and warnings that had come to her mind. "How did you—"

He interrupted her question and explained, "You can thank Sahnassa, in large part, for alerting everyone to what happened. Once she spotted the guards in the windows and heard where you had gone, well, it was just a matter of time before they called down to the Marshall for help." Turning to Cutter and the other soldier, who still had their weapons trained on Tana, he introduced them. "Vanarra, meet Sergeant Cutter of the famous Defense Force Storm Pack. This is his explosives expert, Griz. Good soldiers, this is Vanarra Anasto, and she put the Meeting Den rescue together."

"At least the first one. So nice to meet you," Van said, almost shyly. "Thank you so much for rescuing us." They nodded in return.

Theo then looked towards Tana. "Who may I ask is this?"

Van looked at her and smiled. "This is Tanassadurini de—"

"I was Tanassadurini de Caterra. Now, I'm Tana … Asuala," Tana offered timidly, and Vanarra stared at her in stunned amazement. "Vanarra promised me shelter from my old family."

Theo walked forward, and as he approached her, the guards lowered their weapons. "Sounds alright by me," he agreed. Looking at her seriously, however, he warned, "You know there have to be some tough questions later, right?"

Tana nodded, eyes closed. "I do. I'll cooperate as best I can."

Although Theo smiled and nodded at her, the sergeant wasn't convinced and sounding a little aggrieved, explained, "The regulations say she has to be restrained, Theo."

Without turning away from her, he said, "Of course. However, field manual 27-11, chapter 7, section 4a, paragraph 2 states that operatives in the field may determine the method of restraint to be appropriate and equivalent to the level of the assessed threat." He reached out his paw and took Tana's. "I think this will be sufficient." Cutter groaned, but didn't protest further.

"Vanarra!" The voice from behind her surprised them, and the Chief walked into the room, arms outstretched towards her. She smiled and walked into his embrace, laughing.

"Oh Chief, thank you!"

The Chief broke the embrace and asked, "You alright?"

"I'm fine."

The Chief looked to his left and saw Tana. "You?" Tana clenched Theo's paw in fear, and the Chief looked at their clasped paws. "Did I … uh … miss something here?"

Vanarra touched his shoulder. "She helped me, Chief. She took care of me and helped keep the others from hurting me."

"Well, at least we all aren't crazy," the Chief said, shaking his head. "Looks like we're both going to need new last names, though."

"Yes, but I now know that's what I want." Tana's grip slackened just a little, and Theo squeezed back in support.

"You know," Theo warned, "I think we'd better get a move on, or we're going to have Sahnassa leading the matriarchs and dames in their own assault."

Vanarra asked the Chief urgently, "Can I see Agari? Is he okay?"

"He's still pretty out of it, but yeah. Come on." The whole group exited the room, with Tana and Theo just a few steps in front of Cutter.

Cutter whispered forward, "I hope you know what you're doing, Theo. This isn't exactly as secure as I would like."

"It's hard to find any safer place than the one by my side," he responded quietly. Looking at Tana as they walked, he said, "Thank you for helping her. I know that had to be a very hard decision."

For some reason, Tana felt completely at ease with this kind stranger and confessed, "It wasn't, really, when I met Vanarra. Theo, my family has been wrong for so many seasons. I knew it; I just didn't think I could do anything about it until now. Now, if they can't change, I don't want to be a part of them anymore. I'm tired of hiding … and hurting."

"I understand." Theo nodded as they walked down the stairs to the second level. The Chief opened the door and led them to another room a few doors down, where one of the Lupar medics was checking Agari on the bed. On the floor, in the far corner, a corpse was being zipped into a carrying bag.

"Who was it?" Tana asked.

"Someone named Talnar. I don't think he was de Caterra," the Chief responded.

"Tana," Vanarra said stepping beside her and placing her paw gently on Tana's back. "Was the last name you chose the name of your Anati friend? The one who disappeared?"

"Yes," Tana answered, and then looked at Vanarra and the bag in the corner. She looked back at Vanarra, searching for confirmation.

Van nodded. "He admitted it to me. Called her by name. Your friend has been avenged, Tana. She's finally been given justice."

"And her memory honored by your own choices," Theo added, pulling Tana into an embrace as she started to cry. The Chief nodded, and Cutter and Griz walked over and lifted the body and headed out of the room.

Vanarra crept over to Agari's bedside. His eyes were half lidded, and his nose and lips looked pale. The medic explained, "He'll be fine, but he needs to rest, and we need to get him out of the cold and into a warm bed." Vanarra raised her eyebrow fur; until now, she really hadn't noticed the cold. She could feel it around her, but it didn't seem to bother her.

Sitting on the bed and leaning over, she quietly called, "Agari? Agari, it's me, Vanarra."

"Oh, Vanarra," he said a little drowsily. "You okay? They said you were okay."

Van found herself crying. "I'm fine. I'm sorry Agari. I got you into this." She placed her head on his chest.

"S'okay. S'all a part of the job," he whispered, smiling, patting her head gently with his paw.

"He'll be okay, but we need to get him out of here," the medic reassured her. She sat up, nodded, and kissed him, to which he made a half attempt at a purr-like noise, which caused her to laugh.

Suddenly, they heard muffled shouting underneath them. The Chief, Van, Theo, and Tana jogged through the hall and back down the stairs to the first level. Upon opening the door, they were assailed by the curses and insults being spat out by the dame, who was crouched on the floor, arms tied behind her. To Van, who came in last, it was pretty clear what happened. Seeing Talnar's body being brought in and put right near the row of prisoners was bad enough. Now, with Tana obviously a collaborator, the dame's words were growing choice.

"Shut up, you stupid old hag!" the Chief growled angrily, unslinging his rifle and pointing it butt first in her direction.

"You traitor! You're disavowed scum, all of you! You're not worthy to carry the name de Caterra! Do you hear me?! Not worthy!"

"That name's no longer worthy of me!" the Chief shouted back, pulling back on the rifle, ready to slam it into her face. A paw at his shoulder stayed him; it was Theo. For reasons he didn't quite understand, Chief Tawnston didn't strike, even though he wanted too with all that he was. Instead, he stepped back and saw Theo place Tana's paw in Van's before walking over and squatting right in front of the angry dame.

"What do you want, you Nephti filth?" Dame Katur spat.

Theo chuckled and looked at her as few in her life ever had, with pity. He then said with unwavering certainty, "I want to say this to you, face-to-face and eye-to-eye. Tonight, house de Caterra starts to fall, and it's all because … of you. Throughout history and from generation to generation, everyone will look to this night as the night when the de Caterra's end … began. Your name will be forever recorded in disgrace, your remaining seasons pitied, and your memory reviled. By your deeds you are undone, and your house along with you."

The angry dame's ego was deflated, but she still managed, "We'll see. You are in no place to judge the paw of destiny. We still have many friends, many secret allies, and de Caterra is still a formidable—"

He held his clawed finger right in front of her nose. "House? The foundations of that house are fear, deception, intimidation, secrecy, arrogance, and baseless pride. The support those offered your … family … are now eroding away beneath you. Your house *will* fall. As for you, repent. Repent and you might yet save what meager light still burns in the darkness of your soul." Standing, he said again, "Repent."

Looking down into her eyes, he sent a message into her mind that she knew, unmistakably, came from him. She gasped, because his voice kept speaking into her mind as surely as if her ears had delivered his message. "You mistake me for a simple Nephti? Oh, no, I'm so much more than you could ever guess, and you are so … small, so hopelessly simple and self-deluded. I don't actually know if you're smart enough to find a way out of this prison of lies I see in your mind. It was built so long ago for you, when you believed the lies of others, and sadly, now you believe your own. I know what the de Caterra have done in the dark, when you thought no one was looking. The Anati, the Vulpi, and all the other harm you've done, oh yes, I know all of it – even more than you. Soon, everyone will know."

"Come on, let's go," she half heard him say aloud as the group then turned and left.

Yet the maddening words in her mind kept going. "The blood and pain of all those victims cry out against you and your family. They cry out for justice, and yes, they will be avenged. Oh, I may not be the paw of destiny, but I certainly can shift it. For I am a creature of power and light. Darkness such as yours and that of your family falls before me. Heed my words, confess, and tell all. Find your redemption in confession. It is the very last hope you have." Her mind finally released from the tight grip Theo had over her, the once proud dame screamed in unyielding terror and grief.

Sahnassa was almost bounding down the stairs. Others were trailing behind her as the dames and matrons gladly left what had been their command center since the disaster began. A half interval earlier, Dania reported that only two more of the large flyers were needed to completely finish the evacuation, and those groups were already pre-staged, needing no more direction other than that which accompanied them.

After that, all of those who had waited so patiently and worked so hard to ensure everyone else was evacuated battled an exponentially increasing desire to start their own move towards escape and safety. Still, until the matter of the hostages was settled, all of them stayed at their posts, determined not to abandon one of their heroines. Once word came that the captured were free and would be brought through the buildings on their side of the complex, everyone, even Rahnahi and Buck, couldn't wait to get down to the first floor.

Although Sahnassa's knowledge from Theo allowed her to worry less about Vanarra and Agari, it had been a difficult ordeal not only waiting, but watching the others around her. She had witnessed Buck go through terrible anxiety and dread to arrive at unbridled joy when he finally heard all was well. She could see that he truly loved her. She would also tell Vanarra later, if (but more likely when) it was appropriate.

Rahnahi was something else altogether. Quietly and firmly, she had directed the actions of the dames and matrons as the intervals dragged on, but when the troops stormed in, there was no matriarch anymore. There was a young and uncertain soul in that older poet's body that came to the surface; one that cried openly with joy and relief when Vanarra was reported safe. Dania had to assume the mantle of leadership once that happened and did so very ably. Still, Sahni could tell the dame also hurt seeing Buck suffer so.

Now, holding candles, the remaining matrons lined the very hallway where Sahni and Van had been so unceremoniously ejected not so long ago. The group was moved by equal parts awe and honor, because word had reached them that Vanarra had turned one of the de Caterra and caused her to renounce her own family. Up until that time, such had never happened on Thuria; only the dead or disavowed left de Caterra. When Sahnassa saw the honor the matrons of de Gonari and de Dothnar were about to pay to her friend, she couldn't help but cry as she waited.

The door opened at the distant end of the large, candlelit hallway, and Sahnassa watched as the Chief, Vanarra, a beautiful gold on gold Faelnar, and a rather attractive Nephti stepped through. The Chief ushered them in, and Vanarra held the other two by their paws. As Vanarra stepped forward, Sahnassa saw her friend halt and falter, overcome by the awesome scene in front of her. Sahni stepped into the center and started walking forward. Van saw her and ran, leaving the other three smiling behind her. Sahnassa started to run a little too, but it wasn't necessary at the speed her friend was closing the distance. They embraced each other as tightly as they could, and Sahnassa whispered, "Oh Van, I'm so glad you're alright!"

Vanarra held onto her Nephti friend as if she were drowning. "Oh, Sahni! Oh Sahni! Oh, kit! I wouldn't be here if it weren't for you!"

After a few moments, Sahni felt paws on her shoulders, and she looked back. Rahnahi and Buck were both there, waiting their turns for a tearful reunion. As Sahnassa stepped back and watched, the Chief came and patted her on the back. "Great work, Sahnassa. Great work."

"You, too Chief," she sniffed.

As he stepped forward to offer his congratulations, Sahni felt a presence beside her. "If he only knew," a familiar voice whispered slyly. Slowly she looked around into the face of a Nephti, but she knew better. Theo's eyes shone as brightly in that face as they had in the Vulpi's. "Yes, it's me," he whispered as he gave her a brief hug. "I want you to meet someone," he said a little louder as they separated. "This is Tana. She helped protect Vanarra and keep her safe."

"Oh, Tana," Sahni offered with warmth and affection to the shy and somewhat scared-looking Faelnar. "I'm so grateful to you. Thank you." She reached around and hugged her, and Tana somewhat tentatively returned her embrace, but then fully accepted it as Sahnassa held onto her.

"She's right about you," Tana whispered, sniffling and smiling and chuckling a little as she released Sahni. "I can tell you would have rescued her all by yourself if no one else had been there."

"But thankfully, someone was, Tana! And one of those was you." Again, Sahni hugged the Faelnar.

"See," Vanarra noted happily coming up behind them, "now you have another friend." It wasn't directed to either of them in particular, and they parted just long enough to grab Vanarra in a collective embrace.

The door opened behind them, and in came the medics bearing Agari. The three broke their embrace and walked towards the stretcher. Saletta walked up as well, breaking from her position in line. "Agari," she whispered tenderly, leaning over him.

"I'm alright. Just need to rest." She kissed him gently on the side of the muzzle for his bravery.

Vanarra had an idea. "Then rest, and let us do the work." She reached out and took hold of one of the poles at the head of the stretcher, and understanding quickly, Sahni took the other from the Lupar medic. Theo nodded to Tana, who joined him in taking a position at the end of the stretcher. Calling upon old Thurian tradition, Theo then said in a voice loud enough to reach into the rafters and fall back around them, "Honor to Agari, Honor to Vanarra, Honor to Sahnassa, and Honor to Tana!"

All of the matrons, dames, and even Rahnahi herself responded instinctively to Theo's powerful call for honor with uplifted right paws. As they started walking, all of the voices in the hall returned "Honor, honor, honor, honor!" which echoed and resounded throughout the space. From their broad smiles, Theo could see that Rahnahi and Dania both heartily accepted his call.

When the first response was complete, Theo again called, "Honor to Rahnahi, Honor to Amyra, Honor to Tawnston, and Honor to Buck Harlock!"

Again, as they neared the opposite door, the calls of "Honor, honor, honor, honor" echoed again in the hall. Matrons opened the large double doors to let them through.

Just as they were about to leave, Theo added a new line to the Thurian tradition. "Honor to all! Honor from all! Honor … above all!" All behind them bowed in thanks, paws folded in front of them. As Rahnahi watched them leave, she wondered how she would ever capture all of this in words.

Chapter 18: Finding Rest

A short time later, they found themselves outside in the cold night air, small crystals of ice gently pelting them every so often. They had waited and watched as hooded and shackled prisoners boarded their own flyer and were sped away, vanishing into the dark clouds above the mist covered landing zone. Vanarra was peripherally aware of the scramble around them: soldiers taking down equipment, calling over communicators, and lining up in formation. The matrons and dames had also gathered, and it was clear that while large, this was the last group to leave the Meeting Den. Looking towards the dark outline of its buildings, Van could almost sense its emptiness and sadness.

Out of the sky rumbled one of the giant HVR-17's, and Sahnassa and Vanarra looked on as it settled into position. As the rear doors opened and the ramp lowered, the two of them laughed at the silhouette standing, riding the ramp to the ground. From the stretcher beside them, Agari groaned, "Don't tell me. It's Fillie."

"How'd you guess?" Vanarra chuckled, smiling.

As the engines powered down, others grabbed Agari's stretcher and moved towards the craft. The matrons and all the others began to follow. Sahnassa and Vanarra walked a short distance away, watching the last evacuation group move into the lighted doorway as bright moonlight strained through small gaps in the clouds above them.

"I can't believe it, Sahni. It's finally done," Van breathed, shaking her head.

They were strolling closer to the doors, roughly keeping parallel with the last of the matrons entering the flyer. "I know. It's amazing. I can only guess what would be happening here if there hadn't been a Vanarra Anasto ejected from the prestigious Association of Service and Commerce." Vanarra started laughing. "I'm serious!" Sahni protested.

"I know! I just haven't given that group or their award much thought until now, and I don't think I ever will again. I can't imagine any honors higher than what I've already been given tonight. The most important one is you. Your friendship means so much to me. It saved my life." Van reached out and took Sahnassa's paw, gently clasping it in thanks, and Sahni squeezed Van's paw in return.

Standing with their backs facing the rear door of the flyer, they looked out at the dark buildings a short distance away, and Van sighed. "It … it would have been a nightmare here, I know. The conditions they were in, the lack of food, the cold." She took a deep breath and shook her head. "I only hope we got everyone. It feels … empty. That's right, I hope."

Sahnassa raised her right paw and gestured openly and gracefully, taking in the whole of the Meeting Den. "It's empty. We've done—" She was interrupted by a flash of light from behind her, out of time with the normal pulsing of the marker lights on the flyer. "We've done our task. Come on, don't worry. There's a nice warm bed and a hot meal down there somewhere with our names on it."

Turning towards her friend, Vanarra offered, "Thank you Sahnassa. I've said it before; I couldn't have done any of this without you."

"Nor you." They hugged, and Sahni was aware of that flash of light again.

Hearing the engines start to power up, they turned towards the doorway of the flyer only to be greeted by another flash, which this time was very easy to locate. The loadmaster, her eyes a little wide with awe, lowered her camera apologetically. "Fillie!" Vanarra called accusingly.

"I'm sorry. It's just that I'm a bit of a photographer, and I've never seen anything like you two a moment ago. Both of you were positively glowing, and look, I got it!" The childlike excitement was so uncharacteristic of the Vulpi that they had to look at the image viewer on the other side of the device. For whatever reason, the moonlight came through at just the right angle and created a shining corona of stardust around them, reflecting from the crystals of ice scattered on their fur.

"Wow, can I have a copy of those?" Vanarra asked, and Fillie nodded. "That's a totally weird effect!"

Sahnassa looked up the ramp and tugged on Van's sleeve. "That's not all of the effect." Looking up, Van saw Rahnahi, Dania, Tana, the Chief, and Buck standing in dumbfounded stillness, or perhaps even reverence. The sight apparently had as much of an effect on them as it had on Fillie. Sahni, looking towards the corner of the huge doorway, saw Theo nonchalantly leaned up against its frame. He winked at her conspiratorially, and she smiled. Taking Van's paw again, she walked up behind the loadmaster who had stepped back to the ramp and was nearing its top.

"Fillie, may we?" Vanarra asked, shyly. "I mean, we've seen you do it." Fillie understood, and pushed the ramp control, lifting Sahni and Van off the ground, the very last ones to leave the site of the Meeting Den.

Engines came to life, grass and debris blew away, and the great craft lofted skyward. As it departed, power packs in the vehicles below that had long since been drained finally failed as they should have, and lights all around the landing field went out one by one. A chill and icy wind seemed to rush in as if released from a prison, and ice crystals began to fall in a thick, pelting rain upon the Meeting Den, as if a great sheltering wing had finally removed itself. The cold, dark buildings, empty now of any Thurian, stood alone.

Fillie offered both of her paws to steady them. "Wow! This takes some skill," Vanarra observed, trying to adjust her weight properly to remain standing as the ramp locked into place.

Now back to her normal shouting voice and military manner, Fillie answered, "I've practiced more! By the way, Sahnassa, there's someone in the cockpit who would like a word with you, if you're up to it."

"You want to come?" she asked Vanarra who was just finding a seat next to Rahnahi.

"No, that's okay. I'll save you a seat. Maybe Theo could go with you?" Vanarra tried to suppress a small smile, but her matchmaking antics weren't that easy to disguise.

"Theo?" Sahni asked, hopefully.

"Sure, why not?" He unbuckled and stood, taking her offered paw. They stepped carefully down the aisle, coming to a place about mid-ship where no one was sitting, and their conversation would be well covered by the ambient noise. "You did very well, Sahni. I'm proud of you, and proud of Vanarra, too."

Turning around to look at him she said, "I can't even imagine how to thank you for all of the things you did for us! I'll just say it. Thank you. I … I also wanted to ask – you do remember your promise, I hope?"

"Of course. However, I have to make it a clean departure for Van's sake. Sometime after the storm breaks, I suppose. When you're back at your lair, that first night, then I'll come and get you. Besides, by then, you'll probably have a lot of fun things to tell me." She squeezed his paw in thanks, and they continued to walk towards the front of the craft. Near the front was one of the few round windows. He said, "Put on your glasses, and have a look."

She did and stepped to the window. There, flying alongside them was the front section of the Tashar; its aft section was not visible in the small window. "Theo, that's the best escort I could imagine!"

"I'll be sure to tell them that. They've enjoyed helping. Alright, up this way then." She took off her glasses and stepped up the small ladder to the cockpit gangway. Once Theo was beside her, she opened the door. The cockpit, while still small, was at least double or more the size of what Sahni had rode up in. She expected to see someone other than the pilots, but no one else was there.

Stepping in, she called, "Hi there! I'm Sahnassa. Someone wanted to see me?"

The copilot on the right turned around. "Captain Keel and Lieutenant Crastor at your service! We figured you might want to help guide us down. After all, you gave us such great directions on the way up!"

She laughed at the surprise. "You did this on purpose! Theo, they were the ones who rescued us halfway up the mountain! Thank you both; this is great!" Looking out the windows, she only saw darkness. "Oh, but I don't know if I could repeat what I did last time. I can't see anything!"

"Thankfully, this time you don't have to. We're going up to meet a couple of the HVR-9's that have been acting as guides above the clouds. They'll take us to our descent vector. Would you two like to have a seat and watch?"

"I think we can stay until you actually start your final approach," Theo suggested. "Sahni, I think you'll find the view amazing."

"That sounds wonderful." They both sat down, strapped in, and watched as the clouds slowly started to part.

"Captain, do you mind if I make a call down to Tedarri?" Theo asked.

"No problem. Spare headset is on your right," the Captain said. "Are you familiar with the console?"

"Very familiar. Thank you," Theo answered, popping the headset over his ears and changing the frequency to Tedarri's control center. Sahnassa listened, smiling, as she heard him begin to unfold another small miracle.

Vanarra held Tana's paw on her left, but then felt Rahnahi grab her paw at the right. "You okay ... Honored One?"

Rahnahi grimaced. "I guess that title has to come back out eventually, doesn't it? I was never one for flying. So how are you feeling?"

"Tired, Honored One," Van admitted. "I'm a little hungry, too. I could stand a long, hot shower. In fact, I'm not sure which one of those I want to do first."

"I know what you mean. Take a poet's suggestion. Shower then food then bed, sleep in tomorrow. It may be late, but I guess that with the storm, we won't exactly be rushing off to anywhere soon. As for me, I'm battling with even more confusion than you. That writing side of my psyche wants in, and that's something amazing given how much I want to do everything you just talked about."

They laughed, but Van couldn't help asking, "Honored One, are you planning on a new book?"

"I don't know what it will be, but I can tell you I've never been so tired and so inspired at the same time in all my life! There's so much about what's happened, happened to all of us, that needs to find its way to written word. There are so many lights to shine on it, from so many different directions. I could work for the rest of my life to sort through what's happened in these last two sols!"

Vanarra felt it a unique privilege to see the Grand Matriarch Rahnahi de Dothnar so charmingly inspired and excited. "Well, Honored One, if you would take a caterer's suggestion, relaxing shower, then good food, then a soft bed, and then *really* sleep in. Writing tomorrow ... afternoon."

They laughed, but then Rahnahi asked, "Are you still planning to talk with Amyra?"

"I will, Honored One. I've got to get the amulet back. I left it with one of her dames. I'll make sure I have it before I go to see her."

"It's more than just about that amulet, Vanarra, but I'm sure she'll appreciate the gesture. Remember, *both* of you are nervous. That will help."

Vanarra nodded, and then some dips and bumps of turbulence kept them from talking any more. Vanarra just held onto Tana's and Rahnahi's paws, grateful that this was her last flight.

The HVR-17 slowly settled to the ground watched by a small crowd including the Marshall, Tedarri, several dames, and two Perratti law enforcement officers. As the engines wound down, they walked to meet the lowering ramp. The Marshall accepted the loadmaster's salute, smiling a little at how she always delivered it. Applause and cheers and cries of relief also greeted him as the engine noise finally abated completely.

As they were unbuckling, Theo, who had returned to the cargo bay with Sahnassa a few passes earlier, leaned over to Tana and quietly said, "While we were in flight, I arranged protective custody. Just in case the de Caterra decide to take extreme measures because they don't want you talking, and to allay the concerns of local law enforcement. Once you answer their questions, I think you'll be okay. I'll make sure of that before I leave."

Tana sighed as she stood, "I understand."

Distracted by Sahnassa, at Theo's request, Vanarra hadn't noticed the conversation.

"Very good. I also have some hope that the Dame Katuratatallenar will open up to them, as well."

"Good chances with that, but what you said to her, Theo – I don't think anyone's ever talked to her like that before."

"Someone needed to, a long time ago."

"You two ready?" Vanarra asked, finally realizing she'd missed them talking.

"We are," Tana said.

As they walked down the ramp in the midst of the dames and matrons, Theo started guiding them to a small group assembled on their left. In a moment, pleasant introductions were made for the rest of the group, but Theo intentionally left Tana until the end. "And this is Tana, formerly Tanassadurini de Caterra. She is the one who helped Vanarra."

Tedarri stepped forward, looking a little grim. "We're grateful for what you've done, but you understand we have to take some precautions and follow some procedures, based on what you were involved in."

"I understand."

"What? I don't understand," Vanarra said, realizing where this might be going.

"It's alright, Vanarra. I knew this was coming," Tana reassured, looking confidently back at her worried friend.

"We're going to place her in protective custody and get some testimony from her," Tedarri explained apologetically. "If the local magistrate gives us permission, she'll be free to go. However, Vanarra, we don't have a choice. Tonight, we have to book her."

One of the Perratti law enforcers came over and stated, "Tana, you have rights against self-incrimination. You have the right of representation. All statements and actions made while you are in custody are admissible as evidence in any future proceeding, familial or governmental. Do you understand these rights and warnings?" Vanarra watched in tears as the other Perratti put Tana's wrists in binders.

"Yes, I do."

"Knowing that, do you wish to make a statement or provide evidence?"

"Yes, I do. Two statements. First," and she turned to Van, "I am truly grateful to you, Vanarra, and I will always be so." Turning back to the officer, she said, "Second, I want to give information on the illegal activities of the de Caterra family."

"Very well. We'll take that statement when we get back to the department."

Vanarra was still not appeased. "You're not going to put her with the others, are you?"

"No ma'am, nowhere close. Her quarters will be much nicer than theirs. We'll work through this as fast as we can and try to cause her as little discomfort as possible."

"You see that you do," Rahnahi suggested, slipping her coat off her shoulder so that her matriarchal emblem was visible to them. With a slow, understanding nod, he agreed.

"Very well," Tedarri added. "Let's let them go, and then everyone can head inside for some warm food and sleep."

"Sounds good to me," Rahnahi said. Vanarra walked over, hugged Tana, and kissed her on the side of the muzzle before letting them take her. Sadly, with Theo and Sahnassa holding her paws, Van watched them go.

The Chief and Terrat walked over to Vanarra. "It'll be alright, Van. You'll see," the Chief offered, patting her shoulder.

As he turned to leave, Van asked, "Where are you going?"

Terrat answered, "We're going to get Agari set up in the medical transport, and then shut down flight operations for the night. We've got a couple of final details to settle, but we'll be hitting the sack in about an interval. You should do the same."

"Yes, Marshall. Thank you," Vanarra replied. "Thank you both for everything." She walked over and hugged them.

Everyone else in the group echoed her thanks and then turned towards the main building as the soldiers walked away.

As they entered the warmth of the school building, they found the halls were quieter and darker than they expected. "Most everyone else is asleep. Many of them are already across the street at the tertiary school," Tedarri explained. "If you'll let me take you around to the cafeteria, we can get you some food, and once that's taken care of, someone can lead you to sleeping quarters."

"We can take care of that, sir," one of the dames who had greeted them at the landing site interjected. "We've already made provisions for the matriarchy."

"Very well. Have a good night, and we're all very glad you're safe."

Rahnahi stepped up. "And thank you for all you have done. Ah, what about Vanarra and Sahnassa?" The matriarch had shifted her gaze to the dame who had spoken up.

Seeing the somewhat confused expression on the dame's face, Tedarri offered, "My mate has actually set up our spare bedroom for them, Honored One, if that would suffice. Buck, I guess you and Theo could stay here with the rest of the evacuees. Do you know where to take him?" he asked Theo.

"Absolutely. That sounds like a plan to me."

"Would that be okay with you two?" Tedarri asked Sahni and Van directly. Looking at each other, and presented with the possibility of a bed in a lair as opposed to a cot in a school, they both eagerly nodded. "Honored One?" Rahnahi happily gave her consent.

"Can we come back here later?" Sahnassa asked.

"I can bring you back up tomorrow, uh, I guess it's later this sol when I come back on duty," Tedarri responded.

"Okay then! I guess we'll see you later," Vanarra stated, a little apologetically.

"Not without this first," Rahnahi demanded, and she walked forward and hugged both Vanarra and Sahnassa. "I know lots of Thurians helped, but you two made the big difference. Thank you so much, not only for my life, but for every life you helped save."

"Oh, you're welcome; you're welcome, Honored One! Thank you!" Sahnassa breathed, and Vanarra was simply too overwhelmed for words. That emotion grew greater still as each matron and dame hugged them in turn. Sahnassa, weeping happily, looked at Theo who was smiling, appearing perhaps, just a little proud.

It was not a long ride to Tedarri's home, and his spacious hover made the trip quickly and easily. After entering the two-story lair, they were greeted, very openly, by his mate Denala. Even though Vanarra was more exhausted and emotionally drained than she could ever remember, she still didn't miss when someone welcomed an Anati into their lair. Tedarri's mate had nothing but welcome in her pretty gray face and kind blue eyes, and she seemed to know, full well, how tired they all were. She kept the introductions mercifully short, provided them both with hot soup and drink, and took them straight to the guest room upstairs.

As they walked up the stairs, Vanarra saw pictures of children on the walls, older children: a cub and a kit who appeared to be about fifteen or sixteen seasons. "Fraternal twins, perhaps?" Vanarra wondered. As they entered the comfortable and well-appointed room, a large bed lay invitingly before them. Then, with goodnights from Tedarri and Denala, the door was quietly shut.

"Oh wonderful, wonderful," Sahnassa sighed, sitting down on the comfortable mattress. "A real, honest to truth, bed!"

Vanarra walked over and sat beside her. She had to admit that the bed seemed to have an almost unnatural pull on her. "Hmm. It is nice." She really wanted to lie down and sleep, but the soup resting on a nearby tray was just too appealing. It was a happy dilemma, and she sighed. Glancing over at her friend, Van bit her lip a little before speaking. "Hey, Sahni?"

"Yes?"

"This is the first time we've been alone since … well, since the flyer landed to pick us up from our camp," Van observed a little shyly.

"Yes. It is. I have to tell you, when I realized you'd been abducted, I was so scared! I'm so glad you're okay," Sahnassa breathed, reaching out for and lightly grasping Van's arm.

"Thanks for sending in the troops, kit. I owe you." They hugged, and Van again found herself being comforted by Sahni. "Can I ask another favor?" she carefully inquired.

"Yes?"

"Can we sleep … like we did in the shelter? We'll probably never get to again."

Van's eyes were so sad that Sahnassa felt like she had to reassure her friend. "Sisters always find a way to spend time together. I'm sure we'll be able to, every now and then."

"You think?"

"I do," Sahni replied, smiling at her.

"You don't have to, I mean." Van turned away, seeming unsure.

Sahnassa reached out and gently grabbed Van's head, turning it back towards her. "Vanarra Anasto, remember that this is me you're talking to. I promise, when we get back to the office, I'll be your happy employee, fix your servers, upload and transmit whatever you tell me to, go serve creele at whatever crazy events you sign us up for, listen to your pep-talks, and tolerate all your rants, but for now … like I did before, let me just be there for you. You've been through a tough, tough thing." She saw Van about to interrupt her and placed a claw-tip to Van's lips. "No, I know what you're going to say. Yours was tougher. Yes, I'll sleep with you like we did in the shelter. I'll even brave your tail, although I might be tempted to wrap it in a towel for cushioning."

They both laughed. "Sorry about that," Van apologized.

"It's okay. I'm going to go shower, how about you?"

"I want to, but you go first. I'm going to eat. Maybe think a little." Sahnassa squeezed her one last time, and then bounded off towards the bathroom.

As Van started to eat the warm, tasty soup, she looked out the windows and saw snow begin to fall, visible in the various outside lights. As she ate through the generous portion Denala had served her, she finally remembered something she wanted to do, wanted to ask, and realized that it may be too late. She wanted to get Theo alone and ask him about the strange visions she had while she was being held captive. Her tired mind tried to search through what could have caused those premonitions to happen, but everything reasonable didn't make sense.

She caught herself and had to shake her head and quietly laugh. So very little of what they had been through really made any sense. Her possible reconciliation with the de Gonari, her relationship with Rahnahi de Dothnar, and all of the other losses and gains were simply too much for her tired mind to fathom, so she simply decided not to try. She just sat still, peaceful, watching the snow fall and enjoying her soup.

After seeing Buck off to bed, Theo wandered back up in the direction of the command center. Now that the evacuees were on the ground, the urgency of the place had clearly vanished. Only one lone soul sat with the receiver of a communicator buried in one ear, rifling through papers. As Theo walked in, he heard the last part of the Pantera's conversation.

"I'm very sorry, but we don't have specifics about anyone right now, other than we know that everyone was rescued and was either driven out of here to Shanandrae or is in a shelter right now. No, we didn't allow anyone to call because we had to get everyone into the shelter quickly. Hopefully, we'll start having them make calls soon ... yes I know, but everyone else does, too. I'm sorry. Hopefully, you'll hear something early tomorrow, I mean this sol. Have a good night." As soon as he hung up the receiver, Gaitain placed his big Pantera head in his paws.

"You look like you are about finished! Why don't you go get some rest and let me have a turn?"

He looked askance at Theo standing in the doorway and complained, "They won't stop calling. Over and over again, some of them, and I've got next to nothing in terms of information. I'm sure I've honked off at least two dames and who knows how many matrons!"

"Alright Gaitain, you've had enough. Surrender the LineCom, and get out of here before you get yourself into real trouble."

"You sure? I mean, you're not really part of the staff and all."

"I'm the one that's buying you eight intervals of sleep you desperately need, and you're arguing?" Theo eyed him with a look of uncertainty, as if a psychological evaluation was in order should his resistance continue. The Pantera sighed and stood, thanked him, and then left.

Theo sat down and saw four communications lines flashing, awaiting an answer. "Alright my friends, let's do this together. Create virtual replacements for all four lines should anyone else in the building need to use them. Ensure that no one else can listen to what we're doing. Respond in my voice and transition any conversations you have questions about to me."

Suddenly, all of the lines but one went solid, indicating that someone was connected and helping the caller. Theo punched the remaining line and announced into the receiver, "Windston Emergency Management Center. Theo de Allarrae speaking. How can I help you?"

"Hello. I know—" The elder female voice, talking on speaker on her end of the line, paused for a moment. "I know this may be more information than you currently have, but do you have anything on Sahnassa de Orturu, or any de Orturu?" The voice on the other end of the communicator sounded about like what he'd expected: tired and worried, but still very sweet.

"I most certainly do. I have everything. What would you like to know? Oh, and may I ask who is calling?"

"I am Matriarch Selena de Orturu." Theo smiled. There were times he did "shift the work" of the "paw of fate", but it was even better when things like this just simply happened.

"Honored One. It's so good of you to call! Should I start with Sahnassa?" Theo projected his thoughts out to the call's source and was able to find the caller, seated in a comfortable chair next to a fire, with what had to be Sahnassa's parents and a couple of dames busily taking notes.

"Yes, please. We've heard rumors – rumors that she was somehow responsible for or had a part in the rescue."

"Oh, yes, Honored One. Those aren't rumors. First, let me tell you that she and all of the rest of the de Orturu are safe. All of them were evacuated off the mountain. Six were shipped out by ground transport to Shanandrae, and thirty-six remain here in the shelters. Everyone has had a hot meal and now has a comfortable place to sleep. Would you like the names of all of them?"

"Oh, yes, please. I have someone here to take down the information. You're sure none of them are injured? I heard there was an explosion."

"That's true, Honored One," Theo gravely confirmed. "However, the matriarchs of house de Gonari and de Dothnar realized what was happening and got everyone well away before the blast."

"Amyra de Gonari and Rahnahi de Dothnar? They were there as well?" the voice sounded incredulous.

"Yes. They are both safe. Speaking of safe, I have the names. Is your help ready to copy, Honored One?"

"Yes, please." After a few passes of reading names and providing their status in the upmost detail, Theo paused and heard the matriarch say, "Theo, I cannot thank you enough. We've got a lot of worried family here, and this will set their minds well at ease. I … I hate to impose, but may I ask you for a few details specific to Sahnassa? Her parents are here with me, and they don't know what to think of the stories they've heard."

"What have you heard?" Theo asked.

An officious, but deeply worried male voice answered, "I've heard my daughter was nearly lost down a mountain, but she still managed to call for help. Somehow the military got involved, and she's supposed to have done something there, too, but I don't know what. I would just – we would all appreciate finding out a little bit more about what's happened to our little kit."

"Please," the mother added, "we're glad she's alright. We're just worried how … traumatic this has been on her."

"I know you have so many other calls with which to contend," the matriarch nearly pleaded, "if you could just spare a moment."

Theo's warm smile was evident in the tone of his softly spoken answer. "The other calls are being tended to, so don't worry about that in the slightest. For you, I know this is important. First, let me tell you one simple truth, Honored One. Sahnassa de Orturu, as much as or even more than anyone else, helped make possible the rescue of all of the Thurians trapped on top of that mountain. Had your daughter not been there, they would have likely starved or frozen to death. For whatever struggles you had bringing her up and for all the effort you put into it, you helped bring about the saving of nearly fifteen hundred lives. For that, every house and family touched owes you a debt of thanks, time and times over."

"Thank you. Thank you so much," her father said, "but how?"

"She was accompanying her employer who was scheduled to receive a reward up at the Meeting Den in the Yarvea Mountains. There was a misunderstanding, and she and her employer left early. While they were on the road, the quake hit. A landslide knocked their hover off the road and down the mountainside a couple hundred tracks. When they hiked back up, they found their way blocked by downed bridges or slide covered roads. Not knowing what else to do, they set up camp. Over the next few intervals, they were able to communicate their situation to the emergency station here in the valley. They were surprised that no one from the Meeting Den had called in. That's when Sahnassa made a clever little alteration to her PawLink. With that, she and her employer were able to talk to the de Gonari matriarch and find out how very desperate the situation had become. If Sahnassa had not been able to perform that little trick, there would have been no way to contact anyone atop the mountain. All other communications were out."

"So, Sahnassa relayed the message down to the emergency station, and that started the rescue?" the matriarch asked.

"It did, Honored One, although her employer had to dig deep into her own pockets to make sure there would be enough food and transportation available once everyone was rescued."

"What about the military part?" her father asked. "One of my friends is an air controller with the defense force, and he said Sahnassa did something there, too, but he wasn't sure what."

"By the time the military arrived on site, the weather had turned bad. The military was able to locate your daughter and her employer, but they needed help finding their way any further. Sahnassa was able to sit in the cockpit of one of the flyers and help guide them to the athletic field of the Meeting Den. She remembered the tops of the mountains from when they drove in."

"Our smart little kit!" her mother said proudly.

"She certainly is," Theo agreed. "There is one other event you may not have heard about that happened while the general evacuation was in progress. After being rescued, Sahnassa and her employer stayed at the Meeting Den helping the others evacuate. Sometime later, her employer went missing. Your daughter later discovered that a group of de Caterra had assaulted and abducted both her employer and a soldier. Because Sahnassa was observant and had developed trust in the eyes of the matriarchs and the military, they believed her and rescued the captives."

"What, by Thuria, are the de Caterra doing holding captives!?" Selena's anger broke through her otherwise calm demeanor.

"Matriarch, I believe that in the next few sols, everyone is going to learn that the de Caterra have been doing much more than holding captives, and for quite some time. Regardless if the victims were Anati, the disavowed, members of other families, or even their very own, the de

Caterra have done things that are … reprehensible in the eyes of any civilized house."

"Are you sure about this?" The matriarch's words were deadly serious and warned of great consequences should the speaker be mistaken or taking liberties with the truth.

With the calmness of a court clerk reading a verdict, Theo replied, "Honored One, at this very moment, two of the de Caterra have renounced their own family over this incident, and one of those is giving testimony to local law enforcement." Peering a little further around the valley, he was able to add one other detail. "It also appears that a dame involved in the affair has also just confessed—"

"A dame of the de Caterra family! That would imply that—" Selena stopped talking, taking into account the full meaning of what was being said.

"She has just confessed, Honored One, and she has implicated the matriarch and several other high family officials for a number of rape-matings, kidnappings, and murders over the last fifty seasons." Listening to the stony silence and watching, remotely, the unvarnished look of horror on the de Orturu Matriarch's face, Theo apologized. "I'm sorry to break it to you this way, but you will hear it soon, perhaps by mid sol tomorrow when details start to flow through normal channels. However, what I've told you, you will come to know as the truth, in time."

"We were considering trying to … open a dialogue with—" Selena started to say, standing. "This morning, we were going to – Theo, I … I can't thank you enough. We were going to do that this very morning! Had you not told me, warned me, my entire house would have been in disgrace!"

"But are you sure it's true?" Sahnassa's father asked.

"It's so shocking! I always knew they were … hard, but this?" Her mother was equally as stunned.

"I know it's hard to hear, and right now, Sahnassa's father is right. You only have my word. However, you at least have my word. You and I also both know, Honored One, that lying to a matriarch is neither wise or without cost. Given that, I can tell you I'm taking no risk at all in telling you this. Time will prove me right."

"Oh, Theo, Theo," Selena repeated softly, "I can at least delay upon excuse of illness or other pretense this sol's meeting. When the truth comes out, we'll say we heard. If you're wrong, we have but to reschedule. If you're right, oh, if you're right Theo, I owe you a great debt. How … how would you have me pay it? Beyond my gratitude for telling me all of these wonderful things about our dear Sahnassa and the rest of our family, how am I to repay you?"

Theo's voice was soft and serious. "Sahnassa took a risk in her choice of an employer."

"The Anati caterer?"

"I see you know. Very well. It's clear now that she saw something very special in that individual. Had circumstances never required it, it may never have surfaced, but they did, and together, those two, Sahnassa and Vanarra Anasto, saved hundreds of lives. Repay me by remembering her choice with honor and ensure she is never penalized for daring to reach out to the right soul, regardless of what type of body it inhabits. That will be enough for me, Honored One."

A cautious, almost reverent tone issued from the mouth of the matriarch. "I have the feeling, the sense, Theo, that you are not all you appear to be. Your heart is touched with an uncommon wisdom. You have my unbreakable vow, witnessed before all here. When the truth of your words is proven, I will not only welcome her choice, but her employer into our presence with no disgrace or discrimination."

"Then, I am at peace, Honored One, and full of joy. Pleasant morning and greatest honor to your family. I'll ask Sahnassa to call you as soon as she can."

"Thank you, Theo, with honor."

"With honor, Matriarch of de Orturu, a house most noble and true." With that, the line went quiet.

Chapter 19: Reborn

Vanarra stirred, uncertain of where she was. A click, click sound she couldn't place woke her up. The last thing she remembered was putting her soup bowl down and lying back on the bed to watch the snow. She felt arms surrounding her now, soft blankets over her, and her own tail tucked between someone else's legs. A low groan confirmed the identity of her bedmate. Obviously, Sahnassa had showered, based on the fresh smell coming from behind her, and obviously Vanarra had not, based on her own strong scent, but she didn't remember getting into a nightgown. Van wondered if she really had passed out so completely that Sahni had been able to change her clothes without waking her up.

Opening her eyes and looking up at the windows, Van saw the source of the strange sound. Snow had turned to ice and was building up fast on the glass. "Everyone's safe," she thought. "Even Arnat. Even Sanrat." She thought about Tana, and hoped that she was being treated well. She also thought about Agari; he had been so nice to her. He hadn't judged her at all.

Then, she thought about Buck and what a good friend he had been to her. "Could he be more? Do I want more?" She smiled at the question and knew the answer. "Yes, I do." As she closed her eyes and tried to quiet her thoughts, she finally realized what had kept them apart. Until now, Van never felt like she deserved anyone who would really take care of her, so she just didn't pursue anything more than friendship with the keen Faelnar. Now perhaps, even Vanarra Anasto would open herself up to the possibility of being loved.

As if in response to that thought, the arms around her tightened in a hug and gently released again. "Okay Sahni, I'll do it," she whispered and sighed, quickly falling back to sleep.

Gaitain appeared at the door, holding a hot drink. "Thanks for last night. Any problems?"

"No, no problems at all. There's a list here you might find useful," Theo answered him.

Gaitain walked over and said in astonishment, "Wow! If I had this, things would have gone much smoother."

"It was compiled overnight, and yes, it did make things much easier. It showed up shortly after you left."

"Who brought it?" the Pantera asked as he sipped.

"I didn't recognize him as one of the staff. I can't say."

"Any important callers?"

"We had the de Orturu matriarch, plus several dames from other houses, including de Caterra." His call with the de Caterra matron had been interesting, if relatively business-like. They clearly had no idea what was about to be unleashed upon them.

"De Caterra?! Oh, mange, haven't you heard?"

"What?" Theo feigned surprise as best he could.

"That old dame from de Caterra has started spilling her innards about all kinds of horrific stuff that family has done over the seasons. Confirmed everything the other one, Tana, said. Oh, and don't ask how I know about this."

"I don't have to," Theo chuckled, smiling a wry smile. "You talked to the local law enforcement while they were getting their breakfast. Now, I mean, I know about the rumors, but to have two of them confirming it – that's pretty amazing. That's also pretty damning, too. So what do you think is going to happen?"

"It's really hard to say. This is big; it's shocking, but will anything actually change?"

"We can hope."

"Hope for de Caterra to get its collective tail kicked?" the Pantera joked.

Theo's response was more serious. "Hope that victims finally find peace and criminals find justice. Perhaps some shake-ups of the family order are needed – perhaps some shake-ups of the world order, too. So, are you ready to take the helm again?"

"Sure. It sounds like it's died down though."

"It'll pick back up, and some of the evacuees are going to want to call their families, so someone will have to organize that." The communicator rang again, and Theo smiled. "Well, one last one." Picking up the receiver, he said, "Windston Emergency Management Center. Theo de Allarrae speaking. How can I help you?"

"What!? You owe me an apology!" a young kit's voice insisted.

Theo laughed as he recognized her. "I take it this is the honorable Carinthia de Dothnar? If so, then you have my most humble apologies, Cari. Sahnassa did talk to me; I really did not mean to frighten you. We were just trying to make sure everyone got out."

"But you're okay, right? And Celeste? Is she okay too?"

"Yes, she's sleeping. Where are you?"

"I'm in my room," Cari answered, a little quietly, as if being secretive.

"Safe at home, I trust?"

"Yes. I gave my grandsire back his ribbon, but he said he wanted me to keep it, even though I almost lost it."

"He must love you very much," Theo said warmly, "and he must have been very worried about you."

Cari was matter-of-fact in her response. "He was. When we got home, he couldn't stop hugging me. Mom and dad were the same way, too. Is grandama alright?"

"She's fine. I think she's awake. I'll ask her to give you a call, if you like."

"Uh, you better not tell her I called, if you don't mind," Cari stammered. "I didn't exactly ask permission before I did this. It took me forever to find the right number."

"So you called just to find me, huh?"

"Yes. I did. I … I had to know you were both okay." The voice of the little Nephti was so timid and honest.

"I'm very glad to hear you are too. Now, you give your mom and dad and your grandsire some extra love. Will you do that?"

"I will. Do you think you can come and visit me some time, with Celeste? Do a conjure?"

"I'll do one now. Unless you tell them, Cari, no one will ever know you called. As for visiting you, well you never can tell. You never can tell. Be well, little one. Take good care of yourself."

"Goodbye!"

Vanarra usually hated the thought of waking up not knowing exactly where she was. However, given the perfect mix of a comfortable, warm bed, cool air around her, as well as the smell of good food wafting across her nose, Van thought she might just be willing to make an exception. She heard a strange noise, like shuffling, just beyond her hind paws at the end of the bed. Opening her eyes, the room she had shared with Sahnassa came into focus. No lamps were on, but muted white light was streaming through the windows. She could make out some motion behind the glass – moving tree branches and falling snow perhaps – but it was obscured by the heavy ice on the panes.

A very definite giggle, a young one, issued from the foot of her bed. Sitting up, she saw two stunned little faces, just from the eyes to the ears. Grayish white fur, tinged with black, played in differing patterns around two sets of wide eyes, one pair brilliant green and one pair violet. Using more instinct rather than actual thought, she realized what they were: Anati children. "What are you two doing here?" she asked, surprised.

"We're watching you," a little kit's voice whispered.

"Oh, and am I that entertaining?" Van asked sleepily.

"Tarka thinks you're pretty," the female said and was rewarded with a hard jab to her ribs. "Hey! I'll tell Dad!" she complained, standing up, which allowed Van to get a good look at her. She was a Nephti Faelnar mix, and when he also stood up to protest, she saw that he was the same. There was no trace of Lupar in them, at all.

Interrupting their sibling bickering, she asked, "So you're Tarka? And what's your name?"

"She's Arani, and she thinks you're pretty, too. She was making fun of you, though."

"Why?" Vanarra asked, bemused.

"She saw you sleeping with your butt in the air," Tarka's admission drew a hard slap from Arani on his shoulder, and caused Vanarra's blush furs to actually take flight, something that hardly ever happened.

"Oh, I'm sorry. It was … kind of a hard couple of sols. You two, are you like … twins?"

"Yeah, we are. Our parents left us here when we were really small," Arani answered sadly, "but Tedarri's now our dad and Denala's now our mom." The kit's voice was proud, as if she truly appreciated what a gift she had been given.

"Wow," Vanarra marveled, and meant it. She had not thought much on Tedarri, but she was shocked that she had already formed assumptions about him. Now, those ideas were being proved wrong. "That's pretty wonderful! I know a lot of little kits and cubs who don't have a family." Both of them smiled, as if they had finally found someone who understood them.

"Tarka, Arani?" Denala's voice came from the hallway, and in another moment, the Lupar female was in the room. "You two! Couldn't you let her sleep? I told you to leave her alone."

"It's okay. I was already waking up," Vanarra said. "It was really great to meet them."

"Very well then; you two run along. You need to get on your warm things and help your dad. He's trying to clear off the hover, and I know he could use your help."

"Great," Arani groaned, disappointed, "I hate snow."

"Come on, sis, it could be fun! Let's go! See you later?"

"Yes, I'm sure I will." With that, the two were gone, scampering down the hall. Vanarra said kindly to her host, "They really are precious, and if I understood them correctly, you two are pretty wonderful, as well."

Denala smiled. "I know there are some in town who don't like it, and even our family has given us a sack load, but I just couldn't turn them away. I mean, we had our own twins long ago. Racen is in the defense force now, and Malli works as an intern when she's not in academy. Tedarri and I just got so used to having our own around, well, it wasn't hard to adopt these two, and they're really sweet."

"Did you have to convince Tedarri?"

"Actually not. He was the one who found them. They were abandoned at the emergency center one night. Tedarri was making his rounds and saw a moving box outside of the building. When I got home from playing Roquet with my friends, he already had them fed and sleeping in his lap. He loves helping those in need, and those two certainly were."

Vanarra sighed. "That makes you both heroes in my eyes. I volunteer at an orphanage in Shanandrae, and they have a hard time placing the purebloods, let alone … one of us. From my heart, thank you."

Denala sat down on the bed beside her. "I appreciate that, more than you know. You don't get a lot of positive things said about you when you take in someone who's different, and the children at school have been so ugly to them – well, we've had to school them here. It's hard for us, and it's hard for them, but still, we manage." Denala's look was a little bleak, but then she brightened. "And look at the role model they have now! Tedarri's told me what happened to you and most of what you did. I think that's amazing! I hope you get appropriately honored and rewarded for what you've done. It would only be fair."

"I'll settle for some of whatever that is I'm smelling," Vanarra said, sniffing the air, smiling.

Denala's blush furs raised a little. "Mill biscuits, my own recipe. Another batch is coming out of the oven. Your friend seemed to really like them – I mean *really* like them!"

Van and Denala both laughed. "I'll probably be as hungry, but, oh, I have got to, got to shower! You wouldn't have any clothes that I might borrow?"

"I think I have something that will fit you. Tell you what, I'll go get it and lay it over your bed. I'll also make sure the twins don't find their way back in here. You can just join us at the table whenever you're ready."

Vanarra put her arm around the Lupar and gave her a gentle hug. "Thank you, and thank you so much for opening your home to us."

"My pleasure," Denala replied returning the hug and then stood. "I'll let you get started. I think Tedarri wants to get back up to the schools in a little while, once the roads are cleared. The weather's just a horrible mess, right now. See you in a moment." Denala closed the door, and Vanarra stretched a long and luxurious stretch before heading for the bathroom.

"So, is she finally up?" Sahnassa asked, finishing off another mill biscuit.

"Yes, she is, poor dear. I'm afraid the twins may have woken her up." The LineCom started beeping, and Denala picked it off the counter as she walked by. "de Bosnar residence. May I ask who's calling? Oh, hello there. Yes, yes, she's right here." Turning around, she handed the device to Sahnassa.

"Hello?"

"My precious little kit!" Her mother's voice made her smile and tear up. "I'm so glad you're safe!"

"Oh, Mom, I'm so sorry! I was going to call you; we just got in so late."

"Not to worry, a friend of yours made sure we knew you were okay. Theo, I think his name was. Love, he told us everything you did. Your father and I are just so proud of you."

"Thanks, Mom," she said, half grateful to Theo, and half infuriated that he already told them everything. "I can't wait to tell you what happened myself."

"There will be enough time for that. Now, is it bad there? Are you in a good place?"

"Oh, we're staying with a really nice family, and they have such a beautiful lair! The weather has turned downright awful, though. It's well past mid-sol, and it just stopped snowing. We've had ice and snow all night. Tedarri, that's the regional emergency manager whose home we're staying at, said that it's going to be like this off and on for the next four sols. It'll take me a little while to get home, I'm afraid."

"Just as long as you're safe, love. Your father wanted me to send his love, too. He's helping with the evacuated families. He's arranging free travel for any of those who need it."

Sahnassa inwardly glowed with pride at her father's good-hearted nature. He could be so business-like and formal, but if he saw a real need, he'd jump in. Sahnassa loved him all the more for that, despite their arguments in the past. "Oh, that's great, Mom! Please tell him thanks for me. That's wonderful."

"I will, dear. Also, there's someone else who wants to speak with you."

Sahni heard the LineCom being passed, and then an older female voice said, "Sahnassa, you have given the name of our family great honor."

"Honored One! Oh, it's so good to hear you!" Sahnassa instantly recognized the voice of her Grand Matriarch, Selena de Orturu.

"And you, too, dear one. We have heard so many wonderful things about you and what you have done. I can remember you listening to the stories I told when you were just a kit, and now, I want so very badly to sit and hear your story. When you return to us, please, let's spend some time together. Will you bring your friend with you too?"

"My friend, Honored One?"

"Vanarra Anasto, dear. The Anati – the caterer you work for." Sahnassa closed her eyes, cringing, knowing that she had been caught. "Now, you need not worry. She will be welcomed with honor and gratitude. I've given my word. Your friend, Theo, asked this on your behalf. I … I see the wisdom in your choice, Sahnassa, and your bravery in choosing Vanarra as a friend. There are still many things to understand, dear, but I think you and I need to have a good talk soon. I think that we may have a lot to learn from you."

"Oh, Honored One, thank you," Sahni replied humbly. "I look forward to seeing all of you again."

"And we you. Stay safe, Sahnassa. We will see you soon."

After a wonderful breakfast around the de Bosnar table enjoyed by all six of them, Tedarri finally admitted he needed to get back to the schools and his office. The snow had started falling lightly again, so Sahnassa, Vanarra, and the twins were all pressed into service to clear his hover of snow and shovel out a little path for it to exit the driveway. With only a couple of snowball fights interrupting the proceedings, the three adults were waving goodbye to the kids and Denala from the inside of a nicely warmed vehicle as it pulled out into the road.

"They're great kids, Tedarri. They're such fun!" Sahnassa giggled, looking back as they drove away.

"They have their moments," Tedarri joked. "We didn't know if it would work out, but in the end, the family relented – her mom was the worst about it – but it's gotten better over time."

Van patted his shoulder from the back seat. "You're giving them something I would have given anything to have had growing up, and something a lot of our kind never do."

Tedarri was as appreciative as his mate had been. "Thank you. It seemed like the right thing to do. I just couldn't see letting them get locked away somewhere—"

Vanarra sharply inhaled, having caught herself forgetting something really important. "Tedarri, is there any way you can drop me off where they're keeping Tana? I really have to check on her to see that she's okay."

"Not just you," Sahnassa warned. "I want to go, too!"

"Sure. I could do that, and the officer in charge told me he wanted statements from both of you some time soon, anyway. After that's done, you can pretty easily catch a ride back up to the schools, provided the weather doesn't get worse."

As the hover turned at the next intersection, Vanarra looked and saw that the snow appeared to be falling harder than before. "I wonder what it's like up at the Meeting Den," Sahnassa mused, noticing where Van's gaze was fixed.

"I think Terrat's crew left a monitor beacon up there," Tedarri answered. "I would be interested to know that, myself. Okay, here you are! If they can't get you a ride back, call the school, and we'll get someone to pick you up."

"Thanks Tedarri!" Sahnassa offered as she opened the door.

"Thanks Dad! You're the best!" Vanarra whispered in his ear, leaning forward and kissing him on the side of the muzzle before she left.

As he drove away, looking a little stunned, Vanarra remarked, "I never thought someone like him would have such a soft spot or be so … kind. Denala, too. I've spent too much time in Shanandrae; I guess I missed the small towns."

"Big towns with big families and big influence," Sahnassa mused. "Doesn't seem to apply much out here. By the way, my matriarch called. She knows that I work for you." Vanarra looked at her with a mixture of both fear and disappointment. "Don't look so sad! She wants to meet you and welcome you into our home."

That bit of news didn't do much to soothe her boss. "Are you sure? Are you sure you want me to do that?"

"Van, it will be fine. Come on, let's get inside. I'm getting cold!" She put her arm around Van and led her into the station.

Almost the moment they opened the door, a young male Pantera officer asked them, "Can I help you?"

Stepping up to the window at the end of the small waiting room, Sahni answered. "Yes, please. My name is Sahnassa, and this is Vanarra. We would like to see Tana, if that's possible."

"Tana?" the officer asked, obviously not understanding exactly who she meant.

"A Faelnar that was brought in last night and put in protective custody," Vanarra clarified.

"One moment, let me check with the sergeant."

He stepped away, and Vanarra quietly commented, "I hope they let us. I promised that kit I would take care of her. I don't break promises if I can help it."

"And I really like that about you," Sahni responded, smiling before a rueful look appeared on her face. "I hope they do, too. It's a long walk back to the schools."

"Either that or we spend the next few sols in this waiting room," Van observed, scanning the room equipped with only a few hard chairs.

"Not a good idea, no."

A door near them opened, and the officer asked, "Are you Sahnassa de Orturu and Vanarra Anasto?" They nodded, and he requested, "Could you come with me, please?"

As they walked into the small hallway, Sahnassa whispered, "I feel like we're about to be booked."

"By someone so hot looking? Sign me up," Van quipped, earning a light punch in the shoulder from Sahni.

"This way please," the Pantera said with a little smirk on his face.

"He heard you," Sahni whispered, shocked as they followed him down the hall.

"Nice tail, though," Van whispered back.

They were escorted into a small office where a very tired, middle-aged Nephti male sat at a large wooden desk behind a pile of well-organized papers. "Here they are, sir," the guard announced, startling him out of deep thought, a light doze, or some fitful combination of the two.

He cleared his throat, nodded, and motioned to the chairs on the other side of his desk with a dark purple paw. "Please, be seated. Thanks officer; that will be all." In a moment, the door was closed, and the Nephti walked around and sat on top of the desk facing them. "I'm litigator Tornius de Rossi, and I don't mind telling you two that I've had one heck of a night. I will need statements from both of you about what transpired on that mountain, especially detailed from you Vanarra, since you were actually held by the group. I want you both to know what's happened, so that you're prepared." His statement sounded so grim that Van and Sahni both swallowed hard, almost at the same time.

"What's happened?" Vanarra asked, a little fearfully.

"That de Caterra dame, Katuri … Katuran … well, whatever it is, has been confessing all night to … some really incredible things, some really horrible things that family has done over the seasons. I've been calling jurists and arbiters all night for their opinions, but suffice it to say that with Tana's evidence and Sanratia … Sanratu … oh, heck, Sanrat's too, this is going to be incredibly major. This is going right up to the national court, so we have to make sure we do everything right."

"I understand," Vanarra replied, "but before we do anything else, may I please see Tana?"

"I'm sorry. I can't allow that until you've given your statement."

"Why not?" Sahni asked quickly, trying to preempt what she feared would be Van's less than diplomatic response.

"We can't have any possibility that you would collaborate with her on evidence. I'm very sorry to ask this of you, but this is just too important a matter to take any chances."

"If that's what I have to do to see Tana, then let's get started," Van stated firmly. The litigator nodded and then went to get a witness and an evidence recorder.

After almost an interval and a half of taking full written and verbal testimony from both Vanarra and Sahnassa, Tornius reviewed the now signed and witnessed documents with what seemed like an air of relieved satisfaction. "It all fits. It's all solid. Thank you very much. I guess you can see her now." He stepped to the door and called for an officer, and the Pantera who had escorted them in earlier appeared. "Can you take them to see Tana? The one we have in protective?"

"Right this way," the officer directed, leading them down a long hallway that ran along one side of the station towards the back. Just inside of the city lockup, as so noted on a small sign beside the entrance, was a large metal door with a small window in the center. "Here we are."

He was about to reach forward with keys to unlock the door, but Vanarra raised her paw to stop him. "Wait. You have her in a jail cell? She's locked up? I thought this was supposed to be *protective* custody?"

Defensively, the guard replied, "There is still some question as to if she is truly cooperating or if she has committed other crimes. This is one of the nicer ones, and there's no one else in there with her. We gave her reading material and some other things we don't give the other prisoners. Please, you can see for yourself."

Vanarra walked forward and looked in. What she saw instantly infuriated her. Poor Tana was sitting on one of the bunks, facing the far corner, curled up in a ball, sobbing. A few magazines and other trivial comforts were placed around the room, but it was still very much a harsh jail cell.

After peeking in as well, Sahnassa realized that Vanarra's anger was about to get the better of her, and she tried to step in. "Officer, we've given statements, and she's given statements. Surely the locked door isn't necessary anymore."

"I ... want ... her ... out ... of ... there!" Vanarra growled, barely able to control her rage. "I ... promised her that she wouldn't be treated like ... a prisoner!"

"I'm sorry, ma'am. I'm not authorized to do that."

"She saved my life, for the love of kit and cub! How can you keep her locked up!?"

"I'm sorry, ma'am. I can't release her. If you can't calm down, I won't be able to let you see her. I'll have to ask you to leave." He reached around for his stun prod, just to have a paw on it.

Seeing no hope in the guard's expression, Vanarra was desperately frustrated. "Oh, mange, Sahni! What do I do? This is horrible! Officer, if you can't let her go, then I want to be locked up with her, please. I can't leave her alone!"

"Me, too," Sahnassa agreed.

"I can't do that for either of you. I'm afraid you—"

A decidedly calm voice came from the lock-up doorway. "Not to worry officer. I think I have what you need right here."

Sahni and Van both turned in amazement and exclaimed, "Theo!" He was there, standing with the Nephti litigator and the chief of enforcement. In his paws, he held a thin, expensive-looking envelope with a government seal on it.

"At ease, officer," Tornius ordered, his fatigued face now almost alight in excitement. "Come here! You have to take a look at this!"

The officer walked over and took the offered envelope from Theo. Upon opening it and viewing its contents, the hard professional was suddenly gone, replaced by an enthusiastic little cub who had just seen a picture signed by his favorite sports hero. "You're joking! I've ... I've never seen one of these before! I've heard all about them! This is ... like real?!"

"It certainly is," the enforcement chief confirmed, obviously finding his guard's enthusiasm as humorous as it was understandable. "The chief arbiter for the district brought it over himself this morning. He received the image transfer last night, and he was able to verify it."

"Theo, what's that?" Vanarra asked, stunned back into reason by the Nephti's timely appearance and his profound effect on the guard who was about to throw them out not even a pass ago.

The Pantera officer's answer was almost giddy, "It's ... it's a covering of pardon, but it's signed by the Chancellor ... the Grand Chancellor!" Vanarra just stared at him and then at Theo. She shook her head in disbelief.

"May I?" Sahnassa asked. The officer seemed loath to give it up, but finally, he placed it in Sahnassa's outstretched paw.

With Vanarra looking over her shoulder, Sahni began to read, "Upon the earnest petition of an individual of great honor and established service to the good of the state, signed under my paw this sol ... an order for the immediate release and full pardon of Tanassadurini de Caterra, also known as Tana Asuala - upon her voluntary abandonment of house de Caterra. With special consideration being given to both the unique circumstances and character of the individual, covering completely any action or infringement committed here to this moment ... she is hereby released effective immediately and a full and irrevocable pardon is granted—" Lowering the document, she looked at Theo and exclaimed, "You're kidding! Come on, we've got to tell her!"

Van opened her paw, and Sahnassa gave her the pardon. After reading it, Van made a quiet request. "Officer, can you please give me the keys, and can the rest of you please wait outside in the hallway here? I know this is like the most amazing news, and Theo, I'm so grateful for it, but I just want to make sure she's prepared for this, if that's okay."

The officer, the chief, and the litigator looked a little uncertain, but Theo explained, "The moment this was received, no one here has the authority to hold her any longer. If Vanarra is the one who wants to release her, I think we should find a way to allow that."

After looking for a nod from the enforcement chief, the officer gave the keys to her, pointing to the one required and stepped down the hallway so he was standing guard over the other cells. The chief and litigator smiled and stepped back out. Sahnassa walked over to Theo and took his paw. "Thank you," she whispered looking deeply into his eyes.

"You're welcome."

"You two do make such a cute couple," Van observed, smiling. Sahni's blush furs went up, making Van smile even more. "Okay, now that I've thoroughly embarrassed you two, could you wait out here a moment? Oh, and Theo, I really, really want to talk with you at some point, privately."

"Sure," Theo agreed, seemingly unperturbed.

Van took a deep breath, put the key in the lock, and turned it.

It had been a very hard night for Tana, the hardest she had ever known. After leaving the cold landing field in binders, being placed into the caged back seat of an enforcement hover, and being booked as a common criminal, the reality of her situation had set in. True to their word, they had placed her in a cell by herself – one she supposed was nicer than what the others were experiencing, but still, it was a prison cell with a locked door.

Then, there had been interval after interval with the Nephti litigator. She was so tired, but he just kept clawing at her and her story and her honor and her truthfulness over and over again. Like a vicious forest stalker, he looked for any small detail or inconsistency. During that questioning, she understood what it meant to be disavowed. There was no one she could call on for help; she was alone.

He finally left her, in tears, a few intervals ago. She thought his smirking disbelief and vicious tone would stay with her forever, but about an interval later, when she was almost about to nod off, the cell door had opened again, and there he stood. Looking up at him, she saw something more haunting than what she had seen before. The same Nephti stood before her, but all his swagger was gone, and Tornius was visibly shaken. He had sat on the bunk opposite her and stared blankly ahead. Not knowing what to do, she had simply waited in the awful silence for him to speak; finally, he did.

"You … you've never tortured anyone, have you?" She shook her head no. "Assaulted and abducted anyone, except for what happened tonight?" Again, she answered no. "Tana, have you killed anyone or … killed a lot of—" She shook her head forcefully no, with a growing fear in her heart. "Two of your family, or I guess who used to be your family, just confirmed for me that there are … monsters living in the lairs of de

Caterra. What happened up ... up there, at the Meeting Den, was very tame compared to some of what I've just been told." He stood up and placed his head in his paws with his elbows resting on the top bunk.

"What?" was all the question she could manage.

"I think you need to tell me right now if you ever knew anything like that ever happened," he said, not moving.

"No," she responded, horrified. "Rumors and stories do get passed. Sometimes, things happen, but they are passed off as accidents. To question those explanations is seen as doubting the honor of the matriarchy. So as a de Caterra, you're trained not to. It's seen as disloyalty. I ... I never saw anything myself, and I never – I couldn't do those things."

Tornius slumped down and sat on the bunk opposite of her, but he refused to look at her as he spoke. "Tana, I'm just a small-town litigator – property disputes, hover violations, small break-ins, and other such tiny things in the grand scheme. By Thuria, I never thought anything like this would land on my tail. I just got off the wire with the national prosecutor's office. They, they thought I was crazy, at first; then I played the recording. When the storm is over, the national authorities will come for the de Caterra. Everything they have, anyone they associate with, any communications they've sent, and everywhere they've lived are going to be completely searched looking for evidence."

"What will happen to them?" Tana asked, wondering about the impact to her former family.

"Those who have committed crimes or knew they were being committed with any certainty will be arrested and tried, up to and including the matriarch, herself. A whole family, on trial—" He stopped speaking as his eyes lost focus again.

"What ... what will happen to me?" she asked fearfully.

"Right now, they haven't decided what to do with your case, since you voluntarily testified against the de Caterra and you've disavowed yourself. They're seeking clarification, but I don't think we'll have an answer anytime soon." Finally, he looked her in the eye. "I know all of this is hard to hear, but I felt you should know. I'll do the best I can for you. I just hope your paws are clean, Tana, for your sake." Then, he had simply stood and left her.

The next few intervals were the most difficult and lonely Tana had ever known. Her heart and mind could never have conceived of such loss. She curled up and faced the corner as all the dark fears and thoughts started washing over her. Knowing she no longer had a livelihood, nor parents, nor family was overwhelming. Even those she loved in the family would be helpless to aid her. Anyone who tried to help a self-made outcast faced being harshly censured if not disavowed themselves. Even those who were willing to risk that might well have their own problems to contend with as their house was torn apart. After tonight, the name of de Caterra and all associated with it could start to fall, as Theo had threatened.

Her mind filled with images of their ancestral home being searched and ransacked, children being taken from their parents, and those who worked being fired from their jobs just because of their family name. She saw her whole family abused, hated, ridiculed, with other Thurians laughing at them and mocking them like they were … "Anati."

Her mouth moved, but no words came out as the realization hit her. All of the things de Caterra had done, all the evil visited upon those of mixed parentage, were now falling down upon them. Her mind flashed back to what Vanarra told her.

Oh no, kit. You don't understand; it was me they did it to. My father disappeared because someone took him; he didn't leave us – he was stolen from us. We never saw him again. I barely have any memory of him. Later, after letting us live in squalor for seasons, my mother's family murdered her right in front of my eyes. I was on my own as just a kit. I've never had it easy. I was at the mercy of almost everyone.

It was then Tana realized that everything happening to her and everything that could happen to her family was completely justified. The de Caterra deserved no better than to be forever swept away.

As Tana sobbed quietly, grief and loss drowned out all joy as she saw her future drifting away and falling apart. A river of darkness and lonely torment stretched before her with no escape, save one frail, ridiculous hope. Vanarra's certain voice, her steady gaze, and her earnest offer of help took a long while to penetrate the flood of dark thoughts that threatened to drown the poor Faelnar. Despite the choking terrors of fear and abandonment, some bigoted part of her still scoffed at how an Anati could help anyone.

Angrily, Tana screamed in her own mind, "I won't think that way anymore!" Looking through her mind's eye up into Vanarra's eyes, she heard again, "I hope I'm worthy." She knew she wasn't; none of the de Caterra were. She felt the guilt of her whole house searing her very soul, consuming everything she once thought she was.

There was no one she could call out to for help, and no one to whom she could beg forgiveness. She knew that other families held beliefs in a greater power above all; they prayed to it. The de Caterra openly laughed and mocked at such fanciful beliefs; yet tonight, poor Tana wished more than anything that she knew how to pray.

To Vanarra and to all of the Anati harmed by the de Caterra, to any power that wanted to hear, Tana cried softly, "I'm sorry. I'm sorry for what we've done!" The face of Asuala seemed to appear in her thoughts. "I'm sorry, so sorry! I wish I had known; I wish I could have stopped it!" The face turned away in disgust, like it had when Tana had first offended the Anati. "I deserve whatever happens to me – prison, pain, or even death, Asuala, even death. If I am ever free again, then I'll serve the Anati to try to make amends for what my family has done."

A sense of peace started settling over her, easing her great pain. "It's okay. Whatever happens to me, it's okay. I'll accept it. I do accept it." Simply saying that to herself caused her heart to feel relief. She barely noticed the clunk-thunk of the lock and the door opening behind her. She expected to hear a guard ordering her to do something or the litigator ramping up for another questioning session.

A sweet, floral smell met her nostrils, and a warm presence sat beside her on the bed. An arm gently wrapped around her shoulders. Looking slowly around, Tana stared into a set of golden eyes, like her own but seemingly deeper, so much deeper. It was her.

Tana leaned back and looked fully at Vanarra's face, and quietly uttered, "I'm so sorry. I'm sorry for your father, for your mother, for everything that's happened to you, and everything our family may have done to you and those like you. I'm sorry for all of it!" Tana started crying and hung her head.

Vanarra had been struck speechless at how bad Tana looked, her cheek fur matted, her eyes bloodshot, her coat almost a dull yellow instead of the gold she remembered. Instantly, Van understood, having been brought to her lowest point several times in her life. "Oh, kit, come here," Vanarra bade, wrapping her arms around her and hugging her gently at first, and then tighter. "It's okay. What's done is done, and we can go on. It's going to be alright. We're going to get you out of here."

Still not looking up into Vanarra's eyes, Tana sniffed, "How ... how are you going to do that? They said they didn't know what to do with me."

Van pulled the envelope out of her pocket and gently laid it in her own lap, right in front of Tana's face. Hearing the paper crinkle a little,

Tana asked quietly, "What's this?" Her paws released Van and opened the envelope. "What the—" Van released her as Tana read the document. In utter disbelief, Tana read it again, mumbling the words of the text to make sure she was reading it correctly. "Signed by the—" Tana couldn't complete the sentence. Her paw went over her mouth, and she looked at Vanarra in utter amazement.

"That's right, kit, your past, whatever it was, is completely forgiven, and you're free to go. You're free to make a new start." Tana just stared at her, not breathing. "Tana, kit, are you—"

Tana was fortunate that Van was very quick to see what was happening, even before Tana's eyes rolled back into her head. Vanarra caught her and called, "Sahni, Theo! Can you come help me please?" As they walked in, she looked at them in surprise. "I think she fainted! I hope she fainted. I hope that's all this is!"

"Theo?" Sahnassa asked as they helped lay Tana out on the bed.

Touching Tana's neck with a paw and looking at her head, Theo confirmed, "She's out, but just like you said, fainted. Poor thing seems to have had a really hard time. Maybe after awhile, you can get her to talk through some of it. It might help." He took a pillow and placed it under the golden Faelnar's hind legs. "There, she'll come around in a few passes."

"Would you like us to go?" Sahni asked when Tana was settled.

"Oh, no, kit. I thought I was going to do a good job with her, break it to her easy, and look what I got! I would like both of you to stay." Vanarra sat on one bed with Tana, and Theo and Sahni sat together on the other. Van stroked the sides of Tana's muzzle for a moment, but then she looked straight at Theo. "I don't understand how you did this. Is this pardon real? I mean it came so quick, and, forgive me, I've seen more than my share of con jobs."

"It's no con," he said smiling. "The validations have already been done by the local arbiter."

"But how, Theo? I mean, what kind of life do you lead that you can do these kinds of things? Are you like in the government or something? I thought you just worked for Tedarri, but Agari said he knew you from his posting, and that big Lupar, Cutter – you said you had almost beat him on the obstacle course."

Theo smiled. "I lead a rather complex life, and while I'm not in the government, I have fostered some very good connections."

Van's eyes darted to Sahni, and although she was trying to hide it, Van saw that Sahnassa knew something about Theo, something secret, and what Sahni knew pleased her. "Speaking of connections," Van started uneasily, "I ... had some really strange ... I guess you'd call them dreams when I was captured."

"Oh, what sort of dreams?" Theo asked, nonchalantly.

"Dreams..." and Vanarra was suddenly embarrassed, and she continued her sentence a little more quietly. "Dreams about you."

"I hope they were good dreams," Theo responded, earnestly.

Realizing what her next sentence might sound like, her courage failed her. "Yes, they were very ... useful." The edited version didn't sound half as crazy as "well, they told me everything I needed to know about my captors and when the soldiers were going to storm into the building."

"Glad to hear it. Oh, look, she's coming around."

Tana awoke coughing a little, and her vision was still swimming. She felt a paw gently stroking her cheek; it was something her mother used to do when she was very little. Opening her eyes, she looked up into Vanarra's gently smiling face. "I ... uh, I guess I –" Tana was clearly embarrassed, her golden fur on the top of her cheeks lifting almost as much as Sahni's did.

"Yes, you did. Just lay here for awhile. I guess I gave you too much of a shock."

"I didn't just imagine what you showed me, did I?" Van shook her head. "It is real, isn't it?" Van nodded, still smiling. "Vanarra ... I don't—"

"Well, if you're looking for explanations, ask *him*. He brought it for you," she stated, motioning over to Theo.

"Hi there," Theo said in response to her turned head.

"Hi," Tana responded, weakly.

"It's real, alright. Sahni's my witness on this. Last night, as we rode down in the flyer, I made a call from the cockpit. I made a couple of quick calls, actually."

"But to the Grand Chancellor?" Vanarra asked, still unable to comprehend it.

"I helped him out of a pretty serious scrape some time ago. Do you remember the Vogontine affair?"

Sahnassa searched her memory. "Yes, not too long ago, the Chancellor's family was lost on their yacht, the Vogontine. Some pirates stripped off the locator beacons and sunk them in the Altian Ocean. No one knew where it had gone. Until," and she looked at Theo suspiciously, "a certain someone hacked into the satellite network, found the ship, and forwarded detailed information to the authorities. The identity of the hacker was never revealed."

Tana finished the story. "Yes. The hacker provided … the location of the Vogontine, how many criminals there were, and where the Chancellor's family was being held. They sent in the … Storm Pack!"

"They did, and not even Cutter knows the whole story, but his group was as efficient as always," Theo said, smiling. "Anyway, in payment for certain undisclosed services, I told him I had two requirements. The first was that he forgave the intrusion effort it took to collect the information to save his family. The second was that, if asked, he would provide one and only one pardon, upon my request. I told him that if he ever granted the pardon, he would know that he had helped someone who was truly innocent and truly worthy. He doesn't know me by name, mind you, just by code phrase and voice."

"And you used that for me?" Tana asked.

"I know how much Vanarra cares for you, and Sahnassa too, and how badly you needed a fresh start. In the end, it's those things that tipped the scale."

Tana slowly sat up, with Vanarra's help. "What … what can I do to repay you, not that I have much left?"

"You've got more than you think, especially in terms of your potential. Tana, over the last few intervals, you've had some time in here to think. Have you made any decisions; come up with any goals for your new life?"

Tana thought and then remembered. "I decided that if I was ever free again, then I would serve the Anati to try to make amends for what my family has done. I mean that," she asserted and then looked at Van. "In the name of my dear friend, Asuala, and in gratitude to you, Vanarra, I really do."

"Then, that will be repayment enough. I think that above all, you are to serve Vanarra first, because she brought you out of de Caterra just in time, in addition to saving your life at the Meeting Den. I believe she can help you find a place to fulfill your vow, with honor."

"Are you sure, kit? Really?" Vanarra asked. Tana nodded.

"It will take some time to work through the details, so be patient, both of you," Theo cautioned them, much as a father would. "Tana, I want you to always remember this cell, not in a bad way, but in a good way. Right here, in this moment, you've started your new life. I want you to put your whole heart into making that life one that brings light, warmth, and hope to others. Restore your honor, your purpose, and your joy in life through service."

Vanarra was a little overwhelmed. "No, Theo, this isn't right! I've never had anyone serve me before!"

"Sure you have, Van," Sahni put in. "You have a whole crew at your business dedicated to celebrations, photography, and (of course) technical conjuring! You've always given so much time and effort to the orphanage. Imagine what Tana could help you do. Imagine all the children she could help. She could touch so many lives, just through loving them. She just needs you to show her how."

"Will you teach me, Vanarra, please?" Tana asked. "It sounds wonderful."

Theo explained the arrangement. "You would be responsible for giving her food and shelter, Vanarra, or providing her with a way to look after herself." Van thought about it for a moment. With business good, she had been piling up large sums, and she wasn't sure what to do with all she had saved. Provided that the matriarchs were as good as their word and her funds were replaced, she could easily support Tana, as well as give her a comfortable lifestyle.

"I could do that. Tana, if you're sure, I really would love sponsoring you there as a worker. They're really great kids, and they just eat up any love you're willing to give them! When you see them finally find a family who will love them, the feeling is just so … amazing!"

Seeing the echoes of true joy on Van's face, Tana smiled, and then closed her eyes, bowed her head, and quietly promised, "Upon my honor, Vanarra, I am in your service until I breathe my last. You are my family, now."

Theo looked at Sahnassa, and she was shedding tears of joy. She joined the other two, who were already embracing and crying. Theo looked on with a smile from the other bunk until Vanarra saw him. "Don't think you're getting out of this, mister! Come over here!" Happily, he joined them.

"Come on. I have a nice hover warmed and ready outside. Let's get Tana out of here, get her some good food, and get her into a nice bed," Theo suggested, pulling the group up to their hind paws. "Shall we?"

They agreed and started to leave, and the litigator met them as they walked out. "You leaving, too?" Tana asked him.

"Yes, I'm happy to say. I've got to get some rest. Listen, I'm sorry I was hard on you. I have to be. It's part of my job, but you did really well, and I thank you. The evidence you gave will be a great help. Please stop by before you leave town, alright?"

Tana looked to Vanarra for approval, and it took a moment for it to register. "Oh," Vanarra answered, finally understanding, "We both will. I mean we all will, okay?"

"Fine. Take care of yourselves."

"You, too."

The group walked down the saline covered steps and to the large white hover Theo was driving. "What model is this?" Sahni asked a little coquettishly.

"It's a Tashar, but it's an older one," Theo answered, opening the door. Sahnassa burst into laughter, and Tana and Van were confused. "It's an inside joke."

"It's only an inside joke if the heat doesn't work," Van shot back. They all laughed and buckled up for the trip back to the schools.

Chapter 20: Confessing Proof

Once inside the school, Van asked Sahnassa to take Tana to the cafeteria for some food and find her a place to rest. That left Vanarra and Theo together, as she had hoped, but what she didn't expect was at the moment she was about to ask Theo about the "visions" she experienced, the dame she had given the amulet to walked around the corner. At the same moment, the Chief called to Theo from the other end of the hall. "Oh! Theo, this isn't over. I need to talk to you later, okay? Please? In private."

"I'll make sure that happens before I leave."

"I'm holding you to that," Vanarra warned as she turned and darted after her amulet's keeper.

"Theo," the Chief said, walking up. "I've ... I've heard some really weird things this morning. Like the Dame is talking to the authorities?"

"Yes she is. I think things are going to get very interesting, very quickly, for those left in de Caterra. What did Terrat say about your decision?" Theo asked, pointing to the empty spot on the Chief's uniform.

"That I'll need a new name tag, that's all. He told me I'd better pick something decent and short. I asked him if 'Chief' would do, but he said that was okay only if I never wanted another promotion."

Theo chuckled. "He does have a point. Hey, you could always combine – hey what about 'Vanassa'? That's it, Chief Tawnston Vanassa. Consider it a souvenir of the occasion?"

"Might work!" They laughed, but then the Chief became serious. "Hey, I actually came looking for you. We've got one of the flyers on its way back up the mountain, and I figured you would want to see. The de Dothnar matriarch is in there, as well."

"Lead on, then, Chief Tawnston Vanassa!" Theo said, and in a few moments, they were standing in the command center. It was so much a command center now that it was hard to tell it was ever a classroom.

Terrat saw him enter and nodded. "Oh, yes, Theo. Figured you'd want to see this. There's a small break in the weather, maybe one interval before the next band hits, but we wanted to get a patrol up to the den, just in case."

"I don't think you left anyone, Marshall."

"Doesn't hurt to look," he retorted.

"Alpha One to EMC Control." A pilot's voice crackled through the communicator.

"EMC Control to Alpha One. Go ahead," the air controller said.

"We're almost to the site. Just over the next ... oh mange! Can you believe that? Control, I'm going to send you video feed. I can tell you it doesn't do it justice."

The monitor above the air controller's head flickered to life. "By Thuria," Rahnahi gasped in disbelief. Everything in view was covered with thick snow, at least eight tracks deep. The outline of the field was only visible because of the circular lumps that were the buried hover vehicles once used as landing lights. "We would have never evacuated everyone with all that!"

The communicator came to life again. "Oh crap, control! I'm going to fly over this so you can see. You're not going to believe it!" As the flyer moved forward, it drifted over the snow-filled pit that had been the dining hall, and then focused on piles of snow-covered rubble. "I think ... I think that was the main building! It completely collapsed! It would have killed anyone inside when it fell. At least two of the other buildings are also caved in. It's like a bomb went off up here! I hope there's no one left!"

"We counted everyone off," Rahnahi asserted. "Thank all that lives, we counted everyone off."

"Yes. Look," Theo observed. "Building five's had it as well. Our de Caterra friends would have been in for a nasty surprise."

"Alpha One to EMC Control, we're starting to get freezing precipitation again. We're going to have to turn back, end?"

"EMC Control to Alpha One, return immediately," the Marshall ordered into the microphone.

"Roger that, EMC Control. We're making a run for it. Alpha One. End X-mit."

"Bless Vanarra and Sahnassa," Rahnahi said gravely. "We would all be dead without them. Bless all of you, too, for everything you have done, but still—"

"Without those two on the mountain," Tedarri observed, his voice a little awestruck, "we never would have known in time."

"Yeah," the Chief echoed. "Without those two on the mountain, it would have been over for most of you."

"If not all of you," the Marshall added. "Did you record that?" he asked, looking down at his controller.

"Yes, Marshall."

"Make copies, video only. I've heard some grumbling from a few of the evacuees that's really started to singe my tail. I want to make sure everyone sees this and appreciates what they were just saved from. Run it immediately on all public viewers the moment you're done."

"Agreed," Rahnahi said. There was a long silence with just the equipment running as the video replayed in front of them. "What those two did, raising the alarm, finding the resources—"

"They did what any of you would have wanted to do, placed in the same situation," Theo observed, his voice complimentary, not lecturing or flat. "However, much to their credit, they actually did it. With all the challenges, they made it happen. That's the best part of the story."

"I don't think I can remember any story like this one," Rahnahi commented, shaking her head.

"Well then, Honored One, that should make it very interesting to write," Theo observed before quietly leaving the room.

Vanarra profusely thanked the dame as she took back the amulet. The way that the dame gave it to her was a little odd, Vanarra thought, cupping it in both paws and raising it up to her, head bowed. It was almost like a kind of worshipful movement. Van thanked her uneasily, and then the dame backed away, before smartly turning and leaving her.

She replaced the amulet around her neck, leaned against the wall, and then opened it. "Hi Mom," she said, tenderly. She looked at the image for a long time, stroking it gently with her claw tip. After a few moments, the way that dame reacted reminded her of a promise she made, to speak with Amyra de Gonari, Matriarch of the de Gonari family – her mother's family. Regardless of what had happened in the last few sols, there were almost twenty seasons worth of fear to overcome, as well as anger, and hatred, and every other emotion she'd rather not face. Looking into her mother's eyes, she felt a tender rebuke of sorts. "What did you face just by keeping me alive when I was born? Regardless of what anyone says, Mom, the rescue started when you chose to keep me. Surely, I can be half as brave as you were. Just … give me a sol or two."

She closed the locket and walked down the hall. It only half registered that a doctor and nurse passed out of a room ahead of her, leaving the door open. Glancing in, she smiled. There, comfortably resting on the bed was the older Faelnar she had helped transport down with Agari. Walking to the door, she shook her head. That nerve-wracking flight seemed like a lifetime ago.

She leaned against the edge of the door, looking in, absently wondering why the old kit hadn't been taken to the hospital, and she hoped it was because she wasn't in bad shape. "I'm glad you made it," she said at a whisper, and Van was about to leave when the wooden frame of the door popped. It wasn't a loud noise, but it was enough to wake the old Faelnar. Van mentally cursed her own clumsiness; she should have been more careful, she thought.

The Faelnar propped herself up, and, startled, came to a full sitting position. "It's you! Are you okay?" The old one was almost beside herself with worry.

"Yes, of course," Van replied reassuringly as she walked in. "I'm sorry; I didn't mean to wake you up."

Myra was not, as yet, assured. "They told me you were taken captive! They told me your life was in danger!"

A flurry of thoughts flew threw her mind, including "who would bother this poor old kit by telling her that" and "wow, news travels fast." Vanarra pulled up a stool and sat beside the bed. "Yes, yes, Myra, please. I'm fine. It's true. I did have a run-in with some really bad characters, but they're now in jail, and I'm okay. Don't worry, please." Vanarra reached out her paw, and Myra took it.

"Can … can you tell me about it? What happened? Please," the elder Faelnar was nearly begging.

"I will, but I want you to relax. Remember, I'm right here, and I'm okay." She poured a glass of water for the Faelnar and gave it to her. Van then recounted the story, leaving out the pieces about visions or premonitions.

Myra seemed to know some of the Thurians she named. When Van mentioned Talnar, she grunted. "I might have known. Thuria is better without him." When Van spoke about Tana, Myra seemed truly interested and found it compelling. "What a brave, brave kit she was, and you too! I can't imagine how scared you must have felt."

"I guess I put off being scared until later. I've had a life where I've had to think on my hind paws to stay alive at times. I thought I was past all that, but hey, it worked again! Now, that's enough about me. I want to know how you're doing."

Myra sighed. "I'm feeling like the greatest of all idiots. I had been having some twinges of something, but I didn't stay home and go to the doctor like a smart kit. I just went on my trip *hoping* it would go away. I got into a true mess by the time you finally carried me out, but the doctor says I'm tough, and with the right care, it won't be a problem."

"I'm glad. Hey, I'm sorry to have woken you, Myra. I was just walking by, and I was so glad to see you."

"And, I you, dear."

"Then, it was just a good thing I happened to walk by when I did."

"Chance meetings. Life is full of them, it seems," Myra said with a wistful expression.

Vanarra nodded. "I guess we *should* let you get some rest."

"Perhaps that would be best," Myra responded, with a strange tone in her voice. "However, that's not *really* what we should do."

"I ... I don't understand."

"Please, forgive this, but I need just a moment of your time. Do you know one of the most confounded things about being sick is that no one wants you to wear your jewelry? I've had it on me for so long, it's like I'm missing a part of me. Could you go to the top drawer, there, and get it for me, please? It will be in a box with a combination lock. You wouldn't mind?"

"No, no, not at all!" Vanarra walked over and easily found the large, ornate box. She, with some effort, brought it over to the side table and stood near the stool. "Myra, this thing is a safe! I can't wait to see what you've got in here."

"Then wait no more; the combination is 15 – 15 – 25 – 40."

"Interesting numbers," Van said, turning the dials. "Any significance to them?"

"No. I try to pick something easy to remember but that has nothing to do with me."

"There, that's got it. May I open it?"

"Please, dear. Go ahead."

Vanarra popped the lock and opened the heavy lid. Within it was something that made her blood freeze instantly. It was the incredibly beautiful, golden, jewel-encrusted de Gonari insignia and shoulder-piece of the Grand Matriarch. Vanarra stared at it for a moment, not believing, and then she looked into Myra's face. In the green eyes of the elder Faelnar, she saw a majesty and regal bearing that had been hiding in the shadows, and now those qualities had stepped into full light.

Amyra's claw tip reached into the box with practiced ease and retrieved the shoulder-piece and fastened it around her neck and under her arm in a quick but graceful series of movements. Van stood there, dead still, not even daring to exhale.

In a voice that allowed no dispute, Amyra commanded, "I am the Grand Matriarch Amyra de Gonari, and I hereby order you … to breathe." There was a touch of humor in her voice, mingled with concern. Van obeyed, dropping her gaze to the ground. "There, child. That's it. Don't make my mistake. I almost passed out when you and Agari came for me – when I actually realized how close you were." In a much softer, serious voice, she pleaded, "Now, please. Sit with me for awhile."

Van slowly slid back onto the stool, folded her paws in her lap, and kept her head tucked down. Looking like a child at school about to be disciplined, she waited quietly. "Vanarra, dear, I want to start by apologizing. I didn't mean to mislead you about who I was, but in the noise and confusion, you didn't hear my name fully. Because of where we were and what was going on, I was afraid to correct you. I was glad for it though, the misunderstanding, that is. It ... it let me see the real you, how truly kind you are. It also let you see a bit of the real me. So many times, I don't think anyone actually looks me in the face, eye to eye, because of this."

Van ventured a glance up, and Amyra was pointing to the jeweled shoulder-piece. "I wouldn't have it on now, except that what I have to say to you should not be delivered by me alone. When I wear this, I speak for our house, our family."

Amyra's voice became quiet and ragged with emotion. "Vanarra, our entire family is responsible for your mother's death. Our matriarch sanctioned it, and family members instructed to enforce the order did so without questioning how horribly wrong it was. Although we have long ago judged and punished those responsible, all of the de Gonari are accountable for it. We were also responsible for another crime. We could have welcomed and protected your family. To our deepest shame, we did not. Through our actions, we took your mother, and through our inaction, we deprived you of your father. We have no right to seek any kind of absolution or forgiveness from you. Those of us who knew what happened and were too fearful to act deserve the guilt we bear. However, you deserve the truth, and you deserve to hear us say we were wrong, and we're sorry for it."

There was a silence that seemed to last forever, but a deep exhalation from Amyra pulled Vanarra out of her wildly swirling emotions and thoughts within. Van raised her eyes, and she saw Amyra, paws folded on the bed, head bowed. Despite the beautiful ornamentation she wore, the matriarch of house de Gonari looked humbled, resigned to whatever curses Vanarra wanted to call down on her. Van knew she had a decision to make, and she also knew what her mother's death had meant to the elder Faelnar seated in front of her.

Opening the locket, she looked into the face of her mother, for perspective and for strength, realizing in an instant that Amyra had done the very same thing many times before. Looking to the picture on the right, she saw herself, so long ago. There had been much pain in Van's life since that image was taken, but where she was now and the lives that had been saved – so many of them – had been worth that pain. Looking back at her mother, Van now knew the right and just path to take.

"I forgive you, Amyra," she said softly. "I forgive the de Gonari for what they did to me, to my mother, and to my father. I can forgive you because I know you've ... repented; you've changed. I didn't realize it until Rahnahi told me." Reaching towards the bed, she gently took the elder Faelnar's paws in hers. "I have no right to curse the head of the one who held my own mother in her arms as she died. You made sure she didn't die alone on those steps. I can't thank you enough for that. I thank you for everything you've done in my name and in the name of my mother. No matter what's happened to me, what pain I suffered, good did come from it. I've come to realize everything that's happened put me in the right place to help save … so many. My suffering, my pain, as bad as it was, has so little value when compared to that."

They looked into each other's eyes; Amyra seemed so small and pitiful in that moment that Vanarra was compelled to reach out and embrace her, to try to offer comfort. They both cried, for a long time, before Amyra was able to manage a ragged, "Thank you, child. Thank you."

Finally, they both recovered enough to separate. Van looked at Amyra, not as a matriarch, but more as a friend, and whispered, "I … I guess I better go."

Amyra held up her paw and gently said, "There … there is one thing I want to give you. It will shock some to their core, for sure, and I don't know if you will want to accept it, but Vanarra, your family wants you back … if you'll have us." It didn't fully register what was happening until it was too late, but dames and matrons were filling the small room. "Vanarra Anasto is a very pretty name, but would you consider a slight change?" Rahnahi was the last one in, and stood in the doorway smiling at Vanarra.

"I … I don't understand. I'm … I—" Van stammered.

"You have every right to refuse, but if you agree, it will not be Vanarra Anasto who walks from this room, but Vanarra de Gonari, fully avowed and embraced in love, kept by and keeper of her family." Vanarra's eyes went wildly around the room. While seeing Rahnahi's expectant gaze and Saletta's happy and hopeful look may not have been enough, seeing Agari, on crutches, lean in behind Rahnahi, smiling and winking, finally sealed it.

"I … I'm overwhelmed! I … I accept." With that, Amyra bowed her head, and all of the dames and matrons sank to their knees.

In a tearful voice, Amyra said, "We are honored, and we are now complete by what you have chosen. We can only hope that in time, we show you what it truly means, and how much you are loved."

Looking to Rahnahi, helplessly, she mouthed, "What do I do now?"

"Say, 'thank you'," Rahnahi mouthed and motioned back, humor darting in her eyes.

"Oh, thank you … so very much, all of you. I'm … honored," Van wept, tears now streaming down her cheek fur.

With that, they all stood and cheered, and each of them embraced Van calling her "Dear Sister." Van was surrounded by a warmth and joy unlike anything she had experienced before.

As the group departed, Rahnahi walked in and said, "Okay, now that we know you two aren't in here ripping each other apart and everything's good, I'm going to insist that you finally, finally get some real rest!" Her manner was stern with Amyra, but it still had a humorous edge.

"There's one thing I've got to know. How did they all know to come in here at the same time?" Vanarra asked.

A little shamefacedly, Amyra held up a small cylindrical control. "I couldn't remember if it was one for good, two for bad or–"

"Uh, you had it backwards dear," Rahnahi said.

"Oh, sorry."

"It's not like we couldn't figure it out once we got in here," Rahnahi chuckled. "Come on, now, let's let you rest."

Vanarra reached over and kissed the matriarch, now her matriarch, on the side of her muzzle. "I don't know if I'm supposed to do that. You'll have to teach me the rules, Honored One."

"There's no rule for that, my child. No rule at all. For the other things, ask Saletta. She can help you as none other can."

Rahnahi took her at the shoulder and led her from the room. As they crossed the threshold, she said, "Vanarra de Gonari. It sounds very nice."

"To me, too," Agari agreed.

"But … are *you* alright, Agari?" Vanarra asked, slowing as he lagged behind on crutches.

"I will be, sis, I will be," Agari responded, smiling at the privilege to call her sister.

"Oh, this is *too* weird!" Van said, shaking her head.

"It's going to come with its share of difficulties, as you can imagine," Rahnahi warned. "There are going to be a lot of the old guard who are going to be downright angry, but they have no right to oppose

Amyra's decision, and my house stands with her and you, as well. Remember that."

"I will, Honored One. I will."

"I can tell Saletta if you like," Agari offered, "let her know you need some help."

"Oh, Agari, I would be so grateful. But you're laid up, I don't want to trouble you," Van said, stopping as he momentarily readjusted his crutches.

"It's no trouble. They won't let me do any actual duty, so perhaps both of us could help you."

"Oh, I hope I can manage it," Van breathed out intensely, closing her eyes.

"You will, sis, I know you will."

As they walked down the hallway, some of the evacuees were milling about. Seeing Vanarra, they stopped, wide eyed. "Thank you, so very much," a young Nephti female with silver gray eyes said. "I ... I just saw the recording! I couldn't believe it!"

"You're welcome, but what recording?" Vanarra asked, confused.

"The Meeting Den – the video taken this morning! It's a total disaster: buildings collapsed, deep snow and ice, high winds! I ... I wanted to say thank you, from the depths of my heart! We'd all be dead right now if it weren't for you!"

Vanarra walked over and hugged her. "You're welcome. Hey, you are from Sahni's family, de Orturu, right?" she asked as she released her.

"Yes, I am," she said proudly. "Alatta de Orturu."

"Well, remember to thank her, too! She kept me alive. Also, thank everyone in the families and military and down here who helped. However, don't forget yourself. In a really scary situation, you did what you were supposed to: you listened, you helped, and you kept your head and played your part. The real truth is that we all did this together. So thank you, too."

"You're welcome!" Alatta beamed, her blush furs flying high. Vanarra couldn't help but chuckle; perhaps easy embarrassment was a family trait.

"Well said," Rahnahi whispered as they walked away. "Very well said." They smiled and continued their walk down the hall.

Several of the other evacuees also looked long and hard at Vanarra, and it was apparent to Van which ones were de Caterra. Those Faelnar looked at her with a range of emotions from anger to disgrace. "Perhaps," Rahnahi suggested, "you should join *us* for lunch? We have a private dining room set up in the teacher's lounge. I think—" she noted, looking at another group of Thurians who were just as awed by Vanarra's presence, "I think you'll have to if you want to eat in peace."

"I'd like that, very much, Honored One." Vanarra smiled, still not fully over the fact that her literary idol was now her friend.

The group found Sahnassa eating next to Theo at the long table that had been set up in the teacher's lounge. They were looking at a video of the flyover footage, and Theo was describing a couple of key aspects. As the rest of the group entered and took their places, Vanarra was mesmerized by the images of the forsaken ruins, which kept playing over and over again in a loop. After all had seen it a few times, they finally turned it off when food was brought in by the matrons. When Van asked where Tana was, Sahnassa informed her that she had been fed and taken to a rest area, where she had collapsed into unconsciousness nearly just by seeing a bed of any description. Sahni swore Tana was asleep before the door closed.

Sahnassa was stunned and overjoyed to hear Vanarra's news of her "name change," but Van noticed that Theo simply nodded, much as if he'd expected the outcome. She desperately wanted to get him alone, but just as everyone was about to leave and she thought she might get her chance, Saletta entered. Someone else had obviously told her, and Agari was none too happy for having his thunder stolen. He received, however, an instant chiding from Saletta who told him that her information came straight from the matriarch. Saletta suggested to Van that it would be prudent to start going over the basics as soon as possible. The rest of the group soon left the two alone for that purpose.

The next three intervals were very interesting for Van. As much as it was just basic information and rules and expectations, Vanarra found Saletta to be a really delightful teacher, able to explain the "why" as much as the "what" of each facet of de Gonari family traditions and honors. Moreover, she was an excellent listener.

They were just about to pause for a break when the question of sponsorship for adoption into the family came up, more as a footnote. Vanarra instantly thought of Tana and described the situation to Saletta as best she could. She explained how lost the poor Faelnar had seemed, and how, although Vanarra never had a family before, Tana had never been without one. That launched them into another two intervals of story-telling combined with Saletta's view on the rules, and how that, after a period of observed good behavior, such sponsorship was possible.

Van was also pleased to find that she truly liked Saletta; she was young, bright, and very wise for her age. She also treated Vanarra with nothing but complete respect, and Van tried to return that fully. Before they realized it, they were almost too late for dinner, and they had to run to catch the last of the food at the serving line. Only after they finished eating did Vanarra remember that she hadn't even bothered to check on her business, and such would have to wait until tomorrow.

The rest of the afternoon had gone well for Sahnassa, too. She was thrilled to get some time alone with Theo and talk with him about everything that had gone on since he rescued the two of them. Walking down the halls, however, there were frequent interruptions from grateful Thurians. It seemed more and more had been to the library and seen the looped recording of crushed buildings, buried vehicles, and the frozen, inhospitable landscape.

When she questioned Theo privately as to why the buildings collapsed, he reminded her that this storm was far worse than normal, and that even under normal circumstances, the Meeting Den staff would have been up on top of those buildings, getting rid of snow and ice to prevent just such a thing from occurring. Without someone to tend it, the Meeting Den's damage, age, and dated construction techniques caused it to fail. He also told her that every building up there would probably suffer the same fate before the next two sols were done.

For all their time together, Sahnassa still felt a little cheated. Only on the cold walk between the schools could she actually ask him about subjects like the Tashar and how much of the last two sols' events he had secretly helped. She wanted to hear the pardon story in full, but cold and blowing wind got the better of her, and they had to get back inside. She was, however, able to tour the medical transport the military had set up, and the two of them talked with the Chief and the Marshall for a fair amount of time about their service together.

When they returned to the tertiary school, she was cheated once again. Dania, looking very serious, stopped them almost the moment they entered the building. "Sahnassa, may I ask a favor? I need to borrow Theo for a little while, if you don't mind."

Theo looked at her, and in her thoughts she heard, "They're curious about me. They're worried they can't confirm who I am." She shuddered a little; the experience of having his thoughts enter her mind was a little unsettling.

"You'll be okay?" she thought in response, and he nodded. Answering Dania, she said, "Sure, no problem, I suppose. Can you catch up with me later?"

"I will." As Sahnassa left, he asked, "How can I help you Dame Dania de Dothnar?"

"I would like to speak with you in private, for a few moments."

"Certainly, anything to help." They walked in silence until they had reached the school offices where they entered a small counseling room, with two chairs, a table, and only one door. A small bookcase in the corner pointed towards the center of the room. He knew she had chosen the place to convey a serious tone. Her manner of offering him a seat and closing the door did nothing but reinforce the "seriousness."

She sat opposite him on the other side of the table. He could tell she was watching him, too, quite carefully – looking for any nervousness, concern, or even fear. He also knew she was finding that well frustratingly empty, so the long stare before actually starting to speak was a last, desperate attempt to establish control of the situation. Finally, she started. "House de Dothnar has received a request from Selena, Grand Matriarch of de Orturu. That request concerns you."

"I see."

Again, she was put off, expecting a more definitive type of reaction. Still, she pushed ahead. "There have been some questions raised about, well, about your identity, actually. You see, through our house records and the central archives, we have tried to confirm the existence of a house 'de Allarrae', but we've not been able to do so. We were wondering if you could help us explain that."

Theo's response conveyed curiosity while still being friendly. "It puzzles me that you consider my identity to be an item requiring such scrutiny. A search of all of your house records, for both de Orturu and de Dothnar, along with an expedited request to the central archives would have been very difficult to get done in such a small amount of time. Given the present interval, it would have been a very hurried affair, and it would have meant other research work had to wait. So what makes me so important? I'm not saying no to helping you, but I would like to know the urgency that motivates such an extensive examination of my name."

As Theo accurately guessed the effort that had been underway, Dania was feeling increasingly uncomfortable, but still she answered him, grudgingly. "It … it's been observed by some … that you are in a … relationship with Sahnassa. Well, let's say that one may be forming, and the matriarchs look with special favor on Sahnassa for all that she's done for us. They are … concerned and do not want her to be misled or harmed in any way."

With a look of patience and appreciation, Theo answered, "I understand. I wouldn't want any harm to come to her, either."

"Then you can understand why the matriarchy is questioning who you are. If you were disavowed or had committed some crime or fraud well…" Dania trailed off, raising her paw as if towards an invisible set of dishonorable alternatives floating in mid air.

"Yes. That would be cause for concern, wouldn't it? I could be a bad character of some sort, place her in danger, harm her reputation, or use her in some way."

Again, Dania was unsettled that he repeated almost the very words the dames had spoken earlier when deciding on this confrontation. "It's not that what you've done hasn't been appreciated. We've asked about you, discreetly, from many of those who are here without providing any other information as to why. All of them like you and think of you as their friend. Although they have some prior experience with you, you just 'appeared' about half a season ago from nowhere, as far as any record can tell! Your identity and whereabouts to that point are a complete mystery."

Theo nodded, a little sadly. "And my whereabouts will again become a mystery in a very short amount of time. You see Dania, I can't stay."

"What do you mean, you can't stay?" Dania asked, confused. "What have you done that requires you to be so secretive?"

"It's not what I've done, Dania, it's what I am."

"What are you?" Dania was truly starting to get lost.

"I'm just a visitor, and I have to return home. I don't know when or if I'll ever be back," Theo said, his serious tone once again confusing the dame. "And you and your matriarchs are right. Sahnassa and I have become good friends, but she also knows I have to leave, which is why she wants to spend time with me now."

"Why are you leaving? You do care for her, right? Isn't there some way to resolve what's happened?"

"Like you, I have responsibilities that have to be fulfilled," he answered as if she should understand.

"To whom, for whom?" When he just smiled at her and wouldn't answer, Dania started to grow frustrated. "This gets us no closer to understanding where 'de Allarrae' came from. Why do you use this false name?"

He looked at her curiously. "My name is no more false than your own. Take de Dothnar, de Orturu, de Gonari, and de Caterra for example. They all have the same type of meaning. Your family name means 'of the river delta', while de Caterra means 'of the fire plains.' Although I've reformatted my name to match your traditions, my name has the same type of meaning as your own."

"Meaning that you are 'of Allarrae'? But where is that? Could you show me on a map?"

He chuckled. "I can't show you on any map of Thuria you possess. You would not be able to locate my home that way."

Dania was finally too frustrated to continue and stood. "This is getting us nowhere! You're not being truthful with us!"

"Yes, Dania, I am. Now, please sit for a moment, and relax, and, with all due respect, listen attentively and without interruption." Still frustrated, she did, but only for the sake of completing her task. "There, that's better. Now, if I said the words 'green,' 'rock,' and 'flyer,' how much meaning would you be able to parse from those alone? Very little. Why? Because you lack the context of a question or some kind of a statement that helps explain the relationship between those words. What you lack in understanding my answers is the right context."

"Come now, this is all just doublespeak," Dania retorted, shaking her head angrily. "Why won't you answer my questions truthfully?"

"I am answering truthfully, but what I am refusing to give you is the full context of my answers. For you, the real question should be why? Well, on that, I'll answer you. I want to protect you, all of you. There is some knowledge that very few of you are really ready for. So, because I care about all of you, I keep that information to myself. Now, if that doesn't satisfy you, you can imprison me or interrogate me for as long as you wish while I am here. However, when the snow departs, so will I. I will not be where you expect me to be, and I will have become like a vapor. If you let me remain free until that time, I can continue to do good, but again, regardless, when the snow goes, so will I. Either way, Sahnassa will be free to live her own life, and pursue someone else to help her realize her dreams, if that's what she truly wants to do."

Dania was over the conversation and growled out the next sentences through her bared teeth. "I can have you put into prison, a military prison! I could have you kept there, indefinitely! I can make your life absolute misery unless you level with me. You haven't given me one shred of evidence at all – nothing to prove you're not a liar, a fool, or just delusional!"

Theo chuckled a little at the threat. "Okay, Dania, since you asked so *nicely*, how about I give you three shreds of evidence, and even better, these will hint at the context you're missing. Would that suffice?"

"It may. Go on," she answered impatiently.

"Are you sure you're ready for this?"

"Try me," she answered, growling again.

Theo's manner dropped into an icy seriousness. "Very well. When I leave the room, check the recording device you've planted in the bookshelf behind me. You'll find that it has not recorded our conversation, but instead it has been filled with music. That music contains contextual clues, as well. When you leave the room, go to the office or to your matriarch and ask what time it is; I think you'll be surprised. Finally, tonight, at exactly 24.90 by the office clock, stand in back of the tertiary school and look up. For a brief moment, the cloud cover will part, and then you'll be able to see the eye star of Cassius explode, followed by three flame stars that will pass overhead before the clouds close back up. Hopefully, that will be enough."

With that, he stood, and she said, "You're crazy!"

"Do what I ask, and then tell me. You're smart, Dania. Think. I know you can figure this out." He walked towards the door and left.

Stunned by his actions, for a moment she didn't move. She walked to the bookcase, wondering how he could have known about the recording device. Sure enough, when she stopped it and attempted to play it back, she only heard music. It was familiar music, too, and it only took her a moment to place it. "It's the overture from the *Astral Suite*."

She stopped the playback and put the device in her pocket. Looking at her own watch, the time was exactly what she expected it to be, about one quarter interval since they had entered the room. She walked to the door and opened it. Something about the light wasn't quite right; it was just a little darker than it should be. Walking into the main office, she looked at the large timepiece on the wall. She shook her head and blinked in disbelief. It had jumped two full intervals ahead. Looking back at her wrist, she slowly held up her arm until, in her vision, the two displays were right next to each other. Precisely, two intervals difference appeared before her. Presuming Theo had just done something to the clock on the wall, she looked on desks, on computer screens, on communicators – all were two intervals ahead of her own.

"Dania?" the matriarch's voice sounded from the doorway. Rahnahi had a mixture of concern and impatience on her face. "It's been two intervals, dear. Have you been in there the whole time? What's wrong? Did he hurt you in some way?"

"No ... no. I don't know what to – can we talk in private? I'm not sure I would trust anyone else with this."

Rahnahi followed Dania into the small room where she reenacted as much of the conversation as she could. She knew her matriarch was going to think she was crazy, but Rahnahi just listened. She played the music on the recording device and showed Rahnahi the difference between her own timepiece and the matriarch's.

"I ... I just don't know what happened," Dania said, shaken, as Rahnahi sat back, deep in thought. "Did he drug me or hypnotize me or something?"

"Perhaps, but Dania, get on one of the computers out there. Look up the TransNet site for the central observatory. See if they have any information about the eye star of Cassius exploding, going nova ... anything at all that would warn him. Call the observatory in Shanandrae and speak with Otrulla de Dothnar. Tell her to focus and record the eye star starting a full interval before the time Theo gave you. If she doesn't have clear skies, ask her to find someplace else to do it."

Given a task, Dania was able to compose herself. In half an interval, she returned to the matriarch who hadn't really moved much from when she had left her. "Honored One?"

"Yes, what did you find?"

"Otrulla says she will be able to record the eye star tonight, and she has requested that two other observatories on different sides of the continent do the same. We looked through all of the resources, and there is absolutely nothing suggesting any abnormal behavior from the eye star. If something happens, it would be Theo who predicted it, alone."

"Sit for a moment, Dania, please," Rahnahi bade. "I've been thinking about what you told me. Everything he said seems to have had a purpose. I'm starting to piece together a few ... ideas. Now, as crazy as you might think yourself to be, you'll think me crazier when you hear what's turning over in my head."

"Honored One?"

"Think about it. What did he tell you for certain?" the matriarch asked, leaning forward slightly. "He is leaving soon. He's a visitor with responsibilities elsewhere. He is 'de Allarrae', and he suggested that's a place name."

"One we've never heard of. I looked it up, too, and as far as I can tell, that's a completely new word. He has just got to be lying!"

"Careful now," Rahnahi cautioned, "just listen for facts only. I agree he gave us a place name we can't find; that much is a fact. Consider another one; without you suspecting, and without any advance warning, he tampered with your recorder. That's a secured audio recorder, used for evidence gathering by litigators. It's supposedly tamperproof. However, he didn't just stop or randomize the recording; he completely replaced it! I've been listening to it, and it goes well beyond the quarter interval you thought you were in here. It also contains music other than the *Astral Suite*. It contains the *Ballad of the Lone Traveler*, and Atrialli's *Transcendent Soul*, *Light from the Stars*, and a few I can't recognize."

"What does all that mean?"

"From what I gather, he just told us two things for sure. First, he is a master with technology. He never touched your recorder, that you know of, never came close to it?" Dania shook her head in response to the matriarch's question. "So he didn't just swap one for another. Second, his choices all seem to have a direction and a narrative to them. The titles tell a story of sorts. So far, if I rearrange things a little, I get a lone, transcendent traveler ... from the stars?"

"But that's—" Dania reworded the rest of her sentence in deference to her matriarch, "That's not possible."

The matriarch shook her head. "There's a lot that's 'not possible' about what he did. He changed either your perception of time, or he actually moved you in time. Also, what about tonight? If he's able to predict with absolute accuracy the explosion of a star when we know, because our physics tells us, there is no way an observer on Thuria could know about such an event in advance, then what do we say? Perhaps one or two of these things he's done could be fabricated, but to accomplish all three with no warning and no notice—"

Dania swallowed hard. "You mean ... that de Allarrae isn't supposed to be a place on Thuria. He said I would never find it on a map of Thuria, but ... rather could there be a planet called Allarrae?"

Rahnahi leaned back. "I don't know, Dania, for sure. I can only string together what he's given us. It could completely false, but still, there is that small chance he might be telling the truth, and if so, we are way, way out of our area of experience."

"So what do we do about him?" Dania asked.

"We watch the stars tonight. If the skies open, the eye lights up, and three flame stars cross the sky at the same moment, I'm inclined to believe him when he says he's leaving. I don't want to think too much about anything else he's inferred. I also think it would be pointless to try to tell anyone else or confine him."

"What do we tell house de Orturu?"

The matriarch stood and threw up her arms. "We tell them what we can. He's contributed significantly to the rescue effort, doesn't appear to be a threat, and we believe he's leaving soon. Check with Sahnassa, and very nicely and very carefully ask her if that's her understanding. If she confirms it, regardless of how strange the rest of it is, then we've satisfied their request."

As the interval grew late, Tana emerged from her quarters, largely woken by those coming in to begin their night's sleep. She knew her schedule would be off for awhile because of her terrible night in jail. As she stepped into the hallway, she felt very lonely, regardless of how many Thurians were passing by her. She wanted to find Vanarra or Sahnassa, but she didn't know how. "Hello there," a voice from over her shoulder said. She recognized it as Theo's and instantly brightened.

"Theo, it's so good to see a friendly face. Do you know where Vanarra and Sahnassa are?"

"Tedarri's taken them back to his lair for the evening. Van's getting a little anxious about her business and couldn't seem to get to a LineCom around here. She asked about you before she left, and I told her I would look in on you, and help keep you company."

"I'm grateful," she replied. "I still feel like I'm walking on glass floors. It's like I expect the world to fall out from under me and swallow me up."

"I understand. Why don't you come with me, Tana? Let's go get something warm to drink, and then there's an event in the sky tonight you should really see. It's a once in a lifetime."

"Thank you, I would love that. What's happening tonight?"

"The star in the eye of Cassius is going to go nova, so it will glow very brightly, and then disappear out of existence. We should also be able to observe a fire-star or three."

As they began to walk, she asked, "Do you study astronomy? I mean, how did you find out?"

He smiled as he answered, knowing that what he said would probably make it back to Dania and her matriarch. "Oh, I've got a trick or two that lets me see what's headed this way, in terms of these types of events, and it does seem that I spend an inordinate amount of my time star gazing. I enjoy it, though."

"Sounds nice. De Caterra never have a … hobby. We're always schooled and trained and — well, perhaps that's something new I can start."

He smiled and nodded as he ushered her into the cafeteria.

Chapter 21: The Future in Light

Shivering and looking at her timepiece, Dania quietly announced, "It's 24.85." Rahnahi, Dania, and a small contingent of dames stood outside in the cold, in one of the few areas that was not lit by floodlights, the middle of the tertiary school athletic field. They were all looking skyward when they heard paw-steps approaching them from the school. Dania looked at the silhouettes and whispered, "Theo and Tana."

Rahnahi looked at her carefully, and she saw her most steadfast dame visibly trembling not with cold, but with fear. "Relax, dear. I think that if he wanted harm to come to us, it would have already."

"Good evening," Theo's voice called out. "Mind if we join you, Honored One?"

"Not at all, Theo, please. Join us."

"Thank you," he said as he walked closer. "Matriarch, dames, this is Tana, formerly of de Caterra. Vanarra asked me to keep her company tonight."

"Welcome, Tana," Rahnahi offered, politely.

"Thank you, Honored One. I'm very grateful to be here, and most honored to meet you."

"I heard of your pardon, dear. Most extraordinary."

"Yes, Honored One. Theo was able to get that for me, but why I merit such special treatment, I don't know. I'm just grateful."

"Eyes up everyone," Theo interjected, pointing up. "It is time." The night sky was a matted tangle of clouds, but just above them, the intermingled layers seemed to be slipping away from each other. In no more than a pass, a window had formed above them, showing the night sky with perfect clarity. The constellation Cassius was turned slightly on its side, but each of its stars was visible. "In five, four, three, two, one."

When the cadence of Theo's count reached the unspoken zero, the eye of Cassius swelled to a brilliant brightness, its other stars fading in comparison. The bright blue-white glow drew sounds of amazement and wonder from the assembled observers. A flame star streaked by as the brightness seemed to reach a peak and then started to ebb. Two more flame stars shot through the sky a tick later, almost at the same time. In a few passes, the eye had gone out, and the clouds started to cover their field of view again.

"Impressive," Rahnahi finally managed, looking at Theo. "Very impressive." Looking to all of those gathered around, she said, "Why don't all of you return to the building. I would like to speak with Theo alone for a moment. Dania, could you please take Tana and see if there is anything she needs?"

Dania, who was clearly shaken by the event, hesitated. "Yes, Honored One. Are you sure you don't want someone to stay out here with you?"

"Theo and I will be just fine. Now please, go along. We'll be in shortly."

Tana looked to Theo who nodded, and then accepted the paw offered uncertainly by Dania. Theo and Rahnahi were silent as they watched the others leave. When they were safely out of hearing, Rahnahi spoke. "Please, don't tell me that *you* did that." Her claw tip was pointing up.

Sounding a little aggrieved, Theo answered, "No, I didn't detonate an entire star as a conjure stunt! It was simply out of fuel, and the timing was right. The flame stars, well, yes, I did those, and the clouds, yes, those too."

"Uh huh. Oh, and about Dania, you know you've terrified that poor child?!"

While not defensive, Theo's tone was certain and definite. "That was not my intention, but she did force the issue – and under your orders. She's very zealous, that one, which I suppose is a testament to how much she honors you ... and loves you. However, she needs to learn how to snarl far less and listen just a little bit more." Theo stepped closer and said kindly, "I will talk to her and try to ease her fears. Also, when she lies down tonight, she'll find that sleep will come very easily. When she wakes, she would probably swear that she's actually overslept by, say, about two intervals."

"Two intervals, huh? Sounds familiar," Rahnahi said, folding her arms and giving him an appraising look.

"It seems wrong to borrow even time without giving it back," Theo commented.

Rahnahi turned and walked around him. "You know, I haven't figured you out yet. I don't know if you're a secret agent, supernatural being, space alien, conjurer, or con artist. I've thought about the clues you gave Dania, and I think I know the conclusion they are leading me to, but I'm just not sure I can believe it! So, given all that, I have a question, and I would appreciate a straight answer. Why are you here?"

Theo shrugged and replied, "Originally, I was exploring – just having a look. As for all of this, I saw a need, and I wanted to help."

Rahnahi was silent for a moment and then nodded slowly, still looking at Theo with an appraising stare in the dim light. "And Tedarri, the Chief, Vanarra, and even this Cutter say you've been a huge help, wherever and whenever you've shown up. Yet surely in the grand design of all things, what you're helping out with is relatively small. An inspection, a review, working communications—"

Theo interrupted her. "Don't underestimate the importance of the times in which you live. I'm sure you already have some sense as to how even the smallest events sometimes contribute to tremendous change. Thuria is undergoing a transformation, one you helped begin. Each of your books gave little pushes, and now events are starting to roll faster. This is becoming a renaissance, a reawakening in so many ways. Imagine Thuria as a great room with windows, but every one of them is dirty. It's an arguably menial job to clean windows, but when you do, you let in light, warmth, and hope."

Rahnahi remembered the title to one of her own books. *"Light, Warmth, and Hope*? You *are* well read on my writings, aren't you?"

"Yes, I am. You said in *Light, Warmth, and Hope* that those words have more power against soul-crushing darkness than the power of an army. You were right! You've spent much of your life bringing light, warmth, and hope to so many. Do you know I talked to Tana a little bit this evening, just before coming out here? She's actually read a couple of your books! While she was de Caterra, she had to hide them at work, read them in stolen moments in a locked office or in the restroom. Writing a book can be seen by some as a trivial exercise, but look at what you helped

James Todd Lewis

to create in Tana. When Vanarra needed someone to help rescue her, you helped supply Tanassadurini de Caterra, whom you didn't even know."

Rahnahi nodded. "Vanarra also told me that she read my books, and that they helped sustain her during the tough times in her life. You can't imagine what that means to me … and what you just said."

"Exactly! So don't wonder too much about why I help in seemingly little ways. I've learned, over time, those are the ways that work. Public displays with huge movements, grand gestures, or broad exercises of power do not, alone, instill lasting hope or faith. It is compassion, mercy, and the little miracles of the moment that do that."

Rahnahi appeared to relax in her appraisal of him, but only slightly. "I appreciate everything you're saying, Theo, but what about you? What do you get out of all this?"

"The satisfaction of helping, meeting all of you, and seeing things turn to the better. I'm not going to try to convince you that's all I want, because you won't really believe it until I actually leave, and then you'll find I've taken nothing for my troubles. Still, you have my gifts of work, of service, and, in some cases, information."

He paused a bit, as if considering a course of action. He started speaking again in a careful, considered manner. "I will give you and you alone the gift of one vital piece of information. There is a rogue technologist out there who stumbled upon the de Caterra's secured information vault some time ago, and he managed to punch through its defenses. He downloaded all of their secure documents and then erased all record of his intrusion. The de Caterra do not know their security has been breached. However, what our clever little data thief doesn't yet know is that the files in his possession are the de Caterra 'cover records'."

"What are those?" she asked, her manner growing more serious as he explained.

"Simply put, they are the way the de Caterra keep their lies consistent to 'cover' the horrors they have wrought. They also contain instructions and techniques they can use to commit further evil. In the coming sols, news about what that family has been up to will begin to surface and become more commonly known. I guarantee you that when word of Katur's confession reaches the ears of our clever thief, he is going to stop looking at their financial records and start looking through the rest of the files. Having the confession as a guide, it's very likely he'll find and decipher the cover records. Inside will be things so horrifying, so enormous in their impact to your society, there will be no way he can keep them to himself."

"He wouldn't try to blackmail them? Try to get wealth in return for his silence?" she asked.

Theo raised his eyebrow fur as he dismissed the notion. "I very much doubt it! He'll probably be so scared of what he reads in there that he'll run and hide from all de Caterra. After reading only a little, he'll know about how vicious their vengeful streak can be, and he'll want to stay far away. So, he has only two choices: delete what he's found or anonymously release the decrypted records into the TransNet data wells, which will make them publicly accessible to all. Now, if he releases the cover records, all kinds of fires are going to start burning! When that happens, the other houses and families have a decision to make: should they leave every member of de Caterra to burn completely or should they give refuge to those whose names do not appear in the records? There are going to be a lot of very angry and grieved Thurians out there when this information is released, and rescuing the innocent in de Caterra will take advance planning and will certainly not be without cost, financial and otherwise."

"You can say that, for sure," Rahnahi agreed, rubbing her brow with her paw as if trying to clear a headache. "Can this individual be stopped from releasing the records?"

"He could, but anyone who would be sent in, using legal methods, would take and review the records as evidence, and then you're back to the same issue. Someone will stumble upon these sooner or later; it's only a matter of when. Even if he doesn't, then searches of the de Caterra estates, a likely consequence of what's happened here, will probably turn up copies. This is not a question of 'if.' The storm is coming, and I'm giving you warning to prepare, and woe to the house that tries to hide these records, because when they do come out …"

Rahnahi finished his sentence. "…it will make that house look like they were aiding de Caterra and agreed with what they were doing." Rahnahi paced back and forth a short distance. "Well, that's something new for me to worry about, but thank you. I would rather know it's out there than be surprised. May I now ask you a question?"

"Please."

"I … I want to know what would have happened had Vanarra and Sahnassa not contacted us. I can guess at it, and I can have someone at an academy run some numbers, but it would just be a guess. Do you know, with certainty, what would have happened?"

Theo nodded gravely. "Yes, I do. Consider two scenarios, staying or trying to get down the mountain. I know the entire population's age, health, species, and physical abilities – completely. I also know about the Meeting Den damage you've witnessed, but also damage you have yet to see. If you had stayed, about twenty of the fifteen hundred would have survived; the statistical range is very tight, seventeen on the low side and twenty-three on the high."

"Only twenty?! That's not possible!" Rahnahi gasped, shocked and horrified.

Theo's manner was completely certain. "I promise you it is. The ice and snow that will be gone from here in a few sols will linger up there five more. Between exposure, crush injuries from the buildings' collapse, falls, lack of medication, and infighting, only a few would have survived. It gets worse, too. About one third of the twenty remaining would be lost to survivor's guilt within two seasons. The rest would live a … difficult life."

The matriarch shut her eyes as if trying to not see such a horrible outcome. "By Thuria … and if we had tried to leave?"

"If you tried to get everyone off that mountain at first light, then about three hundred and fifty would actually make it to the bottom before the ice and snow started hitting the gentlest slope. Maybe another one hundred or so would make it down after that, but that's it."

"None of those slopes looked in the least bit gentle," Rahnahi argued, looking at Theo and shaking her head.

"You're right. Only those in peak health and with good endurance would have managed it. You would have lost over half of the total number to accidents or falls, and about one half of what did survive would later succumb to survivor's guilt. It's not so hard to understand why, when you consider it would have literally been raining bodies – a real horror."

She walked closer to him and asked, "So there was truly no way out other than what those two precious kits brought us? If Vanarra and Sahnassa had simply tried to go down the mountain themselves, not call out to us, leave us up there, what are the chances they would have made it to the bottom in time and without serious injury?"

It was Theo who now closed his eyes and lowered his head. "Ninety-seven point four percent. They would have been just fine."

"And I don't think they ever gave that alternative a thought," Rahnahi observed, looking into the sky. "For that, may they always be blessed."

"Oh, yes, they should be remembered for that. Also, take this into consideration: if the acts of the de Caterra didn't come out now, houses starting to make overtures of reconciliation to them may have become allies, unwittingly helping them to continue what they were doing. When the cover records finally came to light, de Caterra would have had more allies – namely those guilty by association. What's coming is going to be ugly enough, but it's not as ugly as it might have been."

"One final question?" Rahnahi looked straight at him. "If you wanted to pose a danger to us, is there anything we could do to stop you?" Theo shook his head. "Law enforcement? The military?"

"If you want to imprison me to make yourself feel better, I'll go along with it, but as I told Dania—"

"Yes, I heard. You're gone with the snow?" Rahnahi completed.

"Yes."

"Why then?"

He smiled at her and answered kindly. "Because then the danger will be over, and others can take you back to your lairs. I can leave knowing that you are all safe. Now, I have a request for you. I would like to have what time remains to me free so that I may give some special help to those who need it."

"Sahnassa?" she asked, curious.

"Not so much. More like Tana, Vanarra, and now, I guess, Dania."

She nodded and sighed. "Very well. I grant your request. Speaking of Dania, we'd better get inside. She'll come hunting us with an army if we don't show up soon."

He chuckled again. "I gathered that. She's very effective."

As they started walking back towards the building, Rahnahi noted, "You haven't said 'Honored One' in the entire time we've been talking. Is that just an … oversight?"

"Not so much. No rudeness or disrespect was intended by either of us. We were having a private discussion."

"Between equals?"

"More or less," he responded in a matter-of-fact tone that left Rahnahi wondering as they walked in silence who was more and who was less.

"I'm not going to wait much longer," Dania growled impatiently, Tana nervously at her side. "I wish she hadn't done this!"

"Dame, what's wrong?" Tana asked, concerned.

"Theo! Theo is what's wrong!"

"I don't understand," Tana said, worried that perhaps her pardon would somehow be invalidated.

Dania turned towards her and tried to speak, but every version of an explanation she came up with sounded like utter nonsense. "It's … it's hard to explain." She looked out the door again and sighed, "Oh, thank goodness! Here she comes, and she looks alright."

"I'm fine, Dania," the matriarch stated when she came to the door. "Thank you, Theo, for a good conversation. You'll please see me before you go?"

"Of course, Honored One. May I ask for a few moments with Dania?"

The matriarch actually smiled and nodded at the suggestion. "Yes, I think that would be good. Come, Tana. Walk with me awhile, please," she offered pleasantly.

"Matriarch, I—" Dania tried to plead, but the matriarch was clearly firm in her decision, her paw already in Tana's, leading her down the mostly empty hallway. Looking back at Theo, Dania warned in a whispered hiss, "Stay back!"

"Come now, Dame Dania de Dothnar, think this through! With everything I've shown you, do you think for an instant that if I wanted real harm to come to you, you could do anything to prevent it?" His dead-level stare into her eyes was convincing enough that she shook her head no. "Now, having had that opportunity, did I do anything that physically harmed you?"

She was still backed against the wall in fear. "Two intervals! I lost two intervals of my life! You … could have done anything to me in that time."

"Could I? You would have noticed something, even if it was just a loss of memory. You remember those few ticks between when I left the room and when you did?"

"Yes."

"Any breaks? Any lack of continuity? Can you remember exactly what you did?"

Dania swallowed hard. "Yes."

"I moved not just you two intervals ahead; I moved the whole room two intervals ahead. Have you noticed the timepiece built into the recording device?"

She pulled the item from her pocket and pressed a few controls. "It's two intervals behind, like me."

"I didn't harm you. I just did what I had to so you would know a little more about what I really am and what I can do. Remember, you were questioning me, quite forcefully, as I recall, about my relationship with Sahnassa? You couldn't identify who I was. You didn't know what 'de Allarrae' means. Having seen what I've done, does that surprise you now – that there is no record of who I am?"

"No, but it scares the very life out of me," she said, almost whispering her response.

Theo sighed in frustration. "Perhaps it should. Perhaps that is the normal reaction when seeing something truly new for the first time. Caution and fear have kept many a species alive, after all. In time and with experience, we all learn about new things, even those things we at first don't understand ... and fear. You've seen conjurers perform magic, have you not?"

"Yes, but that's different! I know that's just a trick; I ... I even know how some of them work."

"But even the new ones you see," he countered quickly, "the ones you don't understand, you still know that they're just tricks, right?" She nodded, and for the first time, Theo saw Dania begin to let her guard down and relax. "What does that mean exactly? I'll tell you! That behind every disappearing Vulpi and every Faelnar sawed into quarters there's no real magic, only some technology and intelligence. Agreed?"

"Yes, that's true," she admitted, sounding more thoughtful.

"Everything I've done is like a conjurer's trick. It's magic until you know how it works and what's behind it. Then, it's not so magical anymore. It may be clever, and it may still seem very impressive, but it's not something to be feared, especially not from me. I've only wanted to help, throughout all of this. I also need to be free for what little time I have remaining so that I can finish what I've started."

"And what is that?" she asked, still anxious.

Theo turned and looked down the hallway. "Helping three Thurians find their place again in a world that has radically altered around them."

"Who are they?"

"You're one," he said with a sideways glance before turning to face her. "That's what I'm trying to do right now. Dania, I don't want you to remember this as the time when you started to live in fear; I want you to remember it as the time when your eyes were opened to greater possibilities than you ever knew existed. You are one of the few who will ever be privileged to know that Thuria is not all there is; there's more. What joy, what wisdom there is in that! What perspective there is in that – to look past the events of the moment and see a brighter, larger universe just waiting! Do you think you're there, Dania? Dania who did so much to hold things together up there on that mountain, can you hold things together right here and now, for yourself?"

After a long pause and staring off in thought, she looked at him. "I … I think I can." He smiled and nodded, but still she asked, "Who are the other two?"

"Consider Tana. She's lost everything she's ever known. Consider Vanarra, as well; she's been catapulted into a new place in life she just doesn't understand. All three of you have so much potential for good, and if just by spending a moment or two talking with you, I can help make sure that happens, don't you think it's worth the effort?"

Finally, Dania fully relaxed, smiled, and nodded. "Yes, I suppose it is."

"Good. Now, go rest yourself; the matriarch has already given you leave. I'll kick in a couple of extra intervals of sleep that no one else will notice. I figure I owe you."

Dania walked over and quietly asked, "You won't … do anything to me?"

"You'll be unharmed. Hey, I can give you two more intervals of sleep than the night can truly hold. You won't get another offer like that again!"

"I suppose not," she said, laughing softly. "Theo, I just wanted to say … I'm sorry I threatened you."

He chuckled and patted her shoulder. "It's okay. I understand. It's an occupational hazard for both of us. Now, have a good night, Dania."

"Thank you, and … thank you again." He smiled, and then turned and left. She turned around and, feeling a little drowsy, started to make her way to her sleeping quarters.

Despite the continuing bad weather, the next three sols were oddly pleasant and reassuring for Vanarra, Sahnassa, and a vast majority of the evacuees. The small community within the school's walls spent time talking to one another, calling family, thanking all of those who helped take care of them, and simply getting to know everyone who was a part of this group of survivors. Sahni and Van had even watched in absolute amusement as Theo borrowed a stringed instrument from the music resource room and entertained one evening after dinner. Sahnassa had started a story time in the school library, reading to all of those who wanted to hear, which, to her surprise, was quite a few. Tana, Van, Theo, and even Buck had joined in, at one time reading through a play, each taking a key part. The group grew each time they performed, with Amyra and Rahnahi sitting in one evening, as well. Soldiers were also showing up in increasing numbers.

For Vanarra, some of the de Caterra still shunned her, but word was spreading about the dame's confession, and she had seen Tana pulled into conversations that looked positively desperate. A least five times, Vanarra had been called over and asked to tell her story, about her father and mother. In less than two sols, several more individuals had followed Tana's example and made a public break with de Caterra, witnessed by the two matriarchs. When they did, Van was amazed at how grateful they were to her, and how the lights just seemed to turn on in their eyes. They were like captives finally finding freedom.

Vanarra had actually been to see Arnat in the hospital, and she received a double apology with thanks for their lives from both Arnat and his sire, and, as Theo had coached her, she made sure they understood she was grateful for their part in events, as well.

Saletta spent time talking with Vanarra in the mornings, and over lunch, Theo and Sahnassa would help Van understand or work through the concerns she had about being an avowed member of the de Gonari family. She would briefly check in each afternoon with her office, but her staff told her she had no business calling and should be resting after such a harrowing experience.

In the afternoons, Van would spend more time with Tana. The more she talked with that Faelnar, the more she liked her, and respected her. Tana had a very practical side, and she, too, had been put in scary situations where she had to think on her hind legs. What did disturb Vanarra slightly was Tana's growing dedication to her. The poor kit now seemed to have no other ambition than to be Vanarra's dedicated assistant. Van tried to explain that with Tana's gorgeous looks and obvious book smarts that, avowed or not, she would be a real find for any employer.

Still, Tana seemed determined to live up to her commitment, both to Van and the other Anati. She had been through both schools several times making sure all of the mixed blood were in good quarters, in good health, and had all they needed. Van had walked in on her once, seated at the side of an older male Anati, listening to his life story with tears running down her face. It was clear that something very powerful was happening in that young Faelnar's life, something that felt like it wasn't just a fluke or a promise that would later fail or weather with age. Van was starting to see that Tana was recreating herself in a way that would last for the rest of her life.

In the evenings before returning to Tedarri's lair, Van spent time alone with Buck. He had been so good about giving her space that, initially, she almost had to hunt him down. She found talking to him just as comforting and just as normal as ever. No matter how strange things were, it wasn't hard to talk to him about anything.

Both Sahnassa and Buck were her anchors, for they had known and liked her long before the rescue. With Sahnassa, it had deepened their friendship more than she thought possible, but with Buck, it had rekindled their love for one another and brought it to the surface. She basked in the wonderful feelings being around him, feelings she had never felt with any little fling that dumped her as soon as convenience permitted. Buck loved her, and she felt so secure with him. With everything else that was changing, his feelings for her were unmoved, and she loved him even more for that.

Once at Tedarri's lair, she would play with the twins, love on them, and enjoy the strange sensation of being a guest in a home of Thurians who loved each other. She would drift off to sleep, watching the snow fall or talking with Sahnassa, lying together just as they had in their small shelter.

One area she had been denied any sort of satisfaction was cornering Theo, getting him alone. As more time passed, she wanted to doubt her own memory, but still, the visions happened, and she remembered them. She tried thinking through other rationalizations, but nothing else made sense. She knew she just had to talk to him.

The morning of their fourth sol, Sahnassa, Van, and Tedarri walked outside into a world that was distinctly warmer. The snow had stopped falling, and the roads were almost completely clear. As the three drove the short distance to the school, they noticed flyers lifting off in small groups from the fields and heading out of the valley. "The military is leaving," Tedarri explained, "well at least some of it. The Chief said the Storm Pack had to get back to its digs, and the additional transport wings have to get back to their bases as well. The Marshall's group has authorization to stay a little longer, get some more pictures from up there on the mountain, and assist with any other rescues that are needed. If everything looks good, they'll be out of here in two sols."

"What about the evacuees?" Vanarra asked.

"They'll be leaving, too. I understand the roads between here and Shanandrae are finally clear and are safe up until two intervals after nightfall. We should be able to get enough transports in here to get about half of the evacuees out, and the rest should be gone by tomorrow. You did a marvelous job on the food Van; we'll have enough left of the pre-packaged stuff to send a good sampling back with everyone as they go."

"So, I guess we'll be getting on a transport, too?" Van asked, sounding a little sad.

"You sound disappointed," Sahnassa observed, reaching out to grab Van's paw.

"It'll just be so strange going back to *normal life*, especially when I know it's not going to be *normal* anymore. I've ... I've also really come to like it here. It's a beautiful town, Tedarri, and I would love to come back up here some time and see you and your family again."

The Lupar smiled. "I know they'd love that, too. If you come in the warm season, there's a really nice lake up here that has some good fishing. Reston Lake, I think it's called."

Vanarra sat up straight, as if shocked. "Sounds ... nice, really. I'd love to try it. Sahni, I've *got* to talk to Theo before he leaves!"

"You'd better hurry," Tedarri suggested. "He told me he's leaving in a few intervals."

"No!" Van said with such vehemence that both of them looked at her. "I'm sorry," she offered contritely, "I'm just so frustrated that it's the one thing I've been dying to do; I can't let that chance slip out of my paws!"

"Van, you've spent intervals and intervals talking with him over the last few sols. That wasn't enough?" Sahnassa asked, confused.

"I ... I need to speak with him in private. It's nothing about you, kit or you, Tedarri for that matter. It's just something I ... I really need to talk with just him about. Something private. Sahnassa, I hate to ask you, but could you go see Saletta and tell her I can't join her until I get this done. I'll never forgive myself if I don't!"

"I will. I'm sure she'll understand," Sahnassa replied, patting her friend's paw.

"You bet she will," Tedarri agreed. "Well haven't you two heard? A special private flyer is going to be taking the matriarchs back, and you two and Tana and Buck are riding with them. I'm sure they'll have Saletta along, as well."

"That's ... that's amazing!" Vanarra exclaimed, astonished. "I actually was already thinking about how I could bribe someone so I could get the back seat of a transport."

"First class for you, Vanarra," Tedarri said, smiling.

"See what I mean about normal? Please find her anyway, Sahni. I'd hate to keep her waiting around."

"You really like her, don't you?" Sahnassa asked.

"I do. She's a little naive on some subjects, but when it comes to family politics and procedures, she's got it down cold and in a very practical way."

"Here we are," Tedarri announced as they pulled in. "I'll let you ladies out at the front. Just make sure you say goodbye tomorrow before you leave, okay?"

"I wouldn't dream of leaving without saying goodbye to you and Denala, and those two—"

"Imps? Trouble-makers? Terrors in fur?" Tedarri interjected, smirking.

"No, wonderful joys. They're both great," Van said, shaking her head.

"Thanks!" Tedarri smiled as the two stepped out of the vehicle, and, to no one's surprise, Tana walked from the front of the school to meet them.

"Tana, do you know where Theo is?" Vanarra asked.

Tana nodded her head in a slight bow before answering. "I have seen him; we talked for a long time last evening. This morning, I think he's saying goodbye to the military and taking his leave of the matriarchs."

"Okay, then I have a good idea of where I can catch him. Tana, I need to talk with him alone, if that's okay, kit?"

"Of course it is. I need to make the rounds now, but I was going to wait until I saw you."

Still not fully knowing how to accept Tana's willing service, Vanarra reached out and hugged her. "Oh, kit, thank you! You're so incredible!" They released, and Van stepped forward. "Okay kits, I'll see you!"

"Van? We'll both be here later, if you want to talk," Sahnassa offered, kindly.

"Thanks."

Almost running, Vanarra searched through the halls of the school and caught Theo leaving the de Gonari matriarch's presence. "Ending on a high note?" she asked, trying not to sound as out of breath as she was.

"Not yet," he said, smiling.

"You have time for a ... conversation? A ... private conversation?" she asked in a quiet voice.

"For you, surely. Come on. Believe it or not, I don't think there's anyone out in front of the school right now. We can talk there."

"Great," she replied, and they began walking. "So, where are you headed next?"

Theo hummed thoughtfully a moment before answering. "Not quite sure yet, but I'm either heading home or I'm meeting a friend for a few sols vacation. Feels like I could use one after this."

"I'll bet," she laughed. "Where would you be going?"

"That really depends on where my friend wants to go. They may just want to sit down and watch VidStar as far as I know," he explained, shrugging.

"It's too cold to do anything else."

"It depends on where we end up. Ah, here we are! After you, dear Vanarra."

"Thank you, Theo," she replied as they walked through the door. As it shut behind them, she said, "You know, I've wanted to talk with you alone like this ever since we got down off the mountain. It's only that—" Vanarra started to pace back and forth nervously, obviously trying to work up her courage to explain.

"... now that I'm here, what you want to ask is very difficult," Theo supplied after a moment of watching her pace.

She froze looking at him. "Right! Because the moment I open my muzzle and ask this, I'm going to look like a complete idiot or crazy or ... just ... I don't know – it won't look good!" She went back to her nervous pacing.

Theo's smile was very gentle and understanding as he asked, "Van, do you trust me?"

The question stopped her cold. "Well, yes, Theo. I do."

"Then you have nothing to fear. Ask what you want to ask."

She tried to articulate words, making several false starts before giving up. "I don't know how!"

"Come on. Sit over here," Theo suggested, motioning her to a bench by the curb side. As she sat, he offered her advice. "When you've got something difficult to ask, you generally can take one of several alternatives: you can tell a story, you can start with a different question, or you can just spit it out. Pick one, and see how it goes. I'll be patient, Van. I have all the time in the universe just for you."

Van closed her eyes and tried to breathe. Her words came out in nervous bursts, but she was able to get them out. "When I was … when I was captured up on that mountain, I think they stunned me, drugged me or maybe both. I don't know what they used, but it was … it must have been really powerful stuff. I … I had some … let's call them hallucinations – some very *vivid* hallucinations. Some … very direct and to the point hallucinations." She opened her eyes and looked into his. "You were in them."

He nodded. "Okay. Go on."

"Well, what happened in them was that you and I – oh, this is so embarrassing – we were laying in hammocks on a floating platform in the middle of a lake, Lake Reston … which isn't far from here, only it was the warm turn of the season and evening, and we were just relaxing, nothing like intimate or anything and … and … you told me I had been captured. You told me … you told me the names of my captors and something important about all of them. You … gave me advice that … actually … kept me alive! It kept me from screwing up and doing the wrong thing! There, I've said it! Now, you can tell me I'm a total rabid, wacked-out Anati, and I don't know what I'm talking about!"

Theo looked at her, nodded slowly and said, "I think you know exactly what you're saying. Was there more?"

Vanarra swallowed hard. That wasn't the reaction she predicted, but in some ways, it was the reaction she was more afraid of. "Yes, when the soldiers were just about to break into the room, I nodded off or something, and then I heard you again. You told me that the raid was coming, and you told me what to do! If I hadn't done it, they might have killed poor Tana!" She looked towards the ground, already feeling grief for how great a loss that would have been.

"You told your story," Theo said calmly. "Now, what is your question?"

She looked at him with a long, searching look before answering. "Did ... did you somehow ... talk to me when I was unconscious? Did you somehow talk to me that second time when the soldiers were about to break in?" she asked in a timid, small voice.

At that moment, the sun started to show over the mountains beyond, and the light seemed to make Theo's face almost glow as she looked at it. "Look at that, Vanarra. See how perfectly the sun shines between that cloud line and the mountains? It's like someone took a giant paw and created just enough of a gap for us to see the sun, for the first time in sols. Feels good, doesn't it?"

She looked out at it, and she had to admit, even as nervous as she was, he was right. Van closed her eyes and felt the warm radiance striking her face. "It's nice. For awhile on that mountain, several times in fact, I didn't think I would ever see it again." She opened her eyes and turned towards him.

"I understand. When you see something like that sunrise, orchestrated so beautifully, you know it's something that no Thurian could ever truly reproduce. Some higher order or power is creating that elegant cloudscape above the mountains. Some say it's physical laws or nature. Some say it's the creator of the universe, and some say it's physical laws being used by the creator of the universe or the other way around. Whatever you believe, you are caught up in the majesty of knowing there are things in the world greater than yourself, and greater than what you know. There are things we simply can't explain right now. In the future, someone may be able to, but now, you can't."

"True. So what I experienced is just ... one of those things?" Van asked. "Something I'll never be able to explain?"

"You miss my point ... the one about a higher order. Did you experience those visions?"

"Yes."

"Did they help you? Did they provide you details you otherwise had no way of knowing?"

"Yes."

"Then, perhaps, Vanarra, you have to accept that a higher order was in play somehow: not a god, but certainly no ordinary Thurian."

Vanarra sat for a moment, just trying to think of anything to say. "You're saying that the visions I experienced were real? That something – some higher order – put them there?"

"Can you deny what you saw in your visions?"

"No! Both of them were … just amazing!"

"Then look at them as a gift, one you can't and shouldn't try to explain. If some power beyond your experience put them there, if something wanted to favor you in that way, then accept it. Don't try to talk yourself into thinking they didn't happen. You know they did. Simply accept the gift, and move on."

"But Theo, who … who do I thank? Is it you? Is it you that I thank?" She looked at him anxiously, unsure of what to make of him or the conversation.

"If you want to. It's a mixed blessing being through something strange like this and carrying the questions around always wondering. You have to forcibly decide to lay your questions down and just be grateful. For some, it's very hard to do this and keep a blessing from becoming a curse. If you can simply enjoy the blessing, only then should you give thanks. Will you do that?"

Vanarra closed her eyes and took a deep breath. "I'll do it. I'll stop worrying about it, letting it bother me. I'll just accept the gift and say thank you, Theo, thank you."

He hugged her gently around the shoulder, saying, "Then my work here is complete. Take care, Vanarra. I'd wish you the best, but I think you're pretty close to that already."

She opened her eyes and turned towards him to return the good wishes, but found, to her amazement, he was gone! She stood quickly and darted back and forth, but he wasn't there. "Oh my gosh," she shouted. "Theo? Theo?!" She looked at the ground, and no paw prints in the melting snow led away from the bench, only towards it. Her heart was beating so hard in her chest that she almost didn't hear a nearby door opening. Running towards it, she called "Theo?"

"He's not here, Van," Sahni answered, stepping out. "I guess he's just left; did you catch up with him?"

In her mind, his words echoed, "lay your questions down and just be grateful."

"Yes. Yes I did," Van answered, trying to calm herself.

"Did you … did your talk come out alright?" Sahnassa asked, concerned.

Van thought for a moment before answering. "Not like I expected, that's for sure, but yes, yes it did." Light seemed to glow all about them, and they turned towards the mountains.

"Oh, it's all so beautiful," Sahnassa said as the sun shown in brilliant beams through the clouds so both mountains and sky glowed as if they were filled with a new inner light. Sahnassa walked out in front of the school, and Vanarra joined her.

"Yes it is, kit. Every bit of it." Placing her arm around Sahnassa, Vanarra truly accepted everything that had happened to her as an inexplicable gift and a blessing, and she simply let gratitude, as warm and brilliant as the sun, wash over her.

The End of the Rescue

Epilogue

On a warm and beautiful morning, the elderly Grand Matriarch of the de Gonari family looked out the window of her flyer as it passed the eastern range of the Yarvea Mountains and descended into the valley just south of Windston. With house de Orturu unable to attend because of the recent loss of their matriarch, the matriarch of house de Gonari wanted to ensure that the opening of the Windston Historical Museum would be well favored with dignitaries. The Vice Chancellor sat to the matriarch's right, looking out the large window at the scene beyond. The matriarchs of house de Dothnar and house de Debonar sat beside them. The rest of the vehicle was packed full, every seat filled with all of the other aides and attendants.

As the pilot located his landing zone, he circled once giving those on the right side of the craft, the dignitaries, the chance to see the entire complex. Within the elegant and graceful gardens and well-tended grounds, there was a single white building of exceptional artistic merit.

The building started with a two-story rounded dome, followed by a long concourse reaching out and widening to a four-story dome almost one hundred and fifty tracks away from the first. Flying arches of white transected the domes and concourse at regular intervals, growing in splendor and magnificence as they progressed towards the larger of the two half spheres. The entrance of the building, in the smaller dome, faced out to a large traffic circle with the lowest arch elongated over the road to act as a cover against the elements. Even from their height, the matriarch and her distinguished guests could see that the center of the traffic circle had been left empty and cordoned off from the large crowds waiting just beyond.

Very gently, their flyer, also spotless white – as was planned for the occasion – descended, hovered, and touched down in the center of the grass island in front of the entrance. As the doors opened and the attendants walked out to prepare the way for those of higher rank, the de Gonari matriarch rubbed her temples as cheering assailed their ears. She was glad it was nice weather and the crowds were happy. After the disappearance of her closest friend, the matriarch truly needed those things in her favor.

After stepping out and waving to the crowd for a few moments, watching fathers place their kits and cubs on their shoulders just to get a look at her, the matriarch smiled, waved a final time, and followed her two closest attendants to the door. Walking over the threshold brought that intake of air sound she had finally gotten used to, that sound made by others when she walked into a place. A petite, beautiful Faelnar-Nephti mix stepped forward and bowed humbly.

"Honored Ones, Vice Chancellor, I am Arani de Bosnar, curator of the museum. If you'll step this way," she offered, bowing low.

"You're not getting off that easy, Arani," the matriarch said, smiling. "Come over here." With arms open, she embraced the small female who was about thirty seasons her junior. Carefully avoiding entangling any of Arani's fur in her golden, bejeweled shoulder-piece, the matriarch whispered, "Oh, dear kit, it's so good to see you! How's your brother doing?"

"Still leading the Storm Pack, causing trouble for evil-doers everywhere. He's a mess – refuses to retire," she replied, embarrassed as all of the other staff looked at her curiously. Releasing the matriarch, she stated at a normal volume, "It's so good to see you again, Honored One."

"I'm so sorry I haven't been able to come and see this sooner," the matriarch said, apologizing. "The life of a matriarch and all. I can't wait to have you show me and my friends around this place. It looked so wonderful from the air."

"We hope you'll be as pleased with what you find inside, Honored One. If you will all follow me." They walked in between the information desk on one side of the dome and the gift shop on the other. The matriarch had to softly chuckle at the titles and covers of the books on the shelves. "As you walk through the dome, let me point some things out to you. The lights above have been placed in the correct star positions for the night of the quake, and you'll notice that the eye of Cassius in this dome is still lit. In the dome at the far end, that's not the case. The two domes and the structure between them literally track the passage of time. We're in the starting dome at the earliest point in time, and the ending dome represents the latest point in time. Visitors coming into the museum will actually enter and leave through this dome, making a full circuit."

"So they go forwards and then backwards through history?"

"Yes, Vice Chancellor. The concourse is divided so that visitors get two perspectives on the events. As they walk down the right side towards the far dome, they get the historical facts – biographies of the key figures in the Meeting Den rescue, the time-line and logistics of the rescue itself, as well as its immediate aftermath. When they arrive at the far dome, they'll see an amazing display that I'll just leave as a surprise for now. As they begin to make their way back to this point, they see what many have found to be the most moving part of the exhibit. As guests return, they walk backwards in history, but this time they encounter the thoughts and remembrances of those who were a part of the events on the nearby mountaintop."

"That's very clever," the de Bosnar matriarch said, obviously proud of her house's daughter.

"Thank you, Honored One. The credit for the building and its artistic design goes to Leonat Tersano. You may remember that he was serving as a kitchen helper when the den suffered its first explosion, and he was pretty badly burned. Later, he became one of Thuria's most talented architects as well as one of its most gifted designers, and we are completely thrilled that he designed our building. Now, the museum is meant to be a self-guided tour, and we wanted you to see it as it was intended to be seen. However, I've asked one of the senior staff to accompany each of you in case you have questions."

Three of the others who had been lingering in the background walked forward and took their place beside a dignitary. Arani stepped up beside the de Gonari matriarch. "Won't your own matriarch miss you?"

"No, Honored One. We discussed this in advance. It was my request, if that's alright?"

"It's fine, kit; it's fine. Shall we go in?" Arani nodded, and the pair led the rest of the group into the concourse. The displays began with the Meeting Den's construction and a little bit of the town of Windston's history. One of the most fascinating things for the matriarch was the three-dimensional model of the Meeting Den, in all of its original glory. "I … wow, I can actually remember it when it was like that. That's a great model."

"Thank you, Honored One. There are four of them in this side of the concourse, and each took several moons to research and build."

"Impressive." The matriarch moved on to other displays, citing the founding of the Association of Service and Commerce under the title of "Flawed Beginnings." Another showed Vanarra Anasto standing outside of her first rented office, looking very young and smiling proudly under the title "The Survivor." A second showed Sahnassa de Orturu, looking even younger and stunningly beautiful, sitting on the steps of a local park; her title was "The Key." "I like that," the matriarch said, after reading through Sahnassa's history and seeing the various pictures of her growing up.

"We struggled for a long time with that title, Honored One. I'm very glad you're pleased with it."

"I am, Arani. I am. I think that describes her well." As they moved on, the matriarch looked up and noticed that she had missed something. "You didn't show me that!"

"It's meant to surprise you, Honored One. It began only a few tracks behind us." Attached to the ceiling were other displays showing the matriarchal lines of house de Gonari, house de Dothnar, and house de Caterra. After turning around and pointing it out to the others, they all walked back a few steps and saw long ribbons that intertwined and separated, with de Caterra and de Gonari closely associated and then, as time moved forward, de Gonari and de Dothnar became close while de Caterra grew ever more distant and reduced in size.

"That's really clever!" the de Bosnar matriarch proclaimed.

"I'll say," noted the Vice Chancellor. "I could spend intervals in these few tracks alone, but it's so well done that it's easy to pick up the basics even on a quick walk through! That's astounding!" The normal, reserved nature of the distinguished male Lupar was completely absent as he ran to a section of the wall and pointed. "Look here! Here is the formation of the Storm Pack! My dear, you and your staff have done an amazing job!"

"Thank you so much, Vice Chancellor." Arani's blush fur was at full salute, and seeing her discomfort, the de Gonari matriarch took her by the arm and gently led her forward.

"He's like a cub in a creele patch," the matriarch whispered in her ear.

"We're hoping everyone who was associated with the event feels that way, especially you, Honored One."

"It's all mixed feelings for me, as you can guess." They stopped in front of a large display whose title was simply "The Quake." It seemed to encompass all of the clinical aspects of the quake, including dioramas of the Meeting Den and its access roads before and after, with special attention paid to the location of Vanarra and Sahnassa on the edge of the landslide. This was the part where the matriarch had to fight to keep her emotions in check. Seeing things like the model campsite, the recovered remains of Vanarra's Racerra roadster, and finally, the diorama of the Meeting Den with its dining hall destroyed truly threw the matriarch back into her memories. She returned to the full size model of Sahnassa's shelter and leaned on the railing in front of the display, silent.

Arani was going to speak, but a silvery gold paw reached out and stopped her – one of the matriarch's attendants. Two of the matriarch's attendants took their place beside her at the railing. "Was this it?"

"Yes," the matriarch said, trying to control her emotions, "Yes, it was."

"I know how much this place meant to you. I'm glad to finally see it. Does it look accurate?"

"Oh, it's accurate alright," the matriarch whispered, swallowing.

Her other attendant dame remarked, "But it's so small! It looks like it could barely fit one, let alone two!"

The matriarch laughed. "And you should have seen me trying NOT to go in, but it was either that or freeze my tail off." She grew serious, after a pause. "Oh, Tana, Saletta … you dears, I hope you never have to know the lonely type of life I lived up to that point. As much as you are my family now, Sahnassa was my very first family, and completely by her own choice."

"If this is too much?" Tana asked, but the Grand Matriarch Vanarra de Gonari patted her paw, gently.

"I can keep going. Partially because there's something inside of me that keeps telling me she's alright, regardless of what the search parties say."

"I still can't understand why she went out on a boat, in secret, all by herself! It almost looked like a—"

"Saletta," Tana hissed, angrily.

Saletta spoke quietly, "No, I said it almost looked like a suicide, but then again it really doesn't. It's almost like she planned to meet someone after she resigned as matriarch. She left everything in perfect order."

"The letter I received from her definitely wasn't a suicide note," Arani offered quietly, spinning the three of them around. "Oh, Honored Ones? I'm sorry; I thought you knew."

"No, that's news to us. What did it say?" Vanarra asked.

"It was just a thank you letter, really, but it didn't sound sad or resigned or anything bad. It was sent just an interval before she left on the boat. Here, Honored One, I've kept it with me." She gave Vanarra the note, and placing her glasses on, Van read it.

"It's her, alright. Yes, here too. Nothing's wrong with this, see?" The matriarch gave the letter to her seconds who read it in turn. "Come on now, let's see the rest of this, or we'll be late for the dedication."

Stolidly, Vanarra walked through the rest of the exhibits, detailing the rescue and showing the Meeting Den as it finally surrendered to the elements. She noted the ripping and destruction of the de Caterra ribbon above her head, showing some small strands flowing back into de Gonari and off into other Faelnar lines which appeared briefly. Past a certain point, there was no ribbon named de Caterra anymore, which was perfectly in line with history. Model flyers, a diorama of the Meeting Den covered in snow and ice with all of its buildings collapsed, and arrays of pictures from the shelters fitted out most of the rest of the exhibit.

As Vanarra walked into the large open dome, she was amazed. The whole of the far wall was covered with pictures, faces she knew and remembered. "Arani, are they—"

"Yes, Honored One. Every survivor is pictured here."

She walked forward slowly with Tana and Saletta at her side, not really noticing the large group of watchers to her left and right. "Oh my," she breathed out in amazement looking at all of the faces. In the center were two large portraits, one of Sahnassa and one of herself. It wasn't Sahnassa's picture that drew her close; it was Buck's. Both she and Tana reached out and placed their paws on it. "It's … it's good to see him again, isn't it Tana?"

"Oh, yes," Tana breathed, voice faltering. "I miss him … so … much."

As the two spent a quiet moment together, Arani whispered to Saletta, "What … what happened?"

"He passed recently, and he was very special to both of them," Saletta whispered. "Tabuck is Tana's cub, and Arlani is her kit. The Matriarch … couldn't have any children, and she adopted Tana's children as her own. They both—" She had to stop, as the two were turning around.

"Hello, Honored One," a shy, older Faelnar said, walking up.

"Arnat?" Vanarra asked, eyes still tearing. "Oh come here, you!" She reached over and gave him a gentle hug. "I'm so glad you could come. Are you feeling okay?"

"Yes. I couldn't feel better, Honored One. I couldn't feel better."

Arani spoke up. "Matriarch, there are over one hundred survivors of the Meeting Den who came to be with us, to say thank you ... once again. While you get reacquainted, we have some refreshments. Then, with your permission, we'll go into the auditorium."

"Oh, my," she said, stunned by so many coming after so many seasons.

The Vice Chancellor walked forward and said for all to hear, "May I present to you, in honor, now the Grand Matriarch Vanarra de Gonari, but in honor as well, Vanarra Anasto, whose paws guided so many to safety."

"In honor!" the group replied in a strong, enthusiastic response.

Eyes welling again, Vanarra managed, "and honor to all of you, for all you've done. I ... would like to ask that we recognize the one who saved me. Although she is not here in presence, I sense her spirit is with us. May I present to you, in honor, the Grand Matriarch Sahnassa de Orturu," Vanarra said, pointing towards the large portrait on the wall.

"In honor!" the group replied again in chorus, albeit with more reverence.

Soft music started, and servers began working their way through the group. As Vanarra stood with the other dignitaries in a receiving line, she got to hug and talk to Cari de Dothnar, now Dame of her house, and Alatta de Orturu who had a very successful career in property sales for large corporate concerns. As the receiving line ended, and the group of dignitaries waited outside for their cue to enter the auditorium, a young Vulpi female, a very pretty one, walked up to the Grand Matriarch.

"For your comfort, Honored One," she said, offering Vanarra a drink.

"Oh, thank you dear. All of that talking has just about dried me out. What's your name?"

"Celeste," she answered, and then reached into her pocket and offered the Grand Matriarch an envelope. "For your peace of mind, and for your future."

"What's this?"

"It's an envelope," the server explained, politely, "but you shouldn't open it until you are alone, Honored One."

Vanarra was a little annoyed, but played along. "Why's that?" she asked in a conspiratorial tone.

The Vulpi leaned in close and whispered, "Because, Van, if you open it in public, the letter won't say the same thing it will in private. Theo has made sure of that." The scent of the Vulpi hit her nostrils, and she instantly knew it wasn't a Vulpi she was talking to. She knew that scent cold. The voice and inflection were perfect, too.

Leaning up, she looked at the Vulpi stunned. "You can't be," she whispered in awe and disbelief.

"Oh, yes, Honored One. Now, give your speech, enjoy your afternoon, and then read the letter. What happens after that is your choice."

"It can't be. This is a trick."

Somewhat mischievously, the Vulpi answered, "You think so, Honored One? Look there." She pointed to the side door, and there, having not aged a sol, was Theo de Allarrae. He winked and smiled at her. Van turned back towards the Vulpi, but she was now gone. Looking back at the door, she was stunned to see Theo was gone, as well.

Wondering if she was having some type of delusion, she looked back down at the expensive paper envelope. It was still there, in her paws. She quickly slipped it inside her pocket.

Tana was at her side a moment later, "Matriarch, are you alright? You look as if something's bothered you."

"No ... no, I'm alright Tana. Let's go ahead and get this done. I ... I really hate speeches, you know."

"But you are so good at them," Saletta added, "truly."

The dedication ceremony in the auditorium was very well done, and all of the dignitaries added their thoughts and kind words to the occasion. After that, there was the trip through the rest of the museum, which Vanarra had difficulty with. There was so much of her own history captured here, as well as others she cared about. She had to stop and hug Saletta for a long time when they got to the display showing Van holding a badly injured Saletta in front of an angry Anati mob on the very same steps where Van's own mother had died. Saletta always claimed that she felt the life slipping away from her until Vanarra grabbed her, and only then did she know she would survive.

Upon leaving the museum, the flyer returned to the top of the mountain that had once been the site of the Meeting Den. Now, it was a national monument. The outline of all of the buildings were rendered in short, waist high walls, and facing them from the athletic field was a huge statue of herself and Sahnassa, with Sahnassa's arm outstretched, pointed towards the successfully evacuated Meeting Den. It was based on the pictures snapped moments before the last flyer had lifted off, by then Loadmaster Fillesenalla ("Fillie") de Kestrick. After a few moments walking the grounds, Vanarra felt the urge to return home, the letter in her pocket making her almost want to take the controls of the flyer, herself. Within the interval, all of the goodbyes were said, and she was indeed headed back.

Ninety sols later, very early in the morning, a boat piloted by a lone figure sailed off into the Altian Ocean until it had disappeared from the eyes of the small group who stood tearfully on the shore. The former matriarch of house de Gonari stood at the helm driving towards a destination that only she knew. The locator beacons had been removed and left on the shore, and the thick clouds above would make it nearly impossible for the satellites to see what was about to happen. As she rode, she remembered the text of the letter.

> To my dearest friend, Vanarra. Some time ago, I disappeared from the life I had known for so long, and please know that it was by my choice. You see, you and I are special because before we helped rescue everyone else, a traveler from far away rescued us. Now, as I reached my end, he returned. He's always cared about us, and now he offers us both a new beginning. If it is your wish, you may remain on Thuria, as Matriarch, and end your seasons here. I would never think any ill of you if that were your choice. However, if you do choose to come with us, I can promise you the wonders of the skies and stars will open up before you, and a whole new future will stretch out in front of us both. Here is the location where we will pick you up; come alone in ninety sols if you wish to join us. I hope to see you soon, my dearest friend.

Love, Sahni.

The position sensor beeped, alerting her to the craft's arrival at the coordinates she had requested. She throttled back and pressed the button to drop all the anchors. The sea was rolling gently, lazily almost, when she stepped away from the console and walked towards the uncovered back of the craft. "Well, I'm here. I'm ready," she said to no one in particular, but at that moment, a light buzzing sounded in her ears and everything went comfortably black.

Breathing. She was breathing. Vanarra felt the rise and fall of her own chest before perceiving anything else. Clean air, fresh air, with a light floral scent entered her nose. "That's really nice," she thought. The bed was wonderfully soft and warm. As sensation began to return to the rest of her body, her memory did as well. She opened her eyes and looked up into the faces of Sahnassa and Theo, smiling down at her. "So, it is real."

"Yes, Van, it is, and I'm so glad you joined us!" Sahni said, happily.

"Me too … hey, wait just a tick!" Vanarra was stunned because she tried to sit up, and she had, far faster and more easily than normal. It was then she realized Sahnassa looked almost exactly the same age she did all those seasons ago when they were thrown out of the Meeting Den. Looking down at herself, she saw her own paws, sleek and young, her fur having no silver at all – just reddish brown with gold highlights. Sahnassa laughed happily as she saw Vanarra trying to understand what had happened to her. Theo was smiling, too. "Hey, you two, this isn't – is … is that my voice? Wow! La, la, la, la!" Van trilled up four notes with ease. "Okay, that's cool! Can either of you please tell me exactly what's happened to me?"

Theo was laughing now, too, but stifled it to explain. "All those seasons ago, when the landslide hit, it didn't just graze your vehicle, it pounded it, and both of you were very badly injured. However, I was in the neighborhood, and, believe it or not, I heard Sahnassa's call for help before she lost consciousness. I brought you aboard my ship and healed you both. Because of that, I have detailed genetic records, and consequently, I was able to restore your bodies now to the same, healed condition they were in then."

Vanarra thought for a moment and shook her head. "Wait a pass here. If my body is like it was, how is my memory intact? Have I got a two hundred and forty-eight season old brain inside of a thirty-something body?"

"Your brain is just as young as the rest of you, but it's the mind within that remembers," Sahnassa said, smiling.

"How can he do that?"

"I'm extraordinarily clever," Theo answered, and Sahnassa nodded.

"What happens now?" Vanarra asked.

"Well, we tie up anything you can think of that needs tying up, and then we leave," Theo explained. "I want to show you both my home world, and there are so many friends of mine who have heard your stories and want to meet you. After that, we'll see. There are so many places in need of good souls like yourself that if you want, you can do all the things you did before, lead families, solve disputes, rescue hundreds –"

"Make joining cakes?" Vanarra asked.

They both laughed. "Of course."

"It's just that I actually missed being a caterer. That really made me happy."

Sahnassa teased, "Perhaps we can find a diplomat caterer position somewhere!"

"Don't laugh," Theo said. "I may have just the spot. That is, unless you've reconsidered going with us."

Vanarra took their paws as they helped her to stand. She grabbed them both in a firm embrace. "I can't wait. Let's go!"

The End, and the Beginning...

Abbreviated Thurian Reference

Thuria:

Thuria is the fourth planetary body in a sun-centered system of ten planets. Two moons rotate in slightly different orbits in perfect opposition to one another. Fifty-eight percent of the surface is water, with fairly uniform land masses in the temperate zones. While the poles of the planet are covered with ice, there are no land masses there. Each continent, to varying extents, has its mountains, rivers, lakes, and deserts, but much of the land is arable. While rich in minerals, Thuria lacks fossil fuels, so industrialization and technological advancement occurred slowly, over a long period of time.

Thurians:

Thurians are anthropoid mammals standing erect on two legs covered with thick hair or fur, and the color of fur varies. Most major species of Thurian have fur-covered tails of varying lengths. Ears, muzzles, and eyes are generally somewhat larger than those found in most sentient, bipedal species. Teeth and muzzle betray an omnivorous, but predatory ancestry. Front paws are four fingered with one being an opposable thumb. Claws are imbedded within the end of most species paw fingers, and the inside of the paw maintains a relatively thick paw-pad.

Life spans are long, at approximately 250 seasons (or orbits of Thuria around its sun), and birth rates are lower in compensation. However, this elongated life span allows for families to have nine or ten generations alive at one time. Thurians are social and very familial, with allegiance and membership to a family group passing generally through the male, unless the female is titled (member of the family matriarchy). As compensation, the familial leadership is nearly always female. Thurians are fertile by age 15 and generally lose fertility at around 90 seasons. Usually, mating produces one cub (male) or kit (female). Those terms apply regardless of species. Multiple births are not easily supported by Thurian biology.

Families frequently will raise one child to full adulthood before beginning again.

Thurian Species:

Anati – (*"a-not-tea"*) any mixed-blood Thurian (derogatory term).

Faelnar – (*"fell-narr"*) Purebred species, generally of sleek to average build, with long, short-furred tails. Fur colors range from brown through golden to shades of yellow. Eye colors include gold, green, hazel, and yellow. Noses are black, brown, or yellow brown.

Lupar – (*"loo-parr"*) Purebred species. A large species (second only to the Pantera in size) with gray to brownish fur, with longer than average muzzles. Eye colors are gray to blue to green. Tails are long, straight or curved, and bushy. Fur color ranges from light gray to black and brown.

Nephti – (*"neff-tea"*) Purebred species, generally of average build. Tail fur is long and thick, forming a wide, long, and bushy tail. Fur colors from light gray to black into dark purple through light purple. Eye colors include silver, gray, and shades from deep blue through indigo and violet. Noses are black, pink, or mottled. Striping is prominent, in shades of white, silver, or grey.

Pantera – (*"pan-terr-uh"*) The largest of the purebred species on Thuria. Fur colors range from light gray to black, with no patterning except on the ear ridges (generally black). Tails are short-haired and only of moderate length. Their muzzle is thicker than most other species. Eye colors are blue through hazel to dark brown and gray. While not as sleek and quick as their Faelnar counterparts, they make up for it in muscle. Noses are usually pale pink to pale grey to black.

Perratti – (*"purr-rah-tea"*) Purebred species. The smallest of all Thurian breeds, on average, but sizes can approach average and sometimes exceed it. Tails are small and covered with short hair. Muzzles are long and almost box-shaped, with fur occasionally draping off the sides down the face and muzzle like an upside down "V". Fur color ranges between black, gray, brown, and tan. Noses are uniformly black. Eyes are silver, blue, hazel, or brown.

Vulpi – (*"vull-pea"*) Purebred species. Fur colors include white, orange-red, orange, red, and gray. Patterning is mostly limited to large variations on forearms, hind legs, muzzle, or tail. Eye colors are blue, green, silver, brown, and hazel. Tail fur is thick, forming a wide, long, and bushy tail.

House Matriarchal Leadership Hierarchy
Grand Matriarch or Matriarch
Honored Dames and Dames
Matrons
All other house members

Thurians Prominent in the Rescue
Disavowed (those of no family house)
Vanarra (Van) Anasto – Anati (mixed-blood) caterer
Buck Harlock – Faelnar friend of Van, disavowed from de Caterra

Of House de Orturu (species: Nephti)
Sahnassa (Sahni) – Technician employed by Vanarra Anasto
Selena – Grand Matriarch
Alatta – young adult female

Of House de Gonari (species: Faelnar)
Amyra – Grand Matriarch
Prattura – Honored Dame
Arkest & Arnat – Father and adult son, business leaders
Saletta – Young Matron
Talnar (Tal) – middle aged male

Of House de Dothnar (species: Nephti)
Rahnahi – Grand Matriarch and Literary Legend
Dania – Honored Dame
Carinthia – young female, descended of Matriarch Rahnahi
Delease – middle aged Matron

Of House de Caterra (species: Faelnar)
Tawnston – Air Chief in Thuratani Defense Force
Katuratatallenar (Katur) – mid-ranking Dame
Ocurattiaster (Cur) – young, aggressive male
Sanratatarrae (Sanrat) –scholarly male academy professor
Tanassadurini de Caterra (Tana) –Young Matron

Others:
Regional Emergency Manager Tedarri de Bosnar – Lupar
Marshall Terrat de Debonar – Lupar
Load Master Fillesenalla ("Fillie") de Kestrick – Vulpi
Air Sergeant Korick de Mastif – Perratti
Captain Keel – Perratti
Lieutenant Crastor – Perratti
Leoniry de Nestanum – Nephti business owner
Siflin de Oterbythe – Perratti shift manager of the Meeting Den

Preview of *The Aftermath*

The ship was called the Tashar, and as it broke orbit of the planet Thuria, it went far slower than was its capacity – it lingered, taking its time leaving the beautiful world it had circled invisibly for nearly twenty solar rotations. Not all of that period was contiguous, for the Tashar was also a time ship as much as it was a space ship, and that ability to bounce back and forth across the moments had been used frequently in an adventure its occupant, the mysterious alien Theo, knew he would long treasure – the rescue of nearly fifteen hundred souls at the doomed mountaintop resort known to Thurians as "The Meeting Den."

His involvement with that event had started on a simple premise, searching the universes for other sentients, other beings with self awareness. Probing one galaxy, then another, he had happened upon this relatively young world around a relatively young star and decided to investigate. As he had drawn closer and the probes started downloading their observations, he became more intrigued.

The intelligent inhabitants of this world were not merely of one dominant species with racial variations; there were no less than six dominant species, integrated into a cohesive society. This achievement alone had been surprising, but not as surprising as how many features of less developed creatures Thurians had maintained. They were completely covered in fur; they had tails, and their facial features still bore the long muzzles and largish ears evident in even their own resident lower life forms.

Information about their matriarchal culture, their life spans, and so many other things were just starting to be understood when the Tashar detected an upwelling of magma destined to brush against an ancient fault line underlying a mountain range. Slowing its perception of the passage of time, the Tashar watched carefully as the ensuing quake rolled across the land. Bridges fell, communications systems were destroyed, and structures rocked and crumbled.

Theo then saw a small vehicle, a hovercraft, swept off a mountain road by a landslide and thrown violently down along with the massive flow of debris. When everything came to rest, the two creatures inside the hovercraft were buried, crushed, near death, and left with no hope of survival. His mind reached out and touched one of those frightened souls, a female, who stirred briefly awake – long enough to understand the horror that would be her death. Beside her nearly dead companion, her own heart and internal organs started to fail. Theo made a decision, and brought the two injured Thurians aboard the Tashar.

Their injuries were so severe that the moment they arrived, temporal stasis fields had to be put into place or death would have been almost instantaneous. The ship's computers examined the state of the two victims and determined the one who had momentarily awakened in the rubble, a member of the Nephti species, could be brought back to full health with simple reconstruction, and such was started. The other survivor was of mixed lineage, a combination of what Thurians called Faelnar and Vulpi, but she was in far worse shape. Massive head trauma and other horrible injuries would push the limits of even Theo's advanced science. Still, all the minds aboard that ship plied their resources and techniques to bring back even this one, injured so badly.

As the Nephti reached a point where she could be reawakened, Theo had lightly probed her mind and determined that she was a being who could accept the concept of life on other worlds and all of the significant consequences that devolved from that. Reaching back in time to probe the mind of the mixed blood, named Vanarra Anasto, he found her history far too troubled and difficult to easily tolerate such a huge jar to her reality like the truth of life beyond what she already knew. That one's world had been turned over so many times, to do so again would cause her mind to simply crumble and break apart in disorientation, confusion, and terror.

The reawakened Nephti, however, met and surpassed his expectations. Sahnassa de Orturu was bright, adaptable, and able to converse with him easily about her world, how things worked and why. As she continued to recover, Theo began to understand more and more of the situation that placed them upon the mountain at that particular time –

they had just been ejected from the premises of the grand and storied Meeting Den resort.

The Tashar found this resort not far away, horribly damaged by the quake, completely isolated and under threat from a massive ice and snow storm not even two solar rotations (or sols as Thurians call them) away. This caused him to look at his two guests in a different light – rescued Thurians who could now become the rescuers.

With very little convincing, Sahnassa agreed with his plan and started to assist him. It was also becoming clear to him that the young female Nephti was as grateful to him as she was in awe of him, and he could sense those feelings turning into affection and infatuation very quickly. Still, to his great appreciation, the Nephti put even those intense feelings aside for the task that had to be accomplished. Using the Tashar's powerful abilities, Theo was able to rearrange the hover wreck and place the two rescued Thurians back on the mountain.

Working covertly with Sahnassa using a modified watch and a pair of sunglasses, he was able to help them orchestrate communications, vehicles, food, and eventually, an airlift to shelters in the valley below. Taking the form of a Nephti, himself, Theo was able to work directly with the Thurians to help move things along and overcome problems.

One of these problems occurred with the abduction of Vanarra, the mixed blood he had rescued. By the time this happened, the Tashar understood much more about Thuria than before and the incredible challenges it faced from within. Pondering the Tashar's discoveries, Theo realized that this was a world in dire peril. Internal forces were working toward goals that were as dismissive of the life and freedom of others as they were all encompassing. A darkness was poised to cover this world and change it forever, unwittingly directing its course towards one of self destruction. Theo had lived long and traveled far, and without a doubt, he knew what this world's tragic future would be.

Still, this was an exploratory mission and the full backing of his high assembly was a luxury he did not, for the present, have. In undoing the kidnapping of Vanarra, however, he exercised his prerogative and intervened, at least a little. He planted a seed of confession in one of the dames of de Caterra, who then began telling authorities about all of the misdeeds of her own house. Also, he alerted the head of one of the most noble houses on Thuria, the Grand Matriarch Rahnahi de Dothnar, to the presence of hidden records, "cover records," kept by de Caterra that chronicled their evils in detail. Even if, by some chance, the high assembly did not agree to assisting this planet, he had at least given them some small help in avoiding the calamity that was rapidly approaching. Leaving this promising race in such a state of risk and danger was difficult, but it wasn't, in some ways, the most difficult thing about leaving.

His accomplice on this world, his co-conspirator, Sahnassa, asked that when the rescue was complete, she be allowed to return to the Tashar one last time before he left. In gratitude for all she had done and how much she had grown in that short space of time, he agreed. What followed was truly surprising and humbling, even for a creature as powerful and ancient as he. Kneeling, Sahnassa offered herself up to him – her mind, her body, her soul, and her freedom – as repayment for the debt of saving her life, the life of her friend, and those of nearly fifteen hundred other Thurians. When he touched her mind, he found that she was indeed sincere and utterly enthralled with him – in love and in awe.

Even more than the dark conspiracies on her home world, the young Nephti was a far greater puzzle. He could dismiss her, gently, but then he would have left her feeling that her offer meant nothing, and that her life and all she was, as well, meant nothing. He could take Sahnassa with him, but the toll that would exact upon those she left behind would be far too great to accept. So, for a time, up until the maximum he had allotted for his journey, he gave his time to her. Theo offered her the love and concern and fantasy she so desperately needed, all the while giving her gifts of advice, of music, of information, and many other things of which Sahnassa was completely unaware.

When it came time for him to depart, he had given her one final command, to live her life to its fullest, and to love those she was willing to leave behind – being there for them, instead. Reluctantly, she had agreed and was returned to her bedroom at the very same moment he had taken her away. Now, as the Tashar stood at the threshold of the inter-dimensional gateway that would take Theo home, he literally looked over his shoulder towards her planet, keeping his Thurian form, that of a Nephti, up until this moment. To the watch he had modified for her, he sent one final message – "Stay safe, sweet Sahni. You are so much better than you know. Farewell." Melting from his Thurian form into a radiant sphere of light, he turned his attention back towards the gateway and directed the Tashar to return home.

Continued in *The Aftermath: Secrets of Thuria*

Available now!

About the Author

J̲ames Todd Lewis is a fiction author living in Orlando, Florida with his lovely wife and two children. A native of Warner Robins, Georgia, he is a graduate of the Mercer University College of Liberal Arts and the Great Books program. He's been writing novels and short stories since 1982. At first, he just enjoyed the writing process and the fun of reading his own work. It wasn't until a hard drive crash erased several months of work that his wife, who also enjoyed his stories, insisted on making a printed copy for safekeeping. Seeing his work in print for the first time was quite a moment, and it made him wonder if others would also be interested.

Now, he feels humbled and grateful that others have been entertained by these books – doubly so when someone has been kind enough to post a review!

There is more coming in the Thurian Saga!

LIKE the Thurian Saga on Facebook for updates,

discussions with the author, and more!

Follow the author on Twitter! @hmseagle

Visit the author's website for his essay blog, book descriptions, and more in-depth information: www.jamestoddlewis.com!

www.ingramcontent.com/pod-product-compliance
Lightning Source LLC
Chambersburg PA
CBHW071148250626
47159CB00001B/23